IMAGINE THIS

SW Books
www.ImagineThisTheNovel.com

First published in 2007 by SW Books

This Edition 2008

ISBN 978-0-9555453-0-6

Cover artwork © JagArtist
Cover design © Olamide Adetula

SW Books
PO Box 47197
London W6 6DL
www.ImagineThisTheNovel.com

For my father, may his soul rest in peace.

IMAGINE THIS

IDOGUN

IMAGINE THIS

"The spirit that keeps one going when one has no choice of what else to do must not be mistaken for valour"

African proverb

When I was a child, I spoke like a child, I thought like a child, I reasoned like a child. Now I am older, and wiser. I have put my childish ways behind me and view the world with a weary cynicism that has become hard to shake. How I miss the lost innocence, yet I was never truly innocent. I grew up too soon, too fast, taunted with the knowledge of what I once had but lost.

They say the struggles of a woman begin at birth; my struggles really began in Idogun. I prevailed because to resign oneself to one's fate is to be crippled fast. I survived, not because I had courage, neither was I strong. I simply wanted badly enough what I didn't have and others seemed to have in abundance. So I begin again and as Time turns the page, my journey through life inevitably goes on. This is what was; it has shaped my present and will play a large part in what is still to come, and by learning from my mistakes and my arrogance I can let it shape my future. Who knows, I might even get to live happily ever after like a princess in a fairytale. One thing I have learnt is that no matter how long the night, the day is sure to come.

IMAGINE THIS

"Whatever the eyes of a dead man see in the burial yard is caused by death"

Yoruba proverb

20TH MAY 1977

Dear Jupiter,

Why, why, why, why, why? I hate them all, I want to go home, I don't want to live with my Auntie, I don't want to live in Idogun. I want everything to go back to the way it once was, with Daddy, Adebola and me living at number 4 Edgecombe House.

21ST MAY 1977

Dear Jupiter,

Daddy didn't take notice of my tears, I told him I didn't want to leave Lagos, that I wanted us to live like a family, like we did when we left our foster parents in Kent and went to live with him in London. I sobbed and sobbed till I couldn't sob no more. I promised not to be naughty and to never ever lose the front door key like Adebola and me used to do in London. I told him that I'd be responsible like he is always telling me to be, I promised so much yet he still wouldn't listen to me. He said I had to leave; I had to go and live with my Auntie, Iya Rotimi, because he could no longer take care of me and Adebola. So today I've arrived in Idogun and I'm going to be here forever unless I'm rescued by a handsome prince. It's a pity I don't have long hair or live in a tower, I could've left strands of hair along the way, which my prince could have followed to Idogun and we would have lived happily ever after.

22ND MAY 1977

Dear Jupiter,

Today is Sunday and my Auntie, Iya Rotimi took us to church. I know she doesn't like me so I won't like her either. I don't like the way she looks at me, she makes me feel as if I'm naughty all the time. Whenever she sees me, she rolls her eyes, kisses her lips and claps her hands while moving her head from side to side, and finishes with 'you no go kill me o, I no go let you.' I don't want to kill her, I just want to go back to Lagos and live with Daddy. She turned up out of the blue, Just like when Uncle Joseph came to take Adebola away, there were whispers behind closed doors; I tried to listen through the keyhole but I couldn't understand what was being said. After a while Daddy came out and said I had to pack, I was going to live with her in the village and no amount of sobbing and begging was going to change his decision. I can't wait to grow up and make my own decisions because when I asked him how long I had to stay in Idogun, he said it was till I finished school. That's a stupid decision, I've only just started Primary 4, it will take another three years till I finish Primary 6, and then I'll have to do five years of secondary school. Eight years of my life gone just like that. He never asked Adebola and me what we wanted, he just came home one day and said we were going to go back to Nigeria to live. We didn't want to come to Nigeria, but w came and now he's breaking our family up again. I'll be eighteen, an old woman before I ever see Adebola again, he probably won't recognise me. How could Daddy do this, doesn't he love me any more? Maybe he found out I broke all the glasses on top of the fridge. I didn't mean to, I was just throwing the ball against the kitchen wall because I didn't have anyone to play with.

Everything here is so confusing, I have too many relatives and I don't know how we're related, it seems like I'm related to the whole village. We came to visit once before and I didn't like it then, no one could understand what I was saying then, and they still can't, and now I'm going to have to spend the rest of my life here with no one but you to speak to. I prayed and prayed because Daddy said that God answers the prayers of little children, but I must have been really naughty because God didn't answer my prayer.

We travelled in a rickety old bus, you could see the dusty road through a huge hole in the floor. The seats were wooden and I got splinters in my backside every time the bus jolted over a hole. Most of the roads we travelled on were red dirt roads with huge holes in them. It was worse when we had to go through puddles because the muddy water kept splashing into the bus. Daddy had made me wear my white blouse and tartan skirt, with white socks, he said it made me stand apart. By the time we got to Idogun my blouse and socks were browner than they were white.

We made several stops, people getting off in the towns along the way to stretch their legs and go into the bushes, I'm so glad I didn't have to poo as I had no tissue. We stopped at Ibadan, Ikare, Akure, Owoh and lots of other places that I can't remember. I only remember those four ecause Ibadan is near Lagos, Akure is the capital of Ondo state and Daddy said he went to school in Ikare and Owoh is the nearest big town to Idogun. I wanted to buy some *akara* at one of the stops but I didn't have any money. Daddy had given Auntie some pocket money for me, but she wouldn't let me have it. I hate her very much because after all it is my money. She and her son, who is about five, ate a whole loaf of bread by themselves and didn't offer me any. She's so selfish.

Before it was just the three of us in London, we were like the three musketeers, and before that it was just Adebola and me in Kent. There were no relatives in England, but now I have too many aunties, uncles and cousins and it makes my head hurt trying to remember who is who. When we arrived everyone wanted to pat me on the head and pull my cheeks. I got scared so I bolted back the way the bus had come from. I know I was being stupid, but I was going to run all the way back to Lagos and to Daddy. It doesn't matter that he canes us or makes us stoop down, he's our Dad and I was determined to get back to Lagos, and no one was going to catch me, not even Speedy Gonzales. I was being stupid, it took ages to get here on the bus and I didn't have a clue where I was going; it would have taken me years to walk back. The bus caught up with me before I could even make it out of the village, and the driver grinned at me with his crooked black pirate teeth.

The first time I saw him smile was when he took Daddy, Adebola and me to Idogun that first time. I was so scared of his blackened teeth, I told Adebola I thought he was a pirate but he just made fun of me. The driver was nice to me though, nothing like a pirate, he snuck me some *akara* when Auntie wasn't looking. He persuaded me back into the rickety bus and he took me back home. I suppose have to get used to calling this place 'home.' But I have to say right now — my real home is in London, that's where I was born, in Paddington hospital on March 18th 1968. Adebola was born in Wales, I used to tease him that he was swallowed like Jonah in the Bible and spat out in Wales. I, Omolola Olufunke Olufunmilayo Ogunwole, promise myself that one day I will get on a plane and go back to my friends, I don't know how, but I will, I'll run away as soon as I can. Cross my heart and hope to die.

23RD MAY 1977

Dear Jupiter,

I really hate it here, I really want to go back to London, even living in the two small rooms in Lagos is better than living here. No one understands a word I'm saying, there's no water, no electricity, no television and I have no friends to play with. To make matters worse, I wet the bed last night, so before they all went to school Iya Rotimi put me in a chalk circle and my cousins danced around and made fun of me. Sometimes I'm glad I can't understand what people are saying to me. The younger children thought it was a game, but Yinka with her scarred face enjoyed making fun of me. I know it's because I wouldn't let her wear my favourite dress to church on Sunday. Rotimi, who can speak broken English, said it was going to cure me. Not that there is anything wrong with me, I hadn't done it in a long time, Daddy cured me with the cane and stooping down.

I did nothing all day but sit and cry, not that there was anything to do anyway. I can't go to school because they teach in Yoruba and I can't read, write or even speak it properly yet. Please God, answer my prayer, and let me go back to London. I'll be a good girl forever, I'll eat my greens and I'll be nice to Steve the fat kid in class. The light is almost gone. Rotimi said we have to get up early tomorrow before the cock crows, we're going to the bush to fetch water. I'm scared. What if a roaring lion or a wild elephant attacks us? That's what always happened to the natives in *Tarzan*.

24TH MAY 1977

Dear Jupiter,

Today I got up before the cock crowed to fetch water with my cousins. I'm sure it was still night time but I forgot to look at my watch. All I could hear were scary noises, especially when we left the village. We walked for ages before we came to a little stream in the bushes, I was scared because it was so dark and I couldn't see where I was going. Rotimi lead the way with a kerosene lantern and I made sure I was in the middle just in case a lion or tiger attacked from the back. Not that I'd see it coming, it was as if the bushes were closing in on us as we walked along the path. I wish I had batteries for my torch. I thought we'd be the only people going to fetch water but other people had the same idea, because when we got to the stream, there was a long queue. Rotimi blamed me, he said it was my fault we didn't leave early, they had tried to wake me up, but I kept going back to sleep. Auntie had to pour a cup of water over me. I wish they had just left without me.

The stream wasn't really a stream, it was more like a hole in the ground and we had to use a bowl to scoop the water into our buckets then wait for it to fill up again. It took ages and as we waited our turn, dawn came and the night went away. Rotimi made us wait till the hole filled up before we started scooping the water. He said that way we get pure clean water instead of sandy muddy water.

The journey home wasn't scary but it was very painful. Rotimi wound a piece of cloth into a circle, placed it on my head and I had to walk with the bucket of water on top and fight the tree branches and bushes with no hands. They could walk without touching the buckets, it was a balancing act I couldn't do. By the time I got home, the bucket was half full, I'd spilt most of the water over myself and my neck felt like it wasn't there, it had disappeared into my shoulders. Everyone came to inspect what I'd brought home and it was decided that Mama (my grandmother) should get to drink the first cup since it would be the first fruit from the tree she had planted. Rotimi told me that she said the fruit was sweet. I think that is what he meant, sometimes I don't understand what he means because he gets his words mixed up, most of the time I have to guess from hand waving and watching his eyes. Earlier, he came to get me from where I was playing hopscotch and told me it was time to come and chop. I thought he was going to make me cut up wood and I had visions of chopping off my foot or finger, since I'd never used an axe, but I didn't have to worry. Come and chop means come and eat.

Tomorrow, Auntie says we have to go and visit my grandfather who is blind and never leaves the house. He and Mama don't live together; he's got another wife living with him. Daddy told me that it is the custom for a man to marry more than one wife. I asked him if it was possible for a woman to have more than one husband but he told me not to be silly, which I think is unfair. If a man is allowed to have more than one wife, a woman should be able to have more than one husband too. When I grow up and get married, if my husband decides he wants another wife then I'll have to have another husband. Daddy has other brothers and sisters apart from Iya Rotimi and Baba Dayo, Daddy says I have over forty cousins. Mama lives in the village with her brother Baba Ade and his wife, Daddy's brother Baba Dayo and his wife and their six children. There are only four rooms in the whole house. Mama sleeps in one, Baba Ade and his wife in another, Baba and Iya Dayo and my cousins in the third, the fourth one is a guest room for visitors. It's where we stayed the first time Daddy, Adebola and I came to Idogun.

Apart from my exciting trip to the jungle to fetch water, I've been so bored today, there's nothing to do and everyone else has gone to school. Iya Rotimi has gone to the market, Baba Dayo to the farm. This left me with Mama who doesn't understand anything I say. All my toys are in Lagos. If I had my bike I could have gone exploring, but I was too scared to go further than Mama's house, which is just across the road. If I were in London right now, I'd be watching the *Wombles* or maybe even the *Banana Splits*. Maybe God will still answer my prayer and we'll all go back to Edgecombe House where the chimes of Big Ben woke me up every morning.

26TH MAY 1977

Dear Jupiter,

Went to the stream again and came back with even less water.

28TH MAY 1977

Dear Jupiter,

I hate getting up so early in the morning to go to the stream. I've got horrible blisters on my feet and my neck hurts and I'm never going to grow tall.

20TH JUNE 1977

Dear Jupiter,

Today Rotimi and I had to do an entrance exam to get into secondary school. I don't know why they made me do it because I'm really supposed to be in Primary 4. All the questions had more than one answer and I had to choose the right one. The English exam was okay but the Maths exam was fractions I didn't know, so I guessed most of the answers. I shut my eyes and pointed my pencil up and down the answers five times and if I landed on an answer more than once then that was my choice. I was finished in no time, everyone else was battling over the questions while the evil-eyed man in front swished his cane to and fro. I put my pencil down and tried to catch Rotimi's eye but he was sitting too far away, plus he wasn't looking up.

When the man saw me looking around, he hit my desk with his cane and asked whether I'd completed my exam. I nodded, afraid he was going to cane me because I finished before the time was up. But he just smiled and said he liked to see people finish early and that I could leave. I couldn't leave because I'd come with Rotimi and he still hadn't finished, so I sat on the grass outside and made faces at the children who looked out of the window at me. Rotimi told me that he thinks he did really well in the exam, but I wasn't really interested, I was feeling homesick. I've been missing my friends in London, wondering if they remember me. I wish I could write but there isn't a post office; well there is one, but it's never open.

Dear Jupiter

Why did Daddy do this, why doesn't he want us any more? Maybe he's not really our father and that's why our mother left. She took one look at me and disappeared, so why would anyone else like me? Maybe that's why Daddy doesn't want me to live with him, because I remind him of her. I wonder if I have her eyes and nose, whether her hair is soft and black like mine, or brown like Adebola's. One day when I'm much older I will go and find out for myself, instead of seeing her in every stranger who passes me on the streets of Lagos. I'd know if she were here in Idogun because everybody knows everybody else. When we were in London, we didn't say hello to people we didn't know, not even in Lagos, but here in the village the chances are you're related, maybe your great grandfathers were brothers or something. That's family, and I have a lot of family, everyone is related to me, everyone wants to touch me, they say things I don't understand and then burst out laughing. Rotimi my interpreter is still no good really, his broken English isn't very clear and I have to guess at what he's saying through a lot of hand waving and grunts, but I'm learning to cope and I'm beginning to understand the Idogun language. 'Atiporo' is a 'stool', 'Ka wey ray' means 'where are you going.' I don't really think of London that much any more, only occasionally when things get tough, like when I think of having to spend the next 2,920 days in this village. By then I'll be grown up and able to do what I want when I want. Well today is almost over, leaving me with 2,919 days to go. Maybe tomorrow will be a better one.

Dear Jupiter,

School is out and everyone is on holiday. Today was my cousin, Yinka's, school play, which I didn't watch because she'd told me about her part, so I knew the story already. Yinka played the daughter of a poor farmer with two wives. The first wife, Yinka's character's mother, died leaving the second wife in charge and she hated her step-daughter. I think she would have been perfect in the role of one of the evil step sisters. A wealthy farmer pays the daughter's bride price with yams and *gari* and clothes and palm oil and saves her from her wicked stepmother who can't find husbands for her own daughters. Sometimes I feel like Yinka is my evil step-sister. She makes up stories about me to her mother, who then says to me, 'Don't be bad, is not good.' I can speak some Yoruba and a little Idogun now, but I've given up trying to explain because she doesn't understand me and if she's speaking too quickly I don't understand her, so most of the time I don't even know what I've done wrong.

I wonder how Adebola is getting on with his new life? I hope he misses me as much as I miss him.

Iya Rotimi said that I can't go to Lagos for the holidays and that I will have to stay in Idogun and go to the farm with my Uncle, Baba Dayo. I'm not looking forward to it and I cried myself to sleep yesterday thinking about it. I didn't even know that I could have gone until she mentioned that I couldn't, so I feel like a cockroach or beetle that she's just stepped on. I feel so empty, all I seem to do is wake up, eat and sleep, nothing in between to do. I don't like being sad, I don't like crying myself to sleep and wetting the bed, I don't like feeling alone. I don't know what I've done that's so bad and I don't know how to make it better, I don't know how to make myself feel happy. I just want to be with my dad but I don't want him to cane me for every mistake I make. I want a mother too, one who will plait my hair, kiss me goodnight and read me stories of princes and princesses. I also want my brother and maybe a sister as well, who I can boss around. I'd like a dog, not like the ones here that eat your poo, but like the ones back in Kent at Aunt Sue and Uncle Eddie's. I don't like cats so I don't want one of those but I wouldn't mind a parrot that I could teach to say things like Captain Hook's parrot in *Peter Pan*. I don't care where we live as long as it isn't here. I wish, I wish, I wish.

8TH JULY 1977

Dear Jupiter,

I met another relative today. I've given up on trying to remember who is related to me and how. So I've divided everyone into relative or family. Relatives are those who are related to my grandparents or great-grandparents, though there are exceptions like Baba Ade who is Mama's brother and lives in the same house as Mama. So family includes Iya Rotimi, Baba Dayo and their children who are my first cousins, Mama and Baba who are my grandparents, (Baba has another wife and other children so I have other aunts and uncles and cousins) and Baba Ade. Mama has another sister, but she's a relative because I haven't seen her, she doesn't like going out. Rotimi told me that all her children died, so she just stays at home and talks to herself. She's called Mama Dupe, Dupe is one of her dead children. Once a person has had children, they're not called by their name. They're called by their firstborn's name even if the child dies, but once they become a grandmother or grand-father they become Mama or Baba, so even though Mama Dupe is older than Mama, she's not a Mama, she's a Mama Dupe; if she was younger she'd be called Iya Dupe, like Iya Rotimi. So I've lots of relatives and lots of family too.

9TH JULY 1977

Dear Jupiter,

My neck is sore from carrying a zillion yams, my back is sore from pulling weeds and my hands are sore from making mounds. I've been to Baba Dayo's farm. We woke up very early because it was further than the stream and Baba Dayo wanted to start work before the sun came out. I had to wear my platform shoes because I didn't have any-thing else that was big enough for my feet. Daddy had bought them about two sizes too large because my feet are growing very fast. I used to have to stuff newspaper in them but now my toes reach the top and they are a bit tight. Mama didn't want me to wear them but I had nothing else, I've outgrown all my other shoes, but not my clothes. Even though these are my Sunday shoes, I can't walk around barefoot like the savages in *Tarzan*. That would make me one of them and I don't want to be a savage who doesn't have the sense to hide in a tree when being chased by a lion. Not that I'd be able to run very far in my platforms, I could barely walk properly in them on the uneven paths.

As we walked deeper into the jungle I looked out for any suspicious rustling in the bushes, I wasn't taking any chances. I wasn't scared though, because Baba Dayo was leading the way and he had a really sharp cutlass. The farm is big and Baba Dayo grows more than one crop — there were cocoa-yams, yams, corn, cocoa, kolanuts, cassava, guava and other things I don't yet know the names of. He showed me how to make giant mounds of dirt with the hoe, but my effort didn't match my cousin Aina's. No matter how hard I tried, hers were always bigger. She was also faster when it came to pulling out weeds. Baba Dayo gave her six rows and I got four and she still finished before me. I think it was my shoes and it was so hot, so I kept on resting, plus I got bitten by an enormous soldier ant. It was very painful, I didn't know that ants bit people. There were lots of them marching in a single file. On the sides were the big ones hemming in and protecting the little ones who were carrying bits of food I think. They were marching down my row and I didn't want them there so I used a stick to try and scatter them, but they just kept on making another line so I had to sit and wait until they had gone. That's when I got bitten.

I accidentally pulled up a yam that we ended up cooking for lunch. I thought it was a weed, so I pulled and pulled and dug around it before realising it was a yam. I had to dig it up in the end because the hoe had made marks on the side and Baba Dayo said that if we left it, it would get spoilt. So that was my day, I have to go to the farm again tomorrow and the day after and the day after until school starts again, which it doesn't till September, if I pass the entrance exam.

12TH JULY 1977

Dear Jupiter,

I had exactly the same day as I did yesterday, except today was longer, plus I saw Baba Dayo's thing at the stream and it was huge and had hair all around it, not like

Adebola's, his is small and there is no hair. When he saw me staring he hid it between his legs and he looked like a woman only he had all the hair, which I think is disgusting. I'm still counting the days till this is all over, I suppose if I look on the bright side I won't be spending eight years here, only five. I just hope I pass the entrance exam. If I'd known it would be this important I'd have taken more care when doing the Maths questions instead of just playing guessing games. I have to pass, I hope God will take pity on me and help me pass. After all, I am precious to him. Well, that's what Daddy says anyway, but I don't know if it's true.

28TH AUGUST 1977

Dear Jupiter

For once I have the best news ever, I'm going to secondary school in September which is only weeks away, imagine that. Baba Rotimi reckons that I'll be the youngest student there at nine and a half years old. Rotimi didn't get in so he'll have to repeat Primary 6, he's very upset about this and is blaming me. He said that I failed and he passed and I'm taking his place because the Principal said that he could only allow one of us in. That's what his mother told him. She also told him she had to pay the Principal some money to switch the names, but I don't really think it's true.

He's just trying to make me feel grateful to him like he did me a favour,, but he hasn't because I saw my name on the list and anyway I'm not going to listen to him. I'm just so happy that I'll only be here for five years instead of eight. That's a lot of days, hours and minutes, my head hurts just thinking about it. Maybe if I started counting the seconds, time will go faster.

It's a full moon tonight and I can see all the stars. Everyone is sitting outside. Mama is going to be telling stories soon so I guess I should stop here. I'm not looking forward to going to the farm tomorrow. I don't have a choice though, because during the day there's no one left in the village except the old people who can't walk very far. So there's nobody to play with, which is why I have to go. Soon I'll be in secondary school. I'm so excited.

19TH SEPTEMBER 1977

Dear Jupiter

It has been a while since I last told you anything. Well, a lot has happened. Today I started secondary school. I've skipped the last three years of primary school and here I am starting Form One. I was excited, but today I didn't want to go because I don't know anyone there and Mama had to drag me kicking and screaming all the way. I told them that I didn't want to go but no one listens to what I want. So I hid myself behind the sack of *gari* which Iya Rotimi was taking to Lagos on her next visit. I could hear Mama and Rotimi yelling my name and looking for me.

They eventually found me and Mama dragged me by my hair and said I had to go. When we got to school, all the other students were lined up for assembly, the girls were all in white dresses while the boys were in white shorts and shirts and everyone looked so much older than me. All the girls have breasts and I stood out like a sore thumb because I was wearing my favourite red trousers and a T-shirt and my platforms which are becoming too tight, they're also very dirty from wearing them to the farm. Everyone turned to watch Mama drag me to the front of the assembly. With all eyes on me, I just wanted to die. One of the teachers barked something and Mama explained that I'd just come from London so wasn't familiar with the school customs.

After the teacher had dismissed the assembly and Mama had returned home, he made me walk on gravel with my knees. He told me this was an example for other students who might think he was soft. What we needed was discipline and that is what we would get. I was lucky I was wearing trousers otherwise I would have had some nasty cuts on my knees. I hate school already. I didn't understand anything and Mr Adesanya, the evil man who made me walk on gravel, is the Maths teacher. He kept on picking on me, saying things like, 'Come and show us how this is done in the white man's land,' or, 'Because you have been to the land of the white man does not mean you are better than anyone else.' I never even thought that.

The only class I enjoyed was English Literature and the teacher Mrs Ogunyomi is very nice. She has a daughter, Remi, in 1b, I'm in 1c. During lunch, Remi told me that her father had been to London for business. Everyone wanted to know what it was like living in London, so I told them about how you didn't have to walk a million miles every day to get water and how every house had taps. I also told them about how you didn't have to go into the bush if you wanted to do a poo, that there were toilets, which you just flushed. I told them life was different. They wanted to know what white people were like and I told them that they were just like people. Everyone laughed at this, so I offered to bring some of my treasured photographs of Aunt Sue and Uncle Eddie and the rest of the kids who were staying with them.

Even though I'll only be here for five instead of eight years, it still seems like such a long time. I wrote to Daddy and he hasn't replied yet. I asked him to send me my bike and some of my toys. Iya Rotimi comes back from Lagos tomorrow and I hope Daddy remembers to give her my things; at least I'll be able to get to school on time after going to get the water in the morning.

Dearest Jupiter,

Everything is so awful. Mr Adesanya has made me walk on gravel three times already this week, once for not completing my Maths homework and the other times because I was late. It wasn't my fault, there were too many people at the stream and it took ages before it was my turn. I tried explaining this to him but he wouldn't listen. He said I should get up earlier and that the early worm catches the bird. We got up at 4 o'clock, I checked my watch. Yesterday we ran almost all the way so that we would be the first, but we met people on their way home as we neared the stream.

My knees are cut and sore, I wish Daddy had sent my bicycle, Iya Rotimi said he didn't even send me a letter. He doesn't love me any more, he's forgotten about me already. We learnt a new idiom today in class — 'Out of sight out of mind.' I think this applies to Daddy. I asked Remi today whether her Daddy would mind taking me with him on his next trip to London. I could go back and live with Uncle Eddie and Auntie Sue in Kent, I wouldn't mind if nobody played with me in the playground or sent me cards at Christmas. At least no one there would make me walk in gravel with the sun in my eyes.

Iya Rotimi told me that Daddy might be coming home to Idogun for Christmas. I wonder what presents I'll get? I hope he remembers to bring my bike. Maybe he'll bring

Adebola with him too.

13TH NOVEMBER 1977

Dear Jupiter,

Yesterday I went to the farm with Baba Dayo and my cousins to make palm oil. Baba Dayo had cut the palm kernels from the trees and covered them with banana leaves and left them in the sun. He said this was to make it easier to pick them out of their clusters without pricking one's fingers on the thorns protecting them. We sat beside the little hut made of palm branches and picked the kernels till dusk fell. When we finished, Iya Dayo put all the kernels into two huge barrels and we built a fire underneath the barrels and left them to cook overnight. We had to get up early and Baba Dayo decided we should not go home, so we slept on the farm.

In the little hut there were some sleeping mats, which we spread under the stars. I was anxious because that very day I'd been bitten by another soldier ant and their hill was next to where we were sleeping. Baba Dayo said I didn't need to worry about them, as long as I didn't disturb them we'd be fine, that I should worry more about the mosquitoes. I couldn't sleep though, I kept on thinking of angry ants crawling all over me, biting me and getting their own back. I was a little scared because it was so dark and quiet apart from the insects. I couldn't see beyond the circle of light cast by the lantern, so I stayed close to Aina who wasn't afraid. She taught me some dance steps, we danced around the lantern and Iya Dayo told stories about *Ajapa* the trickster and I forgot to be afraid.

Aina is my favourite cousin; I just wish she didn't snore so much. When she's concentrating on something, she likes to chew her tongue as if she's chewing gum. She laughs a lot and she's not mean like Yinka. I'm older than her but that doesn't bother her like it bothers Yinka. It's really strange that I like Baba Dayo's children but dislike Iya Rotimi's. Yinka walks around as if she's a princess and everyone is beneath her. Rotimi isn't much better, but he's not as mean as her. The younger ones just do what they see their brother or sister doing. Things would be so much nicer if I was living with my Uncle, Baba Dayo instead of Iya Rotimi. Aina told me Yinka got her scarred face when she was a baby. She fell ill and they took her to a witchdoctor who cut her face open to keep her alive. The witchdoctor said the spirits wanted to take Yinka back because she is too beautiful.

When morning came the palm kernels were put into a big tub by the stream, it was made of mud, at the bottom of the tub were huge smooth stones. Once all the kernels were in the tub, Iya Dayo got in and started squishing them with her feet, after a while we all got in the tub and started squishing kernels. We had to separate the outer layer from the kernel while squishing with our feet it was great fun. Aina started making up dance steps as we squished away. Once the squishing was done, we filled up the tub with water and an orange oily gunk rose to the surface, which we just had to scoop off the top. That then had to be cooked until it turned into palm oil. It was amazing, Baba Dayo said that the kernels are then dried over several months. Once they've been dried they are cracked open and the seed inside is used to make skin oil. (Mama uses it and it smells funny.) We cooked yam in the boiling oil and ate it with garden eggs and chilli peppers that Dayo and I picked. The fresh oil was delicious. Nothing on a palm tree gets wasted, the branches are used to make roofs and huts, the leaves are used to make brooms, the kernel is used to make cooking oil and body oil and the dried shell of the kernel is used to build fires. If it was a good tree you can even get palm wine, which is a nice drink after a long hard day. I'm not allowed to drink much, because it could knock me out cold. I can only drink it if it's fresh, not more than three days old, the longer it's kept, the stronger it gets.

I did hate having to carry home the yams, cassava and corn, though. At this rate I'm never going to grow tall and if I'm not careful I'll shrink to the size of *Tom Thumb*. I can't wait to grow up, at least then nobody can make me do things I don't want to, like live in Idogun. Five years is getting longer.

25TH DECEMBER 1977

Dear Jupiter,

As you know from the date it's Christmas, Only it doesn't feel like Christmas. No Christmas tree, no fairy lights, no gift-wrapped presents, no cards. NOTHING. Just two new dresses from Daddy that are too big and an *iro* and *buba* from Baba Dayo. Iya Rotimi didn't give me anything, neither did Mama. And now, I have to go to church.

"Until the rotten tooth is pulled out, the mouth must chew with caution"

Yoruba proverb

Dear Jupiter

Well, Christmas has come and gone and it's the first day of a brand new year. Daddy didn't bring Adebola with him, he stayed in Ekiti with Uncle Joseph; he said I'd get to see him when I go to Lagos for the summer holidays. Maybe during that time I can convince Daddy that we're better off staying together as a family. Christmas was really disappointing because Daddy didn't bring any presents, not even my bike. Iya Rotimi told him that I'd been naughty so I didn't get anything, just two new dresses but they look horrible and don't fit either. He did buy all the other kids sweets, and he gave them all money to spend. Just like *Cinderella*, only instead of the wicked stepmother I've got a wicked Aunt.

If I had a mother she wouldn't let them treat me like this. The other day Yinka accused me of stealing Iya Rotimi's *chin-chin*, I'd never even been near it. A house search was carried out and the nylon pouches were found in my suitcase, as if I'd be so stupid as to steal something and hide the evidence in my own suitcase. No one believed me when I said I hadn't put it there. Because of that I wasn't allowed dinner. Now, whenever something goes missing the finger points to me and I get punished. I never get dinner and I have to wash all the dirty plates when everyone else has finished eating. What's worse is when no one is looking, I lick the plates for a taste of something because I'm so hungry all the time.

Baba Dayo is my knight in shining armour. Whenever Iya Rotimi doesn't give me dinner, (she only cooks once a day) I go over to Mama's house and sit outside my Uncle's room around the time I know he's just about to start having his dinner. It all started when I ran to Mama for help but she believed I'd been naughty too and didn't give me any food. Baba Dayo was eating, I couldn't help myself, and I sat in front of him and watched him swallow each mouthful of pounded yam. I watched him lick the okra off his hand as it slid down towards his wrist. My stomach growled so loudly that he took pity on me and offered me half his meal. It was the best pounded yam and okra soup I'd had in a long time. Iya Rotimi was upset and Mama furious, but he just told them that it was cruel of them to starve me. Uncle Niyi just this Christmas was saying how I looked like a deprived child. I looked it up in my dictionary and 'deprivation' which is listed under 'deprive' is described as 'a state of not having the normal benefits of food and shelter and clothing.' I told Daddy about it but he said I shouldn't steal. I told him it wasn't me but he just made me stoop down. I HATE him, he doesn't love me. When I grow up I'm going to go and find my mother and live with her.

Daddy said she left when I was eighteen months old. My cousins, especially Yinka, say it's my fault she ran away. They heard Daddy telling Iya Rotimi. I wish she would have taken us with her instead of letting Daddy make us stoop down and cane us all the time.

I've got one good thing to report, as of next term I'll be a boarder instead of a day student. I won't have to get up at four o'clock every morning to fetch water or go to the farm every Saturday. The school has a tanker that supplies water for the students. There is also a generator. The other good thing is I won't go hungry any more, as a boarder you get breakfast, lunch and dinner and I'm looking forward to it. In six months it will be the long holidays then as soon as I come back I'll be in boarding school. All of a sudden five years seems bearable.

31ST JANUARY 1978

Dear Jupiter

You'll never believe what has happened now, five oranges have gone missing. It's past midnight and Iya Rotimi has woken us all up to find out who has stolen them. Naturally Rotimi, Yinka and Sanmi are pointing the finger at me, but I never touched the oranges. I think I would have remembered eating them. The others have been allowed to go to bed but I must stay up and wash the dirty dishes, but there is no water. Iya Rotimi was going to make me go to the stream by myself in the middle of the night but Baba Rotimi stopped her. He asked her how would she explain it to Daddy if something happened to me. So she has made me sit outside until I come to my senses.

It's not that dark out and I've got the moon and stars for company, I like the way they twinkle in the black sky. I always thought that the night was silent but I can hear frogs croaking and insects chirping. I sometimes feel like that, silent on the inside but at the same time there's a churning that won't go away and it makes me feel bad.

I saw a shadow in the bushes that I thought could be a lion and I banged on the door but no one would let me in. As the shadow drew closer I realised it was a goat, but I'm still scared, the moon has gone and now all of a sudden everywhere is dark. I can't see what I'm writing so I'll have to stop here.

1ST FEBRUARY 1978

Dear Jupiter

You'll never believe who stole the oranges, for once my name has been cleared. Last night Iya Rotimi eventually let me in, I could tell that she was still angry with me. She said that if I didn't confess then she wouldn't be able to perform the ritual and I would die at dawn. I didn't know what she was talking about so I asked her how this was possible and she said that she had put a curse on the oranges. If anyone took one, they would be struck by lightning. I told her again it wasn't me but she kept on begging me to confess. Maybe I had taken them, but I'm sure I would have remembered. She interrogated me until I started to believe it really was me, she kept on begging me to confess because she didn't want my death on her hands. I found that very hard to believe since she was ready to send me into the jungle by myself in the middle of the night.

Eventually she believed me, so she woke my cousins up and started interrogating them, but everyone kept quiet. We heard a clap of thunder and she broke down in tears and begged the guilty person to come forward, that she didn't want anyone to die. If that was the case I wondered why she put *juju* on the oranges in the first place. I suppose she didn't think her children would steal them. I suspected it was Rotimi because I saw him sneaking into the bushes with a bag and he looked very suspicious.

Iya Rotimi opened the door and the nice clear sky had turned into a stormy one, she made us all look at the bright flashes of lightning in the sky. I could see the fear in Rotimi's eyes, even Yinka started to cry, she kept on saying *'emi ko ni mo ji.'* At first I wasn't sure if she was crying because her tears mingled with her scars and it was difficult to see them running down her face. Auntie told us that if the person didn't confess, then *Sango* would strike them down before dawn. I looked at my watch and the little hand was pointing at the three and the big hand at the nine, dawn was coming and the cocks were about to start crowing. Still no one said anything. I kept on nodding off but she wouldn't allow anyone to go to sleep. I was tired and I didn't actually say that Rotimi stole the oranges, I'm not like Squealer in Animal Farm. I just asked Rotimi in a carrying whisper what he had in his bag when he sneaked off into the bushes. Iya Rotimi of course heard me, I thought now we'll finally get the truth, but he denied it until Yinka said she had seen him take the oranges. I don't know if that was true since it was very difficult to tell Yinka's lies apart, but faced with betrayal by his sister he eventually confessed.

Then came the ritual to soothe *Sango*, the angry God of lightning and thunder. A hole was dug outside and in went the blood of two pigeons, which had just had their necks cut. Rotimi then had to strip to the waist and the blood was smeared on his body. Auntie then took some kola nuts and broke them open, chanted something and threw them into the hole. The last thing she did was pour palm oil over an iron rod and place it in the hole and that was that. Rotimi didn't get a beating or tongue lashing, just a pat on the head for stealing. I wonder what she would have done if it had been me? Guess I'll never know and to be honest, I was glad that for once it wasn't me who all the attention was centred on.

IMAGINE THIS

Dear Jupiter

I am in big, big trouble, what am I going to do? Money has gone missing and as usual the finger is pointing firmly at me. This time it's serious, fifteen Naira and a bottle of oil, I can't even cook, so what would I do with a bottle of oil? When I pointed this out to Iya Rotimi, Rotimi lied and said he saw me take the money and the oil, but I didn't, he was trying to get his own back for the oranges. I've got welts all over my body, she said she was going to beat the truth out of me. I don't remember her beating Rotimi and he was guilty. I might have died today if Mama hadn't stopped her. Even Daddy at his angriest has never beaten me like this. No one will believe I'm innocent, so tomorrow she said that we are going to go and see a *Babalawo* (witch doctor) to find out the truth. I just hope she doesn't take me to Baba Kayode because if you're innocent you end up with a hole in your tongue. That's what happened to a woman from Idoani on the last market day, she was accused of stealing by one of the wives married to her husband so they all came to Baba Kayode to find the thief.

Each person has to kneel in a chalk circle with funny markings, then Baba Kayode chants something under his breath and circles his fist round their head, then throws six cowrie shells inside the circle. Then he places a concoction of leaves on the person's tongue and then he to uses the feather of a hen or cock to drill a hole in their tongue. If you're innocent the feather goes through and you walk around with a hole in your tongue for the rest of your life just to prove your innocence. I hope we go to the leaf man, his is a much more painless way of finding out the truth.

I wish I was somewhere else, I don't care where as long as I can sleep in a nice comfortable bed with a proper mattress. I have to sleep on the floor because Yinka complained that I kept kicking her when she was asleep. So now I've got my own little space in the corridor between the room and store. I don't like sleeping there because the other day when Sanmi thought I was asleep he started to touch me so I kicked him right under the chin and he hasn't been back since, but I try to keep awake just in case.

Well, tomorrow my name shall be cleared and I'll make them all apologise to me.

21ST FEBRUARY 1978

Dear Jupiter

May the Lord be my saviour, my name is still mud and has not been cleared. I have not been found innocent but guilty by the *Babalawo*. I don't understand how because I did not steal the money and the bottle of oil. I have told Iya Rotimi that I'm willing to go and see Baba Kayode because he may not fail me as the other *Babalawo* did. We all went there first thing in the morning after we came back from the stream. The *Babalawo* brought out ten huge leaves. They looked like leaves from a horse-chestnut tree but these were larger and wider. Each of us had to sit opposite him when it was our turn and place our palm in his, face up. He then placed the leaves on top of each other with five of the stems facing me and the other five facing him. He then placed an iron bar on top and chanted for a while then spat on top, called out my name and said that if it was not me that stole the money and oil then the leaves will part without any effort and the iron will fall to the ground. It didn't happen, I tugged and tugged at it but the leaves were stuck together and would not part. So he tried it the other way round, he chanted and spat on it again and said if I did steal the money and oil then let the leaves be parted. As soon as I pulled the leaves came apart as effortless as Moses parting the Red Sea. To be sure, Iya Rotimi made him do it several times but it kept on pointing at me as the guilty one. As she dragged me home all the other kids were shouting, 'Thief' at me. They began to throw stones but Iya Rotimi stopped them just as a stone from Yinka hit the back of my head. I'm going to bash Yinka's head in the moment I get her alone and away from her brothers. To think I've been feeling sorry for her because she has a scarred face. The *Babalawo* they took her to as a baby should have let the spirits take her.

There is still a long way to go till summer but I'm counting the minutes as they go by. I miss Adebola. If he was here he'd stand up for me, he knows I'd never steal. He'd beat up Rotimi and Sanmi for me. I can hear some commotion outside it sounds like someone has just arrived.

Same day, but hours later and you'd never believe who it was. It was Daddy. He turned up out of the blue, he said he had some business in Onitsha so he decided to stop over and see me. He was really mad at Iya Rotimi. Boy was I glad I wasn't the one on the receiving end of his tongue-lashing. It almost made up for all the bad things she's done to me. Now for the rest of the term I'm going to live with Mama, not that she's any better because she always sides with her daughter against me. However, she can't be any worse, and the best thing is that she doesn't have any children living with her so I'll get to eat by myself instead of struggling to eat from the same plate with Yinka who's much faster than me, or having to eat leftovers when

I'm being punished.

I guess the fifteen Naira and the bottle of oil will remain an unsolved mystery. Now I'll never be able to clear my name, whoever said sticks and stones will break my bones but words will never hurt me obviously had never been called a thief. It hurts, every time I think about it I get a pain in my chest and a lump in my throat and I want to cry all over again, especially when I look at my welts. Five years is a very, very, very long time.

18TH MARCH 1978

Dear Jupiter

I'm ten today and no one wished me happy birthday, I didn't get one single present. I suppose those days are over anyway. Yesterday was the start of the *egungun* festival (masquerade) and women and girls are not allowed out after night falls in case we see the *egungun*. Mama said that if a woman sees them before the big dance then she won't be able to have children unless she makes a sacrifice to them, because they are messengers of God descended from heaven to grant our wishes. I've stopped believing everything I'm told ever since the incident with the fifteen Naira. I even stopped speaking to Iya Rotimi and playing with my cousins ever since Mama told me that the fifteen Naira had been found under a sack of *gari*. Since she can't say I put it there because I moved out the day we went to see the *Babalawo*, you'd think she'd apologise for her accusations and beatings but no, not a word. So when she was on her way to the market I told her that I will never speak to her again in my life and so far I've kept my promise. Although it is harder to ignore my cousins, especially Rotimi and Yinka, so maybe I won't be proper friends but just nodding friends and I'll speak to Yinka a little. If I don't, I won't be speaking to anyone and I have to speak to at least someone.

Yinka suggested that we sneak over to the square, which is off limits to women and girls and watch the *egun-gun* preparation, but she chickened out at the last minute so I went to watch by myself. I stood behind some bushes and saw Baba Ade putting on his mask. It was carved from wood and was painted black with feathers sticking out, he wore cowrie shells around his ankles, arms and wrist, red beads around his neck and his chest was painted red. Around his waist he wore a raffia skirt and he looked fierce with his shield made from what looked like the skin of a goat, but I can't be sure because I wasn't close enough. Rotimi was there as well but he didn't get into costume, he just helped the others get dressed. They all had long whips made from the branches of palm trees and when they cracked them through the air they sounded like guns being fired. I heard Mama calling me, so I had to make a quick escape.

I don't like living with Mama, she very rarely cooks because she spends most of her time at Iya Rotimi's. I haven't had a proper meal since I moved here. Baba Dayo still shares his evening meal with me so I guess I won't die of starvation yet. I have noticed that my clothes are too big, I thought as you get older you grow out of clothes, not so me. Even though it has climbed a little I can still fit into my red maxi dress with black polka dots, which I got for my eighth birthday. Daddy did always buy me clothes that were too big, but the problem with this is that by the time I grow into them they have holes, or the colour has faded.

The summer holidays will be here soon and I can go to

Lagos and stop being a deprived child. I'd just be a child deprived of her mother. Maybe I'll meet her this summer, that's my one wish.

Dear Jupiter

Today and yesterday evening was the best day in the village since I've arrived. I saw the *egungun* dancing and they were magical. A twirl of colour in the dust cloud. The drums and the cowrie shells tied around their wrists and ankles spoke the same language as the *egunguns* danced effortlessly to the delight of the crowd. I wanted to jump into the circle and twirl to the relentless beat of the drums. It seemed like they were calling me to pound my feet and gyrate to the rhythm and lose myself, but it was forbidden, women were not allowed to dance with the *egungun* until the last day of the festival. I've got to wait three days, but in the meantime Yinka has been showing me how women are supposed to dance.

Dear Jupiter

I am not speaking to Yinka and I don't think I'll ever speak to her again because she taught me the wrong steps and everyone laughed at me at first when I started to dance. I'll never forgive her even though I did have a good time. As I danced it seemed that I wasn't me any more. I forgot where I was, all I could hear in the background was the beat of the drums and the cowrie shells as they jangled together. I could see people through a haze of red dust and all I could smell was sweat. The feathers sticking out from one of the *egungun's* mask reminded me of a peacock;

they stood straight and proud. I was inside myself but outside myself too, the roar of the crowd brought me back down to earth. And then I would lose myself again. I think it was Baba Ade I danced with but his voice didn't sound the same, although I knew it was him because of the mole on his left foot. I didn't let on that I knew. Everyone congratulated me and I smiled at Yinka and put my finger in my nose to her.

Baba Dayo said that the next couple of moons will bring the coming of age festival for all unmarried women and girls. Mama will have to make pounded yam and sacrifice a chicken to Yemoja the Goddess of the river and sea. He said that in the old days all the women were suppose to get dunked in the river but now it's not necessary because you can bring the river to you.

1st April 1978

Dear Jupiter,

I have some very sad news, my Uncle has died. I didn't know him really, he's not Daddy's brother Baba Dayo. His father was Mama's brother, he lived in Akure and they brought his body home yesterday and there was a lot of crying and wailing. Iya Dayo cried the loudest. When she cried she burst into song at the same time. It was all very strange, her song was about what a good man he had been but how he had been defeated by his enemies, but that there will be justice in his death. Then she started calling his ancestors and asked them to take him on his journey home and guide him safely to the other side.

I sneaked round the back and watched them wash his body. He was just lying on the stone slab of the bathroom, he looked like he was sleeping. How did they know he was dead? I don't want to die, I don't want anyone to bathe me and stick cotton wool up my nose and in my ears. Mama caught me and dragged me away before I could see anything else, she got the cane out but I've learnt to run away as soon as she reaches for it. She told me that this was disrespectful, but all the other children ran when she came after them, so why should I stand there like a fool and let her cane me?

There was a wake, they put him in bed and sat around singing songs, fanning away flies and spraying air freshener. He looked very grey, but he just looked like he was sleeping. He can't be buried till his first son arrives from Lagos. Mama say's he was one of the many relatives who met our plane when we arrived from London, but I don't remember him.

I'm going to have to write to Daddy and tell him not to die, if he dies then I'll be left in Idogun forever instead of five years.

2ND APRIL 1978

Dear Jupiter,

Today was a very sad day indeed, my Uncle was buried in his father's backyard, which is also our backyard. Everyone was crying. Dayo said that the Gods have been asked about his death and they said that he was killed by someone close to him who was jealous of his success. Imagine that. I heard Mama telling Iya Rotimi that he was killed because he was going to become a school principal and it's the wife of the ex-principal who did *juju* for him. Mama Ade (Mama's sister-in-law) tells a different story, she says it's his wife because she found out that he has another wife and a baby. She's younger than his first wife and he kept her in a separate house, his first wife hasn't come for the funeral. Mama Ade says she is spitting on her husband. Imagine.

24TH APRIL 1978

Dear Jupiter

Last night I watched Auntie Bunmi give birth, she had a little baby boy. Auntie Bunmi is Baba Ade's youngest daughter. Mama says she has come home disgraced, she already has one child without a father and now she will have two children without fathers. When I asked Auntie Bunmi how come Seun didn't have a Daddy, she said he did but that he was a useless man who promised her everything but gave her nothing. I don't think she likes Seun, she's always shouting at him and he's only two. She said she gets angry with him because he's almost three and still can't walk. Normal children are supposed to start walking when they're one, but Seun just likes to sit in one place all day. Unless he smells food he rarely moves from his position by the front door where he watches the rest of us playing. When he smells food he crawls to the door of whoever it is that's cooking so that he can't be missed. Even Road Runner couldn't catch him when he starts his crawl from the front door.

Anyway, I got up in the middle of the night to go to the toilet since I'm no longer scared of going outside at night. I don't wet my mat any more, ever since I came to live with Mama. Auntie Bunmi was pacing up and down, I asked her what was wrong and she said she was having a baby and I wasn't to wake anyone up because she didn't want anyone to fuss. I didn't know how she was going to get the baby out without help. We had studied anatomy in biology last term and our teacher explained how children are made. The man has to stick his thing inside the woman's thing and release sperm, which I think is disgusting. You have millions of them swimming to reach the egg and fertilise it. I wonder why it takes so many? After nine months the baby is born with the help of a midwife. The nearest midwife was in the next village which was about a day's walk; although I didn't know what time it was because Yinka had stolen my watch, it was still dark and I didn't want to be the one to go out in the dark and get the mid-wife. Auntie Bunmi said she didn't need a midwife because she had me to help her. I didn't know how to deliver a baby, after all I'm only ten. After pacing some more and doubling over with pain she said she could feel the baby coming and it was time. She lay on her back on the floor and started grunting, she also panted a lot. I saw the soft hair on the head of the baby, with every push the head got larger and I kept on thinking to myself that I'm never going to have children if it was this painful. I hate pain. She gave one almighty push and the baby popped out into my hands with the blood and yuck. She made me pinch his thigh to make him cry and as soon as he started he wouldn't stop and woke up the rest of the household. Mama Dayo took the baby from me and cut the umbilical cord, which according to my biology textbook is what keeps babies alive in the mother's womb. Mama made Auntie Bunmi something to drink to help with the other bit left in her stomach. I know everything a mother eats when she's pregnant, the baby eats through the cord. Mother and baby are now sleeping. I asked Auntie Bunmi how could she stand the pain, but she said it wasn't that bad, but I'm still not convinced.

IMAGINE THIS

Dear Jupiter

All the baby seems to do is cry and eat and sleep. I'm sure I was a much nicer baby, Auntie Bunmi said she didn't sleep at all last night because the baby was crying. I didn't hear him cry and I was sleeping in the passage with Aina. Because it's been cemented it's much nicer than the floor in Mama's room, it's also much cooler. In five days' time the baby will be named, which means there will be lots of food. I can't wait.

1ST MAY 1978

Dear Jupiter,

Today was the naming ceremony of the baby and there wasn't that much food. Auntie Bunmi only made *akara* and that was it, I suppose it was something. The pastor came from church to say special prayers and the baby is now called Olutayo Adegbenro Adefose.

3RD MAY 1978

Dear Jupiter,

I really hate school, especially Mr Adesanya, he always picks on me in Maths and makes me walk on gravel the moment he notices that my sores have healed. My photographs of Aunt Sue and Uncle Eddie have also gone missing along with my watch and I think Yinka has taken them. Of course I can't prove this and I can't accuse her because she has left the village to go and live in Akure with her father. Baba Rotimi has been offered a teaching position there; I heard Iya Rotimi talking to Mama, she won't be going because she says she has a business to run. She buys sacks of *gari* from the farmers and sells them in

Lagos. My red jeans and my favourite red dress and my platform shoes have gone missing as well. I would have given Yinka the shoes and the dress if she had asked, but she never did and I really hate her and I'll never speak to her again even if she crawled on her hands and knees and begged me to.

26TH MAY 1978

Dear Jupiter

I've been sick for the past three weeks. Mama thought I was going to die because I couldn't eat anything. She boiled leaves and the bark from trees and said it would make me better, but I couldn't drink much of it because it was bitter. Everyone was really nice to me, maybe I should get sick more often. Today I feel much better, but I can't remember much of being sick, I just remember being very hot and sweaty and feeling like I'd run a hundred miles and then feeling cold and not being able to get warm. I remember lying on the floor and looking at the door and it seemed as if it was miles away instead of within reach, sounds were hollow and everything was so bright even the light of the lanterns at night. Sometimes it felt like the masquerades were dancing in my head, I could hear their incantations and their whips cracking through the air.

Dayo told me that Mama carried me on her back all the way to the *Babalawo*. I didn't believe him so I asked Rotimi and he said it was true. He said his mother was going to carry me but I became violent and started screaming so Mama had to carry me. Well I don't remember it happening, but I am glad I was horrible to Iya Rotimi because I still haven't forgiven her for the fifteen Naira incident. I'm still very weak and when I walk it feels like a gentle breeze would knock me down.

30TH MAY 1978

Dear Jupiter

Today was my first day back at school since I've been sick, I've missed a lot and exams are next week. My arch-enemy Mr Adesanya has left. Remi says he left because he is scared of Mama. While I was sick Mama went to school to beat him up. Remi said that she chased him around the classroom and screamed at him that if he ever laid another finger on me that she would call my dad and he would come and teach him a lesson. Everyone knows that Daddy is a retired boxer and he'd won medals when he was younger. I never saw them, but Baba Rotimi told me he was the State Champion and he never got beaten once. Mama blamed Mr Adesanya for me being sick because he was always making me walk on gravel on my knees in the sun and he knew I wasn't used to the hot sunshine. All the other students clapped and cheered as she chased him round the classroom. It was the Principal who put an end to it by begging Mama to stop. I wish I was there to see it happen, I can just picture Mama with her head scarf tied around her waist to keep hold of her *iro*, her white hair in plaits and her skull gleaming with oil, wielding the cane that she'd used on me on many occasions. I cackled with sheer delight. It was justice of a sort. Imagine that.

5TH JUNE 1978

Dear Jupiter

I have triumphed over my arch-enemy Emman, my tormentor. I floated like a butterfly then stung like a bee, just like Muhammed Ali who is Daddy's favourite boxer. I remembered watching some of his fights with Daddy on Saturday afternoons in front of the television. Daddy shouting, 'Jab, jab, jab!' and his endless oohs and aahs.

After the fight he'd teach me and Adebola how to box. He'd kneel on the floor, put his fists in front of his face and tell us to try and punch him on the nose while he ducked his head from side to side. We were a family then. Emman has been tormenting me forever — him Goliath, me David. Today I said no more when he stopped me after school and started to pick on me again. I decided not to be a coward and run away like I've been doing. So I put my books on the ground and my fists in the air. Someone shouted 'fight' and before we knew it we were surrounded by eager faces baying for blood. I was Daniel in the lion's den but, like the lion in the *Wizard of Oz*, my courage deserted me, and there was nowhere to run. We circled each other as the crowd shouted and clapped, shouting out, 'Fight, fight, fight!' I remembered Daddy's shouts of 'jab, jab, jab' and in that moment forgot to be scared, I just waited for him to make his first move. When he did, I side-stepped his fist and followed it with a jab. My knuckles cracked with the impact of my fist connecting with his jaw, but I felt no pain as I floated around him. He threw another punch and missed and I followed it with what Daddy called an uppercut, he went down on his knees and I pushed him the rest of the way, jumped on his back and made him eat dirt. I floated like a butterfly, stung like a bee, undefeatable, that's me.

IMAGINE THIS

Dear Jupiter

There has been another tragedy in the family, Baba my grandfather has died. He was sick the last time I saw him, and now he's dead. I was lucky not to have died when I was sick. There is much wailing and crying in the house and there are some women sitting with Mama. I can hear Iya Dayo crying and singing at the same time. Mama has told me I can't go over there to see the body being washed and dressed, I have to stay with her. Mama's face is dry, but she is wailing and throwing herself onto the ground with such force I think she might hurt herself. Each time she lands on the floor the women pick her up and dust her down, she keeps screaming she has to die with her husband and making a dash for it but never getting beyond the front door.

According to Dayo, Mama hasn't spoken to Baba since Daddy went to live in London, and that was over twenty years ago. They quarrelled over whether he should go or not. Baba wanted Baba Dayo to go but Mama chose Daddy instead because he was her favourite, but Daddy told us that he went to London to fight. Dayo and Aina keep telling me they would have been the ones born in London, not Adebola and me.

My Uncle is still at the farm and doesn't know that Baba has died but someone has been sent to bring him home. Aase, the driver who brought me here, has been sent to Lagos to tell Daddy and messages have gone out to my other Uncles and Aunts who don't live in the village. The house is still filling up with people and there's nowhere to sit, so people are standing wherever they can.

Iya Rotimi has just arrived from the market, I saw her leap from the bus and run across to our house as she heard the cries. As soon as she found out that it was Baba who had died, she tied her headscarf around her waist, clapped her hands together and threw herself onto the ground just like Mama, while the other women tried to comfort her. When Iya Rotimi took me to see Baba, he told me that she never came to visit unless she wanted something and that the only time she had come and not wanted anything was when she took me. Now she's very sad because in between her sobs she keeps on asking everyone what she'll do without Baba. I really don't want Daddy to die.

Dear Jupiter, it's the same day but much later. Baba Dayo has arrived from the farm and is on his way to Baba's house, his eyes were red but he wasn't crying. I wanted to go with him but I've been told that no women are allowed out tonight because Baba was descended from the kings of Idogun. Whenever a descendant dies the *egungun* come out to guide the spirit into the next world and as usual I'm not allowed out because I'm a girl. I'm going to try and sneak out when no one is looking.

Mama has shaved off all her long, silky, smelly hair because it is the custom of a wife to shave her hair when the husband dies as a mark of respect. There was a little ceremony before her head was shaved, I couldn't see much of what was going on because there were and still are too many people about. The hair will be buried with Baba. Mama looks strange with a bald head, she's no longer wearing her normal wrapper but the dark blue one she made last year. Baba Dayo and I picked the cotton for her from his other farm which she then spun using just a stick and her fingers. Then she dyed it and wove it into the wrapper using the machine on the wall. I'm not sure what it's called, I'll have to ask Daddy when he comes. Mama's

45

breasts aren't like Auntie Bunmi's, they're like flip flops. Even Mama Ade's look nicer, they don't droop like Mama's. I hope I never have breasts.

Dear Jupiter, same day but much later. Baba Dayo has come back, he said that the body has been washed and dressed and I'll be able to see Baba tomorrow. Mama and Iya Rotimi have stopped throwing themselves on the floor and are much calmer. It might take another two days before the body is buried because we have to wait for one of my other Uncles to turn up. He is Baba's eldest living son. Dayo told me that even though Mama is the first wife, she lost her first three children because Baba's other wife went to a *Babalawo* to do *juju*. So they all died, so now her son is Baba's first child. It's the reason Mama didn't see Baba any more; she didn't want to lose Baba Dayo, Iya Rotimi and Daddy. Which she would've if she was still living there, and I wouldn't have been born. So since my other Uncle is the eldest surviving child he has to be there before anything can be done. He also lives in Lagos so he and Daddy might be coming back together. I'll keep you posted.

16TH JULY 1978

Dear Jupiter

Nothing much has happened yet, there has been a lot of coming and going of people and they are setting up cooking fires in the yard and the front of the house. I don't have to go to school today because I've finished my exams. I can eat to my heart's content, there's a lot of food about, it's just a shame that Baba had to die before it was cooked. Pounded yam with *egusi* soup is my favourite food, I don't like it though when Mama mixes the yam with cassava or corn, I just like the pounded yam by itself. She only makes it that way when Daddy is here, that's also the only time she doesn't pour a bucket of water in the soup. She does this to make the soup last longer, but it becomes so watery that I spend my time chasing the *egusi* and *efo* around my plate. By the time I finish eating, I've got the soup dripping down my arm and on my front. Mama loves hoarding food, she never cooks the tubers of yam I bring back from the farm until they're rotting. She is always saving food for a rainy day, so I guess yesterday was that day.

Last night the *egungun* came knocking on our door, they came to tell Mama that they would take Baba safely over to the other side, I could hear their whips cracking as they danced outside our front door. I wanted to go and watch but it was forbidden. Only Baba Dayo went out to give them some pounded yam and stew. I suppose the Gods have to eat too. As soon as I've had breakfast I can go and see Baba. I wonder if they put cotton wool in his nose and ears like the Uncle who died in April?

Dear Jupiter, I've been to see Baba and he does have cotton wool in his nose and ears. There are more people in his house than there are here. I told Mama that and she wanted to know if there was anyone there who hadn't come to visit her yet. I said I didn't know since there have been so many people.

Mama Tayo, Baba's other wife, has also shaved her head and like Mama is wearing just a dark blue wrapper round her waist, but her breasts are not as flat as Mama's.

I was sitting on a chair next to Baba and got something in my eye, so I used the mirror on the table to try and pick it out, but someone snatched it away and said it was forbidden, because if I looked in the mirror then I'd see the *egungun* escorting Baba on his journey home. If I witness this then Baba wouldn't be able to continue his journey, he'd be stuck here and he'd haunt me. Since I've never seen a ghost before, I'll sneak back later and see if I really can see Baba and the *egungun*.

Daddy and my other Uncle still haven't arrived and people are getting restless, they want to get the body into the ground as soon as possible before it starts smelling. At the moment you can only smell air freshener and camphor balls. I sneaked back to look through the mirror to see Baba on his journey home but I didn't see him or the *egungun* but Iyabo, one of my cousins, saw me looking through the mirror and I had to make a dash for it before I got told off. It's getting late now and I've given up hope of Daddy arriving so I'm going to go to sleep.

17TH JULY 1978

Dear Jupiter

You'll never believe what happened last night! I saw Baba and it wasn't a dream as Mama said. I really did see him, only he wasn't blind like he was before he died. I saw him, he smiled at me then he just disappeared, so I woke Mama up and told her that Baba had been in the room but she just said I was dreaming and should go back to sleep. Well, that was until the *egungun* started knocking on our door and shouting that Baba was refusing to go on his journey because someone in the house was holding on to him. It wasn't me, I wanted him to rest in peace, I just wanted to watch him go on his journey. Iyabo told them what I'd been doing that afternoon and everyone started shouting at me so I started crying. Even Baba Dayo was cross. I told him that I just wanted to see Baba cross over safely to the other side but he said nothing living was allowed to see this. I wanted to know why the *egungun* could but I was told to shut up and that they were messengers from God so there was a lot they could do and see which was forbidden to me.

So another ritual had to be done to clear the path for Baba. This time a goat was sacrificed and I was made to eat the eyes, yuck. They were slimy and, even though they were cooked, I threw up. I read somewhere that eyes are the window to the soul. Does that now mean that I've got the soul of a goat? Mama just said that would teach me to obey my elders because they know better than me. Now I'm not allowed to see Baba until it's time to bury him. One good thing is that I escaped a beating, Mama isn't allowed to do anything, not even lift up food to her mouth. Iyabo said that she's not allowed to eat until after Baba is buried and she can't step outside for three whole moons. So I guess she won't be chasing me for a while.

Dear Jupiter, same day still but much later. Baba's eldest son has arrived from Lagos. Aase said that Daddy wasn't at home when he went to deliver the bad news so he left a message with the neighbours. All fourteen of Baba's children are here except for Daddy and it has been decided that he will be buried tonight. Mama begged them to wait a bit longer for Daddy but my Uncle says that the body will start to smell.

I've eaten three times today and it's still early morning. It was the smell of fried *akara* that woke me up. I loved waking up to the smells of food cooking I can still taste it in my mouth, I want more and I think I might as well stuff myself, because when the ceremony is over and everybody has gone back home, there will just be me and Mama and no food. I think I've over-eaten because I can barely move, but it feels great to have a full stomach, I'd forgotten what it was like. If someone dies every week or so for the next five years then I'll never go hungry again, but I might run out of relatives.

Dear Jupiter, Baba has been buried and with him Mama and Iya Tayo's hair. There were some women – I don't know who they were – who tried to throw themselves into the grave as the coffin was lowered in. There was one *egun-gun* who kept on brandishing his whip and several shots were fired by Baba's hunter friends. All his children (except Daddy), grandchildren (except Adebola & Yinka) and great grandchildren were there to see him get buried. There were lots of people there, but because Daddy wasn't there I had to stand right in front in between Baba Dayo and Iya Rotimi. On our way back to Mama's there was dancing and celebrating and I've just found out that this will continue till the next tomorrow, so I guess I'll be up all night.

19TH JULY 1978

Dear Jupiter,

The festivities are over and everyone has gone home and things are gradually getting back to normal. The ashes in the fireplaces where the women have been cooking since Baba died are still warm and the smell of food still lingers in the air. The women who have been fetching for Mama have also gone home. Daddy still hasn't turned up and I'm worried, the summer holidays start tomorrow and I'm supposed to be on Aase's bus. Mama says that if he doesn't come today then I can't go to Lagos tomorrow because I might miss Daddy. I think she doesn't want me to go because there'll be no one to fetch and carry things for her.

I hope Daddy turns up soon, my suitcases are packed and I'm ready to go.

I've been living here for ages and ages and, even though I hate it, I'm getting use to Idogun. Once upon a time I thought I wouldn't be able to bear another day, but now I'm older and one year wiser and I have adjusted to life in the village. When I first got here and used to cry that I wanted to go back to London, Mama said to me that no condition is permanent and I would eventually move on. Time has passed and instead of five I'm looking at four years and with me being in boarding school next term surely things will be more bearable.

20TH JULY 1978

Dear Jupiter

Daddy arrived late last night and for the first time in my ten years I saw him cry real tears. He was upset with Mama and Baba Dayo for letting Baba be buried in his absence, especially when he wasn't living in London but Lagos. Because of this, Daddy said he was going to dig up the body so he could say goodbye properly, but Baba Dayo said he wasn't allowed to do that. I wondered what he was going to do once he had dug up Baba's body. It's not as if he could wake him up and say goodbye.

Instead, Daddy has to be content with seeing the grave instead of the body. Mama didn't want Daddy to take me with him to Lagos and she was working on him, saying how she didn't have anyone to fetch water for her, or go to the farm since she would be confined to the house for the next three moons. Before Daddy could say okay and let me down again, Baba Dayo said Iyabo will help her fetch and carry. I could tell Iya Dayo wasn't pleased with this decision but there was nothing she could say about it. I just grinned at Mama and whispered to her that I'd miss her a lot, but she knew I didn't mean it. She always pretends to like me when Daddy is around so I did the same thing. So I'm off to Lagos tomorrow and when I get there I'll keep you updated on what is going on. I'm so excited, I'm going to see Adebola again, I bet he's had a better time than me.

26TH JULY 1978

Dear Jupiter

I'm not speaking to Adebola and I hate where we live in Lagos, it's not like the old house where we had lots of room to play and a nice backyard where we could ride our bikes. We now live in Orile Iganmu in two small rooms, one is a bedroom and the other a sitting room. They call these houses 'face-me-I-face-you' and depending on the size you can get up to fifteen families or even more living in them. Our house has ten families including us. Lagos is not like the village where you say hello to your neighbours, it's a bit like London. Our rooms are tiny, there's hardly enough room to move around in, and stacked up on top of one another in one corner are the huge trunks Daddy had shipped from London. One is being used as a table, and the furniture that couldn't be used is also stacked high in another corner, on top of which are our bikes. The worst thing is the toilets and bathroom, which we have to share with the other people who live in the house. The toilets are just a hole in the ground in the back yard and they absolutely stink. I'm afraid to go there just in case I fall in, so I make Adebola stand outside. I think I prefer the bushes of Idogun, they are much safer. But on the other hand I'm glad we don't have the kind of toilet where you have to pay men to carry the poo away. They're called *agbepo* and they come out at night when everyone is supposed to be in bed, but really they start their rounds much earlier. I've seen them carrying their loads on their heads. People cross the street not only to avoid the stench but also to avoid bumping into them, just in case they slip and you end up covered in poo. If you see them coming it's better to cross the street and not make eye contact because if you annoy them, they might decide to chase you. Imagine that.

The bathrooms are next to the toilets and we have to pick our way carefully across the stepping stones when we go to either. There isn't a proper bath tub, just a shed and a bucket of water. At least the smell of soap masks the other odours until I've finished in the bathroom. I miss the bubble baths and water fights we had when we were living with Aunt Sue and Uncle Eddie, things didn't seem too much of a struggle then. We don't really have a kitchen. There is one, but Daddy doesn't use it. We have a kerosene stove and when we need to make anything we just put it in the passage outside our door. Not that we cook much, Daddy gives us money to go to the *Bukkah*, which are the roadside cafés, and they're not always very clean. We're only allowed to go to *Hunga Holo* because Daddy say's it's cleaner than most of the others, but the food isn't as nice as Mama Ibeji's. We haven't caught anything yet so I guess we'll keep going to Mama Ibeji's, Daddy won't know and he'll never find out.

Surprise, surprise, Daddy introduced us to another set of cousins and I can't remember how we're related. They're all older than us except Bayo who's okay. He took us on our first bus ride in a '*Molue*' bus, Adebola liked it but I preferred it when we had a driver to take us everywhere. I don't remember Lagos being this dirty, there's rubbish everywhere and you can see all the green sewage, Adebola says it's where mosquitoes lay their eggs. It wasn't like this last time or maybe I just didn't see it.

Bayo took us to Atitebi, where we met more relatives who oohed and aahed over us as if we were from outer space. I even pretend not to speak Yoruba properly, my efforts amuse them and I get more money that way. One thing is for sure though, I'll have a lot of money when I go back to Idogun and since I won't be living with Mama, I won't have to give it to her. The great thing about having lots of Uncles and Aunts is that there are more people to give you money. This holiday is going to be great, Daddy has even promised to take us to the beach.

3RD AUGUST 1978

Dear Jupiter,

You'll never guess what we saw today, a dead body. Adebola had never seen one. I've seen two, I told him about Baba and our Uncle but I don't think he believes me. Bayo came rushing in to tell us somebody had been hit by a bus yesterday and the body was still there. So we decided to go and have a look. It was a man and he lay on his side with one arm sticking in the air. There was dry blood by his head and green flies were buzzing around him. I wonder if he has a family looking for him.

4TH AUGUST 1978

Dear Jupiter

The dead body is still there but now it's starting to smell and it's all swollen. Adebola wouldn't come with me to see it again because he's just a scaredy cat even though he's older than me. I am worried about Daddy though. What if he gets hit by a bus? How will we know and who will look after us? I've started sitting outside until I see him walking down the street on his way back from work. Daddy has promised to take us to the beach next Saturday. If anything else interesting happens I'll let you know. Now that Adebola and me are talking again I really don't have to tell you everything.

8TH AUGUST 1978

Dear Jupiter,

We went to Bar Beach today after church and it was boring. We didn't even have our swimming costumes on, we just walked on the sand and waded in the water a bit and then Daddy said we had to go home. It wasn't at all like when we went to Great Yarmouth with Uncle Eddie, Aunt Sue and the other kids. At church we saw Mrs Julius and her children, they just came back from London and are here on holiday. I wish I was just here on holiday and going back soon. I was very jealous and refused to talk to Nike who was my best friend when we went to church in London. Adebola thinks I'm silly, so we had a fight and I'm not talking to him either. To think that I even missed him. Next time I see him sucking his thumb I'll make sure I slap him like Daddy said to do and if he hits me back he'll get into trouble. If we're still not talking tomorrow, it's going to be a very boring day.

5TH SEPTEMBER 1978

Dear Jupiter,

We don't know what to do, I caught Adebola crying and he's finally told me about living with Uncle Joseph. He has to wait until everyone has eaten and he gets the leftovers, Uncle Joseph doesn't allow him to sleep on a bed even though there is a spare one. He's treated more like a servant and Adebola hates living there. Things are not good, we were thinking of running away but we don't have anywhere to run to and no money. I don't know what we can do or where we can go. Who will have us? First our mother left us, then Daddy carted us away to live with relatives. If they don't want us, who will? If we were still in England, we'd probably end up in an orphanage like Oliver Twist and be forever asking for more. Which one is better, living with relatives who don't love you, or in an orphanage where you just get porridge? We were happy with Aunt Sue and Uncle Eddie. Why couldn't Daddy leave us there if he couldn't look after us?

6TH SEPTEMBER 1978

Dear Jupiter

The good times have come to an end once again. Adebola has gone back with Uncle Joseph and I'll be leaving tomorrow with Iya Rotimi. I've lost my brother once again. We begged Daddy to let us stay with him, we promised not to complain about the bathroom and toilets. We were such good children he didn't even make us stoop down once. He wouldn't listen to us though. At least now I have Adebola's address and he has mine so we'll be able to write to each other.

9TH SEPTEMBER 1978

Dear Jupiter

Back in Idogun once again, nothing much has changed here apart from Mama's hair which has grown a bit. She's still her same evil self. I'm still not speaking to Iya Rotimi. When she came to pick me up I just started crying and told Daddy that I didn't want to go back. That got me out of saying good morning to her. I knew Daddy wasn't going to be swayed by my tears. He has made me cry too many times himself to feel guilty for his one and only daughter shedding lots of tears. What I need is a fairy godmother, like *Cinderella*, someone to come and rescue me.

Daddy didn't get me all the things I will need as a boarder. I'm supposed to have two check dresses for prep time but Daddy only got me enough material for one. He didn't make me a cupboard to put what little provisions I've got into. I had to beg him for days before he eventually gave in and bought me what I have, which is better than nothing. I've got a packet of cabin biscuits, a small tin of *Blue Band* butter, a small tin of *Milo* even though I told him I preferred *Ovaltine*, a packet of sugar and six cans of milk. When I told Daddy that this can't possibly last till the end of term, he just said that I'm supposed to be fed in school. I still need a cutlass and hoe for Labour Day. Daddy said I should ask Baba Dayo for one since he's a farmer. I also don't have an iron and I've only got one pair of sandals and no slippers. I guess I'll just have to manage.

11TH SEPTEMBER 1978

Dear Jupiter,

I wonder why Mama hates me so much. When I told Daddy how she treats me, he said she brought him up and he's turned out all right. I'm not sure about that though. He said I needed to learn discipline and experience hardship, that way I'd be a better person. I don't see how being unhappy and starving will make me a better person, I don't think I'm a bad or naughty person. If I ever have children I will always love them and give them whatever they want and make sure they're happy.

Mama cooked one of her rare meals today, pounded yam mixed with cassava with okra soup and as usual she gave most of it to her other grandchildren, that is her daughter's children, which means they get to have two meals. I told Mama that this was unfair but she said she couldn't cook and watch her grandchildren starve. So why didn't she give any to Dayo or Aina or the rest of Baba Dayo's children? When I have grandchildren I'll love all of them. Well, I'm going to boarding school next week so I won't have to put up with her any more. Being a boarder should be really interesting. Rotimi told me that he heard Daddy telling his mother that when he told the Principal that he wants me to be a boarder instead of a day student, he refused. He told Daddy that it would spoil the rest of the children, so Daddy had to write a letter to the Governor to tell off the Principal. Now every time I do something wrong like not wake up early enough to fetch water, Mama uses it against me, she says I can't be taken anywhere and anywhere I go or anything I touch always spoils. She said that's why my mother left Daddy. One day I'll find her and ask her if it really is my fault. I HATE MAMA.

14TH SEPTEMBER 1978

Dear Jupiter,

Mama and I have had a big fight. I got fed up with going hungry when there's food in the house. So I bought some fish from the market today and made some stew, the pepper I picked from the farm and the palm oil I used was from one of the many containers she's got hiding under her bed. She's also got half a sack of rice left over from Baba's funeral — the yam and cassava are from those I bring home from Baba Dayo's farm that we never eat because if we did, we wouldn't have anything left for a rainy day. It's a rainy day every day as far as I'm concerned. I was just very hungry and as I sat on the floor looking at the food under the bed, something just clicked in my mind. Why do I have to wait for her to cook? I should cook for myself, then I'll never be hungry. She'd gone to the market, (it's her first outing since the death of Baba in June) to sell her *ogi*, which meant she wouldn't be back till the evening, that gave me enough time to cook eat and wash up.

I'd finished cooking the stew and had just put the rice on when she walked through the front door. She was home early because she had sold all her *ogi*. Since no one else was home she wanted to know who was cooking, so I told her I was making myself some rice. She wanted to know where I got it and I told her it was from the sack under the bed, and that's when she changed into this thing, screaming and cursing me and calling me a thief. She ran to the backyard, drained the rice that was already half cooked and poured water over the wood so I couldn't continue cooking. That's when I changed and turned into the same thing. It felt good to scream and curse her in return. She put the rice in a tray to dry out in the sun and I just grabbed the tray from her, spilling the rice everywhere for the pigeons and hens to eat, then I went into the room and started to drag the bag of rice out from under the bed. I wanted to spill it all for the pigeons as well. She tried to grab the sack from me but couldn't, that's when she got her cane and started on me, but still I wouldn't let go. Somehow, I don't know how, I couldn't feel anything apart from the anger and hate and

I just wanted her to hurt as much as she hurt me. Baba Dayo had come back from the farm early and was in his room sleeping until our fighting woke him up. He came out of the room shouting at Mama, which surprised me, he normally ignores her if she's beating me, but not this time. He said *'Wetin this pikin do you, why you dey beat am so, na your pikin, na your child, na wetin; you no go change?'*

She told him that I was evil and I was going to be the one who killed her with my evil ways. He told her to remember that the child becomes the parent and that if hunger forces a farmer to eat both his yam tubers and the seed-yams, the years to come will be worse for the farmer because he will have no yams to eat and none to plant. I don't know what he meant but it made her pause for a second. By this time Iya Dayo, Mama Ade and Iya Rotimi had come from the market. Then of course there had to be a family meeting. Iya Dayo and Mama Ade couldn't believe Mama had been hiding a sack of rice under the bed. She was meant to share it with the rest of the house but she lied to them and said there wasn't enough to go round. I think by the end of the meeting she was wishing she had let me cook my rice and eat it, at least then no one would have found out she was hoarding so much food under her bed. She's always complaining she doesn't have enough to eat, but now everyone knows the truth. Iya Rotimi is always saying that since all lizards lie prostrate, how can a man tell which one has a belly ache? I would say that that is very true.

"Joy has a slender body that breaks too soon"

Yoruba proverb

17TH SEPTEMBER 1978

Dear Jupiter

Today is my first day as a boarder and this morning Rotimi and Emman helped me carry my suitcase to school. Mama didn't even say goodbye, she just hissed and said I would be back in no time, as soon as the Principal sees sense — she's just upset that she's losing her personal slave. All the other girls came with their parents and they hugged and kissed each other goodbye. I wished my parents were here.

There are about twenty bunk beds in my dorm and I share mine with Dorcas who I don't like, as she picked on me all through last year. The great thing is that Remi has also become a boarder, her mum has moved to another school in Owoh and Remi couldn't go. She's in the dorm next door. Remi and I are the only ones without any breasts and the older girls think it's funny.

After school we had to go back for prep time, this was after the day students had gone home, it's not the same as during the day. Everywhere is quiet and scary; we are surrounded by bush so I'm sure it will be easy for the bogeymen to pick us out. On our way back to the dorm I made sure I was in the middle of the line. We went back to the dinning room and had dinner, it was beans and *gari*. The beans were very watery and had lots of creepy crawlies. I spent most of the time trying to pick them out,

Remi and I had a contest to see who had the most. She had thirty-eight I had twenty-nine. The boarders from last year say that the only good meal they cook is rice which is Friday lunch time and Wednesday dinner time.

20TH NOVEMBER 1978

Dearest Jupiter

I keep forgetting to tell you things that have happened to me, I don't want to forget. Maybe one day I'll look back with fond memories, right now I have to live each second as it comes and hope I survive.

Because I'm small the girls think they can pick on me. They keep telling me they are old enough to be my mother and if it wasn't because of education they would already have given birth to a child my age. They are just jealous of me and Remi because I've been to London and Remi's dad goes there on business. So we've both started walking around like really important people, which annoys the rest of the girls.

Dorcas and I had a fight because of it, I called her illiterate and said that she couldn't speak proper English and she shouldn't be in secondary school. I told her she should go home and have those babies and that an education was wasted on her. Everyone started laughing, so she pulled my hair and tore my uniform, but I made sure I bit and scratched her. Mr Abraham the new English teacher saw us fighting, he gave Dorcas ten lashes of the cane and said that because she's older she should not pick on somebody smaller than her. He also made her kneel down in front of the class. Mr Abraham likes me because I'm the only one who answers his questions in class and I got a hundred in the last test we had. If it was Mr Ife the Maths teacher, he would have beat me instead. I don't know why Maths teachers don't like me. First there was Mr Adesanya who Mama chased away with a cane and now there's Mr Ife. But before that there was Daddy, he only liked me when I got the questions right when he taught me Maths, otherwise it was lashes from the cane and him yelling 'Stoop down there until you become smart young lady,' or I had to repeat, 'Education is everything and no one can take it away from me,' which I did until the words ran into each other and it seemed I was talking another language. I miss Daddy but I don't miss that.

The Christmas holidays are coming soon and Daddy wrote to me and said he is coming home with Adebola. There is going to be a memorial service for one of my ancestors who died ages ago and the whole Ogunwole clan from near and far are coming home for it. Even Bimpe, the current Oba's (King) daughter knows about it. She said that some of my great Uncles came to invite her father, they brought a goat, kolanuts and other things. I've never seen the Oba, Bimpe says that he never goes out unless a goat is killed and a little ceremony is performed. So I guess that's why he doesn't go out much, if he went out every day there wouldn't be many goats left in the village. Mama once told me that the Ogunwoles were supposed to rule Idogun but didn't like the rituals involved so they gave up the throne. I'm not sure how true that is. Bimpe says that if her father dies then the whole village will have to kill a goat each and mourn for three moons and that they would have to bury one of his wives with him. I asked Mama if this was true and she said they don't do that any more. I'll ask Daddy when he comes home.

IMAGINE THIS

Dear Jupiter,

The most horriblest thing happened to me today. It was so awful and I was so scared and I know the girls will never let me forget it happened. After lunch when the day students had gone home and the boys had gone back to their hostel to prepare for prep, I went into the bushes to do a poo. My stomach has been feeling funny all week, I think it's the nutritional beans they make us eat. So I went to poo and it was the soft and smelly nasty poo. I thought I finished but I could still feel something there so I used some leaves to wipe my bottom and there it was — a giant worm sticking out of my bottom! So I screamed and started running with the worm still in my bottom dangling behind and when the girls heard me scream they all rushed out to see what was wrong and they saw me with my pants around my ankles and my uniform around my waist. They all started laughing at me and no one would help me pull out the worm. I stood there crying with my pants down, dress up and a worm sticking out of my bottom and no one would help me.

Lucky for me Miss Opeyemi, the student teacher, was passing by and saw what was going on. Not so lucky she was with Mr Duro the Agriculture teacher, who saw me too. I'll never be able to go to his class again, not that I ever liked agricultural science anyway, I don't care about soil and erosion and fertiliser. It's okay if you want to be a farmer, which means being stuck in Idogun like Baba Dayo who only went to Lagos once to meet us when we arrived from London. Although I don't remember him being there, but I was only little then and there were a lot of people who came to meet us.

Anyway, Dear Jupiter, this day shall go down as the most horriblest. Miss Opeyemi took me into the bush where no one could see us and pulled out the worm. It was so long and horrible and I get the shivers just thinking about it. Miss Opeyemi said I should go to the health centre tomorrow instead of coming to school. I HATE IDOGUN, I wish I was back in London, at least I didn't get worms in my tummy. Time is moving so slowly.

30TH NOVEMBER 1978

Dear Jupiter,

Everyone thinks that Fatima is a witch because she keeps fainting all the time. Remi says that when she faints she is actually visiting her fellow witches. So tonight all the girls in the hostel are going to confront her. I'm just glad they are picking on someone else for a change. Everyone in school knows about the worm incident and I mean everyone, from the teachers to the juniors and I know they are all talking about me. No one dares to make fun of me after Miss Opeyemi heard Dorcas calling me 'Worm Girl' and made her clear the bush behind Class 1b. The thing is, I know they're all laughing at me on the inside but there's nothing I can do about that, There's nothing I can do about much when I think about it really.

Dear Jupiter, it's the same day but much later, I don't know what time since my dearest cousin stole my watch. Everyone has gone to bed and it's lights out, I'm writing this under my covers with a torch, which is dying, so that I won't get caught. I can hear Fatima still crying in her bed, I wish she wasn't in my dorm. Remi thinks she might take revenge on everyone who picked on her tonight. We all made a circle and she was made to kneel in the centre, then we all started singing church songs and trying to invoke the Holy Spirit like they do in Daddy's church. But the Holy Spirit didn't fill anyone, so they all started praying for her soul and tried to cast out the demon by hitting her with palm fronds. All the time Fatima was crying and saying that she wasn't a witch. I felt very sorry for her, I don't understand how fainting makes her a witch.

1ST DECEMBER 1978

Dear Jupiter,

Everyone wants to pick a fight with me because I'm the smallest and the youngest. Yesterday I was on my way back from the staff room, I'd gone to hand in my Maths home work, when stupid Akin bumped right into me and instead of saying he was sorry, he said, 'Look at this small girl, watch where you dey go or next time I go beat you.' All his friends started laughing at me, it made me so mad. He is bigger than me and I didn't want to start a fight, so I stood there hands on hips and told him to go and kneel down in my class since he is a year below me. That's when he started abusing my mother which was fine by me, I don't see why I should defend her. But when he started on Daddy, I wasn't having any of that. I saw Miss Opeyemi coming towards us so I slapped him right in the face and, before he could do anything, Miss Opeyemi was there and wanted to know what was going on, so I told her and she made Akin kneel down in my class until the next lesson. He says he's going to get me, but it'll be a long time before that happens.

I really hate school, I'm miserable. Apart from Remi and some of the teachers, everyone hates me. I don't know whether it's because I was born in London or whether it's something I've done. They just try to put me down all the time, it seems like I have a fight with someone every day and I'm getting tired. WHY CAN'T THEY LEAVE ME ALONE? I HATE THEM ALL. Maybe I'm not really here, maybe this is a dream. I keep pinching myself but I'm still here. What I need are Dorothy's red slippers, but where is home?

3RD DECEMBER 1978

Dear Jupiter

My hair is always itching and today I've found out why. I have lice, that's what Remi says is living in my hair. The white stuff in my hair are the eggs of the lice, Remi kept on picking them out and crunching them between her fingernails. She say's the best way to get rid of them is to put kerosene on my head and tie a scarf round it and wait for two hours. We are going to do it after prep but I'm not sure I can wait that long, I've just caught another one on my neck. Why is it that all of a sudden I'm the friend to all these creepy crawlies? First the worms and now the lice. In biology the other day we had a lesson on the human intestine and Mr Duro the biology teacher (he also teaches agricultural science) made a point of looking at me when he was talking about tapeworm. Everyone in the class laughed so I ran out and I'm never going back to any of his classes again. So that's two classes I'm not going to go to, maybe even four because I hate Mr Ife and he takes Maths and Geography, so I won't go to his classes either.

It's the same day but much later and I have been in agony. After prep Remi and I came back to the dorm and she poured kerosene over my hair then tied a scarf around it. Minutes later I was jumping up and down with the pain which was so bad it made me cry. All I wanted to do was put my head in a bucket of cold water but Remi said I have to wait until it all dried up so that the lice would die. So I lay on my bed crying with pain and praying that the two hours would go by quickly, but they went by very slowly indeed. When the time was up Remi took the scarf off and I sat on a white sheet and we combed my hair into it — and, wow, did they start dropping or what. They where all dried up and it felt like she was taking off my scalp when she started combing but it was worth it to see all the blood suckers dead, some still had life in them but we crunched them between our nails. Now I've just got to get rid of the smell, I could be mistaken for a lantern, I can just imagine them adding that to the growing list of names I'm called already. It's dark out and my scalp still hurts so maybe I should wait till tomorrow, it's also lights out. Goodnight, Dear Jupiter.

4TH DECEMBER 1978

Dear Jupiter,

Once again it has been a miserable morning at school, I've decided not to go to any classes except for English and Literature which are my favourite subjects. The Principal Mr Ogunyemi, called me into his office and told me off. He said that I set a bad example for the other students and that I have a disruptive influence, and whatever that means I know it can't be good. He is a bit like Mama, always nice to me when other people are around. He expelled Moyin from school this morning, not that I'm sorry to see her go, she was always mean to me. He called her to the front of the assembly and strutting up and down like a peacock said in his nosey voice, 'It has come to my notice that you have brought shame to my school, you can no longer be a part of this esteemed establishment, let this be a lesson to all you girls who cannot keep your legs closed. You are expelled!'

It was mean of him to expel her just because she didn't keep her legs closed. Maybe if I kept my legs open I'd also get expelled and Daddy would have to find another school for me to go to in Lagos.

5TH DECEMBER 1978

Dear Jupiter

I made myself get caught today, I was hiding under my bed when Mr Ife checked the dorms. Normally I can hear him coming and I climb out the window and hide in the bushes until he has gone, but today I wanted to go to the Principal's office and get expelled like Moyin. Mr Ife dragged me by the back of my uniform all the way to the Principal's office while I made sure I screamed as loud as I could, and he slapped me so hard that for the first time I saw stars. Now I know why Tom has stars floating round his head when Jerry hits him on the head with a hammer. I can still feel his hand on my face. I can't wait to grow up, I'll be able to hit back when someone hits me. I will never let anyone push me around when I become a grown up, and if I ever have children, which I don't think will happen to me because I don't like pain and I remember the pain Auntie Bunmi had when she had Tayo, I will never hurt them.

Well anyway, when I got to the Principal's office he wasn't there so Mr Ife made me kneel facing the wall and wait for him while he, that is Mr Ife, went back to his class. The moment his back was turned I got up and sat on the chair with my legs wide open like Adebola when he sits down. I had to wait ages before the Principal turned up, and he didn't even ask why I was there. He just knuckled me on the head twice and said to get out of his office that he doesn't want to see my face in his office for the rest of the term. So much for being expelled, but I haven't given up hope yet, I'll keep on opening up my legs until he expels me.

6TH DECEMBER 1978

Dear Jupiter,

I feel so stupid. I told Remi my plan to get expelled so that I can go and live with Daddy in Lagos and she just laughed. Moyin didn't get expelled because she kept her legs open, but because she got pregnant. Remi reckons that's why she has been sick and throwing up all over the place especially in the mornings. I'm never getting pregnant if it makes you sick, why would anyone want to get sick like that? Remi also said that Dorcas told her that she thinks it's Mr Ogunyemi's baby, because one day when she walked into his office without knocking he was touching Moyin's breasts. I think that is disgusting, I never want breasts. The boys hang around with the girls with breasts so Remi and I don't have any boyfriends. Anyway, I'm still in love with Seun from church, he is the only person who has kissed me on the lips. Just before we left London, he came to our house with his mother and we played hide and seek. I found him hiding in the cupboard and he kissed me and said that he loved me and he was going to miss me. I haven't written to him since we've been in Nigeria, I wonder if he's forgotten about me? Maybe I'll see him again one day.

Last week when we went to church I saw Mama and

pretended I didn't see her. It was the first time we had gone to the Anglican Church in Ishara, normally we go to the Methodist in Ugbe. Everyone wears their Sunday best but we are only allowed to wear our blue check smocks. I am glad though that I'm not living with her, being a boarder I get to eat three meals a day. And with the memorial service coming up, there will be food so I'll be okay for the holidays.

9TH DECEMBER 1978

Dear Jupiter,

Even though I was promoted last year to Form 2 I didn't do too well, I came last in the whole school. Daddy wasn't too pleased I can tell you that, but I see no reason why I should have to learn Commerce or Biology or Economics or any of the other boring subjects. I only like English because it's easy, Literature because I like the stories and History as well, because in a way History is a story of the past instead of a made up fairytale like *Cinderella* or the *Ajapa* stories Mama tells in the evenings. Well, anyway, I've missed most of the classes this term, so I'll probably end up at the bottom of the class again. I'm hoping that Daddy will sit up and take notice, maybe he'll eventually say enough is enough and put me in a school in Lagos where he can keep an eye on me and make sure I get my homework done.

Everyone is in school and I'm alone here in the dorm. Evil-eyed Mr Ife has just done his rounds, I don't think he's very smart. Now if I was doing the rounds, the first place I'd check would be under the beds. I saw his scuffed shoes up real close, I could've spat on them but I decided that would be asinine — that's my new word for today, it means stupid which I think Mr Ife is. Yesterday's word was asseverate, which means to state firmly and solemnly. Mr Abraham said that I need to widen my vocabulary so I've started reading my dictionary, there's nothing else to read anyway. I've finished all the books we were given for literature, Mr Abraham said that we'll be doing Shakespeare next year and he's given me his copy of Julius Caesar and I don't understand half of what they're on about, I've got to keep looking up the meaning of the phrases. Daddy would hate it if I was the antepenultimate student in my class. Dictionaries are fun, they've got weird and wonderful words and I'm only still on the A's. I'll have to learn at least five new words a day, I just hope I remember them.

"The teeth are smiling, but is the heart?"

West African proverb

18TH DECEMBER 1978

Dear Jupiter,

School is out and I've failed woefully. That doesn't matter, it's all part of my master plan, to get out of here quicker. Daddy will have to do something about it. I'll tell him I'm simply not getting a good education here because I'm so miserable and sick most of the time that I can't concentrate in class, that way he'll have no choice but to let me live with him in Lagos, then we can be a family again.

I watched parents come and pick up their kids. Dorcas my arch-enemy has an older brother, very much older, who came to pick her up. No one came for me, I knew no one would come but I couldn't help wishing for a mother to drive up in her nice car get out and call my name anxiously then hold out her arms as I ran into them. She'd then hug me and kiss me and say how much she missed me, she'd ask me about school and I'd tell her how much I hated it and she'd tell me not to worry, that she'll find another one for me just to make me happy. Then she'd take me home and cook me rice and stew with *moi-moi* and I'd eat until I was bursting. I imagine her holding my hand or stroking my head and telling me everything is going to be all right. If I ever do find her, I wonder if my life would be like a fairytale where I get to live happily ever after.

Dear Jupiter,

I'm so happy, Adebola has arrived from Ado Ekiti where he's been living with Uncle Joseph, and Uncle Niyi (Uncle Joseph's brother) has suggested to Mama that I should stay with them in the family house in Ugbe. Mama wasn't pleased but Uncle Niyi made her see sense. Daddy hasn't arrived yet, he'll be staying with Mama in Ishara while Adebola and I stay in Ugbe.

Adebola thinks Mama is nice, but I told him that she's only like that when other people are around. She's a wolf in sheep's clothing. He said Uncle Joseph is like that too. He's their servant and does all the domestic chores. He's not allowed to bring friends home or go out for more than five minutes and he has to take care of the baby when he gets back from school. He wants to tell Daddy to let him stay here in Idogun with Mama instead of going back to Ado Ekiti. I told him my master plan of trying to get myself expelled but he doesn't think it will work, he thinks Daddy will just cane me and make me stoop down. We'll see.

The house here in Ugbe is a nicer house, it's not like the one in Ishara. For one, it's been cemented and painted, the upstairs windows are glass louvre, which I don't like because there are no curtains and anyone can see inside at night. Downstairs has wooden windows which makes the rooms look darker during the day because they don't let much light in. Uncle Niyi brought a generator from Lagos so we're the only house in the whole village to have electricity. He brought a small television too but the picture isn't very good. Last night it seemed like we had the whole of Ugbe round to watch the football. We have a tanker to deliver water so there's no getting up in the morning to walk millions of miles for a bucket that doesn't last the day. There's lots of room and Adebola and I will be sharing our room with Uncle Joseph's children and Soji, Uncle Niyi's son. No one has to sleep on the floor because we've got bunk beds. We also have two sitting rooms, the upstairs sitting room is for us and the downstairs sitting room is for visitors and the adults.

The other good thing is that there's toothpaste, I can't remember the last time I brushed my teeth. I've been using a chewing stick and I hate it because my teeth never feel clean afterwards and I know I've got bad breath. We're going to the farm later with Uncle Niyi to collect some palm wine, and we'll be driving there. I'm not sure how far we can go before we get stuck in the forest, we'll probably have to park and walk the rest of the way. I don't mind, I won't have to carry a zillion yams on my head, I've shrunk enough already. I wish I could stay with Uncle Niyi, I really like him and I think he really cares about me because he's always hugging me and he even makes me sit on his lap sometimes.

20TH DECEMBER 1978

Dear Jupiter,

The celebrations have started, the old women with the beaded gourds have already come round dancing, a goat has been killed along with some pigeons and a sacrifice has been made to the Gods. The masquerade will come out, but only at night and as usual I'm forbidden to see it just because I'm a girl. Adebola has never seen a masquerade before so he's looking forward to it. It's so unfair, I'm going to try and sneak out when it starts.

It's much later and the cow that is going to be killed for

the party has just arrived, it's got horns, I didn't know that cows had horns like antelopes. Daddy has also arrived, he wanted to take me back to Mama but Uncle Niyi stopped him. Daddy said that Mama needed me to help her out, but Uncle said that I need to be with Adebola so that we could bond again, whatever that means. I think he still very much thinks of me as a deprived child. He's been making sure that I eat every two hours. I'm glad Daddy didn't make a fuss. Mama can be so evil sometimes, she came here yesterday and saw that I was having a good time and she just wants to ruin it. Right, Dear Jupiter, I'm off to dance. The male dancers have turned up and I can see Uncle Niyi and Adebola having a go but Adebola's not fast enough. I'd better go and show them how it's done.

Same day but much later. Uncle Joseph caught me, just as I was sneaking through the door he was coming in. He asked me where I was going and I said to the bathroom, so he walked me to the bathroom and stood outside but I couldn't go because I'd already been. So I stood there hoping someone would call him. He couldn't see what I was doing because I'd covered the front of the bathroom with my wrapper. I was about to admit defeat when the *egungun* turned up again. Uncle Joseph made me stay where I was because if I had been seen they would've probably demanded another goat sacrifice and made me eat the eyes like last time.

I had to stand in the bathroom and couldn't see anything through the palm fronds, which are thicker than the ones used to make Mama's bathroom back in Ishara. If you have a bath and don't throw a wrapper over all four sides you can be seen through the palm fronds. I've seen Baba Ade and Baba Dayo naked and I saw Auntie Bunmi once.

The masquerade called out everyone's name, starting from the youngest person who is Soji. They said a prayer for the living and said our ancestors are looking after us from the other side. I imagined them looking down from heaven and nodding their heads sagaciously, I wanted to say with sagacious approval but sagaciously sounds much more important because it's a longer word. While I stood in the bathroom, in my mind's eye I could picture the *egungun* hopping nimbly from foot to foot and shaking his cowrie shells, gyrating to the beat of the drums. For the first time in my life I wished I was a boy so that I could dance with the *egungun*.

Dear Jupiter, it's much later, in fact it's very later and Uncle Niyi and Uncle Joseph are arguing because of me. It's all my fault. When the *egungun* left Uncle Joseph dragged me back inside by my ear and pushed me against the wall. I banged my head and started crying and he said I was never to disobey him again and he gave me four lashes of the cane while his kids made fun of me. Uncle Niyi came back and saw me crying and wanted to know what happened, so I told him that I was on my way to the toilet (I couldn't tell him I was on my way to see the *egungun*) when Uncle Joseph caught me and he beat me because I got caught outside when the *egungun* turned up. I told him that it wasn't my fault and that if Uncle Joseph hadn't been standing there then I'd have been able to go. So now they are arguing and everything is my fault, I should listen to my elders because they are sagacious. (I'm not sure I like the word any more, it doesn't sound right.) One person I can say I don't like is Uncle Joseph. I thought he was nice like Uncle Niyi but he's not. Adebola said that I was lucky I didn't get more than four lashes, and he showed me the marks on his back. Uncle Joseph never stops at four with him and he doesn't use a cane, belt or ruler, he uses a *koboko* (horse whip), which according to Adebola is much more painful than the rest, he said it cuts into your skin and leaves gashes that take ages to heal. He must be telling the truth because when Daddy caned us he never cut our skin and made us bleed, he just left big welts which still hurt. When we were younger, Daddy would use the ruler on our knuckles, then he started using the cane on our palm and if a cane wasn't available he'd use his belt. I hate the belt, because when Daddy says give me your hand the belt has a way of snaking under the back of the hand so it's like you are getting beaten twice, on the palm and on the back of the hand.

They are still arguing. I hope they don't send me back to Mama, I really hate Uncle Joseph now. Uncle Niyi is my knight in shining armour just like Lancelot. Baba has come back and they've stopped arguing. Baba is my grandfather's brother and Uncle Joseph and Niyi's father. He's telling off Uncle Joseph, I better stay clear of him tomorrow. I like Baba, he's like Uncle Niyi, nice, my knight in shining armour too.

21ST DECEMBER 1978

Dear Jupiter,

I said good morning to Uncle Joseph and he smiled at me and asked whether I was feeling better today, maybe he feels guilty because I've got a bump the size of a football on the back of my head. Just thought I'd let you know.

Would you believe Adebola is being asinine, he said I shouldn't be calling him Adebola, that I should call him 'Brother.' He's beginning to get on my nerves, he's only one year older than me and he says I have to show him respect because of that. So what if he's older? I don't see why I should call him brother or broda, I've always called him Adebola and I will always call him Adebola. When I told him this he said three hundred and sixty-five days is not a joke, now what does that mean, am I laughing? No, I don't think so. Well, he's not talking to me at the moment but he will, he always gives in first, besides it's the two motherless children against the rest of them. Uncle Niyi's wife, Iya Soji, has just arrived, she's a teacher and couldn't get away in time. I don't like her because she doesn't like me. I can always tell when someone doesn't like me, it's in their eyes, no matter what the mouth is doing the eyes usually tell me another story. When Baba and Uncle Niyi look at me there is a sparkle in their eye and a warm smile on their lips. Baba's eyes crinkle up and I can almost count the wrinkles around them. Uncle Niyi has the same smile but no wrinkles. Mama's smile is more forced, her eyes more cold when she looks at me, but not when she looks at Yinka, I wonder why? What do I keep doing wrong? I don't want her to hate me and I don't know what to do to make her like me just a little.

Dear Jupiter, we've just come back from what I would call a relative greeting. That is Adebola, Soji, Uncle Niyi and me went together. Iya Soji and the rest of the women cooking were not pleased when I took off with them. They said that a woman's place is in the kitchen and I should help fetch and carry, but I had no intention of missing out on the fun. Uncle N just told them that there's a time for that when I'm grown up, and I didn't need to start this minute. We had to go see Mama first. I could tell that Yinka, who is back for the holidays, and the rest of my cousins, were green with envy when they saw us pull up in Uncle N's car. (He really does need a new one because this one is falling apart and it groans and grunts a lot.) Mama gave me the evil eye as usual, but hugged Adebola and Soji, who's a pest really. He always wants to follow Adebola and me wherever we go, he's five and speaks a different language entirely. He's okay though; I just boss him around and make him do the fetching and carrying. I wish I had a little brother just like him. We went to see some other relatives then went back to Mama's to pick Daddy and Baba Dayo up and take them back with us to Ugbe. Lots of the relatives are here, I've counted at least 35 not including children and there are more to come. The cow is about to get its neck cut, and we're not allowed downstairs but we can watch from the balcony, it's a great view. Uncle Joseph and Daddy have bald patches on their heads.

The cow has been killed and at the moment it's being carved up, a hole had been dug this morning and when its neck was cut all the blood drained into it. It took one blow of the machete, the hunters tied its legs together and also its horns so one person was pulling the legs one way and the other person was pulling the horns the other way. With its neck stretched out over the hole, kolanut and schnapps were offered to the Gods and our ancestors. Baba Alaba chanted something, raised his cutlass and down it came. The blood spurted like a fountain and the cow's body started jerking and it tried to get up then it became still, and that's when the gun went off. Well, it's not really a gun, it just sounds like one, it's really a tube dug into the ground, gunpowder is put into it, then a string is lit and it goes bang just like a gun. We're off to play cowboys and Indians and Soji and I are the Indians,

Adebola and Bose are the cowboys. Adebola always gets to play cowboy, and I always get shot dead. I'm going to have to teach the Pest how to pow-wow.

Dear Jupiter,

It's four in the morning and I'm having a good time, everyone is still dancing. I've made about thirty Naira from dancing, so I'll be able to buy provisions for next term, as I know Daddy probably won't give me enough for the term. He's mad at me, because my school report wasn't too good. All he has to do is take me back with him and my school work will improve. I heard Uncle say that we were supposed to have Sunny Ade but he was fully booked so we have to make do with Danny Kay, the local band, who's just as good. Adebola and I are going to stay up till the morning because there's another ceremony and we don't want to miss it. Daddy is throwing money in the air for the kids and everyone is scrambling to get some. When I asked him for some he said he didn't have any. Why do grown ups always lie? I'd never lie to my children if I have them. I'm still not sure whether it will be a good idea for me to go through all that pain like Auntie Bunmi. I told Adebola but he didn't believe me, he thinks I'm making it up but my imagination is not that big. I am really tired now maybe if I close my eyes for a second I'll be okay.

23RD DECEMBER 1978

Dear Jupiter,

All the ceremonies are over, I missed yesterday's and disaster has struck, something terrible has happened to Adebola and it wasn't my fault. It was his suggestion that we play cowboys and Indians and as usual he was playing the cowboy so I had to be the Indian again. The hunters had forgotten to take the gun in the ground with them and Adebola, being the cowboy, had to have a gun, so we raided Baba's room and found some gunpowder, which we stuck down the tube. We used a stick to press it down and lit the piece of string like we had seen them do but it wouldn't go off. So Adebola went to see if it was okay and it went off in his face and now he can't see and his skin has come off. Baba broke some eggs over it and Uncle Niyi has driven him to the medical centre in the next village.

Adebola is back and his face is bandaged up, Uncle Niyi says that he has second degree burns and it will heal without a scar if he's lucky. He still can't see though, he might become like Baba who died blind. That would be horrible, not being able to see. He's blaming it all on our absent mother and I agree with him, because if she was here we wouldn't have left London. If she hadn't left then we wouldn't have been in foster care with Aunt Sue and Uncle Eddie, and Daddy wouldn't have had to leave London because they were going to take us away from him. She would have been there to look after us properly since he couldn't. So if she was around she would've stayed at home and we would've had someone to come home to instead of an empty flat and biscuits for dinner. But Uncle Niyi says that Adebola is just being silly. 'Are you stupid? How can you blame your mother for your actions? Did she force your face there? Did she say Adebola put your face in front of the cannon? Look at this boy ke, have you no common sense? They no de teach am for London?' He became very angry with Adebola and I agree with Uncle N too, Adebola really shouldn't have made us play cowboys and Indians with real gunpowder. Uncle Joseph is leaving after Christmas which is only two days away and I'll have to go back to Mama. I'll miss Adebola all over again. I wonder if Daddy got me anything this year, probably not.

25TH DECEMBER 1978

Dear Jupiter,

It's Christmas day and I woke up very excited, because I knew Uncle N got me a present. He gave me a pair of orange shorts and a book — Little Women, which I read when I was six, but I can read it again as I can't remember what happened. Adebola got a pair of shorts too and a book on aeroplanes. We're back from church and everyone was in their Sunday best even though it's Monday. The whole family went for a blessing and we all wore the same outfit, Uncle N calls it 'and co,' it was nice being part of a family gathering.

Adebola leaves tomorrow and I won't see him again for ages, but we have vowed to write to each other. He would rather stay here in Idogun than go back with Uncle Joseph, but what can we do, we have no say in how our lives are run. Everything is for our own good, when Mama is beating me black and blue it's for my own good, when I'm starving it's for my own good, I'm being forced to live in a village where I don't have any friends except Remi, but it's still for my own good. I wish somebody would do something that isn't for my own good for a change, or even ask me what I want for my own good, because I have lots of thoughts on that subject. I think for my own good we should all go back to London and our old school and live happily ever after, without the canes though. If that's an impossible wish then, for my own good, Adebola and I should live in Lagos with Daddy as a family because families are meant to be together. But what would I know? I'm only ten, well almost eleven now. I wonder if Daddy will send me a present when he goes back to Lagos. I'd really like my bike. Off to make the relative rounds again, then to the farm to pick some oranges, then in twenty hours' time Adebola will be leaving me.

26TH DECEMBER 1978

Dearest Jupiter,

You are the only one who listens to my woes, my brother who I sometimes love and sometimes hate has gone, I ran after the car so that I could keep the picture of his bandaged face in my mind for as long as possible. Sometimes it's hard to remember what he looks like. Now all I'm going to remember is the blast going off in his face and the bandages covering the burns. I just hope it heals and he doesn't have a scarred face. I waved and waved till I could see him no more. Well, at least Uncle Niyi won't be leaving till after New Year's Day. Iya Soji is going back tomorrow though, which is good. She really doesn't like me I can tell, like I said it's in the eyes.

1ST JANUARY 1979

Dearest Jupiter,

The good times have come to an end once again. Uncle N leaves for Lagos tomorrow and I have to go back and stay with Mama until school reopens. Daddy leaves tomorrow as well, Uncle N is going to give him a lift back. Mama has been telling tales about me again, she says that I don't respect her and that I abuse her. When she tells me that I'm stupid or crazy or that my head is not correct, I just tell her there's nothing wrong with me. How can that be abusing her? But Daddy says that when an elder is telling me off I mustn't reply back and if I do then I am being disrespectful. I think she's being disrespectful calling me horrible names and putting curses on me just because I'm young. When Rotimi says things, she doesn't complain to Iya Rotimi, only when I talk back.

9TH JANUARY 1979

Dear Jupiter,

It's my first day back in the dorm and I'm the only one here, not that I'm surprised. Most of the other girls probably won't be here till tomorrow which is Sunday. I'm sure their parents won't want them to go too soon. Mama was being her usual evil self so I decided to come back today. I just hope someone else will turn up because I don't know how to put the generator on and I can't sleep here all by myself in the dark.

Dear Jupiter its night and I'm all alone and I'm scared. There isn't a moon or stars, it's black out and the frogs are croaking and I can hear some owls hooting as well. I don't think I'll be able to sleep, I need to go but I'm too afraid to go outside.

I've done it in Dorcas's bowl, I'll throw it into the bush when it's light and if she asks me if I've seen her bowl I'll just say no. I think I can hear whispering; maybe it's the witches waking up for their midnight meeting. Mama said that this is the time for them to come out, when everyone else is asleep. Only I can't sleep because I'm afraid that if I do that I'd become one of them. Mama said that the only way a person can become a witch is to accept food in one's dreams and eat it, and I haven't had dinner. I could have one of my dreams again, the one where I'm sitting at a table that has all kinds of food, lots of ice-cream and Mama's *egusi* soup that she cooks once every three months with piping hot pounded yam. There's also *jollof* rice, fried rice, *akara*, the apple pie Aunt Sue used to make and much more. All the food I like, no beans with creepy crawlies, no cooked carrots and no *ogi* either. Now how will I be able to resist that when I'm so hungry? But then again if I become a witch maybe I'll get superpowers and I'll be able to hurt all my enemies, I'll make them starve and make them afraid of me. Or maybe — even better yet — I'll make myself a potion that every time I drink it and put my hand in my pocket, I come out with a 10 Naira note. That way I'll never be hungry again. I'll be able to buy any food I want. The cooks didn't think anyone would turn up today, which is why they didn't make dinner. If I had a home, I know I'd rather be there than here, but I'd rather be here even though it's scary, than back in Ishara with Mama.

10TH JANUARY 1979

Dear Jupiter

It's Sunday and all the other girls have arrived with their parents. I watched from the window as they waved their goodbyes. Dorcas has brought more food than anyone, her parents spoil her because she's the only girl and she has five older brothers. So anything she wants she gets. I've decided to try and be her friend this term, especially since I did it in her bowl. I feel really bad about that but I couldn't help it. I didn't sleep a wink last night, all I did was jump at every hoot the owls made or every croak from the frogs. I'm pretty sure I saw a ghost but I can't tell anyone that, they'd think I was a witch. If I did become a witch I'd like to be a good one, I'd feed all the starving people like Jesus did with his five loaves of bread and fish. I'd create a potion and anyone who drinks it will never go hungry. I'd make all the bad people like Mama do good things only and I'd make Daddy love me and my mother come back and live with us so we could be a family. The bell is ringing for dinner.

15TH JANUARY 1979

Dearest Jupiter,

More bad news, there won't be any boarding at the end of the year. I'll have to go back to living with Mama, unless I can get myself expelled before then. Either that or I deliberately fail and Daddy wouldn't have any choice but to keep me under his watchful eye. Imagine that, let the good times roll. Dorcas update, we're talking to each other like friends, I'm not sure if she likes me properly yet or if she's just tolerating me. I'm helping her with her English, her grammar is atrocious, which is another word for terrible. Mr Abraham is impressed with my improved vocabulary. We had to write an essay on what we did over the holiday. So I wrote about how Adebola got his face blown off during the festivities. I hope he's all right, I'll write him a letter.

17TH JANUARY 1979

Dear Jupiter,

Tragedy has struck our dorm, Fatima has tried to kill herself. The girls (I didn't take part) decided to try exorcising the witch in her again since it didn't seem to work last time because she still had fainting fits and still goes into the other world. So yesterday night they all gathered in a circle with Fatima on her knees in the middle with a Bible balanced on her head. Whenever the Bible dropped to the ground she was knuckled on the head seven times or whipped once. Jumoke, who was the person who started it (she's also Remi's half sister) said that it is a taboo to drop a Bible and normally punishment is by death because it means you are not worthy of living because you do not respect the word of the Lord. I don't know whether this is true or not, since I haven't read the Bible cover to cover. I only like some of the stories, like when David conquered Goliath or when Daniel was put in the lion's den. Whenever I have to go into the bush by myself I always imagine myself as Daniel, that way I'm not as scared. Jesus said in the Bible that faith can move mountains, so I try and have faith, I have to believe that one day I will leave Idogun. Because I believe that it makes it easier to carry on. I still sometimes count the days, but not the hours because there are too many.

Well anyway, Fatima was so upset she cried through the night and when it was morning she wasn't in her bed. Titi, her best friend, found her in the Labour Shed, she'd drank half a gallon of gamoline which is used on the cocoa plants to stop insects eating them. Jumoke forced palm oil down her mouth and she kept on choking and throwing up. She's been taken to the hospital in Owoh which is the nearest (it takes two hours.) She can't go to the medical centre because they only have bandages and aspirin. I hope she gets better. Jumoke has to report to the Principal tomorrow, she might get expelled. Maybe I should say it was my fault as that way I'd get expelled instead. I'll go and talk to her.

It's still the same day and Jumoke is such a coward, she's

already told all the girls to lie for her. When I told her I'd say it was my fault, she jumped at the chance of me taking the blame. Remi isn't too happy about it because she doesn't like Jumoke. They've got the same father but not the same mother. Her dad has three wives and Remi is the second born and Jumoke the first. But he married Remi's mum first and when she couldn't give him children in time, he married Jumoke's mum who got pregnant before Remi's mum. Then to make matters worse for Remi's mum, she only had Remi and no other children but Jumoke's mum has two boys and two girls. Remi thinks she's a witch who has put *juju* on her mother because she wants the riches for herself. Remi and her mother, before she moved to Owoh, lived in the backyard and Jumoke's mum and her children live in the main house with the third wife who is a bit older than Jumoke, and pregnant too. I wouldn't want to live in their family. Besides, I don't see why if a man can marry more than one wife, the wife can't do the same. That's what I'll do if it happened to me. Remi and I are kindred spirits, we both suffer. Her more than me because at least I have Adebola. Even if he's not right here with me, I know I'm not alone. I'd hate to be alone. When you think about it, I suppose that's why she got the name Oluremilekun. It means 'God has stopped my tears.' So maybe her mother had been crying a lot when she couldn't have a baby, then she was able to have one because God didn't like seeing her crying.

18TH JANUARY 1979

Dear Jupiter,

I am not a happy person, my plan did not work. I thought I would be expelled for sure but when I went to the Principal to tell him it was me, he put me on Labour for three days. This means that I have to work on the school farm for three whole days and I'm not allowed to attend any classes, so I'm going to miss double Literature tomorrow, my favourite class, it's just not fair.

19TH JANUARY 1979

Dear Jupiter,

I don't have to work the three days any more because Remi came to my rescue, so did my new friend Dorcas. They both went to the Principal on my behalf and told him that it was Jumoke who started the witch-hunt, and that she said she'd beat me up if I didn't say it was me. So Jumoke got ten days Labour, six for the original three and four for threatening to beat me up. She doesn't like me very much at the moment, but it's not my fault because if she wasn't such a coward in the first place she would only have three days

31ST JANUARY 1979

Dear Jupiter,

I got a letter from Adebola today, for the first time my name was called out in assembly when they were giving out letters.

Ivy Secondary School
P.M.B 13002
Ado Ekiti
Ondo State

12th January 1979

Hi O,
Happy New Year, did you make any New Year

resolutions? I couldn't think of anything I needed to change apart from leaving this place and it's not in my power to change that. How are you anyway? I hope this letter reaches you in good health. Things have gone from bad to worse with Uncle J, he's still working me like a servant instead of treating me like his nephew. Lola, we'll have to do something about our situation, maybe running away would be the better option because quite frankly I can't take much more of this. I think we should've taken off when we had the chance in London. It will be harder here but I'll get a job and take care of you since father isn't really up to the job, we'll just have to wait till I'm a bit older.

All I seem to do is clean, clean and clean. If anything needs doing, whose name is it that gets called? ADEBO-LA. Adebola do this, Adebola do that, go here, go there. According to Uncle J, it's training for when I get married. If my wife can't clean then I can shame her into it by doing it myself. When I get married I will have a house girl or boy to do all the hard work.

I've been ill, but I'm getting better. Uncle J says it's as a result of the blast in the face that I got during the memorial. I thought I was going to go blind, but my eyes are okay and the skin is healing gradually. I haven't been to school since term started so I have a lot to catch up on when I do go back. The good news which I should have told you first is that I got a letter from Daddy and I'll be able to board next year. I'll only see Uncle J during the Christmas and Easter hols. the long ones we'll spend together with Daddy in Lagos.

So I'll be seeing you in July, or is it August? Anyway, when we see each other we can try softening Daddy up and see if he'll change his mind. We might get lucky, but don't

get your hopes up, I don't think he wants us living with him. Remember that I love you even if you are a pain, sometimes I miss you (when I don't remember you as the stubborn donkey you can sometimes be).
Lots of love and xxxxxxxs
Adebola (Your one and only handsome and suave brother)

He's so silly, sometimes I think they made a mistake with our birth certificates and I'm the eldest. He obviously didn't look up the meaning of suave before he wrote it down, because according to my dictionary it means having smooth and sophisticated manners. Manners are one thing Adebola has none of, he can be such a pig, like burping in my ear after he's finished eating or farting in my face. I'll write back and tell him he won't become Prince Charming if he carries on the way he does.

I didn't think of a New Year's resolution, but the one thing I'm going to try and change is living in Idogun. If everything goes to plan, I'll either be expelled or I'll fail so miserably that Daddy won't have a choice but to let me live with him where he can take proper care of me. Daddy always says that its important to be somebody and the only way to be somebody is with a good education, He'll have to make sure mine improves.

5TH FEBRUARY 1979
Dear Jupiter,

Dorcas is sick, well she's mostly sick in the morning; she keeps throwing up and won't eat her food. As her new best friend, she gives it to me, especially since she got thirty out of fifty on the last English test. She sat next to me and I let her see some of my answers, luckily she's got a very long neck.

Dear Jupiter,

Just got back from church. We went to the Methodist in Ugbe and Dorcas fainted. Maybe she's become a witch like Fatima, who isn't coming back to school, or maybe Fatima cast a spell on her before she left. Well, that's what Jumoke said to Remi, not that I believe her.

Dearest Jupiter,

I have the juiciest piece of gossip and I can't wait to tell Remi who's gone to school. I won't be going till third period when I have English. Anyway, I was under my bed as usual when Dorcas came back into the dorm, and just as I was about to come out and say hello the Principal followed her in. So I just hid, all I could see were their shoes but I think he was kissing her. Yuk yuk yuk, they were really K.I.S.S.I.N.G. Then she told him that she wants to become his second wife. 'I don carry belle, we must marry,' is what she said to him. Then he said, 'You're pregnant, how can you be pregnant, why you go carry belle?' He kept on saying, 'This is bad, how can you be pregnant?' I wish I could've seen his face, he didn't sound very happy. I could see his shoes turning round in little circles and I imagined him shaking his head, his left arm behind his back as he listened to Dorcas begging to be wife number two. She wants her own house separate from his other wife. Imagine that, Dorcas pregnant and the Principal is the father. It must have been true about him and Moyin then.

Anyway, the Principal said that he loved her, but he has to think of his job and how to feed the seven children he already has. If he takes her as his second wife, then people will know that he got her pregnant and he might lose his job, so she'll have to get rid of it and he'll pay for it. I wonder how that happens. Dorcas started to cry and said that if her parents found out that they'd kill her and him. He just said there was nothing he could do and that he had to think of the many instead of the one.

I almost got caught because I almost sneezed. If that had happened I'm sure he would have done some juju to kill me. He left first then she cried some more then left. I didn't think she'd like it if I'd let her know I heard everything. Imagine, Dorcas and the Principal? She probably did it to get good grades, Remi calls it bottom power. She came last in class last term, just behind me. She is so dumb, at least I'm not at the bottom of the class because I'm dumb. I just refuse to learn because I have a plan. I want to be expelled or I want Daddy to rescue me. Imagine that, Dorcas and the Principal in the tree K.I.S.S.I.N.G! I'll only tell Remi because she's my friend.

9TH FEBRUARY 1979

Dear Jupiter,

Dorcas's secret is round the whole school. I only told Remi though, so she must have told other people even though I swore her to secrecy because Dorcas is now my friend. Gbenga her boyfriend is very upset and he smashed the windows of the Principal's car. I thought he was going to have a fight with the Principal but Mr Abraham took him away to calm him down.

Dear Jupiter,

Gbenga, Dorcas's now ex-boyfriend, has been expelled from school. The Principal called him out on assembly this morning. He did the walk that he does when he's about to say something important, he put his left arm on his back while his right hand stroked his chin, and as he wandered up and down in front of the assembly, his head was bowed as if he was carrying firewood on his head. He told us all that due to his act of vandalism and hooliganism, Gbenga was no longer welcome at school. Gbenga started to call him horrible names and said that he's nothing but a womaniser who keeps on giving his female students babies. Of course he tried to deny everything, he said that these were false rumours and he has never given a student a baby (something along those lines anyway). I wish I could have come out and told what I heard, but Dorcas is my friend and she's already starting to suspect I started it. She doesn't know for sure though.

Dear Jupiter,

I got called into the Principal's office today. He wanted to know if it was me who started the rumour but I denied it. Then he wanted to know where I was yesterday morning so I said I was in class. He pulled out the register and showed me that I was marked absent. I just told him that I was late and the register had been marked before I got to class. Although I want to be expelled, I don't think he would have expelled me for repeating what is true, he probably would have given me a whole month of Labour and lashes from his horse whip, the one her reserves for his special students. He hasn't used it on me yet, he knows that Daddy is an ex-boxer who might come and beat him up if he hurts me. Or maybe he's frightened of Mama coming round with her own whip. Although thinking about it, Daddy and Mama would probably be cheering him on, saying flog her harder; it's for her own good.

13TH FEBRUARY 1979

Dear Jupiter,

Dorcas went home yesterday, (I think she went home). Aase picked her up very early in the morning on his way to Lagos. I gave him a letter to give to Daddy, there wasn't really anything much to say other than that I'm having a miserable time and that I miss him and that I want to go back to London and I'd also like my bike.

The cooks want more money so they have refused to cook, the food stores are locked so we have to go to the school farm and dig up some yams. We'll have to eat them with palm oil and salt which is the only thing not locked up in the store. Remi and Jumoke have decided to go home and come back in the evening. I could go to Mama's, but there won't be any food there so I'm better off going to the school farm.

14TH FEBRUARY 1979

Dear Jupiter,

The cooks are still not cooking so the Prefects had to choose some of the big girls to cook for the whole school and it tasted better than what those cooks make. I hope they don't come back, they should let the girls always cook for the school. We had rice and beans on a Monday; we normally have cold nasty *eba* and watery okra. I'd take watery okra over starving any day though. All the girls apart from Remi and me got a Valentine's card today. The boys are only after the girls with breasts, I hope I never get any.

Dearest Jupiter,

All this trouble is my fault, I should have kept my big mouth shut. Gbenga's mother came to school today very upset. She tied her head-scarf around her waist, her hair was all messy and needed to be plaited again. Anyway, she turned up during assembly and started crying and begging the Principal to let Gbenga come back to school, since he's the firstborn son he needs to get a good job so that he can take care of his brothers since their farm isn't doing too well. The price of cocoa has fallen and they didn't have a very good harvest last year, so things are rough and will get worse too. I felt so bad, she kept saying, *'I beg una, im be doctor, I beg.'* The Principal just said there was nothing he could do, and that he has to set an example and remove the bad apple from the cart.

If I hadn't told Remi, then no one but me would've known and Gbenga would still be in school and his mother wouldn't be in tears. I'm such a bad person, but I didn't mean to be. I wonder if my mother would cry if I ever got expelled from school? Would she get down on her knees like Mama Gbenga and beg the Principal to show mercy? Just imagine that.

Dear Jupiter,

Today was the day where bottles flew and stones whistled overhead. There was a riot between our school and Ireakari Grammar School which is in the next village. It was our turn to host the unfriendly football match. Last time it was in Idoani and we won two-nil. We beat them on their own ground and victory was sweet. Not that I saw the match, I heard all about it the next day. I didn't feel like walking the eight miles it would have taken to get there, so most of the girls stayed behind and the boys went off and came back singing sweet songs of victory.

In the last game we played we had Gbenga, who is the best footballer in the whole school. His nickname is Pele and as soon as he gets the ball a roar goes up. Anyway, since he'd been expelled I overheard Mr Abrahams say that winning would be like digging a well with a needle. Not much hope there in the rest of the team. Anyway, the game starts and before you know it we were three down and didn't look like scoring a goal, that was until Mr Bamijoko decided to put Gbenga on even though he was expelled and no longer a student. By half time we were level and it wasn't even Gbenga who scored the goals. Then Alaba and her big mouth told her brother, who happens to go to Ireakari, that Gbenga is no longer a student. Of course he had to go and tell his sports teacher, who then wanted him off the pitch. Tempers rose and fists flew, then stones then bottles. They broke most of our classroom windows, but we chased them back to their school (not all the way). I don't think the Principal will be too pleased when he finds out what's happened to his school, they even trampled all over the flowerbeds. A stone hit Jumoke and I think it was Remi who threw it, but I'm not saying anything. I even saw Titi and Veronica fighting, I think it must have been over Dipo. He likes them both but he liked Titi first, but now he likes Veronica who is prettier, so now they hate each other and they used to be best friends. I'd never fight with my best friend over a boy, it's just stupid, they should be able to share him, like I had to share my toys with Adebola when we were younger. I still haven't received a reply to my last letter, I hope he's better now and Uncle Joseph isn't being horrible to him.

22ND FEBRUARY 1979

Dear Jupiter,

You'll never guess what happened today. The Oba, who never leaves his palace unless a sacrifice is made (it's not like a proper palace like in the fairy stories), came to school with Iya Gbenga today. I wonder how many goats they had to kill. It was third period and I had English (the only reason I was in school at that time). Two men held a big umbrella over him. It wasn't a rain umbrella, it was larger and had golden tassels on the edges. Another two men were carrying him on a chair and the last man was carrying a large feather fan, which he was using to fan the Oba, as today has been very hot. They stood outside our classroom which is next to the Principal's office and Mrs Jacobs, his Secretary, had to bring the Principal out because it is a taboo for the Oba to enter a house without there being a sacrifice to the Gods and his *Ifa* consulted to make sure it is safe to enter. When the Principal came out, he had to prostrate in front of the Oba, which was unfortunate because he was wearing his favourite white suit, It wasn't very white when he eventually got up. The Oba wanted to know why the Principal wouldn't let Gbenga back in school and that he is a young man with his future ahead of him and it wasn't for the Principal to snuff out his bright light. The man with the fan put his foot on the Principal's back and wouldn't let him get up, but he still managed to fan the Oba. The Principal must have said something because then the man with the fan hit him on the head and we thought he was going to give him lashings of the cane.

Mr Abraham tried to continue the lesson but we were too busy gawking at what was happening to the Principal. I wonder if he'll take it out on Bimpe. When he was allowed to get up, there was a big footprint on his back and his front was dirty. I felt really sorry for him. Only for a little while though because he gave me the evil eye and I had to try and pretend that I didn't see what happened although that was sort of difficult considering that all the students were looking through the broken windows. I overheard Mr Abraham say that it is not good for a chicken to challenge the lion who is the king of the jungle, because it stands no chance of winning. I suppose the Principal is the chicken and the lion is the Oba, who has given an almighty roar and frightened poor Principal into submission. Looks like Gbenga will be coming back to school, the Principal dare not go against the Oba's wishes. Not if he wants to live in our village.

23RD FEBRUARY 1979

Dear Jupiter,

Gbenga is in school again, just as I thought he would be and he has been transferred to my class which is nearer to the Principal's office. We're the first ones who get into trouble for making too much noise. By the time he has finished with my class the bush wire has gone through to the other classes that he's on the move. I've only been caught once, but since I've swapped my desk for a window one, I keep one eye on his office door and the other on whatever fun is going on. If someone I don't like is making a lot of noise, I don't alert them when he sneaks out with his cane in hand. Because of this I've noticed that most of them are nice to me, especially Seyi who buys me lunch every so often. He even gave me his mathmatical set, pity I can't stand Maths.

1ST MARCH 1979

Dear Jupiter,

Dorcas is back and she is no longer pregnant but she still looks sick. She arrived this morning with her parents and one of her brothers who is very important. I was hiding under my bed when they arrived and I dared not come out. If I had, Dorcas would've known for sure it was me who spilled the beans. They dropped off her stuff in the dorm and then went to school. I wondered if the Principal would have to prostrate again, because Dorcas told me once that her dad is an Oba too, which I don't believe. If it were true, he'd have two people carrying him and one fanning him like the Oba of Idogun. The only thing that made him look like an Oba were the beads he was wearing round his neck. He was fat and he also carried a horse's tail and a carved stick. I followed them but didn't find out what happened; maybe I'll worm it out of Dorcas. I wonder what happened to the baby.

3RD MARCH 1979

Dear Jupiter,

Dorcas is not talking to me, I think she knows it was me who started the whole mess. I bet the moment she fails the next English test she'll be my best friend again.

IMAGINE THIS

Dear Jupiter,

Now I know why Seyi has been nice to me, why he gave me his Maths set and why he's been buying me *akara*. He sent me a note in class today saying he wants to be my boyfriend, as if I would. I sent him one back with one word in giant capitals — 'NO.' Because he'd bought me lunch and given me his Maths set he thought we were going to be a couple. Now he hates me, he wants me to pay him back for the *akara* he'd bought, he also wants his Maths set back. I told him to get the *akara* he'd have to slice me open, or better yet he can go into the bushes after I've finished number two. I will give him back his Maths set in the morning. Imagine that, he couldn't get any other girl so he thought he try his luck with me. He isn't the nicest looking person, his school uniform has holes in it and I saw him digging for gold and eating it. Even the way he walks is wrong, his head moves like a chicken even when he's standing still. I'm not opening my legs for a Maths set or *akara* and I don't care how hungry I get at lunchtime.

8TH MARCH 1979

Dear Jupiter,

I've been beaten up by Akin, he's been planning his revenge for a long time. I've got a bruise on my head and a cut on my knee and I think I'm going to have to go to the medical centre because it won't stop bleeding. I left class after fourth period Literature with Mr Abraham and he must have followed me. When I was halfway back to the dorm and my hiding place, he pounced on me. If he hadn't taken me by surprise he wouldn't have been able to beat me up. I think he was waiting in the bushes for me because I didn't see him on the path. As I walked by his hiding place, he hit me on the head with a branch, which is how I got the bruise on the back of my head. I didn't see it coming, there was a thunk on my head and I went down which is when I cut my knee. He kept on saying. 'Who go save you now eh? Where your teacher? Ah, im no dey come o,' as he beat me with the branch. I hurt all over; I will get my own back on him and make him very sorry he laid a finger on me.

9TH MARCH 1979

Dear Jupiter,

My knee hurts so much I can hardly walk. I cut it on a rock when the beast hit me over the head and I fell to the ground. I'm still plotting my revenge and it won't be pleasant. If Adebola was here I'd get him to beat him up. Why do people always pick on me? I haven't done anything to them, but it seems that my very existence annoys them. All I have to do sometimes is open my mouth and someone starts to make fun of me, it's just not fair.   It seems I'll have to work harder at failing the end of the year exams. Not that it would be very difficult, since the only lessons I've attended are English and Literature.

His Evilness wouldn't let me go to the medical centre, not that I could have walked there, I even have a better excuse to stay in the dorms for the next week. If any of the Prefects find me after bed check I'll just tell them I can't walk to class. I've had to tear off the edge of the wrapper Mama gave me to bind the wound so that flies won't get in and lay their eggs. Baba Dayo showed me what leaves to put on a wound to make it heal. I've picked some from the bush and all I have to do is rub them against my palm, then squeeze the sap into the wound and cover it with the mashed leaves. I'll go to the medical centre when it gets better and I can walk properly. It's Saturday tomorrow and I won't be going to the farm with everyone else. I wonder how long this agony will last, because I don't think I can take much more. I wish Adebola was here with me, things aren't so bad when he's around. I'll just have to wait till the long holidays to see him.

14TH MARCH 1979

Dear Jupiter,

I think my leg is getting worse and not better, it's all swollen and yellow stuff mixed with blood is coming out when I squeeze it to try and make the swelling go down. I had to go to school today because the Principal did the bed checks and when he saw me lying there he made me get up and put on my uniform. I hate him, he wouldn't leave the room to let me change, then he asked me where my breasts were or didn't they grow them in England. When he saw I really couldn't walk he gave me a lift in his smashed up car. He's going to bring me back to the dorm and pick me up in the morning, which means I can't even leave class because I can't walk properly.

15TH MARCH 1979

Dear Jupiter,

I got a letter from Adebola today, posted almost a month ago and he doesn't sound too happy. It's got two sides so I can't paste it in, but he says that he's still a bit ill and that he hasn't gone back to school because Uncle Joseph says he has to stay at home and get better. But all he does is wash the dishes, wash and iron the clothes, clean the house, go to the market, and to also make sure there's food on the table when everyone comes home I suppose he'll have to keep remembering the brighter side of things, soon he'll be in boarding school (I'll be back living with Her Evilness) with no worries at all.

16TH MARCH 1979

Dear Jupiter,

Aase just came back from Lagos and I got my first birthday card from Daddy in a long time, he wrote me a letter as well. He's got a new job and we're moving from the nasty rooms in Orile to a flat in Ikoyi. Adebola and I will have to share a bedroom because there's only two, but that's okay because we've always shared the same room. Maybe this means that we can finally become a family now that we've got a flat. I really didn't want to live in those cramped rooms with the smelly toilet and bathroom in the courtyard shared among the other families. I must write to Adebola, he'll be pleased we're finally going to live in Lagos. I'll have to be on my best behaviour all the time because Daddy has a short temper and I really don't like stooping down or getting the cane. I'll miss Remi, she's the only friend I have here and without her I don't think I would have been able to bear it much.

I've got some biscuits left, so on Sunday (my birthday) I'll make chocolate drinks for Remi and me and I'll fry the biscuits in butter using the iron and we'll celebrate my birthday in style. Maybe I'll make some chocolate as well with what's left of the Ovaltine. What I wouldn't give for chocolate cake, vanilla ice cream with strawberries, Liquorice All-Sorts and Curly-Wurlys!

17TH MARCH 1979

Dear Jupiter,

Uncle Niyi has just turned up at school and I've been told that I have to pack some things and go with him. I wonder if Daddy sent him and I'm going to live in Lagos and he's come to pick me up. This is so exciting, even the Principal was nice to me and he said he'll think happy thoughts for me. I bet he's just glad to get rid of me. Uncle N glared at him when he said that though. Uncle N is pacing up and down the corridor outside the dorm, I wonder what's eating him. I've never seen him like this before, he looks like he's been crying. Well, I'd better finish my packing, not that there's much to pack. I think my leg is getting worse, Uncle N was not pleased at all when he saw that I could barely walk. He was furious with the Principal and told him he should be looking after me properly. It made me feel special. I really should finish packing, I just thought I'd let you know what was going on because I'm so excited.

I refuse to believe it, how can I believe it. Oh Jupiter the agony, the absolute agony. Where there were two there is now one, I'm all alone, all alone. Adebola has left me, Uncle Joseph has killed my only brother. Adebola is dead and his body is lying in the other room. When Uncle N pulled up outside Mama's house, she rushed out to enfold me too. I was confused, people were crying as if someone had died. I couldn't think who. Mama was holding me so it couldn't be her. I didn't know what was going on, Uncle N gently led me to Mama's room and there he was, there was my brother lying there with cotton wool stuck up his nose and in his ears. I think I must have screamed, I don't really remember, just that I have no voice, I can't seem to utter a word. I tried to wake him up, I shook him, I took the cotton wool out of his ears so he could hear me calling his name, I tried to make him sit up but he was heavy and cold, then they dragged me away. So here I am, now I'm all alone, who will take care of me now, who will stick up for me, who will I run away with when I'm older? What will I do? I don't know what I'll do now that the only person who really loved me is dead. Killed by Uncle Joseph, the moment Daddy had decided to send him to boarding school. I feel such rage, I want to scream till I can scream no more, I want to kill Uncle Joseph. An eye for an eye, just like in the Bible. I feel so mad, so mad, so mad. No one can explain to me why, can someone explain to me why. Why did it have to be my brother? What have I done wrong that I lose the important people in my life? First my mother now my brother, can someone please explain why? Where is Daddy, why isn't he here? The pain is too great, I don't think there are any words to describe the grief, maybe I'll die from it too because I don't think I can bear much more. I see black and I see red and someone is playing the masquerade drums inside my head. Someone please tell me why he had to die. What do I do, what shall I do? My throat is closed and I can't speak, the pain in my knee is nothing to the pain in my chest. I'm all alone, Adebola is dead.

31ST MARCH 1979

Dear Jupiter,

I can't remember much of what happened, most things are a blur to me. The pain is constant, I still can't speak, I try and utter the words but then my throat closes up and I can't seem to find the sounds. Maybe my voice has died with him, he has betrayed me and left me just like our mother and now I have to try and live without him. I want him to burp in my face like he did when I was eating, or pull my plaits like he did when he was annoyed with me, but he'll never do those things again. He'll never write to me, he'll never chase away my monsters, he'll never stick up for me and he'll never smile at me again. I didn't know how much I'd miss his dazzling smile, the gap in his teeth. My suave and sophisticated brother is gone forever.

He was buried on my birthday, the 18th of March 1979, happy eleventh birthday, Lola Ogunwole. I thought only old people died, he was only twelve. After I tried to wake him up, I think I must have gone a little crazy, I remember Uncle N holding me tightly in his arms, his tears soaking into my neck, but I didn't want to be held. I tried to push him away but he wouldn't let me go. He held me tightly and kept on saying that everything would be all right, that the pain would ease. But he was lying, the pain has not eased, every time I remember his smile or his laugh, my chest hurts so badly and I want to die too. I just want him back. I think I may have tried to jump into his grave when they lowered his body. I wake up from nightmares and all I can hear is the thud of soil as it hits his coffin. There were no masquerades to make sure he got safely to the other side. I even looked through a mirror to see if I could see him one last time. But he didn't come and say goodbye like Baba, so maybe Mama was right and I was just dreaming when I thought I saw him. There was no music, no dancing women or hunters firing guns, no masquerade to guide him on his journey. There was just wailing, a different kind of wailing. I still feel such rage against Uncle Joseph. I think I may have cut him with Baba Dayo's cutlass, then again it could've been a dream. I remember blood, lots of blood,

Mama holding her hands in the air with her headscarf tied round her waist, tears pouring from her eyes, but not like when Baba died. I keep thinking this is a dream and that I'd wake up, but I'm still sleeping because Adebola is still dead.

Father turned up late; I refer to him as father now because that is how I think of him. Daddy is someone you love, someone who kisses away your tears, tells you everything would be all right with your world, someone who is there for you. Father is someone who had a part in your germination but didn't bother to water the seeds so that they would bloom into flowers. A father doesn't care and that is what I have, a father. I've wished with all my heart that I had a Daddy, but as Mr Abraham always says to me, 'If wishes were horses, beggars would ride.' If I had one wish it would be for him to come back so we can be a proper family, so he can take care of me and chase my monsters away.

Father stood by the grave with me, his hand on my shoulder. His eyes were red as if he hadn't slept. He wasn't supposed to be there, neither was I, it's taboo; a parent never sees their child being buried, it's an abomination. But Father didn't care about tradition and custom, he wanted to see Adebola buried. They buried him in the graveyard between Ugbe and Ishara, the graveyard is on the way to school and I'll have to walk by it every day. Will I ever stop hurting? Will everything really be okay like Uncle N said? I remember Uncle Joseph asking Father to forgive him, he hadn't realise how sick Adebola was. Father just looked straight through him and didn't say a word, how could he not say anything. Why is HE not upset that Adebola is dead? I HATE HIM and I'll never forgive HIM for as long as I live. If we hadn't left London, I'd still have a brother, he'd still be alive, it's all HIS fault.

I'm in Lagos right now, HE took me to the hospital to have my leg checked. The doctor said I should have had it treated sooner and that I'm lucky I won't lose my leg. As if I care if I lose a leg. I shall not be jumping with joy, or dancing to the beat of the masquerade drums. I shall never be happy again. How can I? They say be careful what you wish for, I wanted so badly to live with HIM in Lagos and here I am and I'd rather be in Idogun. I remember Mama and Father taking me to see the *Babalawo* because I can't talk. He consulted *Ifa* (the oracle) and was told I had something to hide about Adebola's death. Maybe he died because I wished too hard; anyway, they think I'm a witch and I killed him. I've already been accused of being a thief by a *Babalawo*, why not add witchcraft to my list of crimes? Yet I don't remember eating anything in my sleep. This time I couldn't protest my innocence, the words would just not form, so I just sat there quietly while the *Babalawo* consulted with his cowrie shells. He told Mama that there was still time to save me, there were rituals, chickens and pigeons were killed and more sacrifices were made to pacify my fellow witches. I simply sat in silence, this is my punishment for wishing too hard.

We left Idogun the day after his burial. Father now has his own car, a Mercedes, Uncle N came back with us. He comes to see Father every day after work. I'm glad we now live in Ikoyi. Unlike in Orile, where I shared the sitting room floor with Adebola, now I have a whole room to myself. But if I was given the choice, I'd take the floor and Adebola. I can shut the door and keep everybody out, but then I'm left with my thoughts. I spend most of my time in this room, there is nothing else for me to do but read.

I've found a book on Greek mythology in one of the boxes; maybe I could go to Hades and bring Adebola back, like Orpheus went to bring back his wife Eurydice, only I won't forget not to look back. Uncle N tries his best to make me talk and I want to but I can't seem to, so he sits on the edge of my bed and holds my hand and strokes it, telling me he'll take care of me. He really is a knight in shining armour.

I've missed what's left of the rest of this term and I'm not likely to do too well, not that it even matters any more. I miss Mr Abraham and his idioms and proverbs, he had one for every occasion. I wonder what he'd say to me now. Father hasn't done anything about finding me a new school. I don't see him much, he goes out a lot and comes back late. I don't need him here anyway, besides I've got Uncle N to care for me.

21ST APRIL 1979

Dear Jupiter,

Easter has come and gone. I prayed for a miracle, the miracle of resurrection. I prayed to God to bring my brother back to me like he did with Jesus. Everyone keeps telling me that he's gone to a better place. Why couldn't he have waited until I was old enough to take care of myself?

Father once said that if I pray hard and believe, then God will answer my prayers. So maybe like Job he is testing my faith. I will continue to pray and keep vigil, I shall also fast for forty days like John did. Then when I'm pure in spirit God will listen to my prayers.

Dear Jupiter,

Today is my ninth day of fasting and I'm weakening for food, but I must be strong. I have gone longer without food while living with Mama. Father doesn't know what to make of me, he has a woman coming round every day to cook for us. I think she's more than a cook though. She never calls me by my name and when I refuse to eat her food she gets quite upset and starts whispering to Father in his bedroom. She spends a lot of time cleaning Father's bedroom before going home.

Dear Jupiter,

I am at the halfway mark of my fasting, I've been drinking only water to keep my spirit pure so that God will listen to me when I pray to him on that final day. I am very weak and can't walk very far. Father's cooking woman looks at me with the evil eye because I don't eat her food. I've written her a note to let her know that I'm fasting for forty days so she won't tempt me with the delicious aromas of pounded yam and *egusi* soup. The other day she made *jollof* rice and I almost gave in. It was a struggle at first, then I remembered why I was fasting and it became easy.

Uncle N came to visit yesterday, I think he's quite worried about me. He keeps stroking my arm and asking me to talk to him. He doesn't seem to realise that I can't talk because I'm being punished for wanting too much and because I wished to be in Lagos. Adebola was taken in return for that wish to be granted. It's the way wishes work. I'll pray to God for my voice back on the final day of my fasting.

12TH MAY 1979

Dear Jupiter

Father came into my room last night to tell me he's taking me to the hospital so that the doctor can cure me and, if necessary, force feed me because he does not want to lose another child to sickness. He showed me the note I'd given his 'Cook Woman' friend and glowered at me and said I have to stop fasting or I'll die of starvation. Like he really cares. Where was he when I was starving in Idogun? I will bring Adebola back and he can't stop me.

14TH MAY 1979

Dear Jupiter,

It has been a horrible day. Father took me to the clinic and left me with the doctor who just kept hitting me and pinching me to try and make me talk but I couldn't. No sound would come, only tears rolled down my face as I cowered under his desk in an attempt to hide from him. When Father came back and saw my bruises he started shouting at the man and almost beat him up, but some other doctors came rushing into the room and pulled them apart. Then I saw another doctor, he had kind eyes and he gave me a mint sweet which I put in my pocket. I wrote him a note to let him know that I'm fasting so he wouldn't be upset I didn't eat his sweet. He told Father that I was suffering from a word beginning with 'T', but I don't know how to spell it and that with time I'll talk again. He weighed me and told Father that I was underweight and might not last the forty days. What do they know, anyway he said that I needed nutrients and I couldn't get that in the one glass of water I was drinking each day. He's written out a diet plan for Father. I wrote him a note telling him that I can't eat anything that has been living, I'm not sure, but I think he understood.

23RD MAY 1979

Dear Jupiter,

Ten more days to go and I will finish my fasting and God will bring Adebola back to life. I keep hearing his voice, his laughter. I see his smile in my dreams. I remember how he used to defend me in the playground when we where living in London. Snotty Derek used to pick on me and make me cry until Adebola made him eat dirt. He went crying to Mrs James who gave Adebola a note for Father. We had to carry two encyclopaedias balanced above our heads and stand on one leg when we got home. Father said we needed strong discipline. I won't discipline any child of mine, I'd want them to be happy and discipline does not make me happy.

Father's Cook Woman stayed in Father's room all night. They don't know that I know. She left very early in the morning then came back about three hours later. She smiles at me a lot more now that I eat the *egusi* soup she makes for me. I don't eat it with *eba*, pounded yam or *amala*, just the soup with no meat or fish. She makes it really thick, not like Mama's *egusi*, she likes to pour in lots of water to make it last longer. Cook Woman isn't a very good cook but I eat it because it's better than a glass of water. Besides, I don't want to go back to the doctor, and Father said he'd take me if I didn't eat the soup. I am a bit worried about eating vegetables because they were living once upon a time. I wonder if they have feelings too.

27TH MAY 1979

Dear Jupiter,

In church today I prayed and prayed and prayed that God will return Adebola to me because I need him to take care of me, I need him so that I can talk to him. He's the only one who understands what I'm going through. Even the elders of the church prayed for me, they formed a circle around me and said special prayers with candles. There were twelve candles, one for each of the Apostles of Jesus. I know God will hear my prayer and grant my wish. Four more days to go.

28TH MAY 1979

Dear Jupiter,

Three more days to go, even writing this is an effort.

29TH MAY 1979

Dear Jupiter,

Two more days to go. Faith is all I need and my prayer will be answered, he has to come back to me.

30TH MAY 1979

Dear Jupiter,

One more day and I'm counting the hours. At midnight tomorrow my fasting comes to an end and Adebola will come back to me. Thirty-one hours and twenty-five minutes to go.

31ST MAY 1979

Dear Jupiter,

Today is the day of Adebola's resurrection. Like Jesus and Lazarus he will rise from the dead because God will perform this miracle. I've fasted for forty days to become pure in spirit like it says in the Bible. I wonder if he'll remember lying in his grave, maybe he would have even see Grandfather and all our ancestors who the Masquerade has called on. Tomorrow I'm going to have *jollof* rice, some pounded yam with *egusi* and a bottle of Coke. If I walk to Obalende I can get if from Mama Ibeji in the market. Adebola likes her food and I'd rather eat there than swallow anything Father's cook friend makes. Even I can cook better than her. She's going to have to go.

"The moon moves slowly but by daybreak it has crossed the sky"

Yoruba proverb

7TH JUNE 1979

Dear Jupiter,

I have exciting news! After days of despair thinking my fasting and prayers had not worked. I woke up and Adebola was sitting on the end of my bed. It is truly a miracle! God does listen to the prayers of children. I wanted to wake Father, but Adebola didn't think that was a good idea. It is still only four and NEPA, the electricity people, have taken light as usual, but I'm using my trusted torch because I just had to tell you about my exciting news.

Adebola didn't seem to want to talk much, he just said everything will come in good time and that all that matters is that he came because I need him. He's still dead I think, because I couldn't touch him. Maybe I'm supposed to dig up his body in Idogun so that his spirit will have somewhere to live again. I'll have to wait for Father to wake up, he'll dig up Adebola like he wanted to dig up Baba when he died, and we'll live happily ever after.

8TH JUNE 1979

Dear Jupiter,

What a day! I spent all day waiting for Father to come back from work because I fell asleep again and missed him in the morning. When he eventually got back at nine, the Cook Woman told him I've gone mad and that I'm talking to myself. What does she know, I've tried explaining to her that Adebola is back but she can't see him. I did hope that Father would, but he thinks I'm mad too. Why can't they see Adebola? He was standing right next to me and they couldn't see or hear him. Maybe he's only come back to look after me like Randall came back to look after his partner Hopkirk, and only Randall could see him. I told Father that we have to go to Idogun and dig up the body so that the spirit has somewhere to live but he wouldn't listen. He just kept on clapping his hands together and putting them on his head and saying, 'God, I beg you, please o. Na wetin I do?' It was God that answered my prayers. He said he's taking me to the clinic tomorrow.

I'm glad he's come back, but I'm sad too, because I know only I can see him. As far as anyone else is concerned he's gone, but he's not. He's come back, and if only they'd listen to me, we can get him a body to live in.

9TH JUNE 1979

Dear Jupiter,

The doctor thinks Father should take me to the mad hospital. I'm not mad and I'm not going anywhere and they can't make me.

20TH JUNE 1979

Dear Jupiter,

Adebola and I have been relative visiting and I have saved twenty Naira. I make sure that when they give me money they also give me Adebola's share. It looks like I'm the only one who can see him, which is good because that means I have super powers. I can hear them whispering behind my back that I've gone crazy, imagine that.

Dear Jupiter,

I have been scarred for life. We've just arrived back from Ogbomosho, Father took me to go and see a powerful *Babalawo*. He told Father that he needs to make some sacrifices to the Orishas because no child should see into the next realm. I told him I couldn't see into the next realm and that I could only see Adebola who was in the room with us. He put down some cowrie shells and beads and started chanting and calling on *Ogun, Obatala, Oshun* and the rest of the *Orishas*. Adebola and I just giggled; what did he know? I sat patiently while he continued with his chants and when I got bored, I started to tell Adebola about Remi and Dorcas at school.

When he finished his chanting, he told Father that the spirits of his ancestors have been told by the Orishas that Adebola is with me and that his intentions are to take me with him into the afterlife. Father needs to do more than make a sacrifice to the Gods if he wants to keep me here. He wouldn't believe me when I told him Adebola is here, we have to drive miles to listen to a *Babalawo* tell him the same thing I told him. Now I've got three deep cuts on my back where the *Babalawo*, with the help of my own father, opened me up so that he could put some nasty black powder into me. It's supposed to keep me alive. I hate them all and I can't wait to grow up so that I can run away. I am glad though, that it was my back and he didn't cut my face open like Yinka's.

Dear Jupiter,

I heard it with my own two ears. I was standing outside

the door to Father's room and Cook Woman told him that she's carrying his child. Well, one thing I can say for sure is that she's not going to become my mother. Just when my campaign to get rid of her was working. I've been complaining about her food to Father for ages and saying that we need to get another cook. I guessed she was more than a cook, I just didn't want to see it, even Adebola knew there was something fishy going on. Well, I don't like her or her two kids. She brought them round the other day, I don't want them to come and live in my house. Father, Adebola and me are all the family I need and we don't want anyone else. Well, Adebola and I don't, and Father has never cared about being together. I asked him why he sent us away and he just said, 'It takes a village to raise a child.' I didn't want to be raised by a village.

Now he's getting a new family he'll probably send me back to Idogun again, and he hasn't even found me a new school yet. Each time I remind him he just tells me not to worry, that everything is in hand. I should know what school I'm going to. I might not even like it. The schools in Lagos are different to those in the village. Their uniforms are nicer for one thing.

10TH AUGUST 1979

Dear Jupiter,

The impossible has happened. Cook Woman has moved in with her two brats Ronke and Ayo and they're sharing my room. I am so upset. I have been living in a fool's paradise. I thought all I needed to do was bring Adebola back and we'd be a proper family. When rain falls on a leopard, does it wash off its spots? Father never cared about Adebola and me, every opportunity he had he gave us to someone else to look after. He'd rather we were raised by a village than by him. When we were in England it was Uncle Eddie and Auntie Sue, here it's the relatives and the rest of the village. Well I've told those brats that they're not sleeping on my bed. Their mother will have to get them a sleeping mat or they can just sleep on the carpet. Only Adebola and I can sleep on this bed and I've told them so. Ronke, she's the eldest, almost sat in Adebola's place at the table, but I told her to sit somewhere else. Even Adebola doesn't like them and he normally likes everyone.

11TH AUGUST 1979

Dear Jupiter,

Ronke and I got into a fight and I broke a bottle of ice water on her head. There was blood and water everywhere and Father and her mother have taken her to the hospital. I've locked myself in my room. I didn't mean to hurt her, I just lost my temper and threw the bottle at her when she started making fun of me and Adebola. She said I was mad and probably took after my mum, after all only a crazy woman would leave her children and disappear. I didn't think the bottle would hit her; I usually miss when I target something. They'll be back soon and I'll probably have to stoop down or carry encyclopaedias while standing on one leg. I've decided to go and visit Uncle N instead. Since it's Saturday he should be at home.

19TH AUGUST 1979

Dear Jupiter,

Where do I start? Well for one I will never say another word to my Father again. I don't even think he's my Father. Maybe I was adopted and I have a real dad out there who is looking for me. Or maybe I was switched at birth and I was given to the wrong parents. Well anyway, I didn't get to stoop down or carry encyclopaedias. HE stopped by the bushes on the way back to pick up some canes. They were waiting for me when Uncle N brought me back home. Cook Woman started shouting as soon as she saw me, she wanted to scratch my eyes out but Uncle N prevented her. Father was just calmly sitting there. I was going to escape to my room but he said that I couldn't go in there because Ronke was sleeping and I wasn't to disturb her. He then asked me what happened so I told him how she called me and Adebola names and said I was crazy like my mother so I threw the bottle at her. At that point her mother came at me again but Uncle N held her back. She was screaming that I wanted to kill her child and that this house wasn't big enough for her and me and that my ex-father must throw me out, and that she didn't care where I lived as long as it wasn't in the same house as her.

Uncle N tried to calm her down, but she just screamed the more. She even took off her head scarf and tied it round her waist ready to go into battle. Uncle N then asked Father what he was going to do about it, that he should have told me about things and maybe I wouldn't have resented them moving into my house so soon after losing Adebola. He told Father that, 'If you tell people to live together you tell them to quarrel.' Father just smiled calmly and said thank you, he then told me that our talk is long overdue and that it will be done in his room. That's when I saw the canes, but it was too late, I'd already entered the room and he'd locked the door.

There were at least twenty canes and he got through most of them. I just rolled up into a ball on the floor while the strokes kept on landing. In the end I think Uncle N broke down the door and stopped HIM.

I remember Adebola standing there with tears rolling down his face because he couldn't help me, then he started to fade away and I felt the familiar wrench, the pins and needles piercing my heart and I didn't want to live. I was still curled up on the floor and all of a sudden it became difficult to breathe, my arms and legs became heavy and if I'd tried to lift them, I wouldn't have been able to. As I watched Adebola fade, I screamed for him to take me with him and not to leave me. Then there was nothing, everything went black and I woke up this morning here in hospital. The nurses say that I've been asleep since I was brought in. I've only just remembered what happened, it took me a while to remember my name when I first woke up. Only Uncle N has been to visit. He brought me my things from HIS place, HE hasn't been in to see me yet, I wonder where HE is.

20TH AUGUST 1979

Dear Jupiter,

What makes me different? I've tried so hard to be a very good girl and the best daughter a Father could want, but HE'D rather have Cook Woman's children. I'm going to have to live with Uncle N until school starts then I'll have to go back to Idogun and live with Mama. HE said that the house is too small for them and me and it would be better for me to finish my education in Idogun. So I guess I'm back to square one, back to the place I tried so hard to get out of that it cost me the life of my brother. I haven't seen him since he faded and I don't think he's coming back. I still need him. It doesn't matter that he's just a ghost, I liked seeing him because when I did I knew I wasn't alone, I felt that he was looking out for me like a Guardian Angel. I hope one day he'll come back, but I know he won't. I know death is the end but I keep on hoping he'll open up the door and walk in, or I'll see him sitting in front of the television with his thumb stuck in his mouth. Why do we have to die?

Sometimes I do wonder if he really was there. Did I really see him? Sometimes I'm sure I did. If I didn't that would make me crazy, like they say. Has God given me special powers to see the dead? Or was I just seeing things because I wanted to? I really don't know any more, my head feels like exploding.

31st August 1979

Dear Jupiter,

I'm a football, kicked from player to player only I don't know who's winning the game or which teams are playing. I'm an unwanted parcel. I've been staying with Uncle N since they let me out of hospital. My ex-father only came to see me once, but that's okay, I'm used to him not caring now. It hurts but I'll get over it. Uncle N is so nice to me but I don't feel comfortable living here, I know his wife Iya Soji doesn't like me, but how can I expect her to like me when my own Father cannot stand the sight of me? Just to get along, I do everything she says, I wash the kids clothes, cook the evening meal, fetch water and clean the house. One day I'll be my own person, that's a promise.

Tonight is my last night in Lagos, tomorrow I go to Idogun and Mama. So much joy to look forward to. Yesterday when I went to the market with Iya Soji I saw a woman who kept on looking at me. She was wearing an *iro* and *buba* made from blue lace, everyone was calling her 'Madam' and she kept on staring at me like she knew me.

For a second I wondered if it was HER. I smiled at her and she even smiled back. I was going to ask her who she was, but then Iya Soji called and the moment was lost. Her smile seemed like mine. I've been smiling into the mirror all day to see if our smiles are identical but I know that I'm just imagining things. If I wasn't going back to Idogun tomorrow, I would have gone back to the market to try and find her.

10TH SEPTEMBER 1979

Dear Jupiter

Well, we're here once again and nothing has changed except me, I suppose. I've come to accept the fact that the man who gave me life doesn't love me, that my mother never wanted me, my only brother is really dead and never coming back and my grandmother is the meanest person alive. None of it matters any more, now I've got to just take things as they come. If she doesn't want to feed me then I will starve. Maybe I'll have more luck in the next life. I've had to repeat last year, I missed the end of the year exams so I haven't been promoted with the rest of my class. Remi and Dorcas failed their exams. Dorcas I expected, but Remi is smarter when she wants to be. Now there's no boarding school, I don't get to see that much of them. Dorcas lives in Ishara with Baba Ajao, she rents a room from him because it's too far for her to travel home every day. Baba Ajao is related too, but I don't know how; he and Mama don't speak because they had an argument, this was all before I was born. It has something to do with a woman. Mama wouldn't tell me she just warned me not to go to his house.

11TH SEPTEMBER 1979

Dear Jupiter,

You and Adebola will always be the one I share my thoughts with. Even though Remi, Dorcas and me are like the three musketeers, I still can't tell them how I'm feeling because I don't think they would understand. This year I intend to study and be first in my class. All the other girls and boys who passed have been making fun of us and calling us dumb. I had my reasons for wanting to fail, but they're not important any more. There is nowhere for me to go, so here is better than there.

12TH SEPTEMBER 1979

Dear Jupiter,

I really hate Chemistry. I don't understand it and I don't like the teacher, Mr Boye. He's new and just like Mr Adesanya who made me walk on gravel kneeling down. He's mean. I was going to try and be somewhere else during his class but he keeps a strict register and if anyone is absent, he'll make them uproot a tree from the forest that's being cleared around the school. I've got homework to hand in but I don't understand it and there is no one I can ask, Mama can't read or write. I'm going to have to copy Remi's if she's done it. I hope she has because I don't want to get into Mr Boye's trouble. I just want to be ignored and left alone.

14TH SEPTEMBER 1979

Dear Jupiter,

Today I became a Muslim and I went to the mosque. I

had to wash my hands, face and feet before I could go in. I'll only be a Muslim on Fridays though, because that's when we have double period of Labour and I don't like going to the farm and planting stuff or cutting the bush around the school. I still remember the blisters from last year, so I'm going to avoid them this year. I talked Remi and Dorcas into coming with me, they were scared we'd get caught by Mr Boye who takes the Muslims to the mosque. He just looked at us and smiled. It was scary because it was the first time he'd ever smiled at me. I thought we were caught for sure, I thought maybe he didn't recognise me because I had half my face and head covered with a huge scarf, like you're suppose to. He did, I'm the smallest girl in the whole school, and he had to call out our names and stand us in line but he didn't say anything though. Anyway, I'm glad I missed double Labour, especially since I'm going to the farm with Baba Dayo tomorrow.

16TH SEPTEMBER 1979

Dear Jupiter,

Idogun once again is listening to the wails of people in mourning. This time however, someone has taken their own life. Her name is Bisi, she's not related to me. We were in church when we heard the screams, the pastor was in the middle of his sermon, something about worshipping other Gods. I felt really bad because I'd gone to the mosque to worship another God. It wasn't a nice thing to do, especially since God answered my prayers and sent Adebola to me.

Anyway, as soon as we all heard the cries the whole congregation ran out of the church to find out what had happened. The pastor was left there with the choir as his flock scattered before him. All the women took off their headscarves and tied them round their waists as they rushed towards the cries. Mama told me to go home so I don't know what happened or how she died yet.

17TH SEPTEMBER 1979

Dear Jupiter,

It's Monday morning, I've got English Literature but Mr Abraham isn't in yet so we have to read our text book *(The Merchant of Venice)*. Since it's the same one I read last year, I thought I'd tell you what happened yesterday. I overheard Mama and Baba Ade talking about it, I pretended that I was asleep and couldn't hear what they were saying. Bisi was told to go and fetch some water from the stream but she didn't want to go anywhere. She told her husband that if she left the house then she would die, but her husband told her to stop being lazy and that she should come and meet him at the farm when she had fetched the water.

Bisi didn't go to the farm and she didn't go to the stream either. Mama said that she dressed up in her Sunday white lace and went to the river and poured a gallon of gamoline down her throat. Because she killed herself by the river she has angered the *Orisha Oshun*, who is the Goddess of the river. She'll have to be buried by the river and they'll have to appease *Oshun*, or things will go very bad for the village. Mama said she heard from Iya Tayo, who sells fish down the market, that she was with child only it wasn't her husband's, because he can't have any because he lost his thing in an accident. I've got to go now, I've got Maths this period. It's not so bad when I listen to what the teacher says in class.

Dear Jupiter,

Mr Abraham has organised a debate and he wants me to be one of the speakers because I have one of the best commands of the English Language. I told him I didn't want to do it, it's bad enough having to get up in class and humiliate myself, now he wants me to do it in front of the rest of the school. He won't take no for an answer, so I shall just have to be ill on that day. Just so he doesn't get suspicious I'll start my illness two to three days early. The debate is next Thursday, which is the twenty-seventh. It wouldn't have been so bad if people didn't make fun of me, they mimic me and say I speak like I've got something stuck up my nose and I don't.

I saw Dorcas and Gbenga holding hands, I think they are secret boyfriend and girlfriend again. He must really love her, even after she K.I.S.S.E.D the Principal and had his baby. I'm never ever going to kiss a boy, especially since you can get pregnant. I'm keeping my legs firmly closed. I won't tell Remi this time because if I do it will be all over the school and you know who will get the blame. Remi does not know how to keep a secret, all you have to say to her is, 'I've got something to tell you and you're not to tell anyone else' and her eyes light up as she thinks of whom to pass it on to. She can't help herself, she's told me lots of things that I've never repeated to anyone else but they still manage to get round the whole school like a bush fire. She's my friend, I just don't tell her secret things, I can tell you, like Uncle N, you're all that's left in my life that I can trust.

I told you about Baba's death last year, well, there is going to be a memorial service during the Christmas holidays and you know who will be here. I've promised never to speak to HIM again, so I can't be here when he comes with his new family. I just hope Uncle N comes; if he does, then I can go and stay with him. I'd rather suffer Iya Soji's evil glares than watch HIM with his new family.

I have to go now, I'll let you know what happens with the debate and my pretend illness.

23RD SEPTEMBER 1979

Dearest Jupiter,

Today is Sunday and I've just got back from church with Mama. She wants me to join the choir even though I can't sing, I suppose they won't know it's me when I sing out of tune. I think I'll be fine as long as I don't have to sing by myself.

The other day I was bursting to tell Remi my secret, you know the one about seeing Dorcas and Gbenga together. Well, I got as far as saying I have a secret when her eyes began to glow and she kept on licking her lips, she had that same look when I told her about Dorcas and the Principal. I had no choice but to lie and make up something, so I told her that I overheard Titi telling her new best friend, Bolanle, that she was going to beat up Veronica, her old best friend, because she stole her boyfriend Dipo. This happened last term, Veronica and Titi were best friends before Dipo came between them. They've hated each other since. I thought it would be okay to tell Remi that, since it isn't exactly a secret that they hate each other. Well, before you know it whispers went round school that Titi and Veronica were going to have a fight after school. I decided to go home early, not just because I didn't want to get into trouble, but because I decided to start my pretend illness earlier.

The really funny thing about pretending to be ill is that

I really do feel sick. It doesn't feel like pretend, I think I must have made myself sick just thinking of getting up in front of the whole school and have them laughing at me. My head was pounding and I even managed to throw up in front of Mr Abraham. About the fight... I got to school the next day with my stomach in knots and my head pounding wondering what trouble I was going to be in and whether Titi was going to beat me up because of what I told Remi. But no one suspected that I started it. Remi said that after the last bell everyone just ran to the arena. I call it the arena because it's where all fights are held after school, so that you don't get punished by the teachers. It's the clearing in the bushes just after the graveyard on the way back to Ishara from school.

Remi said that Veronica turned up with Dipo walking hand in hand together and as soon as Titi saw them, she just charged at Veronica and knocked her off her feet, sat on her middle and tried to make her eat dirt. Veronica then tried to scratch her eyes out and they were rolling around on the ground for ages while everyone was just egging them on. Especially the guys because they could see Veronica and Titi's panties. When it looked like Veronica was going to win the fight, Bolanle (Titi's new best friend) intervened by pouring nettle hairs (which she got from the farm) down Veronica's back, which left Veronica rolling in the dirt in agony. So Dipo stepped in, then some of Titi's other friends stepped in and before you knew it, almost the whole school was fighting each other because I couldn't keep my big mouth shut. I was glad not to be there though.

I have to go now, food is ready. Mama is cooking one of her rare meals and she gives me two portions, one for me and one for Adebola. The *Babalawo* told her to continue to give me two of everything until Adebola is settled properly on the other side. It wouldn't be so bad being thought of as crazy if it got me enough food to eat, but Mama's portions wouldn't fill a fly. She just divides up what she would normally give me, so I'm not getting anything extra really.

25TH SEPTEMBER 1979

Dear Jupiter,

They're back again and I'm not sure I've done the right thing, not that I had much choice. I've given them to everyone in the house according to Mama and Iya Dayo. Who would have guessed they'd be united on something, a common enemy. I'm not really sure it started with me. Aina has been scratching her head for the past two days, so the lice could have started with her. To keep the peace between Mama and me, also rather than go through hours of agony with the kerosene method, I've had to shave my hair, so now I have none. Today was my first day at school with the new shave and as usual the name-calling started. It doesn't really matter what they call me, it's just another name to add to the long list. I remember when everyone was calling me 'Worm Girl,' Mr Abraham found me crying in the bushes one day and he said to me that what people call me is not important, only what I respond to. It's a famous quote from someone, but I can't remember who. So now I walk around pretending I'm proud of my bald head, but I have to say it hurts when they call me names like 'Worm Girl,' 'Baldy' or 'Bag of Bones.' Why are people so cruel? Even when I don't know them, they point and stare and laugh. What's so funny about having a bald head? Mama had one when Baba died and I don't remember anyone pointing at her and laughing or even daring to call her baldy. I will not give them the satisfaction of knowing. Let them see only my outer shell, the venom of a viper does nothing to the back of a tortoise. I'll bear my pain inside.

27TH SEPTEMBER 1979

Dear Jupiter,

I'm in trouble with the Principal. He's been away and today was his first glimpse of my bald head. He called my name out in the assembly and made me come to the front where everyone could see me. He did his walk with one arm behind his back and his other hand stroking his chin, I knew I was in for it; he told me in front of the whole assembly that a bald head on a girl was not acceptable in his school and was grounds for being expelled. I had to tell him in front of the whole school and teachers why I had shaved my hair. He looked at me as if I was something he'd scraped off the bottom of his shoe. I know my uniform wasn't in the best shape but it's always like that towards the end of the week. Anyway, he wants to see Mama tomorrow. I don't want to be expelled, I don't want to become an illiterate and HE has always said, 'You're no one without a good education.' I want to be someone.

28TH SEPTEMBER 1979

Dear Jupiter,

I'm well and truly caught, I'm a sinner and God is never going to forgive me according to Mama. She caught me on the way to the Mosque during double period of Labour. She was on her way to see the Principal, she dragged me out of line and back to his office and I had to stand outside while they had their talk. I'm not allowed to go to the Mosque, I'm stuck with double Labour on a Friday afternoon.

5TH OCTOBER 1979

Dear Jupiter,

I'm going to be helping Iya and Baba Alaba build their house tomorrow. They live in a tin house, which isn't very safe at the moment. Their roof got blown away during the rainy season, they're going to build a mud house on the same spot. The land belonged to Baba Alaba's great, great, great grandfather or something. Baba Alaba is a hunter and he's always bringing meat home for his family. He's got to share it with us too since he's a relative. I remember the day he came home with a snake. Mama got upset because Iya Dayo's share was larger than hers, it caused a big fight. So now what he does is divide it into portions and then he asks Mama to chose which one she wants.

Tomorrow should be an interesting day, I've never built a house before. Couldn't go to the Mosque today, thought I might be able to sneak off, but the Principal had given Mr Boye his instructions, 'Lola is not allowed.'

6TH OCTOBER 1979

Dear Jupiter,

I'm so tired, I've been building a mud house all day and I think it's going to take ages to finish. It's going to be exactly like Baba Ade's house, four rooms and a passage. Baba Alaba had already dug the foundation and put string round it. Everyone had to carry buckets of water to mix the red mud; luckily we didn't have to go to the stream to get it. Baba Alaba has hired a huge water drum. It looks like the one we had in school when I was a boarder. Once it had been mixed, Baba Ade and Baba Dayo made these round balls, a bit bigger than a football, which we then had to carry to put in the foundation. It was hard work but at least there was a lot of food and Mama couldn't control how much I ate. Iya Dayo, Iya Alaba and Mama Ade started cooking really early this morning. There were a lot of mouths to feed. I don't think anyone went to their farm today, even Baba Ajao turned up and Mama almost managed to ignore him until the end of the day when they got into an argument. Mama accused him of only coming for the food and that he'd hardly done any work. For once she was right, he kept on complaining of a bad back and a weak leg and moaning all the time. Every time I saw him, he was resting and talking to Mama Abeni. Mama doesn't like her much either, she calls her *ashewo* (prostitute) or a female dog. I just felt sorry for poor Baba Alaba because once the argument started, the building of his house stopped and everyone joined in. Mud was flying everywhere, I was tempted to throw some at Mama's back but she looked around and I'm sure she knew what I was thinking. All that was needed for it to look like a proper war were shields and spears. Everything has calmed down now, I asked Baba Ade whether they'll all come back tomorrow to help Baba Alaba and he said we won't start building again till next Saturday. We've got to wait for the wall to dry before we put another layer on top.

20TH OCTOBER 1979

Dear Jupiter,

We've finished building Baba Alaba's house, now all it needs is a roof. A carpenter is going to help him with this. Instead of leaving it as a mud house, he's told Mama that once the roof is on he's going to cement the walls and floor then paint them. When he left, Mama just hissed and said he's too boastful, just because he'll be living in a cement house. She thinks it's Iya Alaba that has turned his head, a mud house is not good enough for her, she wants a cemented one. Iya Alaba isn't from Idogun so she's not one of us, Mama just tolerates her. Mama likes to tell everyone of her dear son who was the first person in the village to go to the white man's country. She swells up like a peacock, her head held at an angle and with a smirk on her face, as if to say can you top that?

Before I forget, we had a freak thunderstorm. I say freak because it's not supposed to be the rainy season. What made it terrible is that Mama Ebun was struck by lightening and killed while carrying her grandchild, though he didn't die or even have a bruise on him. I heard that she was making some pounded yam in the backyard. Mama reckons someone has put a curse on her. That's what would have happened to Rotimi if he hadn't confessed to stealing the oranges all that time ago. Maybe she stole something that someone had put a curse on. Baba Dayo puts *juju* on his farm because thieves keep digging up his yams. I wonder how I'll die. Maybe it will be peacefully in my sleep or maybe Mama will do *juju* and I'll get struck by lightning. I told Baba Dayo that I was afraid to die and he just said there's nothing to be afraid of. He said death is like a robe that everyone has to wear but I'm still afraid.

21st October 1979

Dear Jupiter,

I've violated the eighth commandment — thou shall not steal. I stole twenty kobo from Mama today. It happened when we were in church during the collection. Thinking about it, I didn't steal from Mama, I stole from God, and he'll probably never forgive me. Baba Dayo is always telling me that God helps those who help themselves so when she dropped the money on the floor, which she was going to put in the collection bag, I picked it up and pretended to put it in but I kept it. I wonder if I'll be struck down. What will my punishment be?

28TH OCTOBER 1979

Dear Jupiter,

I couldn't take it any more, I feel like everyone knows that I've stolen from God, so I've begged his forgiveness. HE hasn't sent me any pocket money, so I've nothing to eat during lunch breaks. Remi is always sharing her food with me, so for once I wanted to buy some puff-puff and share with her because she's started to avoid me at lunch time and I don't blame her really. I haven't heard her say it but Akin was calling me a leech the other day, another name to add to a growing list. It felt like I've got a sign on my forehead saying 'Lola is a thief,' so I told the Pastor after church today and asked him to ask God for my forgiveness, as it'll sound better coming from him. I feel much better now since he told me that God forgives us if we repent our sins, and since I'm very sorry there's nothing for me to worry about. I told him not to tell Mama and he said my secret is safe and he gave me one whole Naira out of the collection. If I spend five kobo a day that will only get me one puff-puff to share with Remi, which means the one Naira will last four weeks, or I can spend ten kobo and it will last two weeks. I could stick to buying just *akara* for lunch, which means I could spend three kobo a day. One *akara* for Remi and two for me. I might have to give Dorcas one because she shares her food with me sometimes too.

29TH OCTOBER 1979

Dear Jupiter,

It's been another one of those days where death enrobes another person, this time it's Aase. He was on his way to Lagos. Baba Dayo was with him too but he was going to Owoh and they had an accident and Aase died. Baba Dayo is in the medical centre in Idoani, we're going to see him tomorrow. I hope he's okay, he's the only one who really sticks up for me with Mama and I don't want him to die. I'm not going to have anyone left if he dies too. This is God's punishment for stealing from him, I left it too late to repent. I can't tell anyone, Aase's relatives would never forgive me. Now there's no one to take me to Lagos for the summer holidays. Aase was going to take me then collect the fare from HIM at the other end. He was being kind because he knew I didn't have any money. Now I am truly stuck here forever.

30TH OCTOBER 1979

Dear Jupiter,

Aina, Dayo, Iyabo and me just got back from the hospital. We left early in the morning before the sun came up. It's eight long miles to Idoani. I'm not sure what time we got there but the nurses said we missed visiting hours and we couldn't see Baba Dayo, we had to come back the next day, so I started crying and pleading then Aina and Iyabo joined in. The nurse took pity on us and led us to his ward but said we couldn't go in, just look from the door.

It was horrible, he looked like he was dead, he had red bandages all over him, his leg, head and arm. The smell… I didn't like the smell of the hospital, it was horrible too and it seemed as if death was just hovering round the corner waiting with his cloak. I'm never going back there.

13TH NOVEMBER 1979

Dear Jupiter,

I have blisters on my hands from trying to uproot a tree. But before I tell you about that, I have to tell you about Mama, she's been very ill. She's been ill for ages and Iya Rotimi, who I'm still not speaking to, has accused Iya Dayo of trying to kill Mama because Mama told her to leave so that the curse of Iya Dayo's family won't rub off on ours. Bisi, the girl who took her life, is Iya Dayo's cousin. Baba Ade warned Mama not to say anything but she told him, 'Only a madman would go to sleep with his roof on fire.'

I was in school when it all happened. With Baba Dayo still in hospital Mama could pretty much do what she liked to his wife. Well, Iya Alaba from next door said that Mama gathered Iya Dayo's things and tossed them out and told her to leave. That's when they started cursing each other. Iya Dayo said that Mama was ungrateful and that she will regret throwing her out. Iya Dayo left and went to her mother's house, then went to gather the relatives on both sides to try and sort things out. Mama insists that it's the curse on Iya Dayo's family that has landed Baba Dayo in hospital. She has consulted a *Babalawo* and I just know how right they can be too. I couldn't hear everything that was being said because Mama made me sit outside. But I did hear them agree that Iya Dayo could come back after the rituals had been completed, which was about three days later.

Anyway, soon after that Mama started leaking blood from her bottom. Mama Ade said it was abnormal because Mama is no longer a young girl, so she shouldn't be leaking blood. It was horrible, she could barely move and Mama Ade kept on having to change the rags and the whole room smelt bad. Even the *Babalawo* said that whoever put the curse on Mama had medicine, which was more powerful than his. Iya Rotimi thought she was going to die so they sent for HIM. I managed to keep my promise and not say a word to HIM, I kept out of the way and spent most of my time with Iya Alaba next door. The roof is on the house now, the inside has been cemented which just leaves the outside left to do.

Mama was taken to hospital in Owoh where she was given three bottles of blood and two bottles of water, which Iya Rotimi said was given to her through a needle. The doctor told Iya Rotimi about a powerful *Babalawo* who might be able to help since they didn't know what was wrong. Iya Rotimi said that HE wanted to know where the Doctor had bought his medical certificate from, since he was advising them to seek the services of a *Babalawo* instead of proper medicine. Anyway, they had to buy a goat to kill because the *Babalawo* said that Mama had touched something prohibited to women so she was paying with her womanhood. (I don't really understand what that means.) I reckon they should have waited to come back to Idogun to make the sacrifice, more food for me. Anyway, whatever it was has now gone and Mama is now well and her usual mean self. While she was ill there was peace and no one told me what to do, it was great. I did feel bad that she was ill but at the same time I hoped she didn't get better, because I knew when she did it would horrible all over again. If she had died, there would have been mourners and lots of food to eat

Now about my blisters — remember my Chemistry homework? Well, I copied Remi's and got caught by Mr Boye. So did Dorcas, we had identical papers. As punishment for our sins he made us uproot a tree and we were not allowed into any class until we finished. It was the hardest thing I'd ever had to do. The tree wasn't that big but it had roots that went very deep, so we had to dig deep using a hoe and cut the roots using a cutlass. It took one whole week and a half and the sun showed us no mercy, maybe that's why it took so long. Mr Boye also made sure that we got no help from anyone; he told the whole school at assembly that if he caught anyone trying to help he was going to give them their own little tree to dig up. I can tell you, when I yelled timber and that tree crashed to the ground it was the most satisfying feeling in the world. We hugged each other and danced around the tree. I brought some of the branches home for Mama so she can use it to cook once they dry.

And I never did tell you what happened at the debate last month. It's probably because I've been trying to forget, not that anyone would let me. My illness didn't work; I think I should have just stayed at home that day. Anyway, Mr Abrahams wouldn't let me chicken out, he even helped me write the closing speech and I spent the whole afternoon memorising it. At the end of the debate, which was about corruption in government, bribe v no bribe, Mr Abrahams announced my name and said I was the best English student in the school and I'll be giving the closing speech. It was the longest walk to the microphone. I started with, 'I'd like to thank ...,' then looked up and a thousand eyes were on me and I just froze. The whole speech just disappeared like it had been wiped off a blackboard, so all I could do was keep repeating 'I'd like to thank you,' over and over like one of HIS stuck records. Mr Abraham came up and whispered in my ear, asking if I still had the piece of paper the speech was written on. Luckily it was still in my pocket, so like a magician pulling a rabbit from a hat I put my hand in my pocket pulled out the speech read it at breakneck speed with my voice, microphone and paper shaking so badly I'm sure no one understood a word I said. I dropped the microphone and ran all the way home accompanied by gales of laughter. I didn't even stop to take my school bag. I'm sure you can imagine the jokes. Every time I think about it I just want the earth to open and gobble me up.

17TH NOVEMBER 1979

Dear Jupiter,

Baba Ajao and Mama Abeni got stuck together this evening. Mama is very disgusted by the whole thing. As soon as the bush telegraph went round, Alaba and I raced there to see what was happening but we couldn't see how they were stuck together. Dorcas says they were having sex. Mama Abeni always comes round on a Saturday, they go into his room and they both come out smiling. I don't know how it's possible for two people to get stuck together. I tried asking Baba Ade but he just told me it's not the sort of thing I should be asking or thinking about. They used eggs to pull them apart, I saw them taking them into the room. I don't think Mama Abeni will be showing her face in the market for a while, that's what Mama says anyway.

Aina, Dayo and Iyabo missed it because they went to the hospital to see their Father again today. The good news is that he's getting better, he can now walk a little with a stick and he'll be coming home soon. He won't be able to go to the farm for a long time though, so Baba Ade is helping him look after it. Mama thinks that someone is trying to cause harm to her and her family. Baba Dayo rarely leaves Idogun and the one time that he did, he has an accident. He had a meeting with the people who buy cocoa, something about fixing a price or finding a new buyer who would pay more.

20TH NOVEMBER 1979

Dear Jupiter,

Yesterday was the coming of age ceremonies for all unmarried women in the village. Mama had to make pounded yam and special *egusi* and okra stew for all her female grandchildren. Iya Dayo had to make some too for her children and since Yinka is no longer here, Iya Rotimi made some for me. She brought it round but I refused to eat it, I don't know what *juju* she's put in there. I said thank you and those were the first words I've spoken to her since the missing money and *Babalawo* incident. Rotimi came round later and I gave it to him, he can catch whatever *juju* she's put in it. Well, apart from all the food, which was a real surprise, (I don't think I've had a proper meal since Baba Alaba's house was finished), all the unmarried women had to go dancing round the village in the moonlight. We met in the old market square for a dance competition between the four quarters, Ishara, Ugbe, Ugbesin and Uba. We won, Alaba was the best dancer and she was so fast too. Although it's supposed to be just for the women and girls, there were some men there too. They came because they wanted to see the women's breasts. Mama said in her days as a young girl they would only tie their wrappers round their waists and wear necklaces of cowrie shells around their waist, wrists, ankles and neck, so that when they danced the shells crashed together and they would make music with the drums and beaded gourds.

At the end of the dance I saw Alaba round the corner with Gbenga. I'm not sure if I should say anything to Dorcas. Alaba is a relative and her dad does bring us bush meat, but Dorcas is my friend. I think I'm just going to keep quiet, though it would have made a great story for the assembly. Mr Abrahams has founded The Idogun Broadcasting Club and I'm one of the members. We have to find interesting stories from what's happening in the village and write a news report to read out in front of the assembly. When he first asked me I said no, I still remember what happened at the debate. But he said that courage is the Father of success and if I want to be someone, each time I fall down I must pick myself up again and make sure I stand tall every time. So I've faced my fear and apart from the first stutter at the beginning of my news report, which was very boring — maybe I should have done a report on Mama Abeni and Baba Ajao — I managed to read the report without repeating a line. And I didn't run away at the end. I think not having to look up from my paper helped, I just imagined I was alone in a classroom reading to Mr Abraham.

30TH NOVEMBER 1979

Dearest Jupiter,

I often wonder whether God will forgive me for serving

another God. Not that I really am, I'm only a Muslim on Fridays to get out of double period Labour. I managed to sneak away today without getting caught. I joined the line after Mr Boye had finished calling the names. We've just gotten back and there's nothing to do in class because the teachers are having another meeting. There have been lots of meetings going on. Maybe that is why Mr Boye didn't come with us to the mosque after the register call. I wish there was a boarding school still, then I could have sneaked back to the dorm like I used to. Remi told me that the reason that we no longer have boarders is because we now have free education. The Soldiers used to rule the country but now we've got an elected president who is from the North. His name is Alhajj Shehu Shagari, he's a Muslim and has been to Mecca. Mama doesn't like him.

Mama registered me to vote but I'm too young so she voted for me. Everyone wanted Awolowo to win because he's from the south and he would look after his people. He promised us free education if he was elected President, but even though he didn't win we still got it anyway.

Nothing much has really happened here, all I do is wake up in the morning fetch water, go to school, come back home, have my evening meal if I'm lucky, then go to bed.

When the moon's out Mama tells us the usual *Ajapa* stories. She starts by saying, *'Alo o,'* and we have to say, *'Alo,'* in response and then she tells us the story. *Ajapa* the tortoise is always trying to con someone but by the end of the story he gets his just rewards. Sometimes we sing songs and dance if it's not a hot or rainy night, other days we listen to Baba Ade's boring radio. Some good news though, Baba Dayo is coming home tomorrow. I'm not sure how he's going to get home because he can't walk properly and there's no longer Aase to pick him up. Maybe they'll find a taxi in Idoani, there aren't any in Idogun but Idoani is a bigger village and I heard that some of the homes have electricity like in Lagos or any big city.

7TH DECEMBER 1979

Dear Jupiter,

It's Friday again and I think our holiday starts next week or maybe it's the week after. I'm not looking forward to it because HE is coming home with his new family. I just hope Uncle N comes as well, then I can go and stay with him instead. Anyway I don't even want to think about that right now.

I got into another fight the other day with Veronica. I don't know why everyone thinks they can just bully me because I'm the smallest in the school. I really am going to have to learn to fight properly so that I don't get beaten up all the time. Bimpe (the Oba's daughter) lent me a book to read. It was called *The Slave Girl* and was about a girl sold into slavery by her brother. Well anyway, I was reading this book in class when Veronica came up to me and said it was hers and could she have it back. It didn't have her name on it so I refused because Bimpe told me not to give it to anyone. She tried to snatch it but I just hid it under my desk, which is when she knocked my head against the window and broke the glass. I was lucky that I didn't cut myself deeply, I'll only have a small scar on the back of my ear. She tried to grab the book while I was dazed but I got it first and held on tightly, which is how it ripped into two. Now I'll never know how the story ended because Veronica took half of the book. I was lucky Mr Boye came into class when he did or else I think I would have gotten more than a cut behind the ear. I called her a boyfriend snatcher and that made her mad. We were supposed to meet after school for a fight, but I'm not stupid. I've taken to carrying Mr Abraham's books home. I think I'll ask him to be my school dad and he can look after me. Sooner or later she'll forget about me and start picking on someone her own size.

This is my life in Idogun, me as David fighting against Goliath, and like him I will beat them all one day, I've just got to pick the right fight.

10TH DECEMBER 1979

Dear Jupiter,

Exams are over and holidays start on Friday, not much to do in school. However it's better than staying at home with Mama or going to the farm.

12TH DECEMBER 1979

Dear Jupiter,

I swear it wasn't my fault, but I'm not sorry I did it though — well, maybe I am a little bit. I had to pretend to Mr Abraham that I was really, really sorry and I didn't mean for it to happen, however he had it coming. I finally got my own back on Akin, after all the bullying and the last beating I got from him, which almost made me lose my leg. He deserves what he got. I've got to take Mama to school with me tomorrow, the Principal wants to see her. He didn't know what to do with me, I'm now a hooligan with no prospects, and according to him, I'll end up dead before my time if I carry on this way.

To cut a long story short, Akin came to my class to take our bucket of drinking water. His class had gotten back from Labour early and finished the water in their class, so he came to steal ours. Unluckily for him, I was lurking in the back of the classroom. I'd invented an illness and stayed behind while the whole school was out cutting grass. There were no more classes and the holidays start in several days time so we were put to work. Anyway, when I saw what he was about to do, I told him to leave our water alone. He just laughed at me and said, 'What are you going to do about it?' I think I saw the mythical red mist I've read about because I rushed towards him and wouldn't let him leave. This made him laugh even harder, so I grabbed the bucket determined that he wasn't leaving with our water. By then my classmates had started to arrive back. Someone started the chant of 'Fight' and before I knew it they were all around us shouting, 'Fight, fight, fight, fight!' as if we were animals. I knew he was stronger than me and he'd already beaten me up before so I was slightly scared of him, even before he started his taunt of, 'If I hit you, you go die today.' I didn't back down, I didn't cower. I just told him that if he didn't let go of the bucket of water I was going to slice him open with the machete I had in my hand.

He dared me to, which was the wrong thing. My arm went up, then came down and I cut his leg open at the side towards the back. Suddenly everyone went quiet, then I think it was Veronica that started screaming first as the blood started spurting out. He let go of the bucket and fainted, the water mixed with the blood and it looked like a river of blood had burst its banks. I thought I'd killed him, so I started screaming too. I said I was sorry that I didn't mean to kill him, that it was his fault for provoking me. I was inconsolable because I thought he was dead and I'd taken a life. God was never going to forgive this sin. He was okay though, he'd just fainted at the sight of his own blood. Mr Abraham and Mr Boye were the first teachers on the scene. Mr Boye went to look after Akin and Mr Abraham took me to the staff room and told me to kneel down. At that point I still thought he was dead, I told Mr Abraham that I didn't mean to kill him and that I didn't want to go to jail. I blamed the whole thing on Akin and Mr Abraham seemed to be on my side. He told me to kneel down in the corner until the Principal came. I didn't want to be expelled, where would I go to school? This was the only school in Idogun, HE didn't want me living with HIM in Lagos and I doubt he'd pay for me to go to a different school where I could be a boarder.

I've told Mama that the Principal wants to see her but not why. He had to take Akin to the Medical Centre in Idoani and by the time he got back, school was over so he's told me he'll deal with me tomorrow. There isn't much he can do anyway, exams are over and the holidays start on Friday, and tomorrow is the dance show for the parents.

15TH DECEMBER 1979

Dear Jupiter,

It's Saturday and school is out, the Principal has told Mama that I won't be allowed to come back to school next term. I'm finally being expelled and I don't want to be. I don't know how I'm going to get out of this jam. Mama told him that he'd have to talk to HIM, she has tried her best to beat the evil out of me but she has had no success. She told him that anything he wanted to do to me, he had her full permission. She wanted to cut me open and put pepper in my wounds to teach me a lesson, but the Principal saved me. He told her expulsion is enough of a punishment. I left school in shame on Thursday, with Mama dragging me by my ear in front of the other students and parents. She was cursing me, my mother and my mother's ancestors.

I'll never get out of everyone's bad books. I tried standing up for myself but I'm no David, most of the time I'm just scared and afraid. What I want most in the whole world, I know I can never have. A mother who cares would have been wonderful, to have one that I even knew would be even better.

I sometimes have this dream where we're sitting round a dinner table. HE is Daddy again and has just come back from work, Adebola is by my side, mother has cooked and we're all sitting down to dinner but no one is talking. Everyone just eats their food and leaves until I'm the only one left sitting there with my food untouched. Imagine that.

30TH DECEMBER 1979

Dear Jupiter,

On Friday I tried to run away. I got as far as the market with my suitcase and realised I didn't have any money and had nowhere to go and I didn't want to become a prostitute. So I sat on the dirt road and cried. I don't know how long I was there for but Uncle N found me. He was on his way to Baba's memorial with the rest of them. I wasn't allowed to go and stay with him as punishment for my transgressions so I've been with Mama, HIM, Cook Woman and her brats, who aren't even his children but who HE treats better than me. Here I am wearing clothes that were bought for me when I was eight. I hope that one day will come when I won't have to beg for food or clothes. The reason I ran away was because I had an upset stomach and couldn't go to the stream like Mama asked. There I was rolling around on the floor and all she wanted was for me to go and fetch water for HIM and his new family. HE came into the room to find out what Mama was shouting about and saw me on the floor, that's when he dragged me out the room put a bucket in my hand and said, 'Go and fetch water and stop being lazy.' That's when I threw up in the bucket and fell to the floor. My legs just wouldn't support me and I was sweating really badly. Baba Dayo as usual came to my rescue, he made them see that I was sick and told them to send Ronke to the stream instead since she's not royalty and can carry a bucket of water just as well. Baba Dayo took care of me. Later on I picked up my suitcase and kept walking, I didn't know where I was going, just that I had to get away. Then I realised I had nowhere to go, that's when I started crying and that's where Uncle N found me. He took me back and as we walked through the front door I just remember HIM laughing and saying he was wondering how long it would take for me to get back. I think I died a little again, I'm trying not to think about it, I watched them dance, eat, drink and be merry and I don't even have the will to eat, there doesn't seem to be any point.

31ST DECEMBER 1979

Dear Jupiter,

My eyes are weary with despair, the tears have stopped and my heart is now empty. I feel no pain or joy, I just don't feel anything any more. My life has no purpose, I am nothing. As time goes by I seem to be marking my life as a bookmark in somebody else's story. Shadows are my constant companions. Every now and then a sliver of light peeps through, bringing with it the hope of a new beginning. Then I think for a moment, just a millisecond of time that my life will change for the better, that it will mean something, that finally I will start to live, start to feel. But then the shadows close in and block out the thread of hope and my eyes droop further into the weariness of despair and I ask myself, what is the point of life when you're not happy? Yet I don't want to die, I'm too scared to take my own life. I keep thinking I should give up but then a little voice whispers in my ear that whatever's around the corner can't be all bad, surely it can't be worse than what I've already been through. The only thing I do know for sure is that I can survive anything except death.

LAGOS

"A child does not die because the mothers breasts are dry"

Yoruba proverb

3RD MARCH 1984

DJ,

I'm now a young woman; back in the day of my great grandparents I would have been traded for a goat and married off to a farmer with two wives. A lot of time has passed and it's been a while since I last wrote anything or confided in you. It's not that I didn't want to, I did; but something happened inside me that made me stop. For a while I even stopped being. It's hard to explain. I was nothing and had no one. I was lost in a multitude of relatives who wanted to own me, so that they could say it was they who brought up the daughter of Samuel Ogunwole from London. So for a long time I've just existed, did what I was told, didn't complain didn't say a word. There were times when I wanted to give up; I didn't see any reason to carry on living. I thought of a thousand ways to end it, but each one seemed so painful and so final. Adebola was my constant companion. We'd sit on his grave and reminisce about living in Kent, moving to London and the life we once had. I lived in the past and I lived for the past. Even though I was perfectly sane, they all thought I was crazy. I could see the fear in their eyes, even Mama's. Then one day Uncle Jacob, another relative, came to Idogun and saw me.

I'm now in Lagos living with him. His mother and Mama are cousins, I'm not sure how many times removed though, and they don't even like speaking to each other. I remember Mama once saying; that the more money you have or the more important you are, the more relatives you'll have too. It feels like I've been in a cocoon. I haven't been to Lagos in four years and everything seems different.

I've become used to saying, 'Good morning/afternoon/evening,' to everyone I meet and I find myself doing the same as I walk down the street with its open sewers, and people look at me as if I'm mad. Sometimes I get a response. The noise, the sheer mass of people and the dirt is horrible and it's going to take some getting used to again. One thing that won't take that much getting used to, is electricity and not having to walk ten miles for a bucket of water. I think all the water I've carried on my head has stunted my growth, I feel I should be taller. No more having to grind pepper on a stone either, Iya Foluso, Uncle Jacob's wife, has an electric blender. I can watch television and Uncle Jacob also has a video player; I'd never seen one before or even knew they existed. What else don't I know? I'm sure there's a lot and I'm going to have to learn to be like a Roman, when in Rome and all that. I know I am, but I don't want people to think of me as an ignorant bush girl.

I haven't seen or spoken to HIM since December 31st 1979. Well actually I stopped speaking to HIM before then, just after Adebola died and he moved Cook Woman in. I have a half brother named 'Ekundayo' which means 'sorrow becomes joy.' I've never seen him. He was never brought to Idogun, Mama had to come to Lagos to visit her new grandchild. Cook Woman didn't want me to kill her child. Apparently they've consulted the Oracle that knows all and I'm a witch who killed Adebola because I was jealous of the affection HE was showing him. It's actually almost funny. What affection? I don't know how I survived the years in Idogun. Sometimes I dreamed that the red slippers transported me home, but I am still not sure where home is. Other times I dreamed of flying in a magic car to a far away land where children were cherished and fed. I even imagined myself as *Cinderella*, but I waited in vain for my Fairy Godmother, who probably wouldn't have wanted to help me anyway, especially after I nearly killed Akin.

I missed a whole year of school before the Principal finally gave in to Mama's pleas. Not that it mattered to me, because I gave up on everything anyway. I had no hope and nothing to cling to. I'd resigned myself to spending the rest of my life in Idogun, I had nowhere else to go and no one who cared whether or not I rotted there. So I existed, I opened my eyes in the morning, then I closed them again at night. There was nothing in between. I even gave up speaking to people for a while because I had nothing to say. I just lived inside my own head, then that became too small. All I seemed to be asking myself was, 'Why?' The more I asked myself the smaller my brain became. The question consumed me, my every thought was, 'Why me?' And as the days dragged into weeks, then years, I remembered Mama's saying that no condition is permanent. As I sat engulfed in my thoughts, the world was passing me by, slowly but surely.

If Uncle Jacob hadn't rescued me, I know I would have been stuck in Idogun for the rest of my life. Uncle Jacob didn't really visit Idogun much, which is why I'd only met him twice in the seven years I existed there. He's a busy businessman who builds houses, which is why he was in Idogun. He's building a house for his mother. Mama is green with envy, she has no house to boast about, she just takes pride in the fact that her son has been to the white man's country. She never fails to point it out to people. She'll start a conversation with, *'Igbati ome mi wa ni ilu oyinbo,'* which translates to, 'When my son was in London.' She is envious of Mama Jacob's house. It will have a proper toilet (no more going into the bush for her), an inside kitchen instead of it being in the backyard, a sitting room and seven bedrooms. By the time Uncle Jacob finishes building the house, she'll have enough relatives wanting to come and live with her.

I might have eventually ended up like Remi and Dorcas, unmarried and pregnant, or married to a farmer that hasn't been out of the village since he was born. Not that going to school made much of a difference. I finished high school by failing all my subjects except English and Literature, so it's not as if I can go to University or even do my A levels. Who would pay for it anyway? Not HIM. I'd resigned myself to carrying and fetching for Mama, forever dreaming of escape, yet here I am in Lagos once again. Uncle Jacob was upset with HIM when he saw me; apparently I'm under-developed because at the age of almost sixteen I should have breasts like any normal teenage girl. But I guess there's nothing normal about me. I think that's probably why the boys in Idogun weren't interested in me, especially after slicing Akin open. For a while I walked around with a machete so that no one would bother me. It added to my legend of being crazy. The boys were only ever interested in the girls who had breasts, anyway. Remi and Dorcas had a lot of boys chasing them but they were only ever interested in Gbenga. Which is why they eventually stopped speaking to each other. They wanted the same man and they got the same man too, because both of their children look like Gbenga. I know he had sex with other girls too; he earned his nickname, 'Woman Wrapper.'

The last thing Baba Dayo said to me when I was leaving was that I shouldn't open my legs for any man or I'll end up with a baby and no husband like Dorcas, Remi and Auntie Bunmi. I don't think he understands that boys only like girls with breasts and since I don't have any and they don't look like they're going to grow, I'm safe. Uncle Jacob wants me to go to evening classes and retake my exams so I can go to University and become a doctor or lawyer. I think law would be much more interesting than medicine, besides I don't think I can ever go into another hospital. After Baba Dayo's accident, I get the shivers thinking about it. People go to hospital because they're dying and I don't think I can watch that happen every day. So I'm going to be a lawyer like Portia in *The Merchant of Venice* and argue the quality of mercy. I've already missed last term and most of the second term so I've only got four months till the exams, but if I pass, then I can sit the entrance exam for University next year. I asked Uncle J who would pay my fees, he said he would because he can afford to.

Uncle J is rich, he's always travelling somewhere and we live in a big house in Surulere. We've got two drivers, three cars and a guard who opens the gate. Uncle J drives a Mercedes. The other two cars are Peugeots and one is used to take the kids to school and Iya Foluso, Uncle J's wife, uses the other. They've got four children, Foluso being the oldest and a pest. Although Iya Foluso can drive, she prefers to be driven everywhere by the chauffeur. She looks more important sitting in the back, that way everyone respects her and calls her Madam. I have to follow the other driver to school with the children and pick them up afterwards. Uncle J has told me that it's my responsibility to make sure they have their breakfast and lunch, to make sure their uniforms are washed and ironed and their room is clean. It's not so bad and I'm lucky to be here and part of a family and I get to eat three meals a day too. Now I just have to pass my exams.

I don't think Iya Foluso likes living in Surulere. Things haven't been the same since the family moved from Ikoyi, which is where HE lives. When they lived there Uncle J had more cars and drivers, but then the contracts dried up and Uncle didn't get paid from the government projects he was involved in. They blame the Military. Ever since the coup, which happened on December 31, 1983, things have gone down hill. Maybe the President's New Year's resolution was to topple a corrupt government, especially after the last elections which where rigged. Mama voted for me again even though I still wasn't old enough. I didn't even know there had been a change in government, not until I was in Lagos. I guess I would have found out if Baba Ade's radio hadn't died a sudden death. Mama Ade had thrown and stamped on it during an argument they had.

8TH MARCH 1984

DJ,

I've started my evening classes. It's not at a private school like the one Uncle J's kids go to, it's a Jakande school called Aunty Aduke Grammar School and I have to take the *Molue* bus to Obalende, which is on the Island. HE lives on the Island and I sometimes wonder if I'll see HIM and HIS new family driving by in his latest car. I guess the change in government hasn't been too bad for

HIM. I remember when we lived in a 'face-me-face-you' in Orile and had to share facilities with strangers. HE seemed to care then but I guess I'm just a disgrace to HIM now. I'm almost sixteen, I have no breasts, rags for clothes, no education and I've NFA (no future ambition), but life is wonderful. It's my birthday in ten days and I'll officially be sixteen and a young woman, but most of the time I feel like a kid who knows nothing and understands even less.

Iya Foluso says I should be grateful that Uncle J has taken me in and is providing for me, and I am. I just wish she wouldn't say it all the time when I've supposedly done something wrong. She never says it in front of Uncle J, in front of him she's always so nice. I wish he was here all the time. I was in the visitor's room the other day watching an Indian film with the kids. She'd just come back from the market and found us there. She was upset because they hadn't eaten, which wasn't my fault. I'd asked them if they wanted to eat and they said they weren't hungry, they wanted to watch the new film Uncle J had brought home instead, so I'd put it on. Now I'm banned from the visitor's room. She started screaming at me, 'You ungrateful girl, so it isn't good enough that your Uncle, my husband and the father of my children takes you in feeds you and sends you to school, heh? What is your own father doing for you, heh? And how do you repay his kindness, heh? By starving his children.'

She then threw her hands in the air saying, 'God what have I done to deserve this evil girl?'

She clearly doesn't know what real starvation is. A part of me wanted to enlighten her, to explain what it felt like when you've had no food for days and didn't know where your next meal was coming from, how your stomach turns on you and starts to devour itself as the pangs grip you like a vice, how you become so dizzy with weakness you almost pass out. But what was the point? She'd only tell me I was being rude and disrespectful. She's going to speak to my Uncle when he gets back. I haven't been here up to a month and it looks like I'm going to be sent back to Idogun. I guess it's true when they say nothing good lasts forever; I just pray he doesn't send me back there because I really don't think I'd survive another round in hell.

18TH MARCH 1984

DJ,

I'm sixteen today. Not that I expected any presents or an acknowledgement from anyone on what's supposed to be the most important birthday in a girl's life. Anyway, it's just another day like any other. It's been an eventful week. Yesterday was the twins' birthday party, their actual birthday is the 9th March, but we couldn't have the party last Saturday because Uncle J hadn't come back from his business trip. He got back on Wednesday while I was at my evening classes. They were having an argument in their room when I got back, I don't think they knew I was in the house. Iya Foluso wants me out of the house because I'm not good for the children, I answer back when she speaks to me and I've been starving the children. She doesn't understand why they have to raise me when my father is richer than they are, lives in a bigger house and can afford to send me to school. Uncle J tried to calm her down and said it's the charitable thing to do and he couldn't live with himself knowing that I was languishing in Idogun. It's no life for someone who knows there's more to life. He told her he'd talk to me, which he did the next day when he got back from work. So now I'm going to try and be very nice to Iya Foluso and not get in her bad books. I won't speak unless spoken to and as soon as I get the kids home from school, whether they like it or not, they're eating, even if I have to stuff it down their throats. I've got to try and make this work, I'm living on their charity and, although I'm very grateful, I can't help but wish for a different life.

Uncle J bought me some new clothes and I'm really grateful but he doesn't know what to buy for a young woman. I'm no longer a little girl yet he bought me a pink frilly dress that would look fantastic on a six-year-old. I had to wear it to church today and, even though he didn't know it was my birthday today I'd like to think of it as a birthday present. He also got me a skirt and blouse, which I can wear to classes; I know they've been laughing at me in class because of my clothes. I don't wear the latest fashions and on top of that I don't have any shoes so I wear bathroom slippers. It's always so embarrassing if I get to school late because as soon as I walk in, in my bright red cut-off cords, there's a pin drop of silence and then the sniggers start. It's got to the stage that if I'm late, I don't bother going in to class, I just hang around till the next one. That's how I met Ngozi, waiting behind the classroom in the dark for the bell to go and the next class to start. She's all right and we've become friends. She doesn't make fun of me and all the boys in school are after her, but she's told me she only has rich boyfriends who give her money and buy her clothes. I've seen her being dropped off in several differ-ent cars. She said when she first came to the city people laughed at her clothes and called her bush girl. Her parents are poor and can't afford to buy her the latest clothes so her boyfriends do it. She reckons when I grow breasts that she'd be able to get me a rich boyfriend and that all I need are the right clothes, shoes and hairstyle. She also thinks I need to put on more weight because men don't like girls who look like waifs; they prefer girls with meat on their bones like her. She has a lot of meat on her bones, especially on her backside; you could balance a cup of water on her behind and it wouldn't spill even if she were walking up steps. I've watched the boys in class watching her when she walks into a room, her *yansh* (bottom) rolls from side to side and their eyes roll with it.

Well, anyway, the twins' party was yesterday and the whole street was closed down because they had to set up the chairs tents and a stage for the entertainers. Families turned up in their expensive cars wearing 'and Co.' HE was there with his family, Cook Woman, her two brats, Ronke and Ayo, and also Ekundayo, my half brother, who I saw for the first time. He was playing with the twins and they ran into my room. I was lying on my bed reading one of Iya Foluso's books and I just knew it was him. He tried to grab the book from me and when I didn't give it to him he sat on the floor and started crying. Cook Woman ran into the room to see what had happened, saw me there with her son, grabbed him and hissed at me. I just ignored her and carried on reading. If her son wants a book, then I'm sure they can afford to buy him his own collection, which he can play with.

It's strange having a brother but not having a brother. I know I'll always have Adebola, but I rarely see him anymore. Not since I left Idogun, but sometimes I feel that he's watching over me and keeping his promise to look after me. It's funny that I'm closer to him dead than when he was alive. When I saw Ekun for the first time, I looked for traces of Adebola, did they have the same smile, same eyes or same anything. His face is rounder and his skin darker than Adebola's and he doesn't have the dimple in his chin. I have to admit, that a part of me hates him and wishes him dead, but he's done nothing wrong; he doesn't deserve my hate, but I can't bring myself to love him, and I never will because he's not really my brother.

It's funny, I watched them all decked out in their matching outfits and I felt nothing. Before I used to get this searing pain, but now I feel nothing, I watched them pile into HIS car, which is even nicer than, Uncle J's, and all I felt was relief they were leaving. I understood Iya Foluso's point about looking after me when HE'S got the money to do it. I stayed away in my room for most of the party and for once, Iya Foluso didn't command me to serve the guests. I think it would have been awkward, the rest of the relatives and other guests seeing me dressed in my rags like *Cinderella*. I'm glad she spared me the embarrassment. She does have a heart sometimes. Uncle N came with his family. I haven't seen him either since the day I tried to run away. He came to my room to say hello and tried to persuade me to come to the party, but I told him I wasn't feeling well and needed to rest. He wants me to go and visit him, I said I would soon.

19TH APRIL 1984

DJ,

Nothing much is happening except I think my breasts are growing. I didn't realise until I noticed Wale, one of the boys at school, looking at my chest. He wanted me to lend him my Economics notes and all the time he was talking to me, he wouldn't look me in the eye. I don't even know why he's asking me for my notes, he's one of the people who makes fun of my clothes and sniggers when I go into class.

Ngozi has advised me not to wear my white blouse without a bra to cover my nipples. I didn't realise you had to wear a bra when you've got small breasts like mine. They're not like Mama's, which are flat like slippers, or Iya Foluso's, hers are like big melons and mine are like little limes. I don't want to ask Iya Foluso for the money to buy a bra, it's too embarrassing. What do I say? I need a bra because one of the boys in school won't look anywhere but my chest. I've torn an old wrapper into strips and wrapped a piece round my breasts. Once I've put my blouse on top it won't look too bad, that is apart from the knot at the back.

22ND APRIL 1984

DJ,

I woke up this morning and thought I was bleeding to death. My wrapper and the sheets were covered in blood and it was running down my leg. I didn't realise I had the curse, I thought the curse was one of those women things that would pass me by. I've seen the girls in school when I was a boarder doubled over in pain, I didn't feel any pain there was just a crimson river trickling down my leg and I stood in the middle of the room trying not to panic but not knowing how to make it stop. Eventually, I plucked up the courage to knock on Uncle J's room to tell him I thought I was bleeding to death. He called Iya Foluso and she told me I had started my menses, which means at sixteen I'm now a woman and if I have sex with a boy I'll get pregnant. I HATE BEING A WOMAN. I don't want to be a woman, I'm not ready to be a woman, I just want to curl up and not move. Will the boys be able to tell I'm now a woman and start hassling me? The very thought is disgusting. Boys are disgusting.

Iya Foluso let me stay at home instead of going to church with the family. I was afraid that if I sat down I'd start leaking and I'd have blood all over my clothes, I couldn't risk it. Iya Foluso says it can take up to five days to stop. Looking on the bright side, I'm not getting any stomach-aches. Before she went to church she gave me a pad to wear in my pants, it stops the blood seeping out and staining my clothes. She only gave me the one pad and it was full and icky before they got back from church so I used the strips from my old wrapper. I can wash and reuse them at least. I've had three baths already and I still feel icky. Iya Foluso bought me some more pads on her way back from church. If I run out again, I still have the strips which I can use but the next five days are not going to be pleasant.

25TH APRIL 1984

DJ,

The curse has finally stopped; Ngozi calls it her 'Red Letter Day' which is so much nicer than calling it the curse. I'm glad it didn't go on for five whole days especially since Wale the creep, is having a birthday party and I've been invited. It's on Friday and it will be my first ever disco party, although saying that, I don't know how to dance. I've seen them dancing on TV but it's different to how they dance in the village.

Wale's parents are away in America and his brother and sister are in University so he has the house to himself. Ngozi told me that he's been sent to the evening classes as punishment. His Father has given up on him, they've sent him to some of the best schools in the State and all he wants to do is party and have a good time, have sex with lots of girls and drink his way through life. Ngozi says he's slept with most of the girls in the evening classes apart from me. She did it with him because she wanted him to get her a pair of shoes from America. She said he was in and out in five minutes and he never got her the shoes. Now she collects before she opens her legs for any man. She's advised me not to sleep with Wale. As if I would, especially after Baba Dayo's advice and definitely not for a pair of shoes. I'm what he refers to as fresh meat because I'm a virgin. Well, he isn't having sex with me, he's a creepy crawly, lower than the grass under a snake's belly. Yuk.

According to the invitation Ngozi gave me, the party starts at six o'clock which is when evening classes begin, which means I'm going to have to go straight to the party instead of class, then come home at the same time class would have finished. I know Iya Foluso won't let me go if I ask her, I'm not even sure how I'm going to get out of the house in my frilly dress. It's the only decent thing I have to wear that is remotely like a party outfit. I don't even have any shoes just the slippers I wear around the house. Maybe I shouldn't go, they might laugh at my flip-flops and dress, and they aren't exactly the height of fashion. I'll have to speak to Ngozi and see what she thinks.

26TH APRIL 1984

DJ,

Great news Ngozi is going to lend me a pair of her shoes. My feet are a bit bigger than hers but she's got a pair of sandals that I can squeeze my feet into. She'll bring them to the party tomorrow.

28TH APRIL 1984

DJ,

Yesterday was a bad day. I got caught by Iya Foluso trying to sneak back into the house in my Sunday best and
Wale tried to have sex with me. I couldn't leave the house
at the usual time because Iya Foluso was home and I did-
n't want her to see me leave in my dress, so I put it in my
school bag, went round the back of the house in between
the water tank and the boys' quarters and put it on there. I
gave the Gateman twenty kobo not to say anything to Iya
Foluso about what I was wearing. She wants to know when
I go out, how long I'm out for, whether or not I bring boys
back. She wants to know every burp and fart I make underneath her roof.

Anyway, I got to Wale's house at half past six and was
worried because I got there late. *Molue* buses don't go to
Ikoyi, they lower the tone of the neighbourhood and, since
I didn't have money for a taxi, I took the *Molue* as far as I
could and walked the rest of the way. I hoped Ngozi was
there so she could come out and give me the sandals before
I went into the house. I rang the buzzer and Wale opened
the door. He was surprised to see me and wanted to know
what I was doing at his house looking like a fairy on a
Christmas tree. I wanted to die on the spot. I showed him
the invitation and asked if Ngozi was there and he said
no and that just because six is put on an invitation that
doesn't mean you're supposed to turn up at six. It means
you're supposed to turn up three hours later. I said I didn't
realise and I turned to go back home but he stopped me
and apologised and said he didn't mean to make fun of my

outfit and that I looked quite sweet. He asked me if I wanted a Coke and that there were also biscuits and other stuff for the party. I was hungry so I thought why not, he's apologised and is trying to make me feel welcome, so it would be rude of me not to accept. I guess at that point I should have remembered the Wolf that tried to eat poor little Red Riding Hood. I walked in the front door and I remember thinking that it was a lovely house, bigger and nicer that Uncle J's. There were huge portraits of his parents' wedding on the wall and also pictures of his brother and sister and him when they were living in America. There was a stick in the corner with a glove on it when I asked what it was, he told me that his brother liked baseball, which is a game the Americans play.

I sat down admiring the pictures on the wall, hoping Ngozi would knock on the door and wishing I'd asked her what time she would be getting to the party, because by the clock on the wall I had another two and a half hours before anyone turned up. I didn't think I could sit there and talk to Wale for that long, even though he was making an effort to be nice. He got me a Coke and put a plate of biscuits in front of me then sat down right next to me and touched my leg. I tried to move away but he just moved closer and before I knew it I was sitting right at the edge of the sofa. So I told him to move away, that I don't like him sitting too close but he just laughed and said to stop playing games and that the reason I came to the party early was so we could be alone together and have sex. I got up and ran to the door and tried to get out but the door wouldn't budge. He'd locked it. I was so frightened. I kept thinking of Baba Dayo's words not to open my legs for any man and Iya Foluso telling me that I can get pregnant if a man touches me now that I'm a woman. I wished for the days of no red letters and no breasts.

I begged him to open the door and let me go home, but he just kept on laughing and said I should take off my clothes and I'd like what he was about to do. He came towards me and I ran to the other side of the room praying for someone to come and save me. He showed me the key and said if I want it, I'd have to come and get it, then he put it down his trousers. I threatened to scream if he didn't let me out. He just calmly walked over to the stereo system, put a record on the turntable and turned the volume up really loud and all I could hear was Michael Jackson singing, 'When the world is on your shoulders,' and in that moment I didn't care. It was as if someone had turned a switch in my head, I was prepared to die and all I felt was a calm acceptance of my fate. I knew there was going to be no saviour and if I couldn't save myself, I was going to make very sure he suffered with me. Fleetingly, I wondered if I'd be mourned, but I didn't think so, I had nothing to lose and no reason to stay alive. So I took his baseball stick and started swinging at everything and any-thing. I felt such rage that I just about destroyed his living room. I started with the telly, then the glass cabinet with all the fancy plates and I just kept on smashing and screaming like a mad woman, 'You will not touch me,' over and over. He couldn't come near me because I didn't stop swinging. I destroyed the record collection and stereo and I found myself in the kitchen. I grabbed a knife from somewhere I don't know where and threatened to kill myself. He couldn't open the door fast enough; the guard at the gate had heard all the noise and was pounding on the front door. In the end Wale was the one begging me, but he needn't have, the switch in my brain was back to the right place and all I wanted was to get out of there, so as soon as he opened the door I just ran. The guard started to chase me but Wale called him back. I got round the corner and threw up. I couldn't stop shaking and crying. Everyone is going to know how I destroyed his house and they're going to make me pay, or even worse, throw me into jail. Then I started to panic about being arrested by the police and put into jail. The more I thought about it the more I panicked and the more I threw up.

Eventually, I managed to walk to the bus stop and drag myself back home only to enter another crisis. Iya Foluso was sitting on my bed waiting for me, and I wasn't looking too good either. I had splatters of vomit on my legs and some on my fairy dress, the strap of my flip-flop had broken when I was running and also because it had rained yesterday there was mud on the back of my legs and dress. She wanted to know where I'd been so I lied. I said one of the teachers from school is leaving and she wanted a photograph of her best students, so she asked us to wear our best clothes. I'd obviously forgotten about the time so she wanted to know why I was home early, so I said that they were having a party and since I didn't know how to dance, I decided not to stay. I know she didn't believe my story. She was prepared to take me back to class to find out, but I was saved by the youngest crying and by the time she was settled, it was too late to go anywhere. That's not the end of it though; she's dropping me off on Monday and is going to speak to the teacher. Of course I told her the teacher would be gone by then and that Friday was her last day. I'm not looking forward to Monday. At least one good thing I'll be driven to school in the air-conditioned Peugeot instead of running after a *Molue* bus.

DJ,

Thank God for small mercies. I thought my goose would be cooked today but Iya Foluso was too busy to take me to school. So I didn't get my ride in the air-conditioned Peugot. I waited for her to come back from the market but she had guests with her and when I reminded her about taking me to class, she gave me one Naira and told me to go and catch a *Molue*. She was more interested in discussing me and HIS wealth with her friends. She thinks HE'S a drug dealer just because HE lives on Cocaine Avenue. I hope not, because if HE gets caught HE'LL be executed by the firing squad. I didn't actually go to school, I stayed in the *Bukkah* round the corner and bought a Coke which I sipped every half hour to make it last. I left when I saw everyone leaving for home.

I was hoping to avoid the crowd but I ran into Ngozi and her friends. She told me armed robbers had attacked Wale's house just before everyone got to the party. They pretended to be guests and that's how they got into the house and instead of stealing the stuff they smashed up the whole house and Wale narrowly escaped with his life. Of course my jaw dropped in amazement. The party didn't go ahead but Laja, Wale's best friend, is thinking of having one at his house instead and this time no gate-crashers will be allowed and it will be strictly by invitation. I know I definitely won't be going, my party days are over even before they've begun.

As we walked towards the bus stop Wale pulled up in his Nissan jeep and offered us a lift. Laja was in the front with him. I said no and Ngozi said someone was coming to pick her up. The other girls crowed into the back. Even though there was only space for three people, all six of them managed to squash themselves in like a tin of sardines. Wale pointed his finger and thumb at me like he was shooting me and winked. I think he's plotting his revenge and I can't possibly go back there. I don't want another Akin situation, I'll be thrown into jail for sure. I guess that means no more evening classes for me. I just don't know how I'm going to pass my exams. Thank God no one in school knows where I live.

5TH MAY 1984

DJ,

Today has been very unusual. It's Saturday and looking at the clock on the wall of my room it's three o'clock in the afternoon. The Government are fighting a 'War Against Indiscipline' — 'WAI' for short — and the whole country is involved. And for a change, the streets and most of the mosquito infested gutters of Lagos are clean of rubbish. This has been an amazing achievement. At eight o'clock this morning, every woman, man and child had to leave their house and clean the streets of Lagos, and whoever didn't comply would get arrested and thrown into jail. Since no one wanted to be detained indefinitely, which could happen, everyone complied. Although saying that, I overheard Iya Foluso telling our neighbours that a man was on his way to the hospital with his wife who was about to deliver and the policemen almost killed him before they realised his wife was in labour on the back seat. He was lucky, normally they shoot first and ask questions later.

On the news yesterday a University student was shot

dead because he wouldn't tell them who he was at a road-block. They said they thought he was an armed robber so they shot him and his girlfriend dead. Everyone knows the dead can't tell the truth. Uncle J thinks he probably got killed because he refused to pay the bribe they always demand at the road checks. The only way to get through is to greet them nicely and give them ten Naira to buy food for their children. If you don't pay, you could get arrested and thrown into jail indefinitely, like one of Ngozi's uncles who got caught out after curfew. We didn't believe her so she brought some pictures of him to school; they were before and after his experience. In the first picture he was wearing a white lacy *buba* with a multi-coloured wrapper round his waist and what could only be described as a ceremonial staff in his hand. Ngozi said that the picture was taken when a new chief was made in their village. He had a potbelly and looked like he was about to have a baby, you couldn't tell where his head began and his neck ended. He had a big grin on his face and looked happy. Then you looked at the other picture and it was hard to believe they were the same man. He was hunched over and just had a wrapper tied round his waist, he'd lost so much weight he was emaciated and you could almost count his bones through the skin. The eyes that were filled with sparkle in the first picture were dimmer and lacked lustre, it was horrible.

It all happened when NEPA took light. He'd run out of kerosene for his lamp and since the whole house had settled for the night and they didn't have any candles, he tied his wrapper, put on his slippers and went down to the street to buy some candles from the Mullah. On his way to get the candles he was picked up by the police who didn't believe he was an upstanding citizen, because only armed robbers are out at that time of the night in their wrappers. So off to jail he went. His family searched for him for three months before they finally found him languishing in a police cell. He didn't have any money to bribe his way out, but then that's Lagos for you, her streets are filthy, her citizens poor and her guardians crooked. Although the President is trying to straighten things out, Lagosians don't like him very much; they don't think he's doing a very good job.

12TH AUGUST 1984

DJ,

Nothing much has happened. Every day pretty much is like the previous, the only interesting thing so far has been watching the Olympics on telly when NEPA has deigned to give us light. We're not allowed to switch on the generator unless Uncle J is at home so I missed most of the events. The closing ceremony was today, Lionel Richie sang All Night Long. Nigeria didn't win a lot of medals. I think we only got two but I don't know who won them. Everyone looked like they were having fun. If we'd stayed in England I could've become an athlete. Once upon a time I was a good runner. I sometimes wonder if I'll ever leave Nigeria, but with no education, probably not. I've failed my exams, no surprises there. Uncle J took it quite well, he just said, 'Eh, you can do better next time. If you don't know book you are nobody, you will end up married to a *Molue* conductor, make sure you do better next time, it is the one thing no one fit take from you, it go open doors.'

Life with Uncle J is okay as long as I don't get in Iya Foluso's bad books. I wake up at five o'clock every morning and clean the house with the maid, then I wake the children, starting with Foluso, to get them ready for school. If it's a Saturday I get up at seven instead. On Sundays, we've still got to get up early to get ready for church. After I've dropped the children at school, the driver brings me home and I do nothing. I just sit and wait for two o'clock to come round, then I go and pick up the kids, come home and make them something to eat. The television studio, NTA, doesn't start until five o'clock and I've been banned from touching the video. I'm not allowed to bring any friends over, not that I have any apart from Ngozi. But I don't see her any more since classes stopped. Well, it was actually before then. Ever since the Wale incident, I didn't go back to class. Making no friends and not keeping the one I had, was the price I paid for destroying his house. I guess we're even.

1ST SEPTEMBER 1984

DJ,

Another day of environmental sanitation. I've noticed that enthusiasm for this day has waned greatly. Probably more due to the fact that the police have been told to break down the roadside shacks that are people's businesses, so all the petty traders are not happy. Iya Foluso has a stall at Tejuoso Market. Luckily it's inside the market so she's left alone, but the traders on the streets and side walks aren't so lucky. The police smash up their corrugated stalls then steal what they can. It doesn't seem as if things are getting better, they're going from bad to worse. The Government has introduced some Decrees: Decrees number two and number four. Decree two means that if a person is seen as a threat to the government, then they could be detained indefinitely, and Decree number four means that if a newspaper publishes anything that is embarrassing to the government, the editors can be arrested and thrown into jail.

Fela Anikulapo Kuti, the famous musician who invented Afrobeat, has been arrested, probably under Decree two; the government say he's a dangerous man; he uses his music to try and fight them. Uncle J loves him, he's got all his albums, he told me that in the '70s Fela sang anti-government songs so one day over a thousand army officers raided his house and threw his eighty-year-old mother over the balcony; she didn't survive the fall. So instead of waiting for him to do something wrong, he's automatically found guilty because it is feared he will incite riots. Uncle J calls it a pre-emptive strike, take out your enemies before they can do you harm. I remember his song Zombie; they played it a lot when we first arrived in Lagos all those years ago. It's just occurred to me that I've been in Nigeria for eight years. We arrived at Muritala Muhammed Airport on the 17th May 1976 and walked into a wall of heat; the humidity almost sapped the life out of us as we disembarked from our flight. On the tarmac waiting for our arrival were about fifty colourfully dressed relatives, all decked out in their Sunday best. They surged towards us as our feet hit Nigerian soil, gesturing their welcome and speaking a language I never thought I'd understand. Time shifts perspective.

17TH OCTOBER 1984

DJ,

Am I really a bad person? I try to be good and I know I lie sometimes, but that's only to get out of trouble. It's not always my fault, like today's incident for example, but Iya Foluso doesn't see it that way. As far as she's concerned I'm an evil girl and now she understands why HE left me to rot in Idogun. She thinks I should never have been born. That way I would never have caused grief for my parents and for her and her family. She wants me out of the house and when Uncle J gets back, she's going to tell him it's either going to have to be me or her leaving this house. She can no longer live under the same roof as me because she's afraid for her and her children's lives.

I guess if I was her and someone dropped my baby on her head, I'd feel exactly the same way. What happened? Well, I can tell you this — I didn't deliberately drop Idowu. She wouldn't sleep unless I carried her on my back and I didn't want to because she wasn't wearing a nappy and the last time I carried her without one she relieved herself down my back and on to my good blouse. But Iya Foluso insisted I carry her so I did, and when she fell asleep I went upstairs to put her in her cot. As I loosened the wrapper to put her down, I stumbled over one of the twin's toy cars, Idowu slipped off my back and hit her head on the side of the cot. Her mother rushed upstairs and accused me of intentionally trying to kill her daughter. My motive for this crime is because I had resisted carrying her initially, I wanted to get my own back. How could she think I'd ever hurt any of her children when all I've done is run around after them and treat them like my own brothers and sister? Especially Taiwo, who couldn't speak English or Yoruba before I came; all he would speak to anyone was the Indian language from the films he watches from the minute he's up in the morning. He only needed to watch a film once and the next time he watched it, he would recite it line for line and act out the roles. No one could understand him and he wouldn't speak to anyone in a language they could understand, but he'd always speak to me.

I remember the first day he spoke his first words to me. I was in the kitchen making *dodo* (Fried plantain) for their dinner, he came in, stretched his hand out and said something incomprehensible. I told him he wasn't getting anything unless he asked in a language I could understand and there, in front of his mother he said, 'Can I have some *dodo*?' Our mouths dropped open in shock. The trick to get him to speak is to not give him something he wants at that time, or I just tell him I won't be his friend, and he talks to me. Not that we can have a conversation; he just tells me what he wants instead of screaming the whole house down.

Well, those days are gone now because here I am once again about to be cast out like a leper. I have nowhere to go and no money. I just pray they don't send me back to Idogun, or even better yet, that Uncle J forgives me and calms Iya Foluso down. I guess the fact that I didn't pass my GCE hasn't endeared me to them. If only I hadn't lied to her that day Wale tried to touch me. If I'd told them the truth maybe they would have found me a new school. Will the ripples ever stop? I overheard her speaking to one of her friends. She was telling her how she thinks I've started to follow boys all over Lagos and I haven't been turning up in class. I don't think she knew that for certain; how could she have found out? Obviously she doesn't want me living in her house barefoot and pregnant by a *Molue* conductor because people are going to point the finger of blame at her. After all, when the roots of a tree begin to decay, it spreads death to the branches. People are going to say there is something rotten in her house.

18TH OCTOBER 1984

DJ,

I guess it's true when they say all good things come to an end. I hope all bad things do too. My life seems to be one long bad joke. Maybe Iya Foluso is right and I never should have been born. Maybe that's when the bad things will stop happening, when I give up the ghost. I can't help hoping, though that something good is round the corner. I woke up at my usual time to get the children ready for school, hoping yesterday was just a bad dream, but it wasn't to be because as I went to open their bedroom door, Iya Foluso came out of her room and said she doesn't need me to prepare them and that the house girl would. Instead, she wanted me to leave the house right then. She had already packed up what few clothes I had while I was sleeping and fitted them into two nylon bags. I'd used my battered suitcase to store my school books so the kids wouldn't tear them. She didn't give me a chance to brush my teeth or wash my face. I was only allowed to change into my torn cords and blouse then I was marched downstairs. One of the drivers carried my suitcase and I carried the other two bags. Uncle J was downstairs. I don't know what time he'd gotten back last night but I hadn't told him my side of the story.

I tried to tell him what happened but he said it was too late, he doesn't want any friction in the house, it's the reason he's never thought about marrying a second wife and that's what my presence in his household feels like. What could I say to that? I told him I had nowhere to go and no money to even go to wherever. He gave me twenty

Naira and told me to go and stay with Uncle N. So here I am, sitting on my battered suitcase outside the front gate waiting for it to get light so I can make my way to Festac where Uncle N lives.

People are going about their daily business, a baby is crying across the street, the street traders have started shouting at the top of their voices, the mosque at the end of the road is calling people to prayer, the smell of fried *akara*, roasted plantain and burning wood wafts through the air. Life is moving on, while I sit here being bitten by mosquitoes and wondering what I'm going to have to face next. Is there a point to my life? While others are living theirs, it is rapidly passing me by. I should hate them for throwing me out of their house, but I can't because I'm not their responsibility and they took me in out of charity, and I guess some people's charity will only go so far. So now I'll move myself on and hope for the charity of Uncle N.

3RD NOVEMBER 1984

DJ,

I've been living in Festac with Uncle N for two weeks now. Things have been okay so far but I have to tread carefully where Iya Soji is concerned. I've always known she doesn't like me, so now that I'm in her house again I try not to speak to her unless she speaks to me and I do everything she asks. The flat is quite small. It only has three bedrooms. Uncle N and Iya Soji sleep in separate rooms so the other room is overcrowded. Uncle N's sister and younger brother share it with three of Uncle N's kids. The youngest sleeps with her mum and I sleep on a mat in the living room. Which isn't a good thing, because Uncle N always has visitors so I can't go to sleep until everyone has gone. It also means I have nowhere to hide and write and think.

Things are better though. Uncle N loves me. He's always taking me around with him and introducing me to his friends. A lot of them are women; they smile at me and pull my cheeks as if I was five. Who am I to complain though? I always end up one Naira or more richer for the experience. Most people think I'm eleven so I go along with it because it can sometimes get me money. I'm saving, and once I've saved enough I'm going to buy a ticket and go back to London.

I've got much nicer clothes now too; Uncle N works at the airport as a Customs Officer so he's always buying clothes from people who have travelled abroad. The other day he bought me a really nice pair of yellow shorts and a cream blouse, which I'll be wearing tomorrow when we go to the Apapa amusement park. We've got to go to church first; I'm so excited I can't wait. Iya Soji has given me one of her old church gowns, which is much too big for me, but I guess they're meant to be shapeless.

Uncle N goes to the 'Celestial Church of Christ' — 'CCC' — for short. Unlike Uncle J's church, CCC is spiritual. Uncle J's church was about everyone wearing their Sunday best. Sometimes you couldn't see the pulpit because some Madam had the most elaborate *gele* on her head. The best part of the service was always when it came to collecting the money. The pastor called up a group at a time to come forward, give money and receive a prayer. Most people were in more than one group. Iya Foluso was in the Anglican women's society, the mother's group, the wives group, the market women's group and a lot more. She went up at least five times in one service; she wanted people to see her giving to God.

Each time a group got up to go forward, the choir would start singing, the drums would start pounding, the congregation would be on its feet clapping and dancing but centre stage would be the group strutting like peacocks down the aisles, shaking their *yanshes* (bottoms) to the cacophony of sound as if they were saying, 'Look at me and what I've got.' If you want your neighbours and friends to know what you have, then going to church on a Sunday is a prerequisite. Iya Foluso always worried about what she was going to wear. She had to have the perfect bag and shoes to match and she rarely wore the same thing twice.

Well anyway, Uncle N's CCC is different. They only wear white robes and if a woman is having a red letter day, it is forbidden for her to enter the church because it's a sign of uncleanliness which is why I didn't go to church with everyone last week. It was nice to just be by myself. I met our next-door neighbour's daughter Bidemi, she's half way through secondary school and she has an older brother who has just joined the navy and a sister who is studying law at the University of Lagos. They were all born in London and moved back to Nigeria in 1982. Her brother loves living in Nigeria but she and her sister prefer living in London. Once she's finished her secondary school, she wants to do Accountancy at University. I'm not that much older than her, yet she knows what she wants to do. I don't have a clue, all I keep thinking about is, 'How long will I be staying at Uncle N's before his charity runs out?'

IMAGINE THIS

4TH NOVEMBER 1984

DJ,

Everyone is asleep and as usual NEPA have taken light again and the mosquitoes are having a feeding frenzy. Church today was interesting, one woman received the spirit of the Holy Ghost, well that's how Uncle N described it. She started throwing herself on the floor and speaking gibberish. Uncle N said she was speaking in tongues. She had to be restrained so she wouldn't hurt herself.

Apapa Amusement Park was fun; it wasn't much different to the fairs we went to when we were living with Aunt Sue and Uncle Eddie. Sometimes I forget there was once a 'we;' I have to look at a photograph to remember what Adebola looked like. If he had lived, would my life be different? Who knows. It was because he died and I stopped eating that HE got the Cook Woman, then she became his wife. Not that they got married in a church. The relatives in Lagos arranged the exchange of the dowry for her. According to Iya Foluso who was there on the day, she was exchanged for a cow and some cowrie shells. Every little thing that I do has unforeseen consequences, like a new wife for HIM.

The good news is that Uncle N has enrolled me at Adegoke Remedial School, which is on 2nd Avenue. Classes start at three o'clock after the nursery children have gone home. It's a private school and Iya Soji isn't happy about it, she says that Uncle N loves me more than his own children and they had a big argument about the whole thing. As soon as it started, I made myself disappear next door to Bidemi's so I wouldn't get caught in the middle. Mrs Adeyemi (Bidemi's mum) asked me about where we lived in London and what HE did when we were there. I couldn't really answer most of her questions. It was so strange, for such a long time all I've wanted was to go back, and when I watch programmes like Love Thy Neighbour, Rising Damp or the Carry On films it seems like such a foreign place, not what I remember at all.

DJ,

School has been fun. For once I'm actually enjoying going to school and I've made some new friends. Although it hasn't been plain sailing all the way. Mr Leke, the Economics teacher, asked me a question about supply and demand and it was the first time I'd had to answer a question and I just mumbled the answer. He told me to speak up, which I did, but I kept my head bowed. I was waiting for the sniggers to start, but none came. Later on, when class had finished, he asked me what I wanted to study when I got to University, so naturally I said Law. He then replied saying if that's the case, I'm going to have to overcome my shyness of public speaking because one day I'll be in court defending or prosecuting someone and I'll have to convince the Judge and Jury that the person is innocent or guilty, and the only way to do that is to speak up and with authority instead of cowering.

I've spent so much time hiding in the shadows, trying not to be noticed, because when I am noticed something has inevitably gone wrong. How do I become a person with opinions who doesn't only speak when spoken to? I'm not sure I can do that, so now I'm going to have to drop Law, which doesn't leave me with much else. I can't do Medicine due to my phobia of hospitals, I can't do Accountancy, too many bad memories learning multiplication. Parents want their children to be doctors, lawyers or accountants, nothing else is worthy. I don't know what I'm going to do. Maybe I could become an engineer or an architect like Uncle J. The matriculation exams are in summer next year and Uncle N wants me to sit for them then, rather than wait to pass my GCE's then take them the following year. This way, if I pass my GCE and JAMB (Joint Admissions and Matriculation Board), then I'll be in University in September 1985.

19TH DECEMBER 1984

DJ,

Iya Foluso and the kids have gone to Idogun for Christmas and Uncle N's sister and brother have gone to Ado Ekiti to see Uncle Joseph. I haven't seen him since Adebola died; according to Cook Woman I killed him with my Witch's *juju*, according to Mama he died of TB, but Uncle N told me he died of malaria. He's still dead and the only way I ever see him is as a ghost. Sometimes I think I'm going crazy, I know he's dead and I'm no longer that grieving child, I don't believe in ghosts, but I do believe in what I see and I see Adebola. I hope I never see Uncle Joseph again, but with having to do the rounds of relatives, I'm sure our paths will cross at some point. We're on holiday till the New Year so there's no school and Uncle N has been taking me to work with him, but it's becoming a bit boring now and no one gives me money any more. There's this woman he met and he said I'm to call her 'Mama,' but she looks nothing like my grandmother. He brought her home and they went into his room. I think they were having sex. I tried to peep through the keyhole but his bed was at the wrong angle so I couldn't see anything. I just heard some heavy breathing and gasps like when Auntie Bunmi was giving birth in Idogun, then he turned his radio on.

I've made some new friends in school, Segun and Yolande Baptiste, Charles Okwon (who we call 'Charlie Boy') and Maggie Brown. Segun and Yolande have gone away somewhere abroad for Christmas, Charles has gone back east somewhere and Maggie has gone to Badagry, which is where her family are from. Badagry is famous for shipping slaves to Europe and America. When we first came to Nigeria it was one of the beaches HE took us to. We saw the huts where they kept the slaves chained up. I'm glad I wasn't living then, I'd hate to be a slave.

28TH DECEMBER 1984

DJ,

I have exciting news. I have a boyfriend. Before we broke up for Christmas, Maggie said I needed a boyfriend to take care of me and my needs. It's not natural for a girl to be without a man and since I'm going to be seventeen soon, I'll no longer be a child. Well anyway, Bidemi's brother, the one in the Navy, came home for Christmas. He told me yesterday that when he saw me he just had to have me. We were sitting outside on their balcony and he said he wanted to ask me something, so he dragged me into his room and shut the door. His sisters started making kissing noises and saying, 'Oh, Lola, I love you, I can't live without you.' It was a bit embarrassing, but nothing compared to how I made a complete fool out of myself.

When we entered his room, he closed the door and said, 'Lola, I'm just going to come out and say this, there's no use beating round the bush, I would like to go out with you.' To my eternal shame, I asked him where he'd like to go and that there's a new restaurant that had just opened on 7th Avenue, I knew this because Uncle N had taken Mama and me there and the food was very good. He looked at me blankly for a second, then smiled and said, 'No, I mean I want to be your boyfriend.' I wanted the ground to swallow me up. I said I knew what he meant and my reply was meant as an acceptance and that he could take me to Good Food to celebrate our new relationship. I'm not sure he bought it, but it was my quickest recovery, though I cringe just thinking about it.

We kissed with tongues and I have to say the swapping of saliva was yuk. Tobi says it's what boyfriends and girl-friends do to show each other they care. Well, I'm not exactly sure I care about him because we've only just met. I know he'll want to have sex with me and I don't want to do that yet.

1ST JANUARY 1985

DJ,

A new year and a new beginning. My New Year's resolution is to pass my exams and go to University in September, and also to fall in love with Tobi. He wanted to have sex with me but I said no. I tried to explain to him that I want it to be like it is in the Mills & Boon books. The woman spots the tall, good looking man and she falls help-lessly in love and then, after some misunderstanding, they realise they can't live without each other and they get married and live happily ever after. Well obviously the spotting across a crowded room isn't going to happen. He is quite tall though and he's got a black belt in Karate. He told me that in the Navy they're taught how to kill a person with a single blow using just their hands. I'm not sure I should marry someone who can do that, and the marriage part will have to wait anyway, until I've finished my Degree, which by my reckoning will be in 1988 if I get into University in September. I won't have to get a job because he'll be putting food on the table and I'll be looking after the house. I'm not sure how that is going to work though, because I hate doing housework. Uncle N caught me bribing Soji once. The deal was that I gave him my breakfast tea every Sunday and he cleans the living room and bathroom. Uncle N reckons I'll be an expensive wife to keep because my husband would have to employ a maid to do all the housework. Which is perfectly fine by me. Why bother getting my hands dirty if I could pay someone else to do the work?

I'm still not keen on the swapping of saliva. In the films I've watched, everyone seems to enjoy it, so maybe I'm doing something wrong. Yesterday I decided to keep my eyes open and watch Tobi while he kissed me. He was making these funny sounds in his throat, the kind you make when you've just had a good meal. Well, anyway, I thought I'd better start making some noises too, and that's when he opened his eyes. We stopped kissing and looked at each other, then started laughing. Looking back, I don't even know what was so funny but we were both rolling round on the floor in stitches. I'm going to miss him when he goes back to his ship, but we'll write love letters to each other. Oh, it's going to be so exciting having a boyfriend. Maybe I'll pine for him like they do in the novels I've read, I can't imagine not eating though, it seems a bit much.

14TH FEBRUARY 1985

DJ,

Guess what? It's Valentines day and although Tobi's not here, he left me a beautiful card and a bottle of *Anais Anais* perfume by Cacharel. He gave it to his sister Bidemi to give to me today. Charlie Boy got me a card and I got an anonymous one too. I think it's from Segun but I'm not sure.

20TH FEBRUARY 1985

DJ,

Iya Soji and I have had a row. She got so angry she hit me and Uncle N got very upset with her. She's not allowed to lay a finger on me, traditionally it's forbidden. Iya Soji, however isn't a woman of tradition, she teaches in primary school and she doesn't kneel down for Uncle N when she gives him his food, unlike Iya Foluso. Whenever Uncle J came back from work, Iya Foluso would run to the kitchen to make him his dinner. The meat and pepper were always bought fresh from the market each day. She would cook his food separately to everyone else in the house and when she put it in front of him, she'd go down on both knees to serve him. Iya Soji doesn't do that, she and Uncle N's mother even had an argument about it. Uncle N's mum doesn't think Iya Soji respects her husband, they don't like each other much. When Mama Joseph comes to stay, it's best to keep out of both their ways.

The argument started because Iya Soji said I was being wasteful for throwing away yesterday's leftover yam, especially in this time of austerity measures. I told her it had gone off but she reckoned it was still edible and that we have to make do with what we have because the way things are going, there could be another food shortage and prices are still going up. Apparently, Nigeria owes billions of pounds and dollars to the Bank and they want their money back. I think they should make the men who stole the money pay it back. They spent money that wasn't theirs and should be the ones punished, not me. When Buhari ousted Shagari in his coup in 1983 austerity kicked in, people started hoarding and only the very rich could afford the black market and inflated prices.

Since then, most Nigerians have adopted the '110', '101'or '001' approach to meals since everything is so expensive. '110' means breakfast, lunch and no dinner, '101' is breakfast, no lunch and dinner and so on. At Uncle J's we had all the meals, but at Uncle N's we go for the '101' approach. It's okay during the week because I'm at school. On Saturdays and Sundays we tend to visit one relative or another and in church someone is usually celebrating something so there's always food. Gone are the days when you could buy one *akara* ball for one kobo, now you'd be lucky to even have breakfast. I can't complain though, I still remember a time when I could go days without having a proper meal. They say a chicken eats corn, drinks water and swallows pebbles yet complains of having no teeth. If it had teeth, would it eat gold? Let it ask the cow who has teeth yet eats grass. No, I really can't complain.

21ST FEBRUARY 1985

DJ,

I've been invited to a party and I'm not sure whether to go after what happened the last time I was invited to one. I told Tobi about my encounter with Wale and he wanted to go and beat him up. I had to calm him down otherwise he would have jumped in his dad's car and driven to Ikoyi.

I was touched; no one has ever wanted to do that for me. Instead, he put Wale's name on his list of people who are going to get payback from him some day. There were two other names in his little black book, they were Prefects at his Grammar school who made his boarding life hell on earth. They were bigger and stronger than him and humiliated him regularly. He didn't say it, but I surmised that he joined the Navy because he wanted to become strong and defend himself against his enemies. Now that he's been taught how to kill a person with a single blow, his foes had better beware.

I've decided to go to the party, it's during the day after classes and I'll be going with Segun, Yolande, Charlie Boy and Maggie. Segun and Yolande will be driving, they're taking their mum's car because she's away somewhere. I'm going to ask Uncle N to teach me how to drive.

22ND FEBRUARY 1985

DJ,

I got my first love letter from Tobi today, it is so romantic. He says he's missing me and can't wait to hold me and feel my beating heart next to his. He's only half alive when I'm not around; he loves the way I laugh and the way I walk. I'm surprised he likes the way I walk, Uncle N is always saying I waddle like a penguin and take too much time getting from A to B. He's drawn hearts and kisses on the letter and he's also sent me a picture of him in his white uniform. He looks so handsome. He wants me to send him a picture of myself but I don't have any nice ones. I'll ask Uncle N for some money and go to the photo studio on 23rd Road.

Charles has been trying to toast me ever since we got

back from the school holidays; I've told him over and over and over that I've got a boyfriend already, but he seems to think I should dump Tobi for him. Sometimes I think he's mocking me, as if to say no one could possibly want to be my boyfriend, and that I've made up Tobi. I'm just going to have to show him Tobi's picture, which should get him off my back. I don't think it will be wise of me to go to the party, though, so I think I'll just stay home.

18TH MARCH 1985

DJ,

Happy birthday to me! At seventeen I'm almost an adult, but not quite. I'm not independent and I'll never be free if I don't pass my exams, go to University and get a good job. If the first two happen, there's then the dilemma of how do I pay for it all. Uncle N's generosity will only go so far, and the arguments he and Iya Soji are having over me staying with them are becoming a daily occurrence. If I leave here, where will I go? Sometimes I lie awake at night and cry bitter tears and I wonder if there will ever be a time when I can breathe without my very existence offending someone. I look into Uncle N's eyes and I see pity sometimes mingled with love. I don't want to be pitied, I don't want to be anyone's charity case in their bid for heavenly redemption. All I've ever wanted is to have a family of my own, a Father, a mother and a brother of my own, but I guess that's asking too much. Will I always be walking the shadows searching for light? Will this ache in my heart say goodbye at some point? I don't even know what happiness is any more. I keep thinking to myself that because there are shadows, this means that there is light nearby, I've just got to keep looking for the light. It gets hard, especially when I try to remember a truly happy day but I can only ever remember the bad ones, and today more than anything I experience that sharp pain in my chest and I think maybe this is it, God is going to end my agony. But the pain passes and I see Adebola in my mind's eye as if it was yesterday, lying there with the cotton wool in his nose and ears. He would have been eighteen. I miss him so much, some days more than others. Some days I don't even think about him but I know I'll never truly forget him. I've got to keep searching for the light, it has to be there somewhere, and I go on in the belief that one day I'll find it.

Maybe I should take a leaf out of Ngozi's book. She had about three Sugar Daddies, one was paying for her education, one gave her pocket money and I think the other one gave her money too. It seems a woman can't be anyone unless she has a man beside her, so Ngozi has three. Bottom power will take a woman far, but I'm not sure I have the courage to do that. What would be the difference between me and a prostitute? I've often wondered, if I was a boy would HE have abandoned me? Yet another question that can't be answered, rhetorically speaking. I wonder if Ngozi ever got into Lag (University of Lagos)? Ayo told me that after lectures in the evening the Sugar Daddies come round to the halls to take out their girl-friends, and there's always a queue of expensive cars with a driver and some fat man in the back, who, if it wasn't for the fact that he was rich, you wouldn't look at to spit on. She hates it there and wants to go back to London but her parents can't afford it, so she's stuck.

DJ,

It's Saturday, Uncle N, Iya Soji and the kids have gone to a party. Uncle N's sister has gone to church and his brother went to Ekiti with Mama Joseph yesterday, which for a change means I'm home alone. They were all wearing the same purple lace, Iya Soji bought it for the family for the New Year celebrations. So that I don't feel left out, Uncle N bought me a pair of jeans, which are too short, not that I'm complaining.

The flat was too quiet, so I filled the silence with Al Green and Abba. Al made me think of things I didn't want to and I found myself crying again to How Can You Mend a Broken Heart? I didn't want to be gloomy and depressed so I changed the record and danced around the flat to Abba's Dancing Queen. It's nine o'clock and they're not back from the party, Auntie Bose isn't back from church and NEPA has taken light for the fourth time today. Uncle N is the only one allowed to switch on the generator, so I'm making do with the lantern until they get back. I wanted to play more records and dance while no one was here, because then I'm not thinking about anything. I'd like to let the music wash over me and carry me away on cotton candy clouds. I know it's an ephemeral feeling; however, these days I take each ray of light and hoard it, because all I'm ever left with are the memories and I want happy ones.

DJ,

Today was one of those surreal Mondays. Segun and his sister, Yolande, were forced to go to a society party on Saturday with their mum. It turns out they went to HIS house. I've never been there but how many Ogunwoles can there be living in on Cocaine Avenue in Ikoyi? Their mum got invited because HE is a customer at the Bank she works at. Apparently it was Ekundayo's fifth birthday on Saturday and the rich people of Lagos society were there to celebrate and show off their latest V-boots (Mercedes) and Jeeps. There's a swimming pool, a pool house and extensive grounds. There were a lot of army officers and other bigwigs and a who's who in Lagos society. Yolande reckoned there were more than 20 bedrooms and their whole house would fit into the lounge. I didn't let them know we were related. How do I explain my situation to people? It sounds too dramatic and pitiful and like I said, I never want to be pitied again. So Saturday now makes sense, Uncle N must have gone to the party. He didn't tell me where he was going because he probably didn't want to hurt my feelings. I've accepted the fact that HE has nothing to offer me, maybe I look like my mother and HE remembers her leaving HIM and HE can't bear to look at me, so instead I'm left to accept the kindness of others. I've often wondered if HE'D ever treat me like a daughter again, could we ever go back, was there actually ever a time when HE said I love you or I'm proud of you? I don't remember it, maybe one day HE will say it. I read it in a book that one should believe in miracles but not depend on them.

1ST JULY 1985

DJ,

Exams are over and the summer holidays have started. I have a good feeling about these exams, because for the first time, I actually understood the questions and knew the answers. I've chosen Mass Communications because I can become a news reporter or an actress; I've had enough practice, pretending not to be me. Uncle N is going to pay my fees. Iya Soji isn't too pleased about it. One day I'll be able to show him what his kindness has meant to me.

14TH JULY 1985

DJ,

Another day and another disagreement with Iya Soji, the whole thing is becoming tedious. These days all I have to do is open my mouth and she bites my head off for something or the other. Today's argument started because I asked Uncle N to teach me how to drive in his jeep when he got back from work. That, according to Iya Soji, was insolent of me. I should be grateful for what he does for me and not ask for more of his attention. I guess I just picked a bad day; the trouble is, I never know when it is a good day as far as she's concerned. Every day she comes back from school, I ask her if she'd had a good day and if I could make her something to eat. Sometimes I even offer to wash her clothes but she still hates me and I don't know what I've done to deserve it and I don't know what else to do to make things better.

5TH AUGUST 1985

DJ,

I have the greatest news ever! I've passed my GCE's with four A's in Economics, West African History, English and Literature, three B's in Business Studies, Commerce and Bible Knowledge, I got a C in Biology and Mathematics. This means I can go to University. Hooray, hooray, hooray! I can no longer be considered dumb. The rest of the gang — Segun, Yolande, Maggie and Charlie Boy — all passed too. We're hopefully all going to University next term. HOORAY!!!!

11TH AUGUST 1985

DJ,

Today has been an amazing day for all Nigerians; there are still crowds on the streets celebrating despite the curfew. The Baby Eagles have just won the first ever FIFA/Kodak under sixteen World Cup in China, they beat West Germany 2 – 0. I'm not a great football fan, but it was always fun watching Uncle J watch a game when I was living with him in Surulere. He'd get up from the sofa and start dribbling, kicking or heading an imaginary ball and screaming abuse at the opposition and whomever he was supporting. He'd say things like, 'Ah, look at this one, what are you doing on the field if you can't kick a ball?' or, 'Na your wife teach you how to play?' or, 'Look at this idiot.' Every player was an idiot — 'capital W' — which when translated means 'mad man.' Uncle N is no better, he doesn't do the dribbling, but he gets up and holds his heart like he's having an attack.

NEPA, being the generous organisation that they are, didn't take the electricity at all, although I heard they took it on 7th Avenue. The residents got so irate they marched to the local office and beat up the poor guard who was on the premises as if it was his fault. Why does everything have to end in someone getting hurt? We have an epidemic of armed robbery that is raging out of control, sometimes I'm even scared to walk to the market. The last time I'd gone there with Iya Soji and she had left her bag open, I looked up and saw a man's hand going into her bag as we stood by the pepper stalls. Luckily, she reached in at the same time and twisted round to see where I was. We all had a lucky escape, if I'd said anything I know she would have started shouting 'ole' thief, he would've been lynched and if he managed to escape, he might have followed us home and murdered us while we slept, for revenge.

Charlie Boy told us a story once of how a man got caught stealing in the market. Instead of handing him over to the police, he had a six inch nail driven into his head by an angry mob. Another time, two friends went to the market together, one called the other 'ole' jokingly, he was overheard by someone who raised the alarm and before you could say Lola Ogunwole, they'd put a tyre round his neck, poured petrol over him and set him alight while his friend was begging them and saying he's not a thief. But by then it was too late. The mob wanted justice and someone had to die. I never thought I'd say this to myself, but sometimes I wish I was back in Idogun starving. There I knew what to expect and that nothing was expected of me. I didn't live in constant fear of being murdered in my bed or in the market. Only the very poor are really safe in Lagos, not that Uncle N is rich, but he's not poor either.

28TH AUGUST 1985

DJ,

It's happened again, Buhari is out, Babangida is in. We've had another coup d'état. According to the news it has been a bloodless one. I'm not quite sure I understand what they mean, because some soldiers did die. I guess they aren't important enough on the food chain to warrant a mention. Yesterday Buhari's residence was surrounded and he's now under house arrest, so the country is in even more chaos. I don't think anyone went to work today. Uncle N and Iya Soji didn't, however I'm not sure it's because of the coup d'état, there's been something else bubbling under the surface for a while. I just pray it's not about me. I've been staying out of her way. I don't want to be there when things explode, it will be ugly, I know it. It doesn't help that Mama Joseph is back either. I like it when she's here though, she takes Iya Soji's focus off me.

JAMB results aren't out yet and I'm scared that if I don't pass, I'll be stuck here with her for another year. At least if I'm living on campus and only here during holidays it won't be so bad, I'm a firm believer in the proverb; 'Familiarity breeds contempt and distance breeds respect.' I have to pass.

Segun and Yolande are having a party and this time I think I'll go. I didn't go to the last one, I let my fear take over because I can't dance and I didn't have anything nice to wear. I still can't dance but I've got a nice pair of shorts Uncle N bought for me from work. I can sit and watch and learn the moves. I'm scared, but I realise I can't live the rest of my life in fear of what may happen, let them laugh if they want. When people see me, they think I'm a JJC (Johnny just come) because I wear shorts and not the traditional *iro* and *buba*, or a skirt and blouse, or a dress. Girls aren't supposed to wear shorts or trousers, but if it's all I have, I'd rather they think of me as a JJC than pity me because I can't afford to buy nice clothes.

I got another letter from Tobi today, he's still missing me and he still loves me. I am his moon, his stars, the sugar in his tea, the ink in his pen and even the tyre of a car he doesn't own. How romantic. I have to confess that the initial excitement of having a boyfriend, especially a long distance one, has worn off. I sometimes forget that I'm now in a couple because it doesn't feel that way. I use it once in a while to throw in Charlie Boy's face. He's my most ardent toaster and always wants to take me to a party somewhere. I probably would have given in if it wasn't disloyal to Tobi. I told him this and his response was, 'What Tobi doesn't know won't hurt him,' but I'll know, and how will I ever be able to look him in the eyes if I was double dating him. Charlie Boy's solution is that I break up with Tobi and go out with him instead, but I don't want to. I can't imagine myself kissing him, he's more like a brother and I don't feel any passion for him. According to the books I've read, I'm supposed to feel a tingle down my spine and I just don't get this with Charlie Boy. To be honest, I don't get it with Tobi either, I think he became my boyfriend because he was the first boy to ask me. I wish Segun had asked me, but he never even looks at me, besides he has too many beautiful girls running after him so why would he be interested in me? I sometimes imagine him holding me close and kissing my neck like Tobi did. I think that would be wonderful.

I wish I could put on more weight and not look like a waif, and have a *yansh* that rolled like Ngozi's. Yolande has a big butt, but mine is just flat and there's nothing there. I folded up a blouse and tried stuffing it in my pants to make my bottom bigger but it looked lumpy and asinine. Yolande said I should be thankful I don't have to carry a big *yansh* around. But it's what boys like, it's what Segun likes, I've seen a string of girls come and go and the one thing they have in common is their backside. I don't even have hips; I look like a boy from behind. At least my boobs are a nice size now, so maybe my hips will grow soon.

31st August 1985

DJ,

He kissed me! Segun kissed me on my forehead and it was so soft and gentle and I really think he likes me. Not that he said anything, it all happened earlier after the party we had at the FHA club house. I didn't realise the party was actually to celebrate Segun's birthday. He's seventeen, which means I'm five months older than him. But my age shouldn't matter; I hope he doesn't see it as a barrier. I want to be his girlfriend. Every time I see him my heart does a little jump and the palms of my hands get sweaty, but instead of saying nice things to him I'm always saying horrible things and I can't seem to help myself. Even today on his birthday, I told him that he was like bacteria, he had no culture, but that was after he called me 'telephone wire.'

Well anyway, at the party I was sitting in the corner watching the latest dance steps and knowing I wasn't brave enough to venture on to the dance floor, when Yolande gleefully sat next to me rubbing her hands together. Segun hadn't been on the dance floor because he had two girls there who both believed they were his girlfriend. He didn't want to ask either of them to dance because it would cause a fight, so he asked Yolande and she said no and came to sit beside me, waiting with an evil glint in her eye to see what he'd do. He did the only thing he could, he grabbed me and pulled me up without even asking me if I wanted to dance. I was mortified; that's when he called me 'telephone wire' and I called him 'bacteria.' The music changed tempo and as the DJ started playing Marvin Gaye's Let's Get It On. My heart stopped beating for a millisecond, then went into overdrive as Segun pulled me close, I tried to shuffle my feet to what little beat there was without making a complete fool of myself. As Marvin crooned the words I felt he was speaking to me. I wanted to say something but couldn't utter a word. My palms started to sweat and for a change I couldn't think of anything to say, so I told Segun that I felt honoured he had asked me to dance, and he ought to be careful or people would start to think I was the latest in his long line of girlfriends and that wouldn't do his reputation any good. He told me to shut up or he'd kiss me right there on the dance floor and ruin my reputation. I was tempted to put him to the test but I could feel the daggers from the other two girls. It wouldn't have been so bad if there were other people on the floor but as soon as he started dancing everyone stood round us in a circle. He pulled me closer and I ended up hiding my face in his shirt. He smelt so nice. It was a good thing he was holding me tight because my legs were jelly. I felt him hard against my stomach and I tried to pull back but he wouldn't let me, so we shuffled back and forth in an imitation of dancing and I remembered reading somewhere that dancing is a vertical expression of a horizontal desire, so maybe he did like me and this was his way of expressing it.

The song ended and he led me back to my seat, which I dropped into like a sack of *gari*. He then went to get Yolande and me a drink. I was hot and bothered and wanted to go outside but the two girls where glaring daggers at me, so I dragged Yolande with me. She wasn't pleased. I told her it was her fault and if she'd danced with her brother like he'd asked, I wouldn't have been dragged into this mess. It turned out that Segun had only invited one of the girls and Yolande had invited the other.

Apparently he has another girlfriend who's in University. Her name is Yeside and she's the one he's in love with. They made a pact that when she wasn't in town he could see whoever he wanted, but as soon as she came back, any other girl he was seeing got dropped. So Yolande warned me off and told me to be careful, that as much as she loves her brother he's a womaniser and she didn't want to see me become his latest victim. I heard what she said but my heart was telling me a different story. If he didn't like me, he wouldn't have danced his first dance with me and just dancing wouldn't have turned him on. I've felt Tobi's, but that's only when we're kissing and I wasn't kissing Segun, just dancing.

The rest of the evening passed in a haze. I didn't dance with Segun again or even talk to him, but every time I looked across at him he was looking at me. It was exactly like they describe it in the Mills & Boon books, our eyes met across a crowded room and everyone else disappeared and it seemed like there was an invisible cord connecting our eyes together. But then Charlie Boy stepped in front of me and asked me for a dance and I got dragged on to the dance floor again. Segun was dancing with one of his girl-friends and all of a sudden I had this powerful urge to scratch her eyes out. I managed to resist then the DJ started playing Teddy Pendegrass's, Love TKO and I wondered if I should let it go. We're friends and I don't want to lose that, I don't know many people in Festac. I don't want to fall in love with Segun Baptiste, and I won't fall in love with him just because he kissed me on the forehead.

It all happened after the party. I'd walked there but Yolande insisted Segun drop me at home since it was dangerous for me to walk home by myself. So Maggie went with Charles who brought his mum's car and I went with Segun and Yolande in their mum's Beetle. Yolande wanted to sit in the back because then she'd seem more like a Madam. I didn't personally see how you could look like a Madam scrunched up in the back of a Beetle, but who was I to disagree with her? So I ended up sitting in front with Segun. Then, just as we were about to leave, his two girl-friends came rushing up and asked him to take them home too. They were supposed to go with Charles but they were doing *shakara* so he left without them. I was going to get in the back with Yolande but he put his hand on mine and said no. He let them in through his side and they sat in the back with Yolande. No one was pleased.

The original idea was for him to drop me off then go home, but because Yolande didn't like the girls she insisted on being dropped off first, even though they lived in the opposite direction to me. After we dropped Yolande, I curled up and pretended to fall asleep just so I wouldn't have to speak to him or the other two girls. They were both upset with him and almost started a cat fight on the back seat. He ended up telling them he wasn't seeing either of them and he just wanted to be friends. I could feel him glancing across at me but I kept my eyes firmly closed. I had become an expert at faking being asleep, from back when Mama would try and wake me in the morning to fetch water.

After dropping both of them off, he drove to Uncle N's. He could have dropped me after Yolande but I guess he didn't want to get stuck with the bitches from hell. He tried to shake me awake but I just rolled to face the other way and mumbled, 'Leave me alone.' He got out of the car and came round to open the door, then he squatted down and gently brushed my hair back and kissed my forehead. I still have goose bumps. I think he muttered, 'What am I going to do about you?' but I can't be sure. He shook me again and said, 'Lola, you're home.'

I opened my eyes and stared straight into his and every bone in my body turned to jelly again. I knew if I tried to stand up I'd fall flat on my face, so I smiled and said, 'Thank you,' and closed my eyes again and pretended to go back to sleep. That's when he reached in to pick me up and all of a sudden there I was in his arms and he was holding me like I was a fragile piece of porcelain. What was a girl to do? I put my hands round his neck and my head on his shoulder as he carried me up three flights of stairs to Uncle N's front door. I didn't want him to put me down but he didn't have a choice, he couldn't carry me over the threshold, it wasn't as if we'd just gotten married. Although if he ever asked me I know I'd say yes, but I also know that will never happen. I'm in love with Segun Baptiste. Imagine that.

1ST SEPTEMBER 1985

DJ,

Iya Soji wasn't pleased with the fact that I came in late last night, even though I'd asked Uncle N's permission. The first time I ever stay out late and she wants to have an argument about it. I'm sick of her picking on me. Mama Joseph came to my rescue and she ended up having a squabble with her. Things aren't looking great, I just hope I pass my JAMB exams so I can get out of here. They've announced on the news that the results will be posted at the JAMB offices in Ikoyi tomorrow. I don't think I'll be able to sleep tonight. I think I'll go and visit Yolande.

I've just gotten back from Yolande and Segun's house and she's made me realise how truly selfish I've been. Everything has been about me, and each time I speak to her I seem to whinge more about my situation. I've made it seem that no one else has problems but me, no one is suffering or has suffered like me. Although I'm grateful for the kindness that various relatives have shown me, deep down I seem to have taken it as my right. I've been going around thinking that If HE won't look after me then I become their responsibility and I don't appreciate the hardship they are going through to accommodate me. I've been truly selfish.

For such a long time I've walked around pitying by myself, yet I abhor pity from others. I've been walking around with the weight of the world on my shoulders and blaming HIM and SHE who shall never be mentioned for such a heavy burden. However, the scales have fallen from my eyes and I'm seeing the world in its rainbow of colours. Yolande painfully pointed out the errors of my ways to me. I can't even remember what I was moaning to her about. Probably Iya Soji and her nastiness, but do you know what Yolande said to me? The words will forever be seared in my brain. She said, 'Oh, for Christ's sake, Lola, when are you going to wake up or grow up? Yes, you've had a hard life growing up and it's unfortunate, but do you always want people to feel sorry for you, to point and stare and mutter behind their hands saying things like, "Oh look, there goes Lola, her parents abandoned her and her relatives treat her like a maid?" Well, look around you lots of people are suffering. You're fucking eighteen and an adult, so whatever happens to you from now on is your fault and no one else's.'

I stood there in total shock. She'd never spoken to me like that before. I'd gone to escape another disagreement and thought she was a friend I could talk to but I should've gone to see Maggie instead. I thought she liked me, but there I was standing in her kitchen when she exploded. She grabbed me by the collar of my dress and pushed me against the fridge and said what she did. My eyes started to water and I knew I was going to burst into tears any second. I tried pushing her away but she held on tight, looked into my eyes and said, 'Think about it.' In that moment one of Mr Abrahams favourite phrases popped into my head, so looking straight back at her I said, with fierce pride in my eyes, 'Yolande, never judge a person unless you've walked a mile in their boots, so don't you dare judge me because you don't have a clue.'

We stared into each other's eyes, me with hurt and disillusionment and her with the frustration of trying to make me see. In the end she said, 'Think about it,' again, and then let me go. Even though I'd hardly spent any time there and I'd wanted to see Segun, I told her I had urgent business back home and left. As I walked back to Uncle N's, I let the bitter tears fall. Why did I open my big mouth and tell her my secrets? She did have a point, though; some people don't even have a roof over their head or a food in their stomachs, yet here I am fed and clothed and yet I still have the audacity to complain. From now on I'm going to be as nice as I can be to Iya Soji. Things must be difficult for her with me here.

As I walked home, I did think about it. I wondered about my life, what direction I was going in and I realised that for such a long time I've been drifting, accepting the things that happen to me as fate, so maybe I'm the reason bad things have been happening, it has to be something about me. I've tried racking my brain but I just don't see what I've been doing wrong. Maybe it's because I only do things when I'm asked. I'd rather be putting my feet up in the living room watching TV while someone else does the cleaning and cooking. They say the truth is pure but never simple, or is it simple and never pure? Whichever way I looked at it, here was a bitter pill which I found unpalatable; it is my attitude that has been letting me down, so I've got to change and change so that the Iya Soji's of this world won't dislike me.

2ND SEPTEMBER 1985

DJ,

It's been a disastrous Monday. I didn't exactly fail my JAMB, I missed the cut-off from my Major by five points. I'm devastated that I won't be going to University this year. Yolande's going to Ogun State Uni, but will try and transfer to Lagos next year. Maggie is going to Lag to do Law; I think money passed hands somewhere because she didn't even apply. She wanted to become a broadcaster like me but her dad wants her to follow in his footsteps so he can boast about his daughter the lawyer. Charlie Boy is the only one not compromising on his dreams; he's off to the University of Nigeria to do Engineering. Segun's score was woeful so it looks like we'll be the ones left behind.

Yolande and I have sort of made up. She apologised for what happened in her kitchen, she says she wanted me to realise I have a lot going for me. I know she's right, but she wounded me deeply. Words are like bullets, once they've escaped you can't catch them again. It's going to be hard for me to ever confide in her or anyone else. If I can't reveal who I am to the people I call my friends, I don't know any more. Well, I guess I'll always have you Dearest Jupiter, you've always been with me and I've been able to chronicle my journey, Every obstacle I overcome can only make me stronger, although I can't help wishing for a day where, stretched out before me, is a vista of green grass with no hurdles.

28TH SEPTEMBER 1985

DJ,

We have just got back from Sagamu, we went to drop Yolande off at University. Segun drove us down in one car. Their mother was so proud she couldn't stop smiling. Uncle N came too, would you believe, he's taken a liking to Mrs Baptiste, so he drove the luggage. I just pray he doesn't do anything embarrassing like ask her out just because she doesn't have a husband. Mrs Baptiste insists I call her 'Mummy,' but I feel a bit strange doing that. Although I have to admit she does treat me a bit like a daughter and the last few weeks I've spent more time in her house than at Uncle's. I don't think Uncle N or Iya Soji mind. The less they see of me the less tension there is in the house. I have changed my attitude and it means I'm staying out of her way as much as possible, although it's going to be tougher now that Yolande is in Uni. Even when I was apologising to Iya Soji for disrupting her home, I couldn't help but feel I was apologising for my very existence and I felt a lot of resentment and still do. It's true when they say you can't choose your relatives. I'm still working on changing my attitude but I have to admit that with Iya Soji, it's going to take a while.

Mummy Baptiste likes me, though, I can tell. Maybe it's because I do her ironing for her. Yolande and Segun both hate doing it, so one day I offered to help to avoid an argument between brother and sister. It was the least I could do to repay them for the many dinners I've had at their table. I feel sad. We left Yolande settling into her new dorm, she'll be meeting new people and making new friends. She probably won't want to be friends with me when she comes back on holiday, because who wants to be friends with a failure? At least I've still got Segun, though he hasn't said or done anything to indicate he's interested in me since his birthday party. His college girlfriend has been around a lot and she's absolutely beautiful, I wish I looked like her. Having met her, I can understand why he'd never be interested in a skinny, penguin walking person like me. He's tall, handsome and even funny. His lips are full and sensual; his bottom lip juts out and is a pinkish red. His shoulders are wide and what can be considered as manly. When he walks into a room everyone notices him, he has this presence that attracts people to him; how could he possibly be interested in a telephone wire like me? I wish I was beautiful.

24TH NOVEMBER 1985

DJ,

Life hasn't been that interesting since the rest of the gang have gone to Uni. I'm missing them terribly. I just have Bidemi next door to chat to occasionally, but she's only a kid and still in secondary school. She keeps asking me when I'm going to see Tobi. I can't go all the way to Port Harcourt to see him and he couldn't come for the last summer holidays because he's no longer a Cadet but an

Officer. I'm getting bored with writing love letters, I don't feel any love and what's worse is I'm running out of things to say. I can no longer keep writing things like, 'You complete me,' 'You are my world' or 'You make my heart soar with joy,' when I have to look at his picture to remember what he looks like. And looking at it, I don't even feel an iota of anything.

Segun has been around a lot and I've been round to his house to help Mummy Baptiste with the housework. I think she misses Yolande being there, so I do what I can to help her out. Segun is absolutely useless when it comes to cooking, he just knows how to eat and boy, can he eat! I don't mind doing the cooking, I feel like I have two homes.

4TH DECEMBER 1985

DJ,

It's happened and none of it was really my fault. Iya Soji has packed her bags and moved out of the flat. Uncle N's sister beat her up pretty good too, I couldn't believe my eyes when I saw it happen. She is a Born Again Christian and is always preaching peace and love, however I don't think I'll ever be able to get the picture of her sitting on top of Iya Soji and hitting her with a slipper out of my mind. I had to pull her off before she could do any real damage, although I have to admit I was willing to let her carry on a little more. I even accidentally pushed Uncle's shoe, which was in the doorway towards them, just in case Auntie Bose decided to change her weapon of choice to a more suitable one.

It all started with Mama Joseph wanting *ogi* this morning there wasn't any in the house, so she started to complain that Iya Soji was a bad wife. Well, Iya Soji had reached boiling point and was ready to explode which she did by slapping Mama Joseph. Uncle N wasn't in, the kids had already gone to school and normally at that time Iya Soji would have left too. There was Uncle N's brother and sister and me and I've never seen Uncle N's sister move so fast. We were both in the sitting room when we heard the slap, then Mama start to cry, 'You slap me, you slap me.' Well, Auntie Bose slapped Iya Soji right back and dragged her to the ground. Each time she hit her with the slipper, she'd say, 'Don't you hit my mother again.' Uncle N was furious when he got home. Iya Soji didn't even wait for him to get back. Instead of going to school, she spent the morning packing her bags and she moved out this afternoon. Most of her stuff is still here, she's just taken her clothes, so no doubt she'll be back soon. Uncle N says he never wants to speak to her again. I'm just glad that this didn't happen because of me.

15TH DECEMBER 1985

DJ,

Iya Soji came round today to pick up the kids; she's taken the others but left Soji. Uncle had gone to see his friend Nana from work. He goes there every night after work, ever since Iya Soji left. Sometimes she stays over when Mama Joseph isn't here. He wants to marry her but Mama Joseph won't accept her because she's from Ghana. It's bad enough she's not from Idogun, but to make matters worse she's from a foreign country and speaks a different language.

When I told Uncle N that Iya Soji came round with her relatives to take the children, he just shrugged his shoulders and said they're her children, she can take them. She came prepared to fight tooth and nail for them. It makes me wonder why mine didn't fight tooth and nail for us. There's no point in looking back though. There's only forward to go and I can only hope that the future holds much more than the past.

DJ,

Hooray, everyone is back in town and it's party time. There's a party every day and I'm building up quite a collection of invitations. Charlie Boy is the same joker. The first thing he did when he saw me was grab his heart and go down on one knee and start singing very badly, You Got Me Hanging on a String Now, by Loose Ends. I don't think he knew the rest of the words; he's always serenading me with half a song. Segun has a good voice but he doesn't sing, he likes to rap. He goes out with chunky gold chains around his neck and calls himself Grandmaster S, he's been trying to get a band together and Mummy Baptiste isn't very happy with him. She keeps telling him there's no money in rap in Nigeria, but Segun wants to become a superstar. These days' every time he comes to see me he's playing Atlantic Starr's Silver Shadow at full blast. I think he parks outside the close, waits for the song to get to the part about the world remembering their name and screeches into the close at the same point every time. Uncle N has nicknamed him 'Silver Shadow.' Contrary to the lyrics, he seems to have forgotten Segun's name.

It's really strange. Segun and I are almost like a couple but he's never officially asked me out. He hasn't kissed me either apart from on the forehead. He's always holding my hand when we go out, though and we've been bubbling together. He's a sought after DJ and whenever he's at the party he drags me along. He told me it keeps the girls off his back, but he only ever dances with me and it's always towards the end and to the same song, Secret Lovers. He holds me close and I put my head on his chest and listen to his heartbeat as we slowly move our bodies in a parody of dance. He then takes me home, walks me to Uncle's door and leaves. Each time I've hoped he'd kiss me, but he hasn't. I'm not sure for how much longer I can go on, all I seem to think about is him. I've decided to write to Tobi and break off our relationship; it's just not working out. How can I be his girlfriend if I want to be with someone else? It's not fair on him. I'm hoping he doesn't come home for Christmas, it will be easier writing him a letter rather than telling him to his face. Do I tell him I'm in love with someone else? Am I really in love with Segun? I don't know what love is. I just know he's the first thing I think about when I wake up in the morning and I count the minutes till I see him. When I go to sleep, his face is the last thing I see in my mind's eye, so if that's love then I guess I'M IN LOVE WITH SEGUN BAPTISTE.

I like to listen to him laugh. It rumbles, starting deep in his stomach. When it reaches his mouth, his lips part to meet his eyes and his whole face creases up. Hearing that sound makes me happy, so I try and crack jokes all the time but I'm an appaling joke-teller. I have no sense of timing; I seem to mangle the joke, which he thinks is funny.

1ST JANUARY 1986

2.30AM

DJ,

I've had a lucky escape. It wasn't until I was facing death that I realised I didn't want to die. We were all coming back from a New Year's Party on 21 Road when a guard on C Close pointed his gun at us and demanded to know where we were going. All the stories I'd heard of the police and soldiers shooting innocent people came flooding back. Segun was holding my hand and as my fingernails made craters in his palm, we stood petrified, unable to speak as the soldier barked at us. Eventually Segun managed to raise his arm in the air, pointing in the general direction of the party we were coming from and stuttered that we were coming from a party. The soldier said we weren't allowed to go through the Close, so we ended going round in a big circle, but at least we escaped with our lives. That wasn't the end of our troubles though. We walked Maggie home first and as we were on our way to Charlie Boy's flat, we got stopped and almost picked up for curfew violation. It didn't matter that it was New Year's Eve, we weren't supposed to be out. Yolande and I burst into tears while Segun and Charles started begging for our liberty. We gave them all the money we had, which wasn't much, everything came to a total of five Naira, not much they can buy with that. But thankfully they let us go, telling us that they were going to come back our way and if they saw us, they'd arrest us. Charlie Boy lives in the same close as me so we ran home together, while Segun and Yolande went in the other direction. I pray they got home safely. I keep remembering Ngozi's Uncle. There's no meat on my body to lose.

4TH JANUARY 1986

DJ,

I went to see Tobi in his battleship today, they're going on battle manoeuvres. I'm not sure why, considering there's no war, but I guess they have to be prepared. They docked in Lagos Harbour yesterday and the first thing he did was come and see me. I wasn't at home when he turned up though, so he left a message for me with Soji and Bidemi. I didn't want to go by myself so I dragged Maggie and Yolande along, telling them that I was going to break up with him and needed their support. He took us out for lunch on the Island, but I couldn't find the words to tell him that I wanted to break things off, so I said nothing. I'm such a coward. I've decided to send him a letter instead. He wants me to come alone tomorrow so we can spend time together. He's on duty and not allowed off the boat till evening and by the time he gets a taxi to Festac, it would be too late. I don't want to hurt his feelings so I'm going to have to pretend that I still like him. I just hope he's not allowed to kiss while he's on duty.

5TH JANUARY 1986

DJ,

The rest of the squad have gone back to their various Universities, Yolande had a friend pick her up and I didn't see Charlie Boy leave. I'd already said my goodbye to Maggie yesterday. It's really strange, we seem to have become closer since she went away and she wants me to come and visit her on campus and meet her new friends and go to some of the campus parties. It seems as if she's having a great time. Even Yolande had stories of partying all night and then trying to drag herself to eight o'clock lectures.

I went to see Tobi this afternoon and I still didn't tell him it was over. There didn't seem to be much point in me being there, as he was on duty and couldn't really spend much time with me. I was there for about three hours and I spent most of the time speaking to his friends who weren't on duty. I felt as if I was on display. He'd told them all about me but they didn't believe I existed. I should have sent him that picture I kept promising him. He wasn't allowed to take anyone to his cabin so I only saw the mess hall, which was a shame. I would have liked to look around the nooks and crannies of a war ship. He's off in the morning on a peace mission but he wasn't allowed to tell me where, not that I was interested. I just asked because I wanted to know where to post his letter to, but apparently he'll still get it if I use the old address.

7TH JANUARY 1986

DJ,

I finally did it, I wrote the letter to Tobi. I didn't want him to feel bad so I didn't tell him I'd fallen in love with Segun. I've copied it here because it's my first break-up letter.

> *Dear Tobi,*
>
> *How are you? I hope you are well and my letter finds you in good spirits. I'm not sure where you are right now, wherever it is I pray the sun is shining brightly. Tobi, this is not an easy letter for me to write, I really do care about you but I think we've gone as far as we can with this relationship. You were my first love and I'll always remember you with fondness, you're the first boy I kissed and the first boy who made me feel special. However the time has come for us to move on, it's been hard for me having a boyfriend I see occasionally. I want someone I can bubble with, someone I can show off to friends, but more importantly; I want someone who lives in the same city as me.*
>
> *I will always care about you and I hope you're not too upset by my decision to end things. Just remember you were*

my first love, and will always have a place in my heart. I
hope we can still remain friends.

Your friend forever
Lola xxxx

I tried to keep it as short as possible, but I'm beginning to
think I should have told him the truth. What if he decides
to transfer back to Lagos, what do I say to him then? I just
hope he meets someone else.

16TH FEBRUARY 1986

DJ,

Segun and I had our first argument today. It was stupid
really. I got angry with him because he told me to shut up
because I can't sing, and I was ruining one of his favourite
songs. We were on our way back from class, which isn't fun
without the rest of the squad there. It feels too much like
when I had to repeat my second year back in Idogun. Why
do I have to keep failing at everything I do? I can't even
keep Segun interested in me; even though we still hold
hands (apart from today), nothing has been said about us
being together. Maybe it's because he's still in love with
his ex-girlfriend, or it could be that he thinks of me as his
sister. I really, really hope not. Mummy Baptiste bought
me a dress from work the other day. One of her work
colleagues goes to Yankee and brings things back to sell in
the office. She was going to get me a pair of shoes to
match but didn't know what size I was. Neither do I for
that matter, of all the things not to know about yourself,
shoe size shouldn't be one of them.

I wanted so badly to be in Segun's band. He's audition-
ing for a girl to sing duets with. If only I could sing,

it would be my eyes he stares into as he sings love songs. I know I'm fooling myself but I can't seem to help imagining us together forever. I imagine our lives, our house, our children and grandchildren and Segun at ninety still looking into my eyes and singing to me.

1ST MARCH 1986

DJ,

This morning I got a reply to my break-up letter with Tobi and he's not happy with me. In fact he's pretty peeved, not that I blame him. I know I should have found the courage to tell him face-to-face and explain why. Now he thinks I've been two-timing him, so he's calling me a whore, bitch and a slut.

Uncle N has been in a bad mood all week. Nana has gone back to Ghana, as all the illegal immigrants have been told to go home because the economy can't sustain them. I'm going to miss her, she gave me some of her clothes that don't fit her any more. My favourite is a black dress with yellow flowers; I've got another party dress to add to my growing collection. I don't wear my shorts that much any more, especially since they're looking a bit ragged. The last time I wore them Segun and I were trying to catch a bus back home from Mile Two and the conductor wouldn't let me on because I was showing my legs. We ended up having to get a taxi with the money we were going to spend on *suya*.

If I think about it, I have been two-timing Tobi, I may not have kissed Segun or accepted a proposal of marriage but we've still be acting like we're a couple. Bidemi probably told him what was going on — not that she actually knows anything, how can she? Even I don't know what's going on. I'm going to have to ask him out myself, if I wait for him I might die of old age.

DJ,

It finally happened. I didn't have to ask him. Mummy Baptiste had gone to bed and we were watching a Wrestle Mania video. I was lying on the couch with my head in his lap and he was playing with my hair.

I was trying to dredge up the courage to ask him out when he says in a serious voice, 'Lola, we need to talk.'

My heart skipped a beat as he continued, 'I don't know how you feel about me, but I really like you and I was hoping we could become an item.'

Now I have to admit that I was disappointed, it wasn't exactly the declaration of love that I was seeking, how can he not know how I feel about him? Of all the ways to ask a girl out — 'I was hoping we could become an item' — do I look like a tin of tomatoes on a shelf? I wanted the moment to be more than that; what happened to, 'Would you be my girlfriend because I think about you day and night, and each time I sing a love song I'm reminded of your dazzling smile?'

I don't know why I'm complaining, we are now officially a couple and we kissed and I have to say it was more than swapping saliva. My toes tingled and my heart was beating so fast I thought I was going to hyperventilate. He wanted us to make love there and then, but I kept remembering what Mummy Baptiste said to me when I first started coming round to the house. I think she knew then how I felt about Segun, she warned me about having sex before marriage. She told me that a man will sleep with any woman that lets him, but when it comes to taking a wife they all want to marry a virgin. She was a virgin until the age of twenty-seven, which is when she got married to Segun's father. They met in University in America and he married her because she wasn't second-hand goods. It's just the way the male species think, no matter how modern they think they are, they prefer it if a woman is chaste and pure. Well, I have kissed another man, so I'm not completely pure.

I asked him about Yeside, his ex that isn't really an ex, and apparently she's now seeing someone at Uni and it's serious. Does this mean I'm second best? I love him so much and I'm filled with doubt as to his sincerity; whenever I wish for something, things have a way of always going wrong. I can't ever let him know how much I care, I'll have to secretly love him until a time comes when I know my feelings are reciprocated. It's going to be morning soon and I'll have to go to church with Uncle. I think he's missing Iya Soji now that Nana has left. He used to smile all the time and now he shouts at everyone. He blames Mama for chasing his wife away so she's left and I think Auntie Bose might leave soon if things carry on the way they have. I've spent most of my time at Segun's so I've missed the brunt of his anger. I'd forgotten to tell him that I was going to Segun's first concert. His new band is called 'Voice Out' (he still hasn't found a female lead singer). He was the opening act for Miss LASU (Lagos State University). He's outgrown his Grandmaster S days and is now into Rock and Pop. The students loved it, especially the girls and I felt so special because he chose to be with me when he could have had his pick of the most stunning girls on campus. He even dedicated one of his songs to me. He whispered into the mike, 'This is for my special girl who always believed this was possible, thank you for being you.' It was a beautiful moment.

*"Calamity has no voice,
suffering cannot speak
to tell who is really
in distress"*

West African Proverb

3RD MARCH 1986

DJ,

I don't know what to do, who do I tell? I thought he loved me but clearly I was mistaken. I feel dirty and violated. Did I bring this on myself? Has it been my fault it happened? He doesn't know that I know, I pretended to be asleep because I thought he was going to send me on an errand and I didn't want to get up when he called out my name. I'd settled in on my mat in the sitting room and was thinking about Segun and our day together and I didn't want my quiet time interrupted. But I wish I'd gotten up now and maybe turned on the lights, would he have had the courage to do what he did, while I lay and pretended that I was fast asleep? I can't say anything to him, what do I say? 'Uncle, why were you touching and sucking on my breasts last night?' If I tell anyone he'll send me away and there is nowhere else for me to go, no one else who would pay my school fees. I can't run to Mummy Baptiste, she's got her own children to raise. What can she do to help? No, no one must know my shameful secret, not even Segun.

I feel so ashamed. I wanted to stop him but didn't know how. He's my Uncle, I used to sit on his lap. When Adebola died it was him that held me close and promised nothing bad would happen to me, he promised he'd look after me.

DJ,

He won't stop; who do I turn to now? GOD PLEASE, MAKE HIM STOP. I don't know what to do, I feel so stupid and helpless. I'm almost eighteen and I still can't look after me. Adebola, where are you when I need you, why did you have to die and leave me with these people. SOMEONE MAKE HIM STOP.

DJ,

It started two weeks ago and every night since then he's come to the sitting room to touch these things that I have. If only I could get rid of them so he wouldn't see me that way. When I look at him the next day, he still seems like the same Uncle N who I thought cared about me, the one who was by my side when Adebola died. He held my hand, gave me hugs and told me it would be okay. He's given me a roof and food in my stomach. I think about his kindness and I wonder if I've imagined the whole thing, that the night before was a bad dream, but then I catch him looking at me and I don't understand the look in his eyes, but it makes me feel horrible, and I know it really did happen and I feel sick to my stomach. Segun has noticed that something is wrong with me. He wants to touch me and I go cold at the thought of his hands on my breasts and I push him away. I can't tell him, I don't even know how to tell him, will he think it's my fault? Have I done anything to encourage Uncle N to touch me in this way? All I have are questions and no answers. I don't even have tears to shed, I keep thinking at least he hasn't taken the one thing I do have to offer Segun. If I keep pretending I don't know what he's doing, maybe one day he'll think he can get away with it and want to go below my belly button, and what will I do then? Will I ever feel safe again in this flat? In two days' time I'll be eighteen — happy birthday to me — welcome, Lola, to the sorority of womanhood.

22ND MARCH 1986

DJ,

I've moved into the kid's room with his sister and I've kicked Uncle N's brother out into the sitting room and taken his bunk bed. It was all Auntie Bose's idea. I was in the kitchen making *eba* and not looking too good from the many sleepless nights and she asked me what was wrong and I said I hadn't been sleeping well on the floor, so she told Tayo that since I'm older than him, I should get the bed and he should be the one sleeping on the floor. Despite this, I haven't managed to get a good night's sleep. I keep waiting for him to sneak into the room once everyone has gone to sleep. He asked me why I moved into the kids' room and I told him I'd rather sleep on a bed than on the floor because I was a princess. He laughed and made a remark about me being too mischievous for my own good.

APRIL 6 1986

2.30 AM

DJ,

Yesterday evening was Mummy Baptiste's fiftieth birthday party and Segun was the DJ and he also performed with his band, 'Voice Out.' Yolande brought some of her new friends from Uni. She's even got herself a boyfriend, Segun and I couldn't believe it. She's always acted as if boys were beneath her, guess she met one that changed her mind. Things are still strained, we both tried but there were long silences as we struggled to find common ground. Unfortunately for me, she seemed to resent her mother including me in their family circle. I didn't know what to say when Yolande came out with, 'So she's adopted you now, Mummy's always taking in strays, well enjoy it while it lasts.' What could I say? I realise that no matter how many dresses Mummy Baptiste buys for me, no matter how many times she sends a kind word my way, they'll only ever be scraps from the main feast. Sometimes I sit in their flat and I watch the affection they all have for each other and I want to cry with envy, so I take what I can when it's offered; surely I can't be begrudged that?

3:30 AM
DJ,
Uncle N has just come into the room. Auntie Bose is out at an all night vigil, Soji is sleeping in the bottom bunk and an earthquake wouldn't wake him and Tayo is in the lounge asleep. He came in and was surprised to see me still up. He said he thought I'd fallen asleep with the light on. I told him I couldn't sleep so I was reading a book. He told me not to stay up too late or I wouldn't be able to get up for church. I lied and said I couldn't go anyway, due to the fact that I was on my period. He looked at me suspiciously but he went back to his room. When I heard his door click shut I exhaled deeply not even realising that I'd been holding my breath. Another escape. Next time Auntie Bose goes on a night vigil I'm becoming a Born Again Christian and going with her. Only God can deliver me from this *palava* that I'm in.

13TH MAY 1986

DJ,

Although Uncle N hasn't said anything, I think he knows that I know what he's been doing, because he's asking probing questions. The other day he said, 'Lola, are you all right? You look like you haven't slept properly,' staring at me intently. I just shrugged my shoulders and said, 'I'm fine.' God has been good to me because he hasn't been back. I'm hoping it's because he's found another girlfriend. Her name is Yemi and she's high maintenance with a bad attitude. I don't know how they met and I don't care really. I was hoping she'd move in but she can't because she's a student at Lag and only looking for a Sugar Daddy to buy her the finest things. As long as his attention is on her, it's away from me.

JAMB is over and I think I did okay, I just want out of here and going to Uni will get me away from this place and Uncle N. Although the chances of me having a trouble-free education are probably nil, the students are rioting again. Uncle N reckons it's because The President has made Nigeria a member of the Organisation of the Islamic Conference and the Christians aren't happy. I thought religion was about loving thy neighbour. Uncle N doesn't like the President very much, according to him he's diverting the wealth of the South to the North and building proper roads over there. NEPA never takes light and they have running water in all houses. They get all this because the top positions are filled with Northerners. He reckons there might be another Biafran war. I sure hope not, life is hard enough as it is, you add war on top of that and hell would probably be nicer. Tonight I'll go down on my knees and pray there isn't a war. There's been a mass exodus, to

Yankee and London. On the News it's being called a brain drain because all the people who are leaving are the doctors, lawyers, architects, engineers and anyone with a decent degree who can afford the exorbitant airfares.

17TH MAY 1986

DJ,

Charlie Boy is back in town and it's not even the summer holidays yet. Several students at ABU (Ahmadu Bello University) have been shot dead; the students are rioting so some of the Uni's in the North have been shut down. Charles doesn't think they'll reopen until next term, which means he doesn't get to do his end of year exams so he'll have to repeat his first year.

Nothing much else is happening. There seems to be a party every day that Segun is invited to, which means he takes yours truly. Not that my name is ever on any of the invites, I'm just the 'and friend.' Not that it matters; they're becoming boring now. You go to a party, listen to the same music and see the same faces; the only thing that tends to change are the clothes. They're all trying to outdo each other in the bid to see who's got the best 'spoots' (clothes). I'm all bubbled out, but there's a party next Saturday which I'm excited about, it's someone's birthday and they're having a beach party and the only way to get there is by speedboat. I've never been on one before so it should make things a bit more exciting.

12TH JULY 1986

DJ,

Segun and Yolande have gone away for the summer holidays again, to stay with Mummy Baptiste's brother in

Chicago. I don't know how I'm going to cope without my sweetheart for two whole months. Since we've started dating, I've seen him every single day. I'm missing him already and he's only been gone three hours thirty-two minutes. He gave me a photo of himself in an envelope and said not to open it till he had gone. On the back he's written, 'This is so that you don't forget what I look like, I love you.' He's written down the three little words that I wanted to hear him say so badly.

14TH JULY 1986

DJ,

It's bad, Uncle N has been retrenched which means no job = no money = no food and if I may selfishly add = no Uni for me.

19TH JULY 1986

DJ,

　Things are pretty dire; I think Uncle N is cracking up. He had a huge fight with his latest high maintenance girlfriend, Yemi. I'm still not sure where he picked her up from or how long they've been seeing each other. She wanted money, he had none to give, so she told him she'll find it somewhere else and left. I've started looking for a job, but what can I do? I can't work in a Bank or an office and that leaves selling fish in a market somewhere. My brief stint of selling pepper soup in a *bukkah* gave me nothing but chicken change. I had to leave anyway because the owner, Mike, would only play Michael Jackson's *Off the Wall* album and I couldn't bear to listen to it without remembering things I'd rather forget. I've got to find a way of making money without doing the obvious; I don't want to become

Ngozi with three Sugar Daddies. I'm not naïve, I know what they'll want in return, the question is, can I have sex with a man for money? I'm not quite desperate enough yet. If I can't make love with Segun, the man I adore and would like to marry, can I just give it up for the sake of having the latest clothes, shoes and bag to match? I'd probably have to marry the man for him to pay my school fees. Charlie Boy always says, 'Why I go put petrol inside car I no dey drive?' I've managed to endure the many hardships so far and my burden has been small compared to other people, so I can only hope that around the next corner the sun is shining brightly.

26TH JULY 1986

DJ,

I have to admit I'm feeling a little sorry for Uncle N but at the same time I'm secretly delighting in his misery. He still hasn't found a job since he's been retrenched and he still hates the President with a passion, especially since he can't even afford to put petrol in his car any more. He walks everywhere these days. He tried to get a job with FHA but even they're retrenching staff. He always had so much money before, wads and wads of it. I guess that, unlike Mama, he doesn't believe in rainy days, he spent money like he had a money tree growing in his back garden. I had a dream about finding a purse with only five Naira inside it and each time I took out the money to spend I had to spend all of it, that way the purse would replenish itself with another five Naira bill. I think Uncle N could do with a magical purse right now.

1ST AUGUST 1986

DJ,

When I thought things couldn't get any worse I was wrong, because they just have. While I've been trying to climb out of the black hole that is my life, a greater force has been digging the hole a little bit deeper. I've been knocked out cold and now once again I'm lying at the bottom looking at the light, which now seems like it's a billion miles away and I've run out of energy to try and follow it. Iya Soji has been persuaded to come home, but her one condition is that I not be here when she comes back. I've nowhere else to go, which means I could be sleeping on the streets of Lagos by next Saturday, which is when she's moving back home. I can't help but wonder why now. The way Uncle N has been acting, you'd think he was single. I guess now that the money tree he had in his back garden has been plucked dry and he no longer has a job and Iya Soji still has hers; he'll be needing her money to keep the family going. Uncle N says I shouldn't worry, that he'll find somewhere for me to live. He's taking me to the British High Commission on Monday to see if they can help. Apparently, because I was born in London I'm technically a British citizen and they have to protect me since I'm in a foreign country. I don't know what they can do. Uncle N thinks they'll give me a ticket so I can go back to London, which is a bit unrealistic of him. Assuming they do give me a ticket and say you can go, where exactly will I live? Either way, it seems the streets of either London or Lagos are beckoning, what will be, will be, there's no point fighting the inevitable.

DJ,

Today must have been one of the most humiliating experiences of my life. Uncle N and I caught the bus to Victoria Island to the British High Commission. There were lots of people there waiting for visa application interviews, we took a ticket and waited our turn. The occasional businessman came in, wanting to jump the queue, spouting the usual, 'Do you know who I am?' I've always wondered about that. Why do people say it when most of the time no one really wants to know who they are anyway? The other day I was at the bus stop minding my own b's when a soldier walked straight into me, and did he apologise? Of course not, especially since it turned out to be my fault for standing in his path. He then had the audacity to say, 'Do you know who I am?' when quite frankly I didn't care who he was, all I wanted from him was an apology. Instead, I got a gun pointed in my face for the second time in my life when I replied back to him, 'Do you know who I am?' His answer was, 'You could be nobody in two seconds.'

The red haze descended. The last time it happened I went berserk; curiously, this time it had the opposite effect. I remained eerily calm, but still in that instant I was prepared to die and I think he saw it in my eyes; he expected me to beg for my life but instead what he got was a girl saying, 'Go ahead, kill me in front of all these people.' I really had nothing to lose. A crowd had gathered and were pleading with him to let me go since I was only a child. It was over in minutes, he slung his gun back over his shoulder and carried on walking while I disgorged the contents of my stomach.

Anyway, our number came up and we went to Room Six

and waited. A white lady waddled in and I remember thinking to myself that I hadn't spoken to or seen a white person in over ten years. She had curly brown hair and wore her glasses just on the tip of her nose and her *yansh* was flatter than a pancake. She had a high-pitched voice that grated on my nerves and made me instinctively dislike her. Uncle N gave her the story of how I was born in London and had been abandoned by both my parents, and how he had heard that the British government looked after children who had nowhere to go. She looked down her nose at me and 'ummed', she wanted to know the last contact I'd had with my parents and I had to tell her I'd never met my mother and I hadn't spoken to my Father since 1979. I don't know whether or not she was sympathetic to my plight, however she wanted to see proof of citizenship, a birth certificate or a passport. I had neither, but she said not to worry and wanted to know my date of birth, so I told her. She looked at me with surprise and, after doing the mental calculation, she closed her note pad and said, 'I'm afraid we can't help you.' She explained that they do have an obligation to protect children who are citizens whether or not they live in the country. However, at eighteen I'm an adult and not the responsibility of the British government.

The funny thing was, even though I didn't expect any assistance, I couldn't help but hope that my fortunes would change. Instead, I had to endure the pity of a total stranger but then I remembered what Yolande said, so I sat up straighter and held my head a little bit higher. Uncle N is determined to get me out of the house by Saturday. Tomorrow we're going to see HIM. The way Uncle N sees it, HE needs to take on HIS responsibility instead of pretending that I don't exist.

"My child is dead is
better than my
child is lost"

Yoruba proverb

DJ,

Iguess I should begin on the day of the meeting. I remember thinking to myself that here I was, eighteen years old, and still needing to be looked after. I thought that at eighteen I'd be independent and free, that I'd be able to go out into the world and no longer have to rely on anyone but myself. That clearly hasn't been the case because I'm still walking the shadows searching for light. You're wondering what happened; where do I start? It was more of a family battle that had nothing to do with me. Although everyone was there, they didn't come to persuade HIM to look after me; the relatives had their own agenda.

Uncle J, who I hadn't seen since he kicked me out of the house, started the meeting by saying, 'When there are no elders the town is ruined and when the master dies the house is desolate.' He told HIM, that because he was younger than HIM, it wasn't his place to teach HIM the traditions of their forefathers. However, despite this, he couldn't sit back and continue to say nothing when HE is doing something so wrong. HE lives in a big house with another man's children yet HIS own child has to rely on the charity of others.

He pointed to me and said, 'Look at her, your own daughter wearing a hand-me-down that is even too big for her.' I had nicer things to wear but Uncle N had made me wear one of Auntie Bose's old dresses. He pointed to me again and said, 'Look at her feet, no shoes, just bathroom slippers. How you fit sit there with all the money in the world and ignore your own flesh and blood?' I hadn't seen HIM since the twins' birthday party so I didn't know what to expect, what I'd see in his eyes when I looked at him. But I saw nothing, he looked straight through me as if I didn't exist. I almost broke down but was saved by Iya Soji. She was on form, all the animosity she felt towards me was now directed at him and she let him have it.

She was more interested in finding out how HE made HIS money; I guess she still remembers the two rooms we lived in, in Orile. However, she crossed the line when she accused him of killing Adebola to make money. There was complete silence when she said this. People's mouths opened in varying stages of disbelief at what she'd said. I knew she was only saying what most of them thought — a few years ago we were living in a 'face-me-I face-you' house, sharing facilities with total strangers, now here we were in a mansion he owned. Even though I also speculated about HIS sudden wealth, I did wonder why the meeting suddenly shifted focus from me and became about Adebola and HIS pursuit of the almighty Naira. I thought they were there to convince HIM about his responsibilities towards me. However, it was apparent they each had something else in mind, old scores needed to be settled. As the elders of Idogun are fond of saying, 'A jealous person has no flesh upon them, for however much they feed on jealousy; they will never be satisfied.' No one ever came to visit when we were living in Orile and none of them cared about me except maybe Uncle J and N, yet there they all were asking HIM if he sold his own son's soul or sold drugs. I settled back into my chair and watched the fireworks explode; this was my family. Of course Cook Woman wasn't taking an accusation like that lying down; she took off her headscarf, wrapped it around her waist and went for Iya Soji, screaming abuse. I wasn't sure who to cheer for. After all, they were my two favourite people in the whole world.

Before they could hit each other Uncle J stepped in, I wanted to scream, 'Let them fight!' I almost exploded with the effort of holding back, I wanted to see them bleed and hurt like never before. In the middle of this, Cook Woman's children, Ronke and Ayo, rushed in adding their voices to the melée. Cook Woman accused the relatives of being jealous of HIS success and that it was a family member who killed Adebola and who was trying to kill her son Ekundayo, she knew who it was but she wasn't going to mention a name. Of course she said it looking straight at me. Iya Soji was like a dog with a bone, she called her an illiterate woman who colluded in the death of Adebola and thought she could replace him with another son. I'd never heard that word before and I admit, I had to look up the meaning. I was so happy that her wrath wasn't turned on me because when she starts she can't stop; she has what Uncle N likes to call verbal diarrhoea. Everyone started screaming at each other. Uncle J's wife is a foreigner who doesn't understand the ways of the Idogun family and the role of the wife in it. That was said of Cook Woman too, it seemed the wives who are not from Idogun are to blame for all the ills that have befallen the family. Of course they seemed to be forgetting that my mother was from Idogun, and what a joyful union that turned out to be.

Well, after a lot of screaming and shouting and head-scarves being tied around waists, things calmed down. HE just held his hands in the air and like magic everyone became quiet. HE looked at Iya Soji and thanked her for her role in raising me. His explanation was that it wasn't his intention to let me starve and die, HE thought he was leaving his only daughter in the hands of people who would treat her like a daughter. He pointed to Ronke and Ayo and said that they were not his children but he treats them as if they are. HIS reasoning for sending me away was to gain an understanding of the Idogun culture and the ways, which are different from the white man's. I, apparently, needed de-programming and needed to realise that life can be hard and that it takes a whole village to raise a child. HE didn't know who his father or mother were until he was in school, yet HE was never mistreated by the relatives he stayed with. HE became their son while he lived with them and that's how it should be. HE looked at Uncle N and Uncle J and asked if they gave him a precious package to look after, would they expect to receive it back in the same condition in which it was given or not? At this point, I didn't know what to think; maybe HE does love me but just doesn't know how to show it. HE said that because of the history of bad blood between me and Cook Woman, it wouldn't be a good idea for me to live with HIM. My heart sank just as I was warming to him. I contemplated having to sleep under Mile Two Bridge, but then HE added that I could stay in the old flat. It wasn't ready and I was to come back next week, because the tenant who was letting it had just bought a new house and was moving out. Whoopee, I thought to myself, I'm going to be living by myself with no one looking over my shoulder.

Cook Woman was having none of it, she said that Ronke was supposed to be moving in and she'd promised her the flat. My heart dropped again and I almost started crying, but I'd promised myself I would never cry in front of HIM again. This time HE didn't let me down; he looked straight at her and said, 'It's for my daughter.' HE actually acknowledged me and I almost did start crying, I'm beginning to think that HE doesn't hate me, maybe HE just doesn't know how to show me HE loves me.

Well anyway, Iya Soji wasn't happy about living with me a second longer, but she didn't argue because she knew that my banishment from her realm was only a few days away. Saturday, the day she was due to move back came, and we helped her move her stuff back in, only she decided I wasn't being helpful enough and decided there and then that I had to go. Uncle N had had enough, so he told me to pack my bags and he was going to have to drop me off in Ikoyi. I didn't have much to pack; apart from the frilly dress Uncle J had given me and the clothes Uncle N had bought for me, most of the clothes I had were the ones I brought from London. I don't know why I still had them, they no longer fitted, but they were that last tangible link to a life I once knew. I packed my clothes into two blue nylon shopping bags, along with my journals. I couldn't leave those behind. Looking at the clothes I had, I remember being amazed that I was Segun's girlfriend. It sure wasn't my clothes he liked.

So I picked up my two bags, and was duly whisked away to my new palace. However, when Lola the princess got to the palace, all the king's family and all the king's men, including the king, had gone away somewhere. When we arrived at the gate the guard told me everyone had gone away. I went back to the car to tell Uncle N and he told me he couldn't take me back to Festac, that I'd have to wait for them to come home. So I took my two bags out of the car and bravely waved him away, my smile a bowl to catch the tears that were making their journey down my face.

I turned back to the guard at the gate and asked to be let me in, only to be told that he couldn't because 'Oga', HIM, won't be back for days. I turned back and watched Uncle N's rear lights fade into the night and wondered what I was going to do. I told the guard I was 'Oga's' daughter and to let me in, but he just looked at me with an expression I can't describe. I just remember feeling like an ant. He didn't say much but I knew what he was thinking. There I was in another hand-me-down dress, which was too big. It was a black dress, with pink flowers only the black had faded to a dull grey and the pink had lost most of its colour too. I understood the look in his eyes. There I was dressed in rags, with two nylon bags for a suitcase, with dirty feet and a dirty face, having been dropped off in a car that was falling apart. I looked more like somebody's servant than the daughter of one of the richest men in Lagos.

I begged and pleaded, it was getting late and I was getting desperate, but he had orders not too let anyone in through the main gate. I had nowhere to go, I couldn't go back to Uncle N's or Uncle J's. I thought for a second of going to Mummy Baptise. I knew she'd help but I didn't want to see the look in her eye either. I walked down the street praying for a miracle and wondering what I was going to do. All I had on me was a ten Naira note that Uncle N had given me a long time ago. I had been saving it for a rainy day, and that day it was pouring. I thought about climbing over the walls if the guard wasn't prepared to open the gate, then I remembered the dogs. In the end I decided to swallow my pride and go to Uncle J's. If I went to Uncle N, Iya Soji was bound to slam the door in my face, besides it was quicker to get to Surulere than go all the way to Festac. So I walked all the way to Obalende and jumped on a *Molue* bus.

When I got to Uncle J's, there was more bad news. No one was at home, and according to the guard they'd left the day before. He told me that Iya Foluso's sister who lives in Abuja was getting married, he didn't know me so he couldn't let me in, so I jumped on another bus and went back to Obalende and walked back, hoping that they were back from wherever it was they'd gone, but in my heart I knew they were probably at the same wedding. By the time I got back to the house, NEPA had taken light and only one out of the four houses on the road had put on their generator. It was a blessing in disguise because it allowed me to hide myself without the guard seeing me. So I put my clothes on the ground, prayed it wouldn't rain and rolled myself into the smallest ball, hoping when NEPA brought light back that no one would see me. The mosquitoes were merciless as they supped on me. I couldn't sleep, I just dozed. I was terrified. Every horror imaginable was in my head, I was going to be slashed and my body parts sold to a *Babalawo* to make money. Or maybe I'd have to become a woman of the night and sell my body to get food. I was beyond tears.

As soon as it was light, I left my makeshift palace hoping I wouldn't have to spend another night there. I put my clothes back in the bag and as I walked to Obalende I thanked God it hadn't rained. I only had about eight Naira left, which was maybe enough for two meals, which meant

I couldn't jump on another bus to Surulere. I needed to brush my teeth but I didn't have any toothpaste and in my rush to leave I'd forgotten my toothbrush. That was an easy problem to solve. I bought a chewing stick from a woman in the market. Even though it was just fifty kobo, it was hard parting with what little money I had. My next problem was where to clean myself. I needed a wash and I couldn't get that in the market. Since I didn't know what time HE would be back, I decided to just buy some *akara* to keep me going, as it was cheaper than having a proper meal. I didn't want to run out of money and have to start begging; what little I had, had to go a long way.

I wandered round in my faded black dress, with my two shopping bags filled with my only possessions, and hoped I didn't run into anyone I knew. For a moment I was glad Segun was away on holiday. I missed him terribly but I didn't want him to see what had become of me. I was ashamed of myself, I had only myself to blame for my woes. It wasn't HIS fault I found myself in my predicament, it wasn't even Iya Soji's, it was mine. I was the one who hadn't made more of an effort with her, it was me who came between husband and wife and made it intolerable for her to stay. So maybe I did deserve to be homeless, for all the evil thoughts I'd thought towards her. What is it they say — 'Ashes fly back in the face of him who throws them' — so I was getting my reward for rejoicing when she moved out. She saw the smile on my face. I remember thinking I'd won the battle between us, but I was wrong. I lost the war.

I sat in the shade in Tafawa Balewa Square, trying to sum up the energy to walk back to Ikoyi. As I sat there and time passed, I spent it watching people walk with a purpose; they seemed to be in a hurry to get somewhere, their faces carrying varied degree of expression. Were they happy, were they sad or just numb like me, tired of the cards life had dealt them? But unlike me, were they doing something to change their fate? The one thing I remember clearly from my musings was that my life could not continue on the path it was on, I had to make drastic changes before it was too late. I went back to Ikoyi and HE still wasn't back. I knew in my heart that the likelihood was another night under the stars.

My third night was the worst because that's when the heavens opened up. I was soaked within seconds and, with nowhere to go for shelter, I sat on the grassy verge and let the rain mingle with my tears of self-pity. I thought to myself, 'Even the rain has somewhere to go' as it ran in mini rivers around me. I watched the rainwater make its way to the sewer and wondered where my journey would end. I had run out of money the day before, and my rumbling stomach took me back to those ghastly years living with Mama and I wondered how I had ever managed to fast for forty days. I cupped my hands in front of my mouth and let the droplets of rain trickle in to quench my thirst. At least the rain would keep the mosquitoes away. I was covered in rashes from the bites and I could feel myself becoming ill. It was the same feeling I got when I was in Idogun. My head became heavy and my steps light and it felt as if a gentle gust of wind would knock me over. The only symptoms missing were the fur that normally covered my tongue and the loss of appetite.

I couldn't tell you exactly what happened, but sometime during the night it had stopped raining. NEPA had taken light and it seemed very late, I must have been dozing because I slapped myself awake when I felt a particularly vicious bite from a mosquito. I was cold and tired and, just as I was wondering how soon it would be until the sun came up, to dry me out, than it started to rain again. Since the chances of me getting any sleep were non-existent I decided to try and find some shelter. I put my wrapper over my head for protection against the rain, which was a stupid idea since it wasn't waterproof and I was already soaking wet. I picked up my two bags and set off. That was last thing I remember.

From what I've pieced together from Alhaja, I walked straight in front of their car. They were on their way back from a function. I don't remember being hit, just the walk and then nothing. I've been told that I was in a coma for three weeks. I had no identification on me so they didn't know where I came from. All I had was my two shopping bags containing my paltry possessions. The only thing I cherished were my journals, which have kept me sane. I'm not sure but I think Alhaja read them; it's the way she looked at me like she wanted to take care of me and fight my battles. I didn't want to feel her pity. But the more I resisted, the kinder she was. She bought me clothes, she measured my feet while I was in hospital and bought me a new pair of shoes.

About a week after I woke up, they began asking me all sorts of questions, like what date was it, who was the president, what was my name. When they first asked me, I couldn't remember my name, but it was only for a minute. I was confused and didn't know where I was, so I started screaming for them to leave me alone and that I wanted my mummy. The doctor was shocked, he'd spoken to me in Yoruba and I'd automatically replied in English. I'd looked round the room and didn't see a single face I recognised and I was petrified. I knew I was in hospital, I'd never forget the smell. I tried crawling into a ball, but couldn't even manage to lift my arm. It was then I saw that I had a needle in my arm and was attached to a drip. At that point I passed out. When I woke up again later, Alhaja was the only one in the room and she was stroking my hand and I think, praying under her breath.

Even though I knew I was in hospital, 'Where am I?' was the only question I could think of to ask. She wanted to know where my parents lived but I didn't want to tell her, so I ignored her question and started panicking. Where was I going to go? HE was probably still at the wedding, not realising where I was. I had no broken bones, just a bruised body. The doctor said the mind has the ability to shut down when it can't cope and maybe that's why I went into a coma. When I didn't tell them anything about myself except my name, they thought I had amnesia. I couldn't tell them I knew who I was, where I was born, who my father was. I remembered everything, but I didn't want to be Lola Ogunwole any longer, I wanted to be someone else. I wanted to be someone who was happy, a person who had a sparkling future ahead, a person with no fears. I didn't want to be the person who people pitied.

After days of trying to resist the kindness of a total stranger, the straw that made my house of cards come tumbling down was when Alhaja came in to measure my feet for shoes. The bubble burst, the floodgates opened and she just held me and said they were only shoes. But to me they weren't only shoes, it was her act of giving with no thought of what she'd get in return that was my undoing. So I sobbed into her vast bosom, and I sobbed some more for something I wish I'd had. I think it was then I decided to really become someone else; if they didn't know who I was, they wouldn't be able to send me back to HIM.

Obviously I wasn't thinking straight. How was I going to get into University if I didn't have my certificates? If I did do the exam and pass, how was I going to pay for it? But my biggest problem was Segun. I couldn't let him think I no longer existed, he was the one good thing left in my life that I hadn't managed to mess up. After a week of not remembering who I was, I confessed my identity and told Alhaja how I came to be on the street in the middle of the night during a rainstorm.

I'd already been discharged from hospital and was living with them in Ikoyi by the time I got round to confessing my sin. I realised that they lived around the corner from HIM, just a ten minute walk away. Alhaja said she had suspected, but that she hadn't wanted to push me. Alhaji knows HIM, they are both members of the Ikoyi Club. So it was decided that the next evening we'd go round and let him know I was still alive. Alhaja reckoned he would be worried sick. I didn't want to disillusion her. I knew he probably thought I was still at Uncle N's and I hadn't turned up because everything was okay with Iya Soji. I didn't think it would occur to him to check up on me.

Even though it was just round the corner, Alhaji thought it better that he drive us there because I was still weak. I hadn't been out of the house since they brought me back from the hospital. I was being fussed over by everyone in the house. The houseboy wanted to know if I was hungry, if I needed him to put a video in for me, if I was thirsty. Even when Alhaji came back from work he always seemed to bring something that he thought I might like, usually sweets, biscuits or chocolates. He also bought me a bag to go with the shoes Alhaja bought for me. I was shocked. I almost cried again. He bought me a new watch too and some earrings. He said he was getting Alhaja something and didn't want me to feel left out. I told them one day I'd repay their kindness and Alhaja said to me, 'You have blessed us with your presence and that is repayment enough.' They were thanking me, they had no reason to do that; all they had done was show me kindness and renew my faith in mankind. I had nothing to offer in return, but one day, God willing, I'll be able to offer the world something.

I wasn't sure of my reception at HIS so I asked if I could come back with them and they agreed, as long as I made an effort to try and make peace with HIM. So off we went in the chauffeured car, with me up front and both of them in the back. I deliberately wore my faded, hand-me-down black dress and a pair of my new shoes. I looked incongruous in my faded dress and brand new shoes but I wanted the security guard to remember me. However, I needn't have bothered because he wasn't there. I learned later on that he'd been sacked because he wouldn't let me in. There were a lot of cars in the drive when we arrived. At first I thought they were having a party, but there was no music so I knew it had to be another family meeting. The guard just waved us through and as we went in I spotted Uncle N's scrap heap car. I cringed as I remembered the last meeting and hoped there wasn't a battle going on inside. I rang the doorbell and Ronke answered and stood staring at me for several seconds. Alhaji asked to see HIM and she just moved to the side with her mouth wide open, staring at me as if she'd seen a ghost. Most of the relatives were there; I could smell cooking and voices coming from the kitchen. Cook Woman saw me first and started screaming and before I knew what was going on, the whole house was in uproar and everyone wanted to touch and pinch me.

They all thought I was dead and were there making funeral arrangements for a body in the mortuary burnt beyond recognition, which was supposed to be me. They were having a wake and were going to take the body back to Idogun in the morning and bury it beside Adebola. This person had stolen something from the market in Obalende and the market people decided to give her jungle justice, a tyre doused in petrol round the neck. I couldn't be found anywhere so they made the assumption that the body must be mine.

Uncle N just started sobbing and saying how sorry he was and to forgive him. I don't know what Iya Soji was feeling I couldn't read her eyes. Cook Woman wouldn't stop screaming and I don't know if it was for joy or bitter regret that it wasn't really my body lying in the mortuary. Before I could try and figure it out, I was standing in front of HIM. I tried to think of the last time I'd stood that close and I couldn't remember. HE had lines on his forehead and bags under his eyes and they were puffy and red. The last time I saw those eyes was when Adebola died. They seemed to be filled with pain. He reached out to touch my face and for the first time since I can't remember when, he called me by my full name — 'Omolola Olufunke Olufunmilayo, my child, my daughter,' then he held me close. He hugged me and I was in shock; he kept on mumbling, 'Please forgive me,' and he held me so tight I thought I was going to suffocate. Then he pushed me away and said, 'What happened to you? Where have you been?

You are a bag of bones.'

That's when Alhaji explained what had happened. It was then that another family row almost erupted; HE told Uncle N that he is his blood, but that his wife is no longer welcome in his house; she started shouting that it wasn't her fault and I wasn't her responsibility. All this time I'd been on my feet and the volume was getting to me, Alhaja saw me swaying, took hold of me and said she was taking me back home. HE refused and said he can't let me go, I had to stay with him in the house. Even though I was glad he wanted me to stay, I couldn't. I couldn't wipe out the years of pain just because he hugged me once. As soon as the relatives disappeared and all that was left in the house was HIM, Cook Woman, her brood, and me; whose side would he be on when the chips were down? I couldn't stay with him, too much had already happened so I told him I wanted to stay with Alhaja until I was strong enough to move into the flat and stay by myself. If he wanted to see me, I'd be round the corner. Then, we left.

I stayed with Alhaji and Alhaja for two more weeks before moving into the flat; they wanted me to stay with them but the elders say that no matter how long a log may float in the water, it will never become a crocodile. So I chose to leave and here I am, my future ahead and no more looking back. This is a new beginning, another chapter in the saga that is my life.

"Do not follow the path,
Go where there is no path
To begin the trail"

A West African proverb

30TH OCTOBER 1986

DJ,

I went to see Segun today, not realising he thought I was dead. When he and Yolande got back from America he went looking for me at Uncle N's. He saw Soji who told him I died in an accident. I've spent the whole day with them explaining what happened, Mummy Baptise was upset with me for not coming to her when I was in trouble and, rather than tell her that I didn't want to impose, I said that I didn't have the means to get back to Festac. Yolande knew that this wasn't true. I told her once I'd hitched a ride and the man wanted me to become his second wife within minutes of getting into his V-boot Mercedes. We laughed at how men with money think they could buy anything. We were not for sale, I had Segun and Yolande had her principles, although now she does have a boyfriend.

Segun couldn't stop touching my face and reassuring himself that I was okay. He'd been trying to get hold of Uncle N to ask when my funeral was, but every time he went round no one was in. I think we must've held hands the whole time I was there, apart from when we had to eat. Mummy Baptise told me he's been very upset and hasn't been eating since he got the news. He hasn't been out and all he's done is stare lethargically at the picture she took of us on her fiftieth birthday. She hugged me and told me she was glad I was alive.

The other bit of good news is that Segun managed to secure a place at LASU (Lagos State University); I'm not sure how he managed that feat especially since his score was just as woeful as last years. Maybe it's because he chose a less competitive subject. There aren't that many students clamouring to study History, not because it's not an interesting subject, but because when you finish University there are no jobs to be had. Every one wants a lawyer, doctor, accountant or engineer in the family; no one wants a history graduate. Although I love him dearly he's not very academic, he'd rather be jamming with his band, but his mother would like him to have a degree. I'm just jealous because I should have done what he did. Everyone wants to become a news broadcaster or journalist and travel around the country and the world. I wish I'd listened to Segun's advice when I was filling in the form, but I was so sure I'd pass this time. Mama always said that, 'it's the fly that has no one to advise it that follows the corpse into the grave.' It seems I've dug mine. Tomorrow I'll be going to see Segun at Uni, then he'll be coming back to Ikoyi with me. He hasn't been to my new flat yet and I still haven't told him who HE is; I'm not sure if I should.

2ND NOVEMBER 1986

DJ,

It's Sunday today and I really wanted to spend the day with Segun in Festac. Mummy Baptiste let me spend last weekend with them. I slept in Yolande's room, we spent the day shopping, I helped her cook and iron and we were like a real family. However, Yolande was home this weekend with her friend from University and the atmosphere was horrible. I thought Yolande and I were friends but ever since she went off, she's become some other person. I guess she's moved on and left me behind, but I think it's more than that. Sometimes she looks at me when I'm talking and rolls her eyes as if to say, 'Oh, you're so stupid.' Sometimes she talks to me as if I'm a child; she's also been talking about me to her new friend.

On Friday when she got back we were sitting outside because NEPA had decided to take light and it was too hot inside. Mummy Baptiste made a comment about how students are always rioting about something instead of studying and that she hoped Yolande wouldn't join the mob. I just jokingly said it was because the teachers didn't give them enough homework to do. Bukola, Yolande's new friend from University replied, 'Oh, what would you know about it, it's not as if you've been to University or are likely to in this century.' I was hurt that she could talk about me like that to other people. Segun was good, he came to my rescue, he told her she only probably got in because of who her father was. He seems to be some sort of multi-millionaire who probably got rich not from hard work, but from greasing palms. What else is new? This is Nigeria after all and in money we trust and worship. The man with Naira is the man we bow down to. It is he who jumps the queue because he is too important to wait his turn, his motto, 'Do you know who I am?' Who am I to talk? I'm sure HE got his money the same way and it's what puts food in my belly and a roof over my head so I'm in no position to judge anyone else. Iya Soji always said that 'the bottom of wealth is sometimes a dirty thing to behold.' I think I now understand what she meant.

Well, after that altercation things went downhill.

Yolande got on Segun's case and they almost came to blows. In the end Mummy Baptiste sent everyone to bed. Normally, I sleep in Yolande's room but Mummy Baptiste thought it would be better if I slept in the sitting room. I didn't mind really, but then she said she thought it would be better if I went home the next day. Segun was furious, but Yolande just smirked and went to her room. I calmed him down, it didn't matter too much to me to be sent home, for once I wasn't running away from my own home. For the first time, the flat in Ikoyi really seemed like home; it was my refuge, my space in which to be whoever I wanted to be. I knew Yolande didn't want me in her house, so I didn't mind leaving; I had somewhere to go and be safe. For once I could say what Mama used to say and mean it; she'd say that 'because friendship is pleasant, we partake of our friend's entertainment, not because we have not enough to eat in our own house.'

I knew it was the end of my ever spending a weekend there. I couldn't sleep that night, I kept on wishing I was in my own bed. I was up at three o'clock. NEPA had decided to give us light again, so I ironed the rest of Mummy Baptiste's clothes, some of Segun's and even Yolande's skirt. I couldn't pack because my things were in Yolande's room and I didn't want to wake her, so I sat and waited for dawn. While I sat and listened to the day waking up, I remembered those other times when I'd been asked to leave and had nowhere to go. I felt it briefly that dawn, even though I had nothing to be afraid of because I had somewhere to go, I had a roof over my head and I was no longer hoping for the charity of relatives. Yet still I was afraid and I wondered if that fear would ever go away.

We all had breakfast together and I felt awkward. I

couldn't look Mummy Baptiste in the eye when she was talking to me. She wanted to know what University I was going to apply to next year and her advice was to pick a subject that didn't have students clamouring to get on it. I mumbled something, but it was the one thing I couldn't bear to discuss in front of Yolande. Segun held my hand under the table, his touch worth more than a thousand words. He wanted to give me a lift home, but Mummy Baptiste wanted him to drive her somewhere so he walked me to the bus stop instead. He didn't want me to go so we walked to the park and sat talking for ages. He apologised for Yolande's behaviour and I told him not to worry, it wasn't his fault. I was just glad he still wanted to be with me even though I wasn't an undergraduate. I told him then that I wouldn't be spending any more weekends with him in Festac. I'll come by occasionally but he's going to have to make the trip to Ikoyi and I'll come and see him on campus.

9TH NOVEMBER 1986

DJ,

I've got a toothache and I have to go and see a dentist; I don't think I've ever been. I've got a hole in my tooth and every time I eat meat a big chunk gets stuck in there. Sometimes I can't even chew. I'm still young and already my teeth are rotting. I blame HIM for not giving me money to buy toothpaste and having to rely on chewing sticks. By the time I'm thirty, all my teeth would have fallen out. I wonder if Segun would still love me then, or would he be the type to have girlfriends and second and third wives? I don't think so. Even though he's never said the three words, his actions indicate he does. He also wrote them to me when he went to Chicago so he must. He stayed over for the first time yesterday and we slept on the couch in the sitting room and just held each other. I've told him that I don't want to do it until my wedding night; I secretly hoped he realised I meant our wedding night. I know he's disappointed, but he was okay about it. He sang me his new song, which he's written; he says it is about how he feels about me. I cried because it was so beautiful. I asked him to write down the words for me.

Until the day that I met you
Didn't know what life was
Until the day that I kissed you
All my wishes of love came true
Didn't know how to feel
But now I'm living a dream, so real

Chorus
Lead me now, take my hand
And we will (we will)
Reach the promised land
I was lost & now I'm found
Keep me warm, keep me safe
Keep me wrapped in your embrace
because I will no longer (3x)
Be alone

When I close my eyes, it's you I see
I'll never walk alone
Forever in you arms I'll be
I bless the day that I met you
To you always my heart and soul
Precious babe you've made me whole

In a way, he has said he loves me, and he's used more than the requisite three words.

10TH NOV 1986

DJ,

I went to LUTH (Lagos University Teaching Hospital) today to see the dentist and the doctor said that I need four fillings and I have to have my tooth removed because it has decayed into my gum, which is what has been causing the pain. I've got an appointment for next Monday the 17th. In the meantime I had two fillings done today. I'm going in on Wednesday for the other two, this time lower jaw. It was horrible. I had a student doctor who was so nervous because the senior doctor was standing over him while he was giving me the injection. He kept stabbing me with the needle until I ended up crying like a baby, in the end the senior doctor had to take over. All the time there were other students standing around trying to get a closer look into my mouth. There I was lying back in the most uncomfortable chair, a big light surrounded by bobbing heads shining down on me. It was so embarrassing, especially when he started talking about hygiene and how most of these problems occur due to a lack of education. People thought all you needed to clean your teeth was a chewing stick, which was why if you went to the villages, most of the older population almost had no teeth. I couldn't contradict him because I had the dental student poking around in my mouth. Mama and most of the old people in Idogun still had their full set of teeth. They were yellow and stained from eating too much kola nut, but they still had them all. Which is why I'm surprised I'd be losing one of mine and filing holes in the rest. Oh well, at least I can feel my lips now; if felt like they were swollen out of proportion, but when I got home and looked in the mirror, they were the normal size. If Segun comes by later, there will be no K.I.S.S.I.N.G.

DJ,

Lost my precious tooth today. HE came to see me this morning; HE arrived at five o'clock, banging on my bedroom door and calling for me to come out. 'Omolola, you better come out here now.' I haven't seen him since I moved in, although I know he's been here twice. Each time he'd left me some money for food, I sat in the living room with my wrapper tied around me wondering what atrocity I'd committed this time and whether he was going to kick me out, the neverending fear. My mouth went dry as I watched him pace up and down trying to get a handle on his temper, instead of striking me with one of his clenched fists.

I took my courage in my hands, swallowed some dry spit and asked if something was wrong. Now if it was possible to kill someone with a look, I would be dead right now. Once upon a time, when he looked at me like that, I'd cower with trepidation and confess to sins I didn't even commit. But as I looked at him that morning, it seemed as if I was looking at him for the first time in my life. I saw a fat, pot-bellied man, with a receding hairline and a neck that was disappearing into his shoulders. I looked in his eyes and probed with mine, trying to find his soul, trying to figure out if he really did hate me.

I didn't see hate in his eyes and that encouraged me to ask the question, so I did. 'Why do you hate me so much, what did I do wrong?'

He was shocked. I haven't spoken to him in such a long time that even he'd forgotten what I sounded like. We sat opposite each other like a pair of duellists ready for battle with the line drawn in the ever-shifting sand. I couldn't stop the tears that charted a course down my face as I stared at him; the pain of his rejection and abandonment seemed to fill every fibre of my being.

'Where were you when I needed you; why couldn't you love me; what did I do wrong?' I didn't wait for an answer; I just raced back to my room and sobbed my heart out. HE left me two hundred Naira and I still don't know what brought him here at five o'clock in the morning. I haven't seen Segun since Friday. I'll have to go and see him on campus tomorrow.

18TH NOVEMBER 1986

DJ,

I think, I mean I know Segun is ashamed of me. He didn't want to introduce me as his girlfriend to his new friends. I went to his campus today because I haven't seen him for a while. He was supposed to come round on Sunday but he didn't turn up. I even went to the trouble of cooking his favourite dish, brown rice and pork with pepper stew. Not that I really blame him, he probably didn't want to embarrass me because I know they'd ask me what University I was in. And I'd have to say I'm still at home twiddling my thumbs, having failed to make the grade for the second time. Or maybe it was the way I looked. I watched the girls on campus and they were very sophisticated, walking around in four-inch heels with immaculately made-up faces. I felt I was at a beauty pageant; not a hair was out of place. They were in University to be seen and I saw Segun's eyes following one girl as she came up to say hi to him. She touched his arm and fluttered her eyelashes and I wanted to scratch her eyes out and scream that he was mine. She wanted to know when the next gig was, told him that he was so good this weekend. I was so upset. He didn't even tell me he had a gig; I'd sat at home cooking and waiting for him to turn up. He said it was a last minute request; the original band that was booked couldn't perform because the lead singer was ill so they asked him. So he spent Sunday daytime rounding up the band for a quick rehearsal, before the nine o'clock performance. I told him I would have liked to have been there, but he told me not to be silly, that there would be other gigs. Something was wrong. I asked him what but he just said he had some course work to hand in and he's behind. I left, hoping that he'd come back to Ikoyi with me and spend the night; I was feeling a little bit lonely in the flat by myself. But he's got course work, so I left him to it. I didn't even get a kiss goodbye, just a distracted, 'I'll see you on Saturday,' which is a whole four days away. What am I going to do till then?

19TH NOVEMBER 1986

DJ,

You'll never guess who I ran into on campus while visiting Maggie — Ngozi! I couldn't believe my eyes when I saw her. She got out of some man's V-boot, decked out in her best. Most of the girls I saw were like the girls in LASU, they looked like they were in a beauty contest. I asked Maggie why she wasn't spooted up and she just hissed and said that she doesn't have time for nonsense. The gossip is that Ngozi is into Sugar Daddies, which isn't news to me.

When I was still living with Uncle J and a student at Aunty Aduke Grammar School, she was always being dropped off at evening classes by a different man every day. It's what she does to survive; she doesn't have a rich father to pay for her school fees and put a roof over her head so she has to rely on these men. Maggie doesn't approve, but then she has everything handed to her on a plate. I didn't tell her that though, I just pretended to be shocked. I wondered what she'd do if she was Ngozi?

When I got back from my visit, who do I find on my front doorstep? None other than the incompetent dental student from LUTH. At first I thought something was drastically wrong and I had to go back for more treatment. But no, apparently he really likes me and would like to go out with me. I stood there in shock. I wanted to know how he managed to find out where I lived and it turns out he'd tracked me down through my hospital records. 'How I no go find fine girl like you now, we are meant to be together,' were the words dripping from his mouth. Telling him I had a boyfriend who I loved very much didn't divert him from his mission; he still wanted to take me to dinner. He said he didn't mind sharing and that with time, I'd fall in love with him too and ditch my boyfriend. I didn't know what to say, just as I was wondering how to politely tell him to leave, HE turned up and for the first time in ages I was really glad to see him. The confident medical student with the world before him crumpled before my eyes as HE demanded to know who he was and what he wanted.

It was quite funny actually, but I did feel sorry for the student so I told HIM that Deji — that's what he said his name was — was the doctor at LUTH who took out my tooth and did my fillings. But HE wasn't going to let it go, he wanted to know what he was doing there. 'I just came to make sure she didn't have any side effects from the treatment,' said Deji. HE just glowered at him and replied, 'You think I was born yesterday? Eh, tell me how many of your patients do you visit at home eh? Don't let me see you near my house again or I'll have my men cut off your manhood.' Deji stammered, 'Yes, sir,' and scurried away.

Well, I finally found out why HE turned up at five o'clock yesterday morning; it seems that someone, I don't know who but my money's on Cook Woman, has been telling him that I'm bringing Sugar Daddies here. It seems that I have a Sugar Daddy for every night of the week, they've been buying me clothes, shoes and jewellery. I was so incensed I couldn't speak, so I dragged him into my bedroom and asked him to show me the things I've apparently acquired through lying on my back and opening my legs. I was disgusted he could even think I would do that. I wanted to know who told him these stories but he wouldn't tell me the person's name. I started crying again and he left the room and I promptly slammed the door. He's still out there waiting for me to come out, but I've nothing to say to him. It's whoever's been spreading malicious gossip about me I want to talk to, with my fists and feet.

21st November 1986

DJ,

HE has been coming here every day this week and each time he leaves me some money. I've never had so much money in my life, at last count it was five hundred Naira. But we still don't talk. To be honest, I wouldn't even know what to say and that's sad. I went to see Alhaji and Alhaja this evening and they were very happy to see me. Alhaja had been shopping and she had bought me a skirt and a dress. If HE sees them, he'll probably think they are from some Sugar Daddy. I haven't seen Segun at all this week. I hope he turns up tomorrow especially since Maggie will be here. It'll be like old times with half the gang.

23 NOVEMBER 1986

DJ,

I finally found out what was wrong with Segun. He'd come to see me and saw HIM going into the flat with HIS own set of keys, and since I hadn't told him HE was my father, he thought HE must be my Sugar Daddy. Segun came round yesterday evening just as Maggie and I were wondering what to do with ourselves. We were in my room and HE was in the sitting room. HE'S been spending too much time here. I had to introduce Maggie to HIM and it was an awkward moment. I really wanted to say, 'Meet the man who begat me.' Instead, I said, 'Maggie, meet my father.' It would have been too strange if I'd said, 'Daddy, meet my friend, Maggie.'

Later on, the doorbell rang and I just knew it was Segun. HE was actually on HIS way out when the bell rang. HE was just in front of me as I ran to the front door, but HE got there before me. It wasn't just Segun standing on my doorstep, he was with Yolande. That girl has far too much time on her hands; it seems that every weekend she's back in Lagos for some reason or another. I think she's home-sick; she's never been away from Mummy Baptiste for more than two weeks.

I made the introductions the same way. I said 'Yolande, Segun, meet my father.' They both stood there in shock not knowing what to say. Yolande eventually closed her mouth and said, 'Good evening, sir.' HE, of course, wanted to know where they were from; I told HIM they were my friends from Festac and then HE left. I went to hug and kiss Segun like I normally do and he pushed me away. He wanted to know why I didn't tell him that Mr Ogunwole was my dad. He thought he was my Sugar Daddy. How could I've known that? I can't read other peoples minds; if I could I would very much like to read HIS. We've made up though; he was coming over to have a confrontation and brought Yolande for support. Apparently, it's been eating away inside of him, thinking of me with a man old enough to be my father. I pointed out to him that HE is my father.

Maggie persuaded Yolande to spend the night. I hadn't told her the problems Yolande and I were having so I told her she was welcome to stay. Segun raised his eyebrow and I shrugged my shoulders. If she was going to be my sister-in-law, I was going to have to make an effort to get on with her and once upon a time we were good friends. So Segun went home and we stayed up till around four o'clock. Yolande plaited my hair for me, we talked and cleared the air, but I'm not sure if we'll ever share that closeness we once had, where we could tell each other anything.

HE came back in the morning. We'd all fallen asleep in the sitting room. HE had breakfast with us, it was very strange. HE wanted to know who their parents were and what State they were from. HE knows Mummy Baptiste because she works at the Bank and he's heard of Maggie's dad but they haven't met. I didn't know her dad was the Chief Justice, no wonder he wants her to become a lawyer. HE seemed to be impressed with their accomplishments. HE listened to them and seemed interested in what they had to say and what they were doing. When Maggie talked about her plans for the future, he looked over at me as if to say and what about yours? I sat there trying to remember the last time I'd had a conversation with HIM, or even introduced him to my friends. I was unsure of this new development; I didn't recognise this person in front of me, this seemingly affable man. I was shocked to the roots of my plaits when he said he knew the Dean of the Faculty of Medicine. Apparently, they're a member of the same Club. HE'S never offered to pull any strings for me. Twice I've failed to make the grade and he could have done something. HE meets a perfect stranger and offers her a lifeline, while HIS own flesh and blood is gobbled up by quicksand. I have to admit I never told him about trying to get into University, so maybe he didn't know.

19 DECEMBER 1986

DJ,

It's Friday and six days till Christmas. I'm not ecstatically happy, but I'm beginning to have a warm glow. Yolande tells me I've lost the desperate look that screamed, 'please love me.' I didn't even know I had it. My father and I are getting on better. I like to think he cares but he doesn't know how to be a father to me. We still can't seem to talk to each other. Maybe he finds it easier relating to other peoples children. I can't stand Cook Woman and her brood, so I stay away from the mansion. Father brought Ekundayo to visit me yesterday and he followed me around like a little puppy. He wanted me to carry and cuddle him even though he's almost six. I looked for traces of Adebola, but there was nothing. I still cry silently inside. I miss Adebola and there aren't enough adjectives in the English dictionary to describe how I feel. I know I must keep putting one foot in front of the other, because the tree that cannot shed its leaves in the dry season, cannot survive the period of drought.

They've gone to Idogun today for Christmas, Father wanted me to go too, but I won't go back there, never ever. I told him I'd spend the holiday with Alhaji and Alhaja, besides I don't want to leave Segun.

Uncle N came by today. He knocked on the door and I looked to make sure it wasn't the incompetent Deji. He's been round to the flat twice now and each time I've pretended I'm not in. He caught me once and I told him I'm not interested, that I've got a boyfriend but, like a typical man, he thinks that saying no means I'm playing hard to get. Anyway I peeped through the curtains and saw Uncle N on my doorstep. I hadn't seen him since my 'death' was being mourned at the mansion and I didn't want to speak to him now. So I stood there praying he hadn't heard me come to the door. He banged several times then gave up and left. Once upon a time I would have trusted him with my life.

1ST JANUARY 1987

DJ,

It's Thursday today, the first day of a brand new year and I'm so happy, I seemed to have found the light I was seeking, its intensity banishing the shadows that have dogged my footsteps, filling me with joy and hope for a future. Why do I feel this way? I don't know. Nothing special has happened apart from the fact that I had a New Year's Eve party in the flat and my friends stayed over. Everyone is still asleep, but I just woke up so excited and with an incredible lightness in my heart. I think God smiled on me. This year will be my year, I'm going to try and make an effort with Father. And I know that when JAMB results come out this year, whether I fail to make the grade or not I'm going to be in Lag come September. Father is just going to have to start pulling some strings for me. He's pulled some for Yolande and she'll be transferring to LUTH in September. In Nigeria, what you know is unimportant; who you know is crucial.

I didn't realise how many people you could fit into this flat. Most of the people who came none of us knew. It was a last minute party because nothing better had come up. I thought why not, it was New Year's Eve and Father was in Idogun. Yolande, Maggie and I went shopping for *jollof* rice ingredients and drinks, we made a list of people to invite and the number came up to about thirty. I only had one guest, Alhaji and Alhaja's son Timi over from London. He's the one who wants to be an actor. Alhaji thinks he's wasting his life, he wants him to become a doctor or a lawyer.

The party didn't really cost that much; Father had bought me a bag of rice and we had oil, so we only had to buy meat and pepper. Segun was going to DJ so we didn't have to pay for any music. It was such short notice that I didn't think anyone was going to turn up; in fact, when the clock struck twelve it was just the gang and me there. We counted down the seconds and screamed, 'Happy New Year!' to each other and then Charlie Boy grabbed me and kissed me on the lips before I could react. I thought Segun would've been upset but he just pushed him off and laughingly told him to go and find his own girlfriend. I felt so special. He placed his palms on my cheeks and gently kissed me and looking deep into my eyes, he said the three words to me for the first time. My heart just stopped beating for a second, then it picked up pace and it felt like the masquerades were dancing on my heart. I put my hands round his neck and everything I felt went into the kiss I gave him. I forgot we had an audience. A switch in my brain had been turned on and all the passion I didn't even know I had in me came pouring out. It was exactly like they describe it in the Mills & Boon stories, now I just needed the happy ever after. I was rudely awakened when I heard Maggie's voice from a distance saying there was a bedroom next door. We managed to un-weld our bodies, which seemed to still gravitate towards each other. Yolande handed out the Cokes and we toasted the New Year and I know it's going to be a very good one, because I'm on fire and SEGUN BAPTISTE LOVES LOLA OGUNWOLE.

11TH JANUARY 1987

DJ,

Would you believe I just got back from church? That's not what is amazing, but the fact that I went with father and Cook Woman and the rest of the brood. They came to pick me up this morning; I was still in bed when they arrived. I heard Father calling me, and when I came out of my room they were all seated in the sitting room. I had a flashback to the last time we were all in this flat, 11th August 1979. I'd broken a bottle over Ronke's head and Father decided to teach me a lesson by beating me. The physical scars were still there and so were the mental ones, and I was immediately on the defensive. I didn't mind Father and Ekundayo being there, but I did not want Cook Woman and her other brats in my flat. I was going to say so, but Ekundayo pulled my hand and urged me to get ready for church. The Bishop was going to be there for a special blessing for the Ogunwole clan; I guess that included me.

I stood there for a moment, a part of me glad I was being included, the other part wanting to be left alone. But Ekundayo wouldn't let go of my hand, he almost pulled down my wrapper in his excitement. They were all dressed in the same cream and orange lace which obviously I didn't have, until father handed me a bag containing my outfit. To say I was shocked is an understatement, especially after he produced a bag and shoes to match. To top things off, I had *aso oke* for the headdress and the shoulder wrap. Alhaja knew my size so she got me the shoes and took the material to the tailor to have it made for me. Father told me that Alhaji and Alhaja would also be in church, so would the rest of the family. I had a quick shower and put on my first ever family 'and Co' attire and it felt good and I looked good too.

It seemed that all the relatives were in church this morning, even Uncle N and Iya Soji. And Mama, of all people; they must have brought her back with them from Idogun, I think the driver brought her to Church. I couldn't avoid her because we had to sit on the same pew, which had been reserved for us. 'Good morning' was all I could manage. After the sermon, the Bishop was ready to start the blessing and he called us to the front of the Church. The whole family and relatives got up, but the Bishop stopped everyone; he said he just wants Mr Ogunwole and his two children and wife first, which of course meant Ronke and Ayo had to stay behind. I looked at Cook Woman with a little smile on my face. The moment was sweet, I only wish they had excluded her too. We had to dance our way to the front of the pulpit and it took forever even though we were sitting just two pews away from the front. Cook Woman was showing off, she kept on dancing backward and shaking her *yansh* as if to say, 'everyone look at me.' The Bishop should have left her out of the first blessing; it should have been Father, Ekundayo and me. We knelt down and he prayed for us, for father's continued success and my further education and our general health. Father put a very large envelope in the offerings bag and the dancing commenced again. This time the whole family came forward, then came the friends and the hangers on. We all headed back to the mansion afterwards but I'd had enough of playing happy families so I rode back with Alhaji and Alhaja.

It took forever for Alhaji to get us back to the mansion; he's not the best driver and he'd given his chauffeur the weekend off. His skill was not helped by Alhaja's back-seat driving, even my nerves were shredded by the time we got back. A twenty-minute trip took just over an hour and when we got there the party was in full swing. Cook Woman had changed into her next lace attire, which looked like it cost enough to feed a poor family for a year. Relatives were everywhere. Yinka, my childhood nemesis was serving food to guests, Uncle N was sitting in the corner with Uncle J, having a loud conversation about football. He kept on glancing across at me but I made sure I avoided his eyes.

Everyone was having a good time, the smell of *jollof* rice and *moi-moi* wafted through the house, mingling with fried plantain, each scent battling for supremacy. Once upon a time I would have been in the kitchen stuffing myself till my stomach was full to bursting. Instead, I just watched the festivities unfold. Iya Rotimi was there, her *gele* — headdress — looking like a stiff bird in flight. Mama was relishing her position of family matriarch; she sat on the couch queen of the Ogunwole clan, her subjects bowing before her, congratulating her on her son's success. Her complacent smile said it all. Outside the mansion, guests sat under white canopies, which protected them from the sun's glare and heat. The more energetic ones were rolling their *yanshes* to Sunny Ade's Synchro System, which is a song father played all the time when we were in London. Others were busy swapping the empty beer bottles they'd brought from home with unopened ones to take back with them. Iya Foluso had brought a crate of Star and a crate of Guinness to swap; I watched her surreptitiously sneak the crates into her boot. Some guests had brought food containers; no one leaves an *owambe* party without taking a food pack home. Iya Foluso almost got away with a huge cooler of fried rice, but got caught by Cook Woman who wanted it for her family.

As I watched everyone drink, dance and be merry, I realised I really didn't want to be there; apart from Alhaji and Alhaja, there was no one there I wanted to talk to. I stuck around for as long as I could, then asked father's driver to bring me home. He didn't want to at first, said he had to ask Oga before he can take the car anywhere. He came back and said father wanted to see me, he wanted to know why I was leaving so early, so I told him I needed to study for the JAMB exam. He let me go. The river is never so full that it covers the eyes of the fish. Imagine.

DJ,

Segun and I haven't seen each other in two days. If he doesn't come by today I'll have to go to LASU tomorrow to look for him. I miss him when he's not here. He's been very busy trying to juggle lectures, and Voice Out rehearsals. The band is really becoming successful around the campuses; he's got a show in Ife and Ibadan next week and one at Lag at the end of the week. I'll be going to that one and staying over in Maggie's room. Everyone knows Segun at LASU, which is a bit disconcerting. When I turn up on campus looking for him it's always a case of follow the largest crowd because he's bound to be in there somewhere, entertaining and cracking jokes. I don't even think he goes to lectures any more. I just hope he doesn't become one of those sad students who pays someone else to do their assignments, or cheat during the exams.

17TH JANUARY 1987

DJ,

Last night was fun, I went to Segun's show at Lag. It was actually a fashion show and he was the entertainment. The students weren't interested in the clothes, they wanted to see Voice Out perform and when Segun came on stage the girls started screaming, but it was me he sang to. He opened the show by singing my song, the one he wrote for me. He said, 'This song is for the very special lady in my life.' I was a bit disappointed that he didn't mention me by name, but when I asked him why, he told me he didn't want some jealous fan to scratch my eyes out. I didn't know it was even possible to love him any more than I already do. All I have to do is think about him and my heart sings with joy.

I'm not sure when I'm going to see him next, especially after this morning. HE found us snuggled together on the sofa in the living room. Instead of staying with Maggie, Segun insisted on bringing me home and he stayed over. We were fully clothed and nothing happened, although on this occasion he was getting carried away. We'd kissed and I'd let him touch my breasts — only briefly — but he wanted to touch me down there. He said he understands, but if I really loved him, I'd let him make love to me. I do love him, but I want our first time to be when we're married.

Anyway, HE came home and went berserk. Segun was up and out before you could say 'Speedy Gonzales' and before I knew it, HE started striking at me with his belt. I just stood there, a red mist building in front of my eyes with every stroke of his belt. Then, as if someone flicked a switch, he stopped. Maybe it was because of my non-reaction. Normally, I'd be begging for mercy or cowering in fear, but this time I just stood there until his anger was spent. The whole incident didn't take more than two minutes, and then we stood staring at each other. Then I calmly told him that if he ever laid a finger on me again, that day would be the last day he'd ever be able to refer to me as a daughter. They say 'my child is dead is better than my child is lost,' but I would be lost to him forever if he ever touched me again. Then I calmly walked to my room. Segun is now banned from my flat, but if HE thinks HE can keep us apart, then he's got a lot to learn about me. I will do anything for Segun because he loves me. I've survived without HIM so far All he's done is given me money, and that doesn't make up for a lifetime of hurt;

time is longer than a rope and time is what it will take to overcome the vicissitudes life has dealt me.

1ST FEBRUARY 1987

DJ,

Father seems to have moved himself in; he spends most of his time here. Segun is allowed to come and visit, but only when HE is home and he's not allowed to stay over. Which is okay by me because when we're alone, I'm finding it increasingly difficult to keep Segun's hands out of my panties. He insists that if I love him I'd do it and I tell him if he loved me he'd wait. We have an uneasy truce. He's recently decided we can't be in the same room together. I miss our closeness; why can't he just wait?

Father has ordered a phone line for the flat. I don't know why I'm excited, I don't even have any friends to call. Maggie's got a phone, but she's only home during the holidays. The last time I saw her, I told her Segun wanted to go all the way and she was shocked that I'm still a virgin. I tried to explain that I wanted to wait until our wedding day but she just burst out laughing and wouldn't stop. She seems to think that I've got an outdated notion of romance from reading too many Mills & Boon novels. Her philosophy is to try before you buy, otherwise you'd end up with something that's not suitable and it will be too late to return it to the shop. She doesn't think that Segun is waiting for me, she reckons he'll be getting it from somewhere else. He's a man in his prime and he has needs that I won't fulfil so he's going to look elsewhere.

2ND FEBRUARY 1987

DJ,

Not that I don't trust Segun, but what Maggie said has made me think. So I went to LASU today to see him. As usual, his adoring crowd of admirers surrounded him and as usual he should have been at a lecture but someone else was taking his notes. He still hasn't introduced me as his girlfriend to his new crowd of friends, apart from Bola, his new best friend. They go everywhere together and have even started dressing the same, it seems as if Bola wants to be Segun. I don't like him very much but he's Segun's friend so I put up with him. However, the next time he tries to stroke my arm, he's going to get a kick where it hurts.

We couldn't talk because Bola decided to invite himself along when I suggested we go back to Festac, so I'll have to wait another day. I spent the rest of the day there because I hadn't seen Mummy Baptiste for a while and I had dinner with the family before coming home. Father, of course was waiting for me. He is not happy with me, says that I gallivant about too much and it's because I don't have anything to do. So he has enrolled me in a private school for my JAMB exam, which is in April. Classes start at nine o'clock and finish at three thirty. I start tomorrow. What he doesn't seem to realise is that the term started weeks ago. I'll be the new girl in class with no friends. Why do I feel as if I'm eleven instead of almost nineteen?

3RD FEBRUARY 1987

DJ,

It was just as I expected, but worse. I'm older than all the other students, they're just kids who have just finished secondary school. Ironically, they thought they were older than me and I didn't correct their impression. Mama starving me in Idogun has made me look younger, it's either that or good genes. This must come from my mother's side because father's face is lined with each year of his age. Not that I even know how old he is or when his birthday is. If I were to count the lines, I'd say he was at least sixty.

Luckily I've been studying at home, since I've nothing else to do. So I'm up to date with my Literature and Bible Knowledge. I just have big problems as usual with Maths, my eyes always glaze over whenever anyone starts talking about fractions. I've reread *The African Child, Merchant of Venice and Arrow of God* for the zillionth time until the stories have merged into each other.

At the private school, all anyone seems to talk about is their parents' wealth and who is dating who. I sat in the back of the class and listened. To be honest I was jealous. They were all carefree with not one problem that Daddy and Mummy couldn't solve. I wish I could, but I can't get away from the fact that other people have parents they like to talk about. Even when they hate them for some little misdemeanour or the other, there's a certain look in their eyes, and it's all I can see. I certainly can't talk about Father like that. I've got ten weeks till the exam, and then hopefully in September I'll be a student at the University of Lagos.

6TH FEBRUARY 1987

DJ,

Maggie has just turned up unexpectedly for the weekend. She says she needed to get away from campus so that she can think clearly. Apparently she has some tough choices to make but she hasn't told me what they are.

Father has left for the evening, he's been here too much. Every time I turn around he's breathing down my neck, finding fault with everything. The house isn't clean enough, I'm wearing the wrong clothes, I stay out too late. He's beginning to get on my last nerves; maybe I should go and visit Auntie Bunmi from Idogun who now lives in Ilorin. Olutayo, the baby I watched her give birth to, is nine now.

8TH FEBRUARY 1987

DJ,

I finally found out what has been bugging Maggie. She's joined a secret organisation on campus. She won't tell me much about it other than it's very serious, and that something needs to be done about the bribery and corruption that is rife in high places. Plus the fact that what was once a secular country is fast being turned into a Muslim one and the Christian faith and belief needs to be protected. So that's all I know. I'm not sure what they're planning on doing because she won't tell me. It can't be a coup d'état because they're only students and I hope they don't have any guns to storm the buildings with and take control; she kept on talking about a revolution. Whatever it is, I just hope it's harmless. With new decrees popping up every day, I'm sure they'll think of one especially for them. She told me that the government have banned the National Association of Nigerian Students (NANS) after last year's student riots. That's why her organisation is secret, if they're caught, there's no telling what will happen. She might get thrown into jail with no one knowing where she is, like Ngozi's uncle. He went in a fatted calf and came out a scrawny scarecrow. She's asking for trouble. I told her, 'Whatever the eyes of a dead man see in a burial yard is caused by death.' Mama says that a lot, it fits most situations, especially when I don't know what to say.

DJ,

Another boring day in school. I really wanted to go and see Segun. I don't seem to see him as much as I'd like to any more. Once upon a time we were inseparable. Maybe I am being unrealistic asking him to wait before we make love, but if I do let him and he decides I'm not the right one for him, what do I do then and how will I cope? I can't bear to think about it, so I won't. He doesn't laugh at my jokes like he used to; I miss his rumble. The last time I hugged him he didn't hold me as close; before, we'd snuggle right up; arms wrapped around each other, my head fitting just under his Adam's apple. I could feel his blood pumping from the veins in his neck and it was comforting. When he holds me, I feel safe and protected. I really miss him.

I spent the evening with Alhaja and Timi. I was surprised that he was still in the country. I thought he'd gone back to London, I think he's having too much fun being pampered by Alhaja. He thinks that I should go back to England and study there instead of trying to get into University in Nigeria. Apparently, as a Subject of her Majesty I'll be given money for food and a place to live and the government will even pay my tuition. Once upon a time I held that dream, to go back and live in London, with my friends. But I'm no longer a child and those friends I once had have also grown up and moved on. Maybe one day I will go back, but for now with all its faults, my life is in Nigeria. I couldn't possibly leave Segun. I barely see him now, and four years in a foreign country might kill our relationship. I don't think I do long distance very well, Tobi will tell you that much. I must remember to ask father for my birth certificate and passport, just in case.

DJ,

It's Saturday, it's eight o'clock in the evening, it's Valentines day and Segun Baptiste hasn't turned up. I'm so angry with him. Like a fool I've been at home all day waiting for him to turn up. Happy Valentines Lola Ogunwole. The only way he's being forgiven is if he's been in an accident and is lying in the gutter somewhere with no memory.

15TH FEBRUARY 1987

DJ,

Still no sign of Segun. Maybe he has had a horrible accident and is in hospital. I hope he's not hurt. I kept hoping he'd be round today and now it's too late to go out. I'll go to LASU tomorrow to make sure he's okay. I'm going to have to skip tomorrow's lessons, exams are getting closer and I'm still stupid when it comes to Mathematics.

16TH FEBRUARY 1987

DJ,

Today has been one of those days, so I'll start from the beginning. Well, you know Father has been making a nuisance of himself and spending too much time in my flat. He turns up in the early hours of the morning and watches me leave for school. Then he's here in the evening too, not every day, but most days. Today wasn't much different.

I'm not sure what time he turned up, he was just there as normal and as normal we didn't talk. I went off to school, for the morning lessons. I was hoping to get one of the girls to sign me in for the afternoon lessons. I asked Funke — who sometimes sits next to me — because I did it for her last week when she snuck out, I'm sure to visit her boyfriend. I didn't ask her why she was skipping classes, but she wanted to know where I was going and who it was I was visiting, which was very annoying. I just said a friend. I didn't want her to get too friendly with me, she's such a kid and we have nothing in common. Before I knew it, people started talking about my trip as if it was a big deal. It was so irritating. I left at eleven just before double Maths, I wanted to get to LASU during Segun's lunch hour. While I was waiting at Obalende for a bus, Tunde, a kid from school drove up in his dad's Nissan Patrol. He said he'd been to the British High Commission to get a visa but the crowds were too much. He's going to send the houseboy tomorrow to queue up (I think it's because he's too important to stand in line himself). He wanted to know where I was going, then he offered me a lift. He drove me all the way to LASU. I made sure he knew he didn't stand a chance of going out with me and I was only accepting his offer because it was better to travel in the comfort of an air-conditioned car rather than sit amongst the great unwashed on a *Molue* bus. Charlie Boy had a favourite phrase, and it was 'how I go put petrol for car I no dey drive?' Men never give a woman anything without expecting something back in return, it's the law of the land. If they offer to buy you a drink, it never occurs to them that you accept because you're thirsty and not because you're interested in becoming the second or third wife/mistress/girlfriend.

Well, Tunde took me to LASU and no one seems to have seen Segun since Friday, so on the way back Tunde was kind enough to take me to Festac, but he wasn't there either and now I'm really worried. He didn't tell me about any shows he had.

But now I'm in trouble with HIM because the school rang and said I wasn't there. Would you believe it? I wish HE hadn't installed that phone. This obviously means that Funke, the immature idiot, didn't sign me in for the afternoon session. And why did they have to call HIM. It wasn't as if I played truant every day. I just hope Segun is not in hospital.

17TH FEBRUARY 1987

DJ,

Another bizarre day. Suddenly everyone in school wants to be my friend. Or rather, they want to be friends with who they think I am — a rich spoilt brat like them. Father dropped me at school today. He insisted in coming in with me, it was so embarrassing. I felt like I was eight. He doesn't seem to realise it's too late to play the concerned parent, but then one cannot show darkness by pointing it out. I had to wait outside Mrs Aderemi's office like a little girl. They had a chat, then I was called in and got a severe telling off for my absenteeism. She duly pointed out, as if I didn't already know, that I'm the oldest in the school and have to set an example for the others. I was determined not to cry and I didn't, but I came so close. She made me feel so small and insignificant. Well, after my ordeal I just went straight to class and sat in the back licking my wounds.

At lunch time I went to thank Tunde, who was surrounded by a bevy of girls, and he offered to give me a lift home. I couldn't accept because Father told me he was going to send his driver to pick me up. So I told him thanks, but I was being picked up because Father didn't trust me to go straight home and I walked off. Not long after that, Funke and her gang of girls, who wouldn't even talk to me before because I wasn't part of their little clique, wanted to know all about me. Where I lived and if I had a brother. It was amazing. I told them I did, but I didn't tell them he was still in primary school. I've never had an invitation from them before to their silly daytime parties, but I received several today. I told them I had prior engagements. I'm not sure if they're now talking to me because of who father is or because Tunde, the only boy in the school whose father lets him drive his jeep, is friends with me. Tunde and I came to an agreement that we can only be friends; I've got a lost boyfriend who I hope still loves me as much as I love him. Although he's cute, seventeen is just too young for me.

Still no Segun, and I won't be able to go to Festac until this weekend, which is four whole days away, ninety-six hours, five thousand seven hundred and sixty minutes. I won't even bother counting the seconds.

21st February 1987

DJ,

Segun has been in hospital all this time and I didn't even know. God forgive me for all my bad thoughts towards him. I was expecting the worst, not that him having an accident isn't bad. I'm just so relieved. He'd been on his way to pick me up, there was a party at Leki beach he was going to take me to. The stupid boy was racing his mother's Beetle on the 3rd Mainland Bridge against Bola in his father's Peugot 505 — not exactly an equal race. Anyway, the gear stick came off in his hand and he lost control of the car and ploughed into the side of the bridge. He's lucky the car didn't go over the side into the lagoon, otherwise it would've been a different story. I can't imagine what he went through in those minutes when his life expectancy was reduced to almost zero, and before they finally managed to get him out of the car.

I knew there was something about his friend Bola I didn't like. I blame him. Segun doesn't race, he's always been a good driver. It's the only reason Mummy Baptiste allows him to drive the Beetle, which is now apparently a complete write-off. It's a miracle he came out with only bruised ribs and a fractured ankle. God is good and works in mysterious ways.

Bola was supposed to come and tell me what happened, but he never showed up. I think he's trying to split us up. He lied to Segun that he left a note on Monday, but he couldn't have. There was no note when I got home. I'm going to see Segun again tomorrow, then I'll have to wait till next weekend before I can go to Festac.

22ND FEBRUARY 1987

DJ,

I think Father can read my mind. I've been thinking how to broach the subject of my birth certificate and renewing my passport. When I got back from Festac this evening, he'd left them on the dining table along with an application form and some money.

I ran into Maggie at Segun's; she had heard on the grapevine that he'd been in an accident so she came round to see him. She looked dreadful, unlike her usual immaculate self. Not that she hadn't had a bath, she just looked unkempt. I'm so used to seeing her with lipstick and full make-up and every single strand of hair in place. I tried to find out what was going on but she said it was the pressure of mid-terms and assignments. I think her secret society is weighing heavily on her mind. Yolande was home too, she had just come for the day to see Segun. Anyway, her and Maggie want to spend next weekend at my flat, not because Yolande wants to see me but because her new boyfriend, Ope, lives in Ikoyi and he's coming home for his parents' thirtieth wedding anniversary. I've been invited because she wants to stay over and Maggie's been invited because it would be less awkward between us with her there. I know.

28TH FEBRUARY 1987

DJ,

I just got back from my very brief visit to see Segun. He seems to be much happier than the last time I saw him. I still can't hug him properly but it was nice to just be able to touch and be with him. He's decided to go bald rather than have a patch of missing hair on his head. The nurse had to shave round the cut he got on his head from the accident. I think it makes him look ten times sexier. I've nicknamed him Bullet. He can hobble around with a crutch, but he hates the fact that he's been cooped up at home all week.

I wish I could have stayed longer, but I had to dash back here to meet Yolande who arrived yesterday. I've only got one set of keys and I'm sure if I left her sitting outside she'd hate me for life.

1ST MARCH 1987

DJ,

It's a very small world. It turns out that Tunde from school is Ope's brother, who is Yolande's new boyfriend. Tunde had invited me to a party at his house earlier in the week, but I told him I had some friends coming to visit and we were already going to a party. Even if I didn't have somewhere else to go, I think I would have lied. I didn't want to socialise with Funke and her clique of vituperative Vipers. The claws and daggers are out in school, it's so pathetic. Like Mama always said, if two people raise their voices in the street, how will onlookers be able to tell which one of them is mad?

Maggie didn't turn up. She wanted Yolande and me to spend some time together instead. It wasn't as awkward as I thought it would be, because I hardly saw her. When she arrived on Friday, it was too late for cosy girly chats and in the morning Ope came to pick her up and I didn't see her again till it was time for the party.

I spent the rest of my day with Ekun. Father had brought him over; apparently all week he'd been screaming that he wanted to visit his big sister. He's told me he wants me to come and live in the mansion with them, or he wants to move in here with the rest of the family. There is not a chance that will happen. For a six-year-old, he's very vocal in what he wants, though, and very persistent too. He wanted to help me pack a suitcase, so while I was in the kitchen making us some fried plantain he was busy putting a chair in front of the wardrobe, trying to reach the suit-case at the top. Only when he couldn't reach, he decided to pile some books on top of the chair and climb on top of those. That of, course, was his downfall; I heard an almighty thud, followed instantaneously by a protracted howl of pain. I think he fell on his bottom, and luckily he didn't have far to fall, otherwise it might have been a different story. I can just imagine Cook Woman on my doorstep brandishing a machete, wanting to cut off my head. He survived with no broken bones or severed limbs. After that, though, he wanted me to carry him everywhere so I ended up with him on my back for almost the whole day, and he weighs a ton.

I now know why Father is spending so much time here, though of course it took the babblings of a six-year-old to figure it out. Ekun overheard Father discussing with Cook Woman my coming to live at the mansion, but she is adamant we cannot share the same house. She threatened to leave with Ekun and her brats, which I can't quite see her doing. She likes being Mrs Ogunwole, having the housemaids at her beck and call, being driven around in an air-conditioned car. No, she won't be leaving, not even if he brings home wife number two; she's more likely to consult a *Babalawo* on how to get rid of me or any other interloper. If it wouldn't make my life hell, I'd go and live there just to spite her. Anyway, that's why Ekun has got it into his head for me to live with them. I guess he doesn't want to be taken away from Father.

The party wasn't fun; I wished Maggie had come. Yolande spent most of her time talking to her friends from University and Bukola was there too. Her being there brought back bitter memories of my last sleepover at Segun's. I still remember her cutting words very clearly — 'It's not as if you've been to University or are likely to go there in this century.' As soon as I saw her, I knew it wasn't going to be a comfortable evening.

If it had been anyone else, I would've given up by now, but I keep trying with Yolande because she's Segun's sister. It was becoming more and more clear to me that she didn't want to be my friend; she was just tolerating me, probably for the same reason. I'd had enough and left her there, she came back in the morning to pick up her stuff. As she was leaving, I had this strong urge to ask her whether she still wanted to be friends, but I didn't. Another of Mama's favourite sayings came to me, I could picture her with her wrapper wrapped around her waist and her slipper breasts hanging loose, clapping her hands and kissing her teeth. She'd say, 'There is no point in using our bare feet to search for hidden thorns which we have seen in the light of day, have I not spoken the truth?'

4TH MARCH 1987

DJ,

Tunde was kind enough to take me to the British High Commission today in Lagos. We had to get permission from Mrs Aderemi yesterday. Tunde thought it better to go early in the morning rather than at lunchtime so we took the whole day off. Tunde finally got his visa but they wouldn't accept my application. I've been told to bring photographs of myself and father in Trafalgar Square because apparently everyone take pictures there with the pigeons. I have seen a picture with us trying to feed the pigeons but, even though the evidence is there, I don't remember it being taken. I looked terrified. I wonder what was going through my mind at the time? A picture can only capture so much. I probably only thought about food and sleep, not that much has changed; they still occupy a large part of my brain. If I don't eat, I start to worry. I've finally managed to get some flesh on my bones, not much, but at least I no longer look like a praying mantis.

Life certainly hasn't been the enchanting time I imagined it would be at six. If I could, I would have wished for a different one; but I have to row the boat which I find myself in. Looking back, my life in London seems like a fairytale; I look at old photographs and wonder where the child in the picture went, I wonder what may have been. I close my eyes and imagine undeveloped yesterdays. But these musings are futile exercises. When the door is closed you must learn to slide across the crack of the sill.

I've given the application to Father, he can sort it out. I'm not going back there, it was horrible. We got there really early this morning but there were hundreds of people already queued up. I think some may have even spent the night, because the stench of unwashed bodies was mighty. When the doors finally opened, there was a mad rush to get in, I felt so suffocated that I almost fainted. Father had been so desperate to come back to Nigeria, he told us we'd have a better life here. Now people are so desperate to leave and will do anything to achieve that goal. America and England beckon, but unfortunately the only ones who can afford it are the rich minority. Trafficking in drugs is the new way to riches, either that or stealing crude oil. It was on the news that a woman carried her dead baby on a flight and he was stuffed with drugs. The airhostesses became suspicious because the baby never cried once and didn't eat anything, and she was arrested in London.

It's amazing what we do to survive. What happens to the dreams we have when we're young? I didn't dream of anything much, all I wanted above all else was a family and to go back to London. Not a lot of imagination then, and not a lot of imagination now. I ask myself what do I want to be when I grow up and I'm almost grown up and still don't know. What would I do if I didn't get into Uni in September? Become a *Molue* driver's second wife? I'm sure Segun wouldn't want to marry a girl with no education, he'd be too embarrassed to introduce me to his friends. What job would I be able to get? I'd probably end up hawking wares like a common street seller, and the cars carrying my peers like Bukola and Funke would stop to buy my water, or sweets, or whatever the hell it is that I'm selling. Even worse, I could become the woman with the dead baby carrying drugs. Is that what the future holds? Even if I managed to get an office job, I'd be expected to open my legs and keep them open for any promotion. Why does life have to be so hard? One must row in whichever boat one finds oneself; after all, we live by hope, but then the elders also say a reed will never become an Iroko tree by dreaming. I have to start making my dreams come true.

6TH MARCH 1987

DJ,

Father has taken my application in to the High Commission; I have to pick it up in two weeks. I'm not sure how he managed to get them to accept it, he probably went in throwing his weight around saying, 'Do you know who I am?'

I'm going to see Segun tomorrow. He called me yesterday, said he was missing me. I can't visit him during the week, by the time I get back from school, it's too late to go all the way to Festac because of rush hour traffic. He's taking me to a new Chinese restaurant that has just opened on 5th Avenue. I'm excited because I've never had Chinese food before. I think there's also a party somewhere and he's going to be the DJ.

DJ,

All I can say today is give me a bowl of pounded yam with *egusi* or *edikankong* instead of a bowl of noodles in water and cabbage any time. There was no meat at all, just squid, which was like eating rubber. But I didn't want to appear 'bush' so I ate everything on my plate. I don't think I'll be eating there again.

It's been a good day though. It's been ages since we last went out together or had a proper conversation about us. Segun is really excited about Voice Out, he wants to become the first Nigerian superstar. He'd rather not be at Uni, but he's using it to make contacts. It turns out that Creepy's dad — I've started calling Bola, Creepy — is a music producer and has worked with Fela. Creepy is going to try and convince his dad to come and see a Voice Out show, which Segun hopes will blow him away. Which means I've got to try and be nice to him. URGH!!!!

Segun came back home with me and he's going to spend the night. It'll be like old times, talking through the night whilst holding each other. He's gone to say goodbye to Creepy who gave us a lift back. He seems to have attached himself like a leech. I think he's trying to hit on me. He hasn't done anything overt, but it's a feeling I get when he's around.

In ten days time I'll be nineteen, but I'm not having a party. Whoever turns up will get fed, and I hope I get lots of presents.

11TH MARCH 1987

DJ,

Charlie Boy is back in town, his University has been closed down indefinitely. There's been unrest and the students have been rioting, protesting against the proposed introduction of Sharia Law, whatever that is. I can't keep up any more. He spends more time at home than at Uni. I'm finally beginning to understand what Alhaja was trying to make me see when she insisted I should go back to England and study at an English University. Here, the students are always rioting about something and the government is always closing them down. I'm not even sure whether ABU has reopened since its closure last year. But then how can I leave Segun? I'm not stupid, I know there are girls out there who want to be with him, but he's not interested because he's got me. Leaving would lead to the demise of our relationship. Flowers need water and sunshine to blossom

18TH MARCH 1987

DJ,

Today I'm nineteen years old, next year I'll no longer be a teenager. Father brought Ekun round and he gave me a nice self-made card. Father gave me some money in a brown envelope. I haven't counted it yet. This is the first time since I was a child that he's acknowledged my birthday. This is a year of miracles. I've managed to save five hundred Naira from the money Father and Alhaja have been giving me. Every time I visit, she gives me money or has bought me something. I think I'm the daughter she never had. I try not to visit too often though. Every relationship I've tried to hold onto in the past has always had a habit of turning sour. I'm trying to learn from the past — a man who is trampled to death by an elephant is a man who is blind and deaf. I've got to go to school.

Tunde bought me a bottle of perfume for my birthday. He snuck a look at my passport for my date of birth. He wanted to take me out to a Chinese restaurant in Lagos (urgh) but I told him I was expecting Segun to come round and I think he was a bit disappointed. I've told him we can only be friends but he keeps hoping for more.

Segun turned up with Charlie Boy and we had a great time. Segun bought me another bottle of perfume; he has no imagination. Charlie Boy bought me three Pacesetters novels, I've read most of them apart from *The Delinquent*, and he got me *The Slave Girl*, the book I fought with Veronica over. It was very sweet of him to buy me books to read. I wish Segun was more imaginative when it comes to giving presents.

11TH APRIL 1987

DJ,

Today has been a mad day. I had my JAMB exam this morning, and afterwards I decided to go and see Maggie on campus. I haven't spoken to her in a while. I like being on campus. When I walk through the gates there is an ambience of knowledge that permeates the air I breathe. The students emanate it and I badly want to be one of them, to feel my life has direction and focus. I watch the bookworms in their groups on the open lawns arguing about philosophy, social injustice and any other hot topic of the day. Maggie calls them 'our future professors.' Then there are the students who aren't there to get an education but to make connections. They party all night and pay others for their lecture notes. I want to be a part of this world. I want to broaden my horizons, to learn and to grow, because now I realise the importance of education.

When I got to Lag, there was a small group of students gathered at the entrance. I think they thought I was a student because the next thing was some mad girl grabbing my arm and asking me to come and join the protest against the spread of Islam in government and life. Apparently, there had been some trouble between the Islamic Movement and the Christian Alliance last night and some students had been hurt. I told her I was visiting a friend and she let me go. She reminded me of Maggie during her unkempt days, she had a crazed fervour about her and I don't think she'd had a bath.

When I got to Moremi, there seemed to be a lot of people milling about there as well. Neither Maggie nor her roommate were in so I decided to wait for a while, hoping she'd come back. What a big mistake that was. I should have come straight home. No sooner had I settled on the grass outside when the group from the gate came marching up chanting 'Babangida must go!' I don't really understand what he had to do with the clashes between both religions but I guess it sounded better than chanting 'God must go,' or 'Allah must go.' Babangida is mortal and he's not God, even though he acts like God, so they can pick on him. To be honest I want him to go too; we should have a woman as President, she'll knock the country into shape. Buhari started it, now there's coup after coup as people come to power. The problem is they don't serve the interests of the populace they purport to have wrested the power for. Everyone is fed up, and people are leaving in droves hoping for a better life abroad.

Father was complaining on the phone to someone that he remembers a time when the Naira was on equal footing with the Pound, but now he could only get one pound for four Naira which limited his spending in London. I think he's buying a house, I couldn't make out the details. He saw me eavesdropping and lowered his voice for a while. He raised it again when he got excited but by then I'd missed the crucial titbit of information.

Back to my ordeal. A more sensible person would have left when the chanting started and the crowd started getting bigger, but no, not stupid Lola, I decided to stay and gawp. Before I knew what was happening, I could hear police sirens, and the students then went wild. It was pandemonium as they rushed towards the gate. Bottles and stones where whistling through the air and I prayed from the bottom of my heart I didn't get hit as I watched a girl go down, blood trickling from a wound on her head. The worst thing was when the policemen started shooting tear gas and bullets; my heart was beating so fast I thought it was going to beat its way out of my chest. I had nowhere to hide, the only person I knew on campus wasn't in her room. With tears rolling down my face, I cowered by a tree hoping I wouldn't get hit and prayed for everything to just stop.

I don't know how long it went on for, I lost any sense of time. But after a while I noticed that there was only the occasional whistle of a stone going over my head and the police had stopped shooting. I couldn't breathe, I kept coughing and the gas was stinging my eyes.

Eventually things died down and it felt safe to move so I started heading for the gate. I realised that the reason I was lucky was because most of the fighting had been towards the gate. The police had been trying to keep the students on campus instead of letting loose a rampaging mob in town. They were still there in force at the gate. They wanted to arrest me because they thought I was a student. I begged and pleaded to let me go, that I was only there to visit my friend but she wasn't in. They didn't believe me, and were about to man-handle me into the back of a Black Maria when the stones started flying again, the students had gone to regroup. A bottle hit the guy about to put me in the van and he let me go so that he could clutch his head. I took the opportunity and ran as I'd never run in my life. My shoes came off as I pelted down the street. No way was I going to end up in a prison cell. The image of Ngozi's emaciated uncle was at the forefront of my mind and my legs kept on pumping, I was running on sheer adrenalin.

I'm so glad I'm home. I got a taxi all the way; with no shoes or money I didn't have a choice. Luckily my keys were in the pocket of my shorts, otherwise I wouldn't have been able to get in and pay for the taxi from my savings. The thought of turning up at the mansion with only Cook Woman to ask for money to pay the taxi was chilling. I think I would rather face a night in a police cell. But I'm safe now.

17TH APRIL 1987

DJ,

Yesterday was Good Friday and today was Maggie's funeral. She was one of the two students who got hurt during Friday's riot, that's why she wasn't in her dorm when I went there on Saturday. She was lying on a hospital bed slowly dying from her injuries.

As I stood with Segun at the funeral, the thud of the earth hitting the coffin brought back memories of Adebola's burial. I'm able to manage but it's always bubbling away under the surface like a volcano waiting to erupt. I can't go through that pain again. How do I stop myself from feeling? I wish there was a switch I could flick or even better a tap. With a tap you can regulate its flow. A trickle would be good, maybe a drip. A drip would be even better, or best of all; I'd be able to turn it off and not let a single drop escape. Maggie is gone forever and life still goes on, the sun still shines, the birds still sing and everything ebbs and flows with the tides of time. I wish I could bring them back.

21ST APRIL 1987

DJ,

I decided to leave Lagos and visit Auntie Bumni in Ilorin. It wasn't the smartest idea because I didn't have a clue where I was going and Auntie Bunmi wasn't expecting me. I figured that if she wasn't there, I'd just return home before Father had the chance to read the note I'd left for him. For some strange reason, when I pictured Ilorin I didn't think of it as a bustling city like Lagos, I thought of it as a village like Idogun where everyone knew each other. Stupid really. I hadn't seen Auntie Bunmi since Idogun, which seems a lifetime ago. After Maggie's funeral, I needed to get away, to get out of town and hide myself. Which is a stupid idea, because when a tortoise moves it carries its shell with it, there is nowhere to hide.

I got here yesterday, I didn't know where I was going, and all I had to go on was what Mama had told me and even that wasn't clear. She just told me the area, and that the Adenikes who were relatives of Auntie Bunmi, have been living in Ilorin since the slave trade. They are very prominent in the market and most people know them. The taxi driver who brought me from the bus station was helpful in pointing me in the general direction of their store where they sell lace amongst other things. I asked a woman selling *boli* (roast plantain) and she pointed me in the right direction.

It looks like I came on the right day too, because Auntie Bunmi is finally getting married tomorrow — well, she's getting engaged first, then married later on. Baba Ade isn't here because he's too old to travel. Father was supposed to be here but he couldn't make it, he urgently had to go to London. I was eavesdropping again; it has something to do with the house he's buying. I know he wouldn't have come anyway. There's something going on between the families that I haven't figured out yet. No one from Baba Ade's side of the tree is here but it's okay though, because her mother's people are here in force, and she's got me to represent her father's side of the tree.

22ND APRIL 1987

DJ,

Aunt Bunmi is now officially married. I'm not sure what her 'Mrs' name is, not that it matters, she'll always be called Iya Seun. I missed the introduction, which was last week, it's where both families meet each other. The engagement was fun. I got to dress up in Auntie Bunmi's *aso oke* and pretend to be her.

The ceremony took place at the bride's house. The groom came in with his family and the men had to prostrate themselves, while the women knelt to ask for their wife. The bride's family then asked for compensation for the loss of their precious daughter. First they handed over an envelope of money but then the bride's people didn't find this acceptable. They told the groom that Auntie Bunmi was worth more than that. Which is when they handed over a ram, but still it wasn't enough. The family's response was that now they have offered food for the bride's stomach she needs jewellery to enhance her beauty. Out came the jewellery and the response to that was that she needs clothes to adorn her body as the jewellery will adorn her neck and fingers, so a suitcase full of *aso oke*, lace and jacquard was handed over, and that was her dowry settled.

Once they'd paid, they wanted to see their bride, which is when I came out dressed in Auntie Bunmi's *aso oke*. They took one look at me and shouted out, 'No, this isn't our bride!' Of course Auntie Bunmi is very short so they knew it wasn't her. Then two more women came out, until eventually they brought Auntie Bunmi through. Immediately everyone started clapping, the drums started up and the singing and dancing began.

Once the couple were seated, they prayed for them and blessed their union and that was the end of the ceremony, apart from a little ritual where the Baba conducting the ceremony gave them kola nut, ata ire and honey. The honey symbolises the sweetness of the union, the ata ire is like a pod with seeds, and according to superstition, when the pod is broken, the seeds that fall out represent the amount of children they'll have. I'm not sure what the kola nut represents. The English ceremony was just the signing of a certificate and then the party officially started and went on till the cock crowed at dawn.

I only made about twenty Naira, which isn't much. Auntie Bunmi made over a thousand, I helped her count it. It's unfortunate that no one from her father's side turned up, not even her brother or sister. She might have made more Naira. Maybe she didn't invite anyone; she can be very strange sometimes. I'll never forget when she gave birth to Tayo in Idogun and she wouldn't let me wake anyone until after he'd popped out, all because she didn't want them to fuss over her.

Enough about Auntie Bunmi, I've met a first cousin on my mother's side of the tree. I have to call her Iya Dupe, because she's much older than me. She is the daughter of my mother's brother. I didn't even know she had a brother. Maybe they don't get along. Iya Dupe is taking me to Minna the day after tomorrow to meet her dad. I want to go but I'm a little afraid too, because it's in Minna that there's been bloody clashes between the religions. It's where it all started and I'd rather not get caught up in another riot. I don't even know where Minna is. I know it's the capital of Niger State, I think. I never did pay attention during Geography.

25TH APRIL 1987

DJ,

Today is Saturday and we arrived in Minna yesterday. It's very hot and dry and everything seems to be coated with a film of reddish brown sand. Baba Lara, (Lara is Iya Dupe's name and she's the first born), my mother's brother, lives in a round thatched house; it's just one big cluttered room. The house is made from mud like the ones in Idogun, but the colours are different. In Idogun, the mud is a milk chocolate brown and in Minna it's a reddish brown and they also smooth the outside of the houses, unlike in Idogun. Baba Lara wanted me to stay for a week so he could get to know me but I told him I've got to be back in Lagos on Monday. I couldn't spend more than two days in the hut with all the comings and goings and no privacy at all. Some son or daughter was constantly popping in to say hello; the word had spread that I was there, which made me feel more like a circus act. I think I lost count on the tenth cousin. Baba Lara is a real live Papa Battalion, three football teams plus extra for just in case.

Iya Dupe's advice to me was to make sure I never became a second wife and if I was wife number one, to make sure wife number two was never allowed into the home. Otherwise, there would be a number three, four, five and six and before you knew what was going on, you would be raising another woman's children. I don't think she likes her father very much, maybe it's because her mother was wife number one and he didn't treat her nicely.

Baba Lara had nothing to tell me about my mother. The last time he'd seen her was when she boarded the plane for England in 1965. He showed me an old fading photograph of her when she was still a child. I looked for traces of myself but the image was too fuzzy to recognise any family resemblance. As I traced her features with my fingers, I wondered what her childhood was like. The photograph seemed to have captured an instant of happiness, a frozen moment of time that has faded to a sepia brown. I reluctantly handed the photograph back, I didn't want to deprive him of his memories of her. Baba Lara doesn't like Father much because my mother wrote to him and said he beat her up. If that's why she left, why didn't she take us with her?

1ST MAY 1987

DJ,

I'm back in Lagos. Even though I didn't want to, Baba Lara convinced me to spend a few extra days with him, then I went back to Ilorin to say goodbye to Auntie Bunmi. She's going to London to live with her husband, because he's already a citizen so she'll be able to get a visa. Another Nigerian checking out. Before you know it there'll be no one left here.

Father is back from his trip, we're still not talking other than to say 'good morning' or to leave notes on the table. We only seem to exchange words when he's angry with me. Ekun is still upset with me because I forgot his birthday, which was last month. That child has the brain of an elephant, he never forgets. I'm going to have to take him to the amusement park in Apapa to make up. But not tomorrow, tomorrow I have to catch up with Segun whom I haven't seen since Maggie's funeral. I still can't get the image of her dad sobbing his heart out when we went to visit him. Traditionally, a parent isn't allowed at their child's graveside, it's some kind of abomination, but I have a memory of father being there when Adebola was being buried. He sobbed, tears trickling through the sunken grooves of his face, his eyes puffed up with grief. Those memories are hazy now, because I don't like to remember.

7TH JUNE 1987

DJ,

The gang are at home, their respective universities have been closed indefinitely, and they've been told it's due to circumstances beyond control. I don't think anyone knows what that means any more; all anyone can say is, *'One day e go betta sa.*' Nothing much happens these days. Normally, Segun would be accepting party invitations and we'd be having a good time. There are parties but no one much feels like partying.

DJ,

I finally did it, this is the happiest day of my life. I'm going to be an UNDERGRADUATE at Lag! I can't believe it. I wasn't expecting my name to be on the list of candidates for Mass Communications, but there it was in black and white. Omolola, Olufunke Ogunwole. I'd almost given up hope of ever getting in. I'd resigned myself to being the wife of a *Molue* driver and having to sell water on the roadside. Thank you, Lord! Best yet, I did it without having to ask Father to grease some person's palm. I did it all on my own. I'm so happy. I can't wait to tell Segun.

DJ,

The day I've waited for all my life is finally upon me and I don't know which way to turn. What was it Mama used to say to me? 'A chicken eats corn, drinks water and swallows pebbles. Yet complains of having no teeth, would it eat gold? Let it ask the cow that has teeth yet eats grass.' I've complained bitterly all my life, her absence has been a constant shadow. I see her in the face of every stranger who smiles at me, and now I've been handed the chance to put a face to the shadowy figure that has haunted me all my life, the woman who gave birth to me. She is my mother, yet she's not, I'm no longer a child so I no longer need succour, I no longer need her to kiss my tears away and tell me everything will be okay with my world. I don't need her to slay my dragons, so what do I do? Should I pick up the phone and dial the number on the slip of paper father has just given me? What do I say — 'Hello, this is your long lost daughter, Lola?' That's the easy part; what do I say after that? Where have you been and why did you leave us? Oh, by the way, just in case you're wondering, Adebola is dead. Will she even care, would she want to talk to me or see me? What will it take to pick up that phone and call? Courage? Strength? I have neither.

How did this all happen? Just when my life was beginning to move forward I find myself dwelling on the past. Father came by yesterday, and told me he'd run into an old friend of my mother's at Heathrow airport. Apparently she now lives in Lagos. She was living in Zambia but has moved back to Nigeria. The woman gave Father my mother's phone number. So since we've been living in the same city, she's bound to know we live here now. Father is sometimes in the news, so unless she's deaf and blind she had to have known where we were, but she didn't get in touch. Maybe she doesn't want to know me. She's probably got a new family and doesn't want to be reminded of the past. I'm not sure why, but Father gave me the letter she wrote when she left us. She'd left it tacked to my crib. He came home to find her gone and both Adebola and me bawling. I've copied the letter into my journal because I have to give it back to Father. This is what she wrote:

19th Sept 1969

Dear Sammy,
*   I know you will be wondering why I have taken this sort of decision, yes I wanted to do this since more or less*

my arrival to this country, but due to what I wanted you to have and to know I could not do it and more over when the children came along. Well, we are not cut out for each other Sammy the earlier you realise this, the better. I never loved you and I know within my heart I'll never hate you no matter what you might have done in the past or in the present. Pray for me daily that my soul may find happiness and forgive me if I have offended you and most of all my children. Please try to look after them till I am settled. I am on my way to Nigeria now, I have been paying this fare for a long time without your knowledge. I don't want to waste your time or stand in your way in finding a real love, a true one that God created just for you.

Now you can recollect from the past, you know we were together for only 1 month 12 days when we had a bitter unforgettable fight on the 16th of May 1965. You just imagine this, not knowing each other well enough and instead of trying to understand each other and make a mutual atmosphere, all you ever did was beat, curse and say all those horrible words to me. I'm not your type because what I want you hate and what you want I deplore. Over all, no love, no affection, no passion.

But I must admit that I gain more than what I should have (WHO KNOWS TOMORROW) if I was in Nigeria and not coming to this country at all, my life would be different, but as the elders say — 'E da ko le pa kadara da.' Well I will thank you and also remind you that my life is just like when a person wants a house and give it to a contractor to build. Well I have to thank God, my parents and all those that contributed to my success in life. Now I am a shorthand typist I still pray to God to let me reach further.

It has taken a lot of courage to do this so please, please don't hate me. May God be with every one of us always. You have destroyed my pride as a woman and you make me look like an outcast and I feel ashamed to see or talk to anybody in the house. You have thrown me out against my wish — you have separated me from my children.

I have experienced enough of your cruelty and I can no longer go on like this. There are many defects in my body as the result of your beating me like an animal daily — these defects I have to repair. Your cruelty to me has gone beyond bounds and I do not want any more damage done to me.

All my love to my children, once more this is the most agonising part of it, "MY CHILDREN" and I pray that one day I shall be able to have them with me and cherish them with love, my love and affections.

If I am allowed to write on and explain this it will take me to the end of the line so I just have to stop now once and for all.

Goodbye
Constance Olufemi.

Those are her words. To be honest, I'm surprised Father kept this letter for so long, and gave it to me to read. It doesn't show him in a good light, but then I know what he's like when he loses his temper, he lashes out and many a time when I was growing up I wished I could run away. Adebola and I fantasised that we'd been adopted or switched at birth and our real parents were desperately searching for us. It is his fault she left and I don't blame her for leaving, but why did she leave us behind? She said she'd come back when she settled; it can't have taken her eighteen years. She left when I was eighteen months old, when I needed her the most and not once has she sent a Christmas, Easter or birthday card. Can I forgive her for leaving me to face his temper? I don't know if I can.

Father has never said anything horrible about her. When we asked, all he would tell us was that he came home one day and she was gone. I now understand why, he knew this day would come. He knew one day I'd find out what a horrible husband he was. I could have imagined him being a tyrant husband, because he's not been the nicest of fathers either. Maybe that's why he didn't want us to live with him, because he hated her so much and Adebola and I reminded him of a time he wanted to forget.

I'm so confused, I don't know what to do; should I call her or do I just close that chapter of my life? If I do, I'd forever be wondering, I'd be forever looking for signs of her in the faces of smiling strangers. I can't be afraid she won't want to see me, she said in her letter that she loved Adebola and me; she agonised over leaving us behind. That does mean she loves us, but on the other hand, actions speak louder than words. They say 'by your deeds you shall be known,' her letter means nothing.

11TH AUGUST 1987

DJ,

It's been three days and I still haven't called, in fact I've been sitting by the phone wanting to call. Each time I pick it up I put it down again, Father asked me yesterday what she'd said to me and I had to admit that I hadn't called her. He just "ummed" and went into his room. I asked Segun for his advice but he was very unhelpful, I don't know what's wrong with him. Something is bugging him but when I asked he wouldn't tell me. I've put it down to Maggie leaving us, but I just don't know. I was with him but felt utterly alone; how is that possible? I know he's hiding something from me, he's being miserable about everything. He's not even going to celebrate his birthday, which is at the end of the month.

14TH AUGUST 1987

DJ,

I still haven't called but I'm thinking about it. I almost got up the nerve yesterday, but just as I was about to pick up the phone to start dialling, it rang. It turned out to be Tunde who is throwing a party tomorrow. He'll be going to UniLag too, studying Petroleum and Gas Engineering. He's also leaving for London on Monday for two weeks, a short holiday before term begins. I know he's just going to buy spoots so he can come and oppress us in Uni.

So now I'm sitting here by the phone, willing myself to pick it up and dial her number. I think I'll definitely call her tomorrow.

More news, Father has helped Yolande transfer to UniLag like he promised. I wonder if she'll stop pretending to be my friend now that she's gotten what she wanted?

15TH AUGUST 1987

DJ,

I should have gone to see Segun today, but instead I went to Tunde's stupid party and it was so boring. It was the same tunes, the same people who are much too young and the same dance moves. It was just tiresome, so I left early. Tunde was upset with me, but I just told him I had things to do at home. I think he's been saying things to his friends, but I'm not sure. I just caught the end of Funke's conversation, she shut up as soon as she saw me. I did hear the word *ashewo* (prostitute) and my name, but I decided to ignore her and her clique, they're only little girls after all. So I can't say for sure whether he's been boasting of exploits that never even occurred. If it's true, he can say bye to our friendship. No one has said anything in front of me, so there's nothing for me to deny and it would look pretty stupid, me denying something that no one has said to me. Even if they did have the courage to confront me, the more I deny it the more they'd nudge and wink behind my back.

29TH AUGUST 1987

DJ,

I'm so angry with myself. All the signs were there. I should have guessed but, gullible me, I never thought in a million years that he would betray our love in such a way. So, Lola Ogunwole is a stupid gullible idiot. How did I find out? I probably wouldn't have if his evil friend Bola hadn't called me up to invite me to Segun's surprise birthday party. The party was going to be at his house in Ikeja because he was organising it; his parents are probably away. Little did I know that it wasn't a surprise party; it had been planned by Segun and Yolande, only Segun hadn't wanted to invite me because he wanted his 'not so new' girlfriend to be there. He knew I'd probably turn up, and how would he explain having a party without telling me? Especially after he'd told me he didn't want a party.

So Bola called me up and told me that because it was a surprise, I had to be there no later than two o'clock because Yolande was going to try and get Segun there for three. Which meant it was to be an afternoon bash and, since everything runs on African time, I didn't need to be there till I about four. So, unaware of the evil machinations, Stupid Lola goes and buys her boyfriend a pair of Ray Ban sunglasses. When I arrived, the party looked as if it had been in full swing for a while; people had already eaten which meant they were probably getting ready to go home. I was upset with myself for not getting there on time. I saw Charlie Boy across the dance floor and he seemed shocked to see me. His eyes automatically went to where Segun was sitting with a girl in his lap.

My stomach dropped all the way to my feet. It seemed to take a lifetime but I managed to make my way through a tunnel to him. Everything was blocked out; all my attention was on him and her, although I fleetingly remembered that he used to cuddle me like that. He was so engrossed that he didn't see me coming. I walked up to him and tapped him on the shoulder and whispered, 'Surprise!' Of course he was shocked to see me. I looked at him expectantly, waiting for him to introduce me to the girl on his lap. I think by then everyone in the room could sense the unfolding drama. He stood up and tried to steer me somewhere, but I stood my ground and asked him to introduce me to his FRIEND. He wanted me to go outside so we could talk in private, but what was the point? The scales had fallen from my eyes and I didn't like what I was seeing. I said no, I wanted him to introduce me to the girl. He just looked at me, and I think she got fed up with his lack of response so she introduced herself as 'Bridget, his girlfriend.' 'What business was it of mine,' she asked. After all, according to her, he'd apparently dumped me months ago. She confirmed what I already knew in my heart. I asked her how long they'd been seeing each other and it turns out it's been going on since January — eight months of lying to me.

The anger and adrenalin that had been carrying me dissipated and my heart broke into pieces. There was nothing left to say. I'd always told him if he wanted to date someone else then he should tell me, rather than two-time me. And he told me he never would — just words. So I gave him his gift, looked him in the eye and said, 'Goodbye,' then I turned around and left. Charlie Boy came running after me. All I wanted to do was curl up and bawl my eyes out. I didn't want to speak to him, he'd betrayed me too; he knew what was going on but didn't tell me. It took Bola, my enemy, to spill the beans, his motives no doubt as loathsome as he. I'll survive, I've survived worse, besides I have no tears left to shed for anyone, not even me. I will not cry over him, he's not worth the tissue.

Charlie Boy wanted to take me home but I told him no thanks, that I'd rather be by myself. 'Why didn't you tell me?' I asked him. 'You were supposed to be my friend too.' He just looked at me and shrugged his shoulders; he had nothing to say. I thought I had friends but I was just lying to myself. So I hailed a cab and came home to lick my wounds.

31st August 1987

DJ,

Today is Segun's birthday Once upon a time I'd be around his house first thing to help him celebrate but he's found somebody else and life must go on. Last night I couldn't sleep. I lay awake remembering the times we'd spent together, how he sang me love songs and promised

309

me forever. Where has forever gone?

I remember going to visit him at home. When I got there he was having one of his spur-of-the-moment jam sessions with Banji, his guitarist. As soon as I entered the room he looked up, saw me and smiled. It was a beautiful day, the sun was shining outside and the room seemed to be filled with an incandescent light. The talking drum that is my heart performed an impromptu solo as the corners of his mouth lifted to meet the sparkle in his eyes. We'd been seeing each other for a while, but it was the first time we'd connected like that. He waved me over to the couch, and I sat down and breathed him in. All this happened in the space of not more than five seconds, he didn't pause a beat as he continued to belt out Easy Lover. I sat down with my head in Planet Lola, the place I go to when life is sweet. In my fantasy we were married with two daughters, a house and lots of money. On Planet Lola I had my happily ever after.

I didn't notice Banji leaving, but I think I must have mumbled a goodbye. The next thing I knew I was being cuddled and I was listening to the synchronisation of our talking drums as they beat. He whispered in my ear that he missed me and held me a little bit tighter and I was ecstatic because I knew he was feeling me just as I was feeling him. I was so happy I wanted to cry, but instead of blubbering all over him like a baby I asked him to sing me a song that reflected what he felt about our relationship and me. Without hesitation, he sang me Through the Years and the tears did fall. What has happened to my happily ever after?

DJ,

I didn't do it to try and keep him. I wanted my first time to be special and memorable. Memorable it certainly will be, the moment forever etched in my brain. I wanted him to be my first. I thought we'd one day grow old together. Now I know I was building castles in the sand, but it was all I could think about. It was my dream. Why did I give in? Because I knew he'd never truly be mine again and I needed something special to remember and cling to. Instead of thinking of him with Bridget or anyone else, I'll always have the night we spent together. He looked into my eyes and told me he loved me and only me; maybe he meant it, maybe he didn't, I'll never know for sure. I gazed back knowing I'd never be satisfied with half of him; I wanted all or nothing. I didn't know that when your heart is broken, you experience physical pain. I need that Tap, so I can turn it off.

DJ,

They say when one is in love a cliff becomes a meadow. I really did think we'd be forever. How did I get here? I don't know. I was sitting outside, NEPA had taken light for the third time in two hours and it was only eight o'clock, too early for me to go to bed. Not that I'd get much sleep. I'd already spent most of the day tossing and turning trying to sleep and at the same time trying not to think about him. It worked for a little while, but I can't spend the rest of my life asleep. I might as well be dead. So I was sitting outside thinking about him with her, smiling at her the way he once smiled at me, holding her hand instead of mine. Writing love songs and singing them to her instead of me. I still hadn't cried, I had no friends and the world was a lonely place once again.

I blinked and there he was. He rolled up in his mum's Beetle, which was still showing the scars of its crash only a few months ago. The dent in the drivers' door has been beaten out, the crushed bonnet has also been replaced, but needs painting. He sat in his mangled car just staring at me. I hadn't seen him since the party. I'm not sure how long we stared at each other. With only the light from the lantern to go on, I couldn't read his expression and he probably couldn't read mine either. But then the tears that had held themselves at bay since it happened threatened to make an appearance and I couldn't bear the thought of him knowing I cried over him. It was bad enough I couldn't eat. So as the floodgates threatened, I jumped up and rushed into the flat leaving the lantern outside and the front door wide open. Maybe subconsciously I knew he'd follow. I went into the bathroom, locked the door and opened the tap to wash my face but there was no water left in the tank. He must have gone to my bedroom first, before knocking on the bathroom door and threatening to break it down if I didn't let him in. So I tried to compose myself, when all I really wanted to do was scream and howl with the pain of betrayal rather than let him in.

'What do you want?'

'Can we talk?'

With my eyes sparking, I looked at him and told him there was nothing he could do or say that could change what had happened. I glared at him with all the hurt and pain. The tears started in earnest, and once they started they wouldn't stop. I crumpled to the bathroom floor, wondering what next. He picked me up as though I weighed nothing and took me into the bedroom, where he laid me on the bed. He took off his shoes and lay down beside me. I remembered the other times we'd spent in that same position, hugging each other, making plans, talking about everything and nothing. Whenever he put his arms around me I'd feel safe, but as I remembered those times, I knew I'd never share that with him again. I sobbed harder, he held me tighter and whispered 'sorry' over and over again into my ear. I could feel his tears on the back of my neck. Eventually I calmed down enough to be able to ask him why. 'I thought you loved me,' was what I said to him. I rolled over to look into his eyes as he tried to answer. I couldn't see his expression because I was looking into the light of the lantern, which cast a shadow over his face.

'What I have with Bridget isn't love, it's just sex.' I wasn't shocked, Maggie had tried to tell me. I'd been too naïve in thinking that because I wanted us to wait until we got married, that meant him remaining celibate and faithful to me. He's still young and needs to sow his wild oats before settling down, so if he couldn't get it from me he was bound to start looking elsewhere. I stupidly and naively wanted our wedding night to be special, and now I realise it was all in my head, he'd never even asked me. I just assumed that one day I'd be Mrs Segun Baptiste. Castles in the sand again. I'd started to think of myself as special. There were times I'd look at him and wonder why he was with me, yet ecstatic that he'd chosen to be with me. I never stopped asking myself, 'why me?' After all, I had nothing to offer. I'm not even beautiful, my legs are too long, my head too small and according to Yolande, I'm like a telephone pole, no curves. 'Obey the wind' is one of her favourite ways to describe my skinniness. I sure fooled myself, what was it Mama used to say to me? 'No matter how long a log may float in the water, it will never become a crocodile.'

I don't remember how it started. He was nuzzling my neck and holding me tight. I knew it would be the last time he held me. No matter how sorry he was, he no longer belonged to me and I was dying inside. I had the memories of the good times, but I wanted something more to hold on to. So when his hands started to wander I did nothing to stop them. His kisses became more passionate and I momentarily forgot what had happened. I opened the tap and revelled in the emotion I was feeling. He told me how much he wanted me and that he wanted to taste me all over. I didn't know what to do. I've read the books but none of them actually describe in detail what I was experiencing. I think at some point he asked me if I was sure it was what I wanted.

He told me I was beautiful and that one day he wanted us to get married. I think he said it because he thought it was what I wanted to hear in order to give him my virginity. But by then I'd already made up my mind. I had decided to take what was mine before letting it go to someone else forever.

As I watched the morning sun chase the shadows across my room, I did the hardest thing ever. I told Segun it was over and I didn't want to see him again. He was dazed. I guess he made the assumption that as I'd spent the night with him, all was forgiven and forgotten. Maybe he even thought it was a desperate attempt to hold on to him, but I explained it all to him. I told him I loved him and I probably always would, but I could no longer trust him. I didn't want to be the kind of girlfriend who was always questioning his whereabouts or couldn't let him out of my sight. I couldn't be the first wife who tolerated her husband's infidelities by accepting wife number two, three, four and five. Neither could I be wife number whatever. He doesn't believe it can be over, but I'm not the sharing kind. I made him leave. I'll be fine, after all if one is carrying water and it gets spilt, so long as the calabash is not split one can still get more.

14TH SEPTEMBER 1987

DJ,

Registration is at the end of the month. As usual the opening of most of the universities has been postponed. Thankfully, this time it's not indefinitely. With all that has been happening, I still haven't called my mother. I'll do it tomorrow, I really will. I don't need her as a mother; it's too late for that. But I do need to know what she looks like and hear what she has to say. So before I embark upon my new life, I'm starting with a clean slate. No more looking back into the past, the future is what is important. I've decided to try and make up with Father, we can't go on like this. I'll start tonight by cooking him a meal whilst he's here, then maybe we can sit at the dinner table like father and daughter.

10 PM

My plans have suffered a slight setback due to the fact that Father didn't come by tonight. I've been hoping he would. If he doesn't come tomorrow morning I'll have to go to the mansion. He might be ill or something. I hope not, he's all I have left.

IMAGINE THIS

DJ,

All is well, Father has been busy with work. I went round this morning and pretended that I needed money for something. He was his usual gruff self, the only thing he asked me was, 'Have you called your mother?' I don't know why he's so eager for me to talk to her; I don't think she's going to be singing his praises. In a way I do feel sorry for her, because when she walked away she lost everything. Who's going to look after her in her old age? Then again, she may have a whole new family, I might have brothers and sisters. I will call as soon as NITEL gives me a working telephone line. It's been down since yesterday.

8 PM

Charlie Boy has just left, I wouldn't have opened the door for him, but Father is here. Which was rather fortunate, it avoided a scene. He wanted to go into lengthy explanations about why he didn't tell me. I told him not to worry and that I was over it. He hoped we would remain friends and I said of course we would. I lied to get rid of him. I'm fast learning how not to wear my heart on my sleeve for all to see. If he really wanted to be my friend, he should have told me what he knew.

"When the jackal dies
The fowls do not mourn
For the jackal never
Brings up a chicken"

Yoruba proverb

10:00 PM
DJ,
  FATHER IS DEAD!

11:00 PM
DJ,
It's on the NTA News. He has been murdered.

01:30 AM
DJ,
  I don't know what to do… what do I do now? No one knows who they are or even why they killed him. No one told me he'd died. I've had to find out about it on the television news. Which is probably my own fault, I stopped answering the phone in case it was Segun on the other end. When Uncle N came round yesterday, I pretended not to be in. Father was shot two days ago, he'd been stopped at a police checkpoint, but the men were not policemen. The driver, before he died, said they came up to the car, looked in and just started shooting. He tried to get away but he didn't get very far. It happened on the 3rd Mainland Bridge, the same place Segun had his accident. He was on his way back from a business meeting. The newscaster said

they might have survived if someone had stopped to help, but this is Lagos, no one stops to help another in distress. Someone is knocking on the front door, probably Uncle N coming to give me the bad news.

27TH SEPTEMBER 1987

DJ,

I've been at the mansion since Friday and I've just gotten back. Things aren't too good over there. Cook Woman won't stop crying, relatives are pouring in and out of the place and everyone seems to think I'm going to lose it again like I did when Adebola died. I should feel sad that Father is gone, but no tears will come. I know the relatives are probably all thinking I'm an evil, heartless witch but I don't care. I've come home because I don't want them touching me. I've had enough of the head patting and the stroking. If I'd stayed another minute I think I would've screamed at someone.

Getting into University was the one thing that I wanted above all else this year and it happened. Although he didn't say anything, I know he was secretly proud. I heard him telling someone on the phone that his daughter is going to University finally. Registration is in two days but I find myself not caring about much these days. Alhaja wants me to come and stay with them but I prefer to be by myself.

28TH SEPTEMBER 1987

DJ,

I don't actually think I believed Father was gone, not until today when I saw his body in the mortuary. It was him but it wasn't him. I stood there staring at him for a long time. Everyone around me was crying, clapping their hands together and beseeching God. But I just stood there and stared with Uncle N hovering behind me waiting for me to break down. All I could think was that we are born with one certainty and that is that one day, somewhere, somehow, death will lay its claim to us and those we love.

Death came like a thief in the night to take him away from me and my whole world has crumbled. I rose with the sun this morning and watched it chase the night away, yet darkness has tainted my soul. The birds came out singing with the joy of a brand new day but I feel no joy, not because he is no longer here but because he was never here and now it's too late to correct the mistakes of years gone by. All I can think of is that the promise of hope has been stifled. He couldn't give me what I needed. All I wanted was his love and approval but what I got instead was his distance. He named me — Omolola Olufunke and Olufunmilayo — did I bring wealth, sweetness and joy to his life as my names suggest? I never knew him; did he ever really care? Now it's too late, the sands of time have sealed our fate. Maybe one day…

I don't remember the day he left, only that he was no longer there. I miss him, not what he was but what he wasn't and the possibility of what he could have been. I wish I had the memories to comfort me, but all I have sitting here are regrets of what I couldn't be for him, and what he couldn't be for me. Father and daughter to each other. You left me before I had a chance to ask you why and now I'll never know.

29TH SEPTEMBER 1987

DJ,

It's late and people won't stop coming, I can't escape

them. Everyone wants to know when the funeral is, but I don't know anything. Uncle's J & N are organising everything. They don't want to leave me alone, someone keeps knocking on my bedroom door. The relatives aren't here because they're sorry he's dead, they've been circling like vultures eyeing up what possessions they want. I caught one of them trying to go into Father's room, and I told them all, no one is allowed in. Not until after his body is in the ground.

Segun and Yolande came earlier. I would never admit it to him but it was nice to see a friendly face. I really wish he was here by my side, but it's over and if wishes were horses, beggars would ride. Now all I want to do is to sleep and wake up and find that all this is a dream.

30TH SEPTEMBER 1987

DJ,

I haven't slept much, each morning as I listen to the distant call to prayer I keep wondering what new surprises the day will bring. It got too much last night so I told them all to leave; Uncle N wanted to come by later to let me know what the funeral arrangements are. I've managed to avoid being alone with him. I don't want him coming to the flat. I HATE HIM, I wish he'd died instead.

I know they'll probably want to take him back to Idogun, to where Adebola is. I'm truly alone. I still haven't picked up the phone to call that number and now it may be too late. I never got round to making up with Father. Maybe it's not too late to make up with her.

8:48 PM

Uncle N has just left. I was right, Father is being taken

back to Idogun. We're going to pick up the body from the mortuary on Thursday, we're taking it to the mansion where there will be a wake. On Friday the body leaves for Church, the same one he had the blessing in, in January. I wonder if the same Bishop will perform the ceremony? Immediately after that, we leave for Idogun. Uncle J has chartered four coaches for the relatives, friends and business associates. The whole of Idogun will probably turn out, making the whole funeral into a parade. A wealthy man will always have followers; would all these people, relatives especially, have turned out if we were still living in a face-me-I-face-you in Orile and Father didn't have a single kobo to his name? I'm not so sure.

If I could drive, I'd drive myself there and back. I don't want to get on a coach with them and the constant wailing. I try not to look anyone in the eye because as soon as I do, the hands go up in the air and it's a litany of 'why has God killed our brother, why has God left his children fatherless, why has God done this and why has God done that' yet without a single tear dropping from their eyes. It seems that there's a competition on who can mourn him the hardest. I told Uncle N that I'll be going with Alhaja and Alhaji; their driver will be taking them. Cook Woman, Ekun and her other children, Ronke and Ayo, will be travelling together in one of the other cars. No doubt they'll be squabbles over those.

The day I made everyone leave, I did a sweep of Father's bedroom for any important papers. He had two boxes full and over two thousand Naira under his bed. Everything is now in my room and no one is allowed in. They can squabble over his clothes and shoes, he doesn't have that many here, most of them are at the mansion.

One of the boxes contained all the notes I'd left for him, all the letters I'd sent from Idogun, Adebola's too. I found Adebola's birth certificate and his expired passport. He'd kept our immunisation certificates, school reports from when we were in Kent and living with Aunt Sue and Uncle Eddie, pictures too. It doesn't seem as if he threw anything away. No one knows why he was killed. There are rumours that it was a political assassination, but he was not foolish enough to get involved in politics. He said it was the quickest way to acquire powerful enemies, so he steered clear. Someone is sitting at home with blood on their hands, someone knows why. I never will.

Today is registration, I couldn't go. I don't even know if I'll be able to go to university. Now that Father is gone how do I get my tuition paid? What do I live on, the thought of having to ask one of them to give me money makes me want to scream in anger. I'd finally managed to get them all out of my life and now I'm dependent on them once again.

1ST OCTOBER 1987

DJ,

I saw his body again today; he really is dead. It's too late for him to be the father I wanted, the father he was becoming. He was changing. I wish I'd made more of an effort. I wish I'd been a better daughter. I wish I'd been less angry. I wish he hadn't died. I wish I had more time. When they got him back, some of the women relatives washed and dressed him, but I couldn't watch. I stayed out of the way until they laid him out on his bed. I sat by his bedside for a long time looking at him. He was dressed in a grey three-piece suit and someone had put white gloves on his hands. He seemed smaller; the potbelly that looked so big when he was alive seems to have shrunk. I took a glove off so I could feel his cold, stiff hand, and his skin had the grey tinge of death. I could feel the relatives hovering in the background, waiting for me to do something, to cry, to speak, to scream. Their whispers penetrated the curtain of sorrow that surrounded me. 'Is she good?' 'Has she cried?' How long has she been sitting there?' Uncle N tried to make me leave but I quelled him with a look and he backed away. I wanted to be alone with him but I knew I couldn't, so I tried as much as possible to shut everyone else out. I remembered sitting next to Baba's body, sneaking a peek through a mirror in order to see his spirit make its final trip. He later appeared to me that night. I don't care about taboos, so I did the same with Father. I looked at him through the mirror and hoped I would see him one last time. Before I left, I kissed him on his forehead and realised it's the only time I've kissed him since we moved to Nigeria.

2ND OCTOBER 1987

DJ,

I expected to see him like I saw Baba, like I saw Adebola. But he didn't come to me, I didn't get to say goodbye. I've packed enough clothes to last a week but I'm only staying one day in Idogun. The funeral is tomorrow, we leave straight after the church service.

5TH OCTOBER 1987

DJ,

I'm back in Lagos. Father has been buried next to Adebola. I can no longer see him, but I felt his presence when Father was being buried. Iya Dayo's wail to the ancestors was the only other thing I remember about the actual funeral, that and the thud of dirt as it hit the coffin. As the eldest surviving child, I grabbed a handful of dirt and threw it into the grave. I threw a handful in for Adebola and a handful for Ekun. I whispered, 'Goodbye Daddy,' and tried to walk away but Iya Dayo's wail pierced my heart. I couldn't stand so my body slid to the ground as comprehension dawned. I will never see my father again. Alhaja caught me before I hit the ground and I held on to her with what little strength I had left. 'He's gone,' I kept on saying; *'wan ti pa Daddy mi,* they've killed him, *wan ti pa.'* Alhaja held me tight.

Idogun hasn't changed that much apart from the fact that he'd built himself a mansion there. It had only just been completed last year. With only twenty bedrooms, there wasn't enough space for everyone so most of the people left straight after the burial yesterday. Mama was a portrait of impenetrable sorrow. I stayed for a while because, I knew her pain. Father was her pride and joy, the son who got himself an education, the son whose prowess in the ring took him to the land of the white man, the son who built her a house she'd never filled until they brought his body home to rest. She ignored me and clung to poor Ekun, who doesn't seem to understand what's going on.

Father's burial was a bit like Adebola's. There was no *Egungun* to see him on his way, no dancing or celebrating of his short life. I finally know how old he was. According to the obituary plastered all over the buses he was forty-eight, born July 17th 1939. That's how much I knew him; it took his death for me to know when he was born.

What do I do and where do I go now? I really can't face going to Uni and pretending that my life can just move on.

Every time I try, something always happens to knock me off my feet. I can't keep saying I'll survive; how many times do I have to keep picking myself off the floor? When will it end?

10TH OCTOBER 1987

DJ,

I'm back at home. I went to stay at Alhaja's to avoid all the relatives who are trying to move in with me, especially Yinka, my childhood nemesis, who has been thrown out of the mansion by Cook Woman. I think she's gone to stay with Uncle J. It's been nice staying with Alhaja and avoiding everything and everyone, but I couldn't stay there forever.

I finally got round to looking in the second box of papers and they're Father's bank and house details in London. I've also got an account at Barclays Bank. I don't know if there's any money in either account but at least things don't look completely hopeless.

I started to read some of the letters I sent from Idogun. They were all the same. *'Dear Daddy, when are you coming to get me... I hate living here... I want my bike... Mama hates me... I want to live with you... I'll be a good girl...'* To the scared unhappy nine-year-old girl, five years seemed forever. Time is not an endless vista, twenty years hence, soon becomes tomorrow. It's a hard lesson to learn. Harder for me to accept is to finally find out that my brother's life could have been saved if Uncle Joseph hadn't been so negligent. This was his last letter to Father.

IMAGINE THIS

At Home

1st March 1979

Hi Dad,

I hope you're well, I'm not. I am very ill but Uncle Joseph won't take me to the hospital. I'm a bag of bones and can even feel my ribs now. Please Dad come and get me, I really need to see a doctor. Sometimes I find it difficult to breathe, the other day I had a coughing fit and there was blood in my phlegm. I've never been this ill before and everyday I'm getting worse. It's worse at night, I start sweating and wheezing.

I'm so tired all the time but they think I'm being lazy. Despite my illness they won't let me rest, I still have to do the chores and everything takes ten times long because I have no energy. If you don't want me to live with you, can I at least move to Idogun and live with Mama and Lola. I asked Mama the last time I was there and she didn't say no to the idea. Please Dad come and get me, I don't mind living in Idogun if I can't live with you, I have to leave this place, I don't want to become a boarder I want to leave Ado Ekiti forever and never come back.

Your loving son
Adebola

Why did Father rely so much on his family to bring us up? Why couldn't he have let us live with him? Why did he have to believe that it takes a village to raise a child? Why, why, and more whys. All I have are questions and no answers.

21st October 1987

DJ,

I've had enough, the fighting and pettiness just keeps on

going. The vultures have picked everything clean. I never thought I'd say this but I feel sorry for Cook Woman, while a part of me is jubilant that she got her just rewards. On the other hand, she is Ekun's mother and she has to look after him. Uncle N has moved himself and his family into the mansion, it all happened two days after we got back from Idogun. Cook Woman had to stay (another tradition) when everyone else left. I think she was supposed to stay for forty days, but she could only manage two weeks before Mama probably drove her mad. She got back home to find Uncle N and his brood living there and there's nothing she can do about it. They've already divided up his assets between themselves. Uncle J chaired the family meeting. I thought there would be bloodshed but everyone seemed to accept what they'd been given except me. He wanted me to move out of the flat into the mansion with Uncle N and Cook Woman so they could rent it out. I told him he'd have to kill me first.

31ST OCTOBER 1987

DJ,

They say a man does not run among thorns for nothing. Either he is pursing a snake, or a snake is pursuing him. A venomous snake is definitely pursuing me and I've decided it's time for me to leave. Let them have their flat and their cars and their money. Those possessions mean zero to me, there is nothing left for me here, my anchor has gone and it's time to sail away. Alhaja advised me and I know it's the best thing to do. I can start again in London. I hope there is money in the accounts over there. If there isn't, I'll still survive. According to the papers I've found he has a house, which is now mine. I'm so glad Uncle N gave me Daddy's death certificate for safe keeping. He wanted me to give it back to him the other day but I pretended not to know where I'd put it.

The government will pay for my tuition and give me money to survive on. It's a better option than the one I have here. Living again on the charity of Uncle N, enduring the hate of Iya Soji; no, I can't go back to that, so on Monday I'm going to buy my ticket and by the end of next week I'll be starting a new life far away from here.

1st November 1987

DJ,

I tried. I finally dialled the number Father had given me. I didn't know what I was going to say. I just knew I couldn't leave without speaking to her and hearing her voice. Her letter said she loved us, I wanted to ask her why she never came back, so I dialled her number. A young voice answered, 'This is the Banjo residence, who are you and who do you want to speak to?' I didn't even know what her last name was, I didn't know if she was Mrs Banjo or a guest of Mrs Banjo. I told the girl, who could be my half-sister, that Lola Ogunwole wanted to speak to Mrs Banjo. She put the phone down and I could hear her screaming, 'Mummy, Mummy Lola Ogunwole wants to speak to you.' I could hear a muted conversation between mother and daughter.

'You are sure, are you sure?' asked the mother.
'She said her name is Lola Ogunwole,' the child responded.
'Quick give me the phone now.' There was a scraping noise and then I heard her say, 'Lola my child, is that you?' I wanted to say something but I had no words, so I listened to her voice. I finally know what my mother's voice sounds

like. As I sat listening to her plead with me to say something, I remembered the childish scenarios I'd imagined. Talking to her for the first time on the phone didn't feature in my happy reunion. I wanted to talk to her, but the words wouldn't come because I wasn't strong enough to deal with her reasons. I didn't want to know why she hadn't come back for us. I'm going back to London; it's better to go without baggage from the past.

2ND NOVEMBER 1987

DJ,

I went to the BA ticket office and they won't sell me a one-way ticket to London in Naira, I have to pay in pounds because I have a British passport. I don't know what I'm going to do. If I convert the Naira into pounds it's nowhere close to what I need. I have to be able to buy a ticket, they have to let me leave. I don't want to be here any more.

3RD NOVEMBER 1987

DJ,

I'm almost there, Alhaji knows someone. All I need is a letter from some Ministry stating that I'm allowed to purchase my ticket in Naira because my father is, I mean was, Nigerian. He's going to sort it out for me tomorrow. I've given him the money and my passport and as soon as he gets the letter, he'll buy the ticket. I'll be staying with Timi until I manage to sort out the house and bank accounts.

4TH NOVEMBER 1987

DJ,

I've got it! I've got my ticket and I leave on Saturday

evening! I've already packed. I don't have any warm clothes I just hope it's not too cold. All I can remember of England is that it's cold, wet and grey. I remember always having to wear mittens and I was always losing them. I remember tea and biscuits when we got home from school. Will I recognise anywhere?

I thought of just disappearing, but Alhaja say's that's cruel. So tomorrow I'll say my goodbye to the only person who once mattered to me and I'll give Alhaja a letter to give to the Vultures.

5TH NOVEMBER 1987

DJ,

I played the role of big man's daughter today. I dressed to the nines and went to the mansion to appropriate Cook Woman's car and driver. I just told her I was taking the car, I didn't care if she needed to go out. I wanted to show Segun what he has missed out on. I became what I've always despised, a rich, spoilt brat.

When I got on campus, I could see them all looking and wondering who I was. I'd been there enough times to know where I'd find him, and there he was sitting under his usual tree with his adoring fans. He's so used to seeing me casually dressed that he didn't recognise me straight away, but Bola did.

I'm not sure what reaction I expected from him. None, I guess. He's moved on, as was evident by Bridget clinging to his arm. I got the message. Even if she didn't say anything, her body was screaming, 'Hands off!' I just smiled at her. But she is welcome to him. I am moving on to greener pastures, which is what I told him. I gave him a letter to give to Mummy Baptiste; she came to Idogun for

Father's burial and I hadn't had a chance to say thank you to her.

Because it was the last time I was going to see him, I kissed him one last time and told him he'd always have a place in my heart. I think the only reason Bridget didn't start a fight with me was because she heard me say I was leaving the county for good. Segun was still standing there in shock when I got in the car and left. He never uttered a single word in the five minutes I was there.

7TH NOVEMBER 1987

DJ,

I started this journal as a little girl and sometimes I think you're the only thing that has kept me going and kept me sane. I started writing my thoughts and feelings down all those years ago because I felt lost and had no one to talk to, so I vented in your pages. I could pour out my thoughts feelings and frustrations without fear. To you I bared my soul and now that a new chapter in my life is to begin, I look back and I ask myself who is Omolola, Olufunke, Olufunmilayo Ogunwole? I don't truly know, but I do know that she's no longer a lost little girl looking for salvation.

I don't know what the future holds; all I do know is that when it is the turn of a man to become the head of a village, he does not need a diviner to tell him he is destined to rule. The time has come for me to start my life.

THE BEGINNING